"A watershed novel: From now on, ~~Canadian~~ will pressed to portray contemporary Toronto in all its multiracial colour and polyphonic sound." —*National Post*

"This is a straight-ahead narrative, craftily conceived so that the relationships morph and the tensions build."
—*NOW* magazine (Toronto)

"It's great that Brand locates these places of grace in funky Toronto bars rather than some lake in northern Ontario or windswept prairie in Saskatchewan. For that, Canadian literature owes her a debt of gratitude." —*Toronto Star*

"It is not too much to say that Brand writes Toronto in this new novel as it's never been written before. . . . Brand's talent for putting that uniqueness into language and art comes through with profound intelligence, humour and realism. . . . The craft of *What We All Long For* solidly establishes Brand as a literary contender. She writes desires like no one else." —*The Globe and Mail*

"Brand's characters and situations are vivid and compelling."
—*Canadian Press*

"*What We All Long For* [is] complicated, curious, heartbreaking."
—*The Gazette* (Montreal)

"The story of Quy . . . enthralls the reader with its strength and intelligence." —*Winnipeg Free Press*

"[Brand's] novels seem her most powerful work, and this one is no exception. . . . *What We All Long For* is easily Brand's most accessible novel and yet she hasn't given up a thing."
—*Xtra!* (Toronto)

"*What We All Long For* is a wonderfully layered and polyphonic novel. . . . I have always found a radiance and warmth in Brand's writing (tough and unflinching though it inevitably is) that I find in few of her peers." —*Vue Weekly* (Edmonton)

DIONNE BRAND

WHAT WE ALL

a novel

LONG

VINTAGE CANADA

FOR

VINTAGE CANADA EDITION, 2005

Published in Canada by Vintage Canada, a division of Random House
of Canada Limited, Toronto. Originally published in hardcover in
Canada by Alfred A. Knopf Canada, a division of Random House
of Canada Limited, Toronto, in 2005. Distributed by
Random House of Canada Limited, Toronto.

Vintage Canada and colophon are registered trademarks of
Random House of Canada Limited.

www.randomhouse.ca

Library and Archives Canada Cataloguing in Publication

Brand, Dionne
What we all long for / Dionne Brand.

ISBN-13: 978-0-676-97693-9
ISBN-10: 0-676-97693-X

I. Title.

PS8553.R275W43 2006   C813'.54   C2005-901318-4

Text design: Kelly Hill

Printed and bound in Canada

12 14 16 18 19 17 15 13 11

For Marlene, still.

WHAT

WE

ALL

LONG

FOR

ONE

THIS CITY HOVERS above the forty-third parallel; that's illusory of course. Winters on the other hand, there's nothing vague about them. Winters here are inevitable, sometimes unforgiving. Two years ago, they had to bring the army in to dig the city out from under the snow. The streets were glacial, the electrical wires were brittle, the telephones were useless. The whole city stood still; the trees more than usual. The cars and driveways were obliterated. Politicians were falling over each other to explain what had happened and who was to blame—who had privatized the snow plows and why the city wasn't prepared. The truth is you can't prepare for something like that. It's fate. Nature will do that sort of thing—dump thousands of tons of snow on the city just to say, Don't make too many plans or assumptions, don't get ahead of yourself. Spring this year couldn't come too soon—and it didn't. It took its time—melting at its own pace, over running ice-blocked sewer drains, swelling the Humber River and the Don River stretching to the lake. The sound of the city was of trickling water.

Have you ever smelled this city at the beginning of spring? Dead winter circling still, it smells of eagerness and embarrassment and, most of all, longing. Garbage, buried under snowbanks for months, gradually reappears like old habits—plastic bags, pop cans—the alleyways are cluttered in a mess of bottles and old shoes and thrown-away beds. People look as if they're unravelling. They're on their last nerves. They're suddenly eager for human touch. People will walk up to perfect strangers and tell them anything. After the grey days and the heavy skies of what's passed, an unfamiliar face will smile and make a remark as if there had been a conversation going on all along. The fate of everyone is open again. New lives can be started, or at least spring is the occasion to make it seem possible. No matter how dreary yesterday was, all the complications and problems that bore down then, now seem carried away by the melting streets. At least the clearing skies and the new breath of air from the lake, both, seduce people into thinking that.

It's 8 A.M. on a Wednesday of this early spring, and the subway train rumbles across the bridge over the Humber River. People are packed in tightly, and they all look dazed, as if recovering from a blow. There's the smell of perfume and sweat, and wet hair and mint, coffee and burned toast. There is a tension, holding in all the sounds that bodies make in the morning. Mostly people are quiet, unless they're young, like the three who just got on—no annoying boss to be endured all day. They grab hold of the upper hand-bars and as the train moves off they crash into one another, giggling. Their laughter rattles around in the car, then they grow mockingly self-conscious and quiet, noticing the uptightness on the train, but they can't stay serious and explode again into laughter.

One of them has a camera, she's Asian, she's wearing an old oilskin coat, and you want to look at her, she's beautiful in a strange way. Not the pouting corporate beauty on the ad for shampoo above her head, she has the beauty a falcon has: watchful, feathered, clawed, and probing. Another one's a young black man; he's carrying a drum in a duffel bag. He's trying to find space for it on the floor, and he's getting annoyed looks all around. There's an enviable loose physical allure to him. He has a few days' growth on his face, and when he smiles his eyebrows, his eyes—his whole face can't help its seduction. The third is another woman, she might be Italian, southern. She's bony like a mantis in her yellow slick plastic coat, except her mouth has a voluptuousness to it, and her eyes, the long eyelashes weigh them down. The Asian woman points the camera at her, coaxes her for a smile, and the flash goes off and she looks startled. It's obvious they've been out all night. They're talking now about some friend of theirs whom the young man loves. But all three are finally subdued by the taut silence around them, as if succumbing to some law they'd broken. Who wants to hear about love so early in the morning?

Mornings are like that on the subway trains—everyone having left their sovereign houses and apartments and rooms to enter the crossroads of the city, they first try at not letting the city touch them, holding on to the meagre privacy of a city with three million people. But eventually they're disrupted like this. Anonymity is the big lie of a city. You aren't anonymous at all. You're common, really, common like so many pebbles, so many specks of dirt, so many atoms of materiality.

Now that conversation has entered everyone's heads, and will follow them to work; they'll be trying to figure out the rest of the story all day. Now they'll be wondering where those three were last night, and someone will think, Why isn't my life like that? Free like a young person's. Someone will go off into a flight of imagination as to where they'd been—probably the railroad tracks, probably High Park, probably smoking dope at a party, drinking beer and dancing. Definitely dancing. And some other jealous rider will think,

That bunch of free loaders! Never worked a day in their lives! Life will get them hard some time, don't you worry.

And jammed in a seat down the car there's a man who hardly understands English at all, but he hears the tinkle of laughter, and it surprises him out of his own declensions on fate—how he ended up here and what's to be his next move, and how the small panic that he feels disgusts him. He rouses himself from going over the details of his life, repeating them in his head as if to the woman reading a newspaper next to him. The laughter pierces him, and he thinks that he's never heard laughter sound so pure, and it is his first week in this city. Only when he was very, very little—a boy—then he heard it, he remembers.

What floats in the air on a subway train like this is chance. People stand or sit with the thin magnetic film of their life wrapped around them. They think they're safe, but they know they're not. Any minute you can crash into someone else's life, and if you're lucky, it's good, it's like walking on light.

There are Italian neighbourhoods and Vietnamese neighbourhoods in this city; there are Chinese ones and Ukrainian ones and Pakistani ones and Korean ones and African ones. Name a region on the planet and there's someone from there, here. All of them sit on Ojibway land, but hardly any of them know it or care because that genealogy is wilfully untraceable except in the name of the city itself. They'd only have to look, though, but it could be that what they know hurts them already, and what if they found out something even more damaging? These are people who are used to the earth beneath them shifting, and they all want it to stop—and if that means they must pretend to know nothing, well, that's the sacrifice they make.

But as at any crossroad there are permutations of existence. People turn into other people imperceptibly, unconsciously, right here in the grumbling train. And on the sidewalks, after they've emerged from the stations, after being sandpapered by the jostling and scraping that a city like this does, all the lives they've hoarded, all the ghosts they've carried, all the inversions they've made for protection, all the scars and marks and records for recognition—the whole heterogeneous baggage falls out with each step on the pavement. There's so much spillage.

In this city there are Bulgarian mechanics, there are Eritrean accountants, Colombian café owners, Latvian book publishers, Welsh roofers, Afghani dancers, Iranian mathematicians, Tamil cooks in Thai restaurants, Calabrese boys with Jamaican accents, Fushen deejays, Filipina-Saudi beauticians; Russian doctors changing tires, there are Romanian bill collectors, Cape Croker fishmongers, Japanese grocery clerks, French gas meter readers, German bakers, Haitian and Bengali taxi drivers with Irish dispatchers.

Lives in the city are doubled, tripled, conjugated—women and men all trying to handle their own chain of events, trying to keep the story straight in their own heads. At times they catch themselves in sensational lies, embellishing or avoiding a nasty secret here and there, juggling the lines of causality, and before you know it, it's impossible to tell one thread from another. In this city, like everywhere, people work, they eat, they drink, they have sex, but it's hard not to wake up here without the certainty of misapprehension.

Quy

Quy. It means, well, it means "precious," and people underestimate me all the time because of my name. How do I start to tell who I am? Talking is always a miscalculation, my father, Loc Tuc, used to say.

I was a boy at that time. It was night. Because it is at night that these things happen. I was with my parents and my sisters. We had left the place where we lived and travelled along a road. We were picked up by a lorry on this road. I held a lime in my hand that my mother had given me to squeeze and to smell when I felt nauseous. We travelled in the lorry for half a day, and we arrived at a place by the water, a bay, where we waited for a boat. This boat didn't come. We waited two weeks in the back room of a house. There were many other people waiting in that house. My father paid extra money to get me milk, which I liked. My parents loved me. My sisters loved me. I was loved. One day my father told us we would travel in two more nights. My parents prepared. My sisters were terrified, but I was only a small boy; nothing terrified me. I would have been frightened if my mother and my father weren't there. I only ever had nightmares about not seeing my family.

No one would suspect I had diamonds in the belt around my waist. That was almost all of my parents' savings.

It was a cloth belt, and my mother had sewed the diamonds into the seams.

At the boat site there were many people. Some of them had been waiting for weeks. Only two boats arrived. There wasn't enough room. Some of the goods and some of the people would have to be left behind. My sisters walked in a small knot, holding each other, my mother held me, my father held me, they passed me between them time and again. One of them put me down. I won't say who. The water was cold and lapping. People were pushing. There was that quiet fighting-pushing people do when it's dangerous to make noise. I was swept along, my feet were getting wet. It was dark. It was night, of course. The sea was humid. The air was humid. I jumped up and down looking for my parents. I made out my father's legs. I followed him. Someone lifted me into a boat. I sat next to my father's legs. I said nothing. I put my lime to my nose. The boat sailed, and I fell asleep. It was cold. It rained sometimes.

We were in the middle of what I later knew to be the South China Sea when I understood that I was alone. I was a small boy, so I cried. The sea was endless, it was like travelling to the sun. I drank water from the ocean and my belly hurt and my lips cracked. The lime in my hand hardened. It was eight days before the boat arrived at Pulau Bidong, but I didn't belong to anyone on board. I followed the legs I had mistaken for my father's.

It was fortunate, I learned later, that I wasn't thrown overboard by the others. Though I was mistreated, beaten back when I reached for the good water or when I cried for food. Well, it would surprise some, I suppose, that people running to democracy are capable of such things. Why? You would think I would've turned out better myself. I didn't.

This is how I lost the diamonds. On the fourth day of that ugly sea we were boarded by Thai pirates. Six of them. They had three guns and many knives. They were disgusting men. They separated the men from the women, and a few of them raped the women while the others searched the rest of us. They found my belt and wrenched it from my waist. My poor father and mother didn't know this was a well-known hiding place. The pirates pulled me around like a rag. One of them said he would take me with them to make me a whore. I didn't know then what a whore was. They decided to take some women too, and the girls. What did I know about these things? I only know that I saved myself by biting one of them and getting knocked unconscious for it. When I woke up I was still on my way to the place I didn't know yet was Pulau Bidong.

After they left, the boat was a sick place. All the food was gone and people were more depressed, so I was an even worse liability. Human kindness is supposed to set in now, and it did, though it wasn't human, just chance. We reached the place called Pulau Bidong. From there on I was treated with a mix of goodness—some would call it disinterest but at the time I thought of it as goodness—and brutality. I never knew who would bring me which.

When you look at photographs of people at Pulau Bidong you see a blankness. Or perhaps our faces are, like they say in places, unreadable. I know how you come by such a face. I was paralysed when we unfolded what was left of ourselves onto the shore of Bidong. I felt like you do with sunstroke. I felt dried out, though, of course, a child doesn't have these words, but don't give me any sympathy for being a child. I grew up. I lived. I've seen the pictures. We look as one face—no particular personal aspect, no individual ambition. All one. We might be relatives of the same family. Was it us or was it the photographer who couldn't make distinctions among people he didn't know? Unable to make us human. Unable to help his audience see us, in other words, in individual little houses on suburban streets like those where he came from. Had he done it, would it have shortened my time at Bidong?

9

In one photograph you can see me stooped at the dress tail of a woman who could be my mother. She had two sons, and in the photograph I look like a third. Staring together into the camera's lens, perhaps by then we knew we were transformed into beggars for all time. I for sure had none of what you would call a character. Pulau Bidong was a refugee camp. A place where identity was watery, up for grabs. Political refugees, economic refugees—what difference? I was too young then for beliefs and convictions, thank heavens. Only at first I looked for love, for goodness, for favour. But after, I lived by one rule: Eat. Eat as much as you can. Nowadays I try not to make too many rules. You probably think if I hadn't lost my mother and father, if they hadn't lost me, I would've been a better person. Don't be sentimental. Don't ascribe good intentions. Who are you to judge?

I spent seven years at Pulau Bidong as an orphan, and I wished the Thai pirates had taken me with them. I would have had a destination and another fate. As it was, I ran to be photographed each time some news reporter or refugee official arrived. Perhaps I hoped my father or mother or my frightened sisters would find me. How did the pictures turn out? Do you recognize me? I'm the one who is smiling brilliantly less and less and then giving up on that more and more. I don't suppose it showed up in the pictures. Bidong became my home.

Once in Bidong I met another boy like me. There were many of us. He asked if he could play with a metal toy I'd made, the last sign of my innocence. I told him no, bluntly. He asked if I knew of his mother and father. I said, "Why would I?" He asked if he could be my friend. I said, "Suit yourself." I don't know what became of him.

What happened next? What happened next happened. That's the one thing Pulau Bidong taught me—shut your mouth.

TWO

RAIN HAD FALLEN the night before, but today the sun lit the studio, and the clutter of wood, canvasses, paper, and the general debris that Tuyen considered to be the materials of her art. Tuyen looked out of her window facing the alleyway. Overflowing garbage cans and a broken chair rested against the wall of the building opposite hers. The graffiti crew who lived on the upper floors there had painted a large red grinning pig on the wall. She hadn't noticed the chair there before and examined it from above, thinking of what she could make with it.

She was still wearing the old oilskin coat, waiting for her brother Binh. She hadn't bothered to take it off when she got in. Carla had gone to her own place next door, and Oku had left them three stops before their own on the subway line. Just as she entered her door, Binh had called to say that he was coming over. That was an hour ago. "Be outside," he'd said in an irritated voice, "I'm coming right now." But Tuyen knew better than to trust his sense of time, and she knew he was only annoyed because he'd been sent to visit her by their father. Though she'd kept her coat on just to be ready.

She was contemplating the discarded chair when Binh's Beamer turned into the alleyway. He pulled up and immediately leaned on the horn, then he put his head out the car window and bellowed her name. She opened her window and fixed him with an exaggeratedly bored stare. Binh leaned on the horn again, not letting up until she slammed the window shut and made her way down the stairs to the alleyway.

"That is so childish," she said to him when she got there.

"Well, you know I hate to come to this dump. Why do you live here anyway? Suffering for your art!" His tone was caustic and slightly envious at the same time.

"What's it to you?"

"Well, I wouldn't have to come here, would I?"

"I didn't ask you."

"No, you wouldn't know about obligations."

"Blah, blah, blah. You're so funny."

"Oh, take this!" he said distastefully, passing her two plastic bags from the passenger seat. "And here," he said, handing her a small envelope. "Money, I guess. Can't you get a job?"

"Thank you, sweet brother." Tuyen ignored the barb.

"Well, can't you? Why don't you go find work to do, huh? Or a husband?"

"As soon as you find one, you fag."

"You're the one with secrets, not me, okay." He waved a finger in her face.

"So, fine. Thank you very much. Goodbye." She turned to go back into the building.

"Hey," Binh said, stepping out of the car. "Hey, I want to talk to you." He was dressed immaculately, his hair long and groomed over his collar, a pair of expensive shades on his eyes.

"I don't want to talk to you. And don't we look fashionable? What d'you want anyway?"

"I'm going to Bangkok . . ."

"What for? A little child-sex tourism?"

"Don't be disgusting. Can you open the store for me?"

"Not in this life." Tuyen turned to go.

"Come on! I'll pay you."

"Are you for real?"

"It's not for me. It's for Ma, you know, and Bo. They can't leave here. They're . . . Ma's terrified . . ."

"When did you cook this up? Did you ask you? Are you leading Ma on again?"

"Forget it. Anyway, thanks."

"Stay out of things. Why don't you let them forget instead of encouraging them, eh?"

"Listen, I'm not encouraging them. I haven't even told them I'm going there, all right!" He removed the shades as if to underline his honesty.

"Just leave it alone. Don't go digging around and then it'll be more disappointment for them." Tuyen stepped closer to him, trying to be intimidating.

She was slightly shorter than he but in every other way as striking. The same thick black shoulder-length hair, the broad high cheekbones, the perfectly arched eyebrows—only she was dressed in a second-hand shirt and a baggy pair of paint-splattered pants she had made herself.

"You surprise me, Miss Great Artist. Aren't you curious? Don't you want to know what happened? Don't you wonder about him? With all your soul searching and finding yourself, don't you want to know?"

"It's not my stuff, it's theirs, and it's painful to them and I don't want you going digging around in it."

"And who are you to tell me what to do?"

"You asked me, so I'm telling you. Don't be selfish."

"*Selfish?* I'm going to try and find out what happened, what happened to him. How am I being selfish?"

"I don't know, but that's how you are."

"Okay, fine, never mind. *Chao chi!*"

Binh got into his car, and rolling up the window, he revved the engine and sped up the alleyway.

"*Chao anh* to you too!" Tuyen yelled at the car speeding away.

14   Tuyen received these visits from Binh every time her parents hadn't heard from her for a while. Her mother, Cam, would send food and her father, Tuan, would send a brown envelope with money. They never came themselves. Cam would have liked to visit her daughter, but Tuyen's father had forbidden it, thinking that they had to maintain a solid front in their objections to Tuyen moving out. The front always wavered though, as their anxiety made them send Binh to give Tuyen money. Binh refused to go up to the studio apartment because he said the staircase was filthy, so he would always lean on his car horn or scream her name up the alleyway until she came down. She was younger than Binh by eighteen months, but she felt she was much more mature, since he seemed to need their parents' approval far more than she. Here he was going on another fruitless search trying to get their attention again, she thought, as she made her way up the staircase.

Tuyen's studio apartment was a mess of wood rails and tree stumps, twigs and rope, debris, really, which she had picked up walking along the beaches, and lumber she'd bought, all of which she was making into a great figure, a *lubaio*, which, when she was finished, she said, would fill the entire studio apartment from ceiling to floor. She'd enlisted her friends, Carla, who lived across the hall, Oku, and Jackie, to help her stand one of two railway ties up on its end while she tied it to iron hooks she'd hammered in at the four quadrants of the room. For months the railway ties had lain diagonally across the floor. Every now and again she bumped her toes trying to get by, until she decided that she would make a signpost.

Stolen is what they were, the railway ties, but "come by" is what she and Oku laughingly called it, recalling their nighttime raid on the railway yards. Tuyen had happened on the idea of the *lubaio* when she was cutting across the railway yards on one of her searches. She hadn't counted on the weight of the railway ties and the difficulty of moving them around at will. But Oku had used his father's old gas guzzler, a windowless sea scow of a Buick Plaza, and they'd harnessed the ties to the top of the car and driven home slowly and stealthily through alleyways. First the ties sat up the staircase for months, then, when they finally arrived in Tuyen's studio at the top, she got her friends to help her raise one to standing.

"Christ, this thing is fucking heavy," Jackie had screeched. "You must be out of your mind. If I get one single scratch, my fucking career is over."

"What '*fucking* career,' Jackie? Hold your *fucking* end up."

"Don't make me drop this on you, Oku."

"Drop it on me, girl. Just like you drop it on that German guy."

"Don't go there, man. Don't front. You couldn't handle it."

"Well, test me, girl, test me!"

"Stop, stop." Both Tuyen and Carla said this at the same time, laughing, the railway tie tilting precariously.

"Why the fuck do I bother with you guys?" Jackie said dismissively.

"Because we love you, sweetie." Tuyen finished tying off the pole.

"It's your Jones for me, baby." Oku wrapped his arm across Jackie's waist.

"Anyways—" Jackie gave Oku a freezing look, at which he dropped his arm limply, then turning to Tuyen—"And what the fuck are you making now? Is this some ancient Vietnamese shit or something?"

"I'm making a *fucking lubaio* . . ."

"Okay, honey, say no fucking more." Jackie examined her nails and her long legs. Jackie could use the word "fuck" as every part of speech, in every grammatical construction.

" . . . because I am not interested in the idea of life, death, fertility, hope, or anything, and because Dali's *Reclining Woman Wearing a Chemise* looks like a dead slaughtered doll, and I can see preying eagles, broken arrows, and jazz musicians in Jackson Pollock, and because I believe that Man Ray and Duchamp were lovers."

"Word!" Oku.

"And because there's some ancient Chinese-Vietnamese shit that's my shit and I'm taking it. Okay?"

"Oh Christ, turn her off." Carla. "But I thought you were Vietnamese?"

"How long have you known me?" The words sounded dangerous in Tuyen's throat. Carla had ventured into a sensitive place.

"Whatever," Jackie said, noticing the sudden disruption. "Maybe you're a fucking genius, but you're nuts is all I know, girl. This place is a fucking mess!"

"Okay, let me explain. You know those fake carved posts they've put in the middle of the road down on Spadina? In Chinatown? Well, they're kitsch down there, but they're supposed to be signposts. Like long ago people would pin messages against the government and shit like that on them. So my installation is to reclaim . . . Of course, regular electric posts already have notices on them like flyers and stuff . . . Well, I still have to think it all through, but . . ."

Breaking off, she explained the plan to make a pulley with a seat so that she could move up and down the *lubaio*, engraving and encrusting figures and signs. At the planned installation, which was to be her most ambitious, she would have the audience post messages on the *lubaio*. Messages to the city.

Jackie began to make snoring sounds. "Anyways, very interesting honey, but . . ." she said, pausing pointedly, "catch you all later. Much. I got business."

Tuyen was devoted, as devoted as she could be to anyone, to Carla. That is, Carla reminded her of a painting she loved by Remedios Varo. *Madness of the Cat.* If you saw Remedios Varo's painting, you would see Carla—without the cats but with the electricity, all kinetic electricity, all the supernatural otherworldly energy. That was how Tuyen saw her, and indeed there was a striking resemblance to the girl in Remedios's painting. The wraithlike face, the high cheekbones, the reddish hair, kinked in Carla's case not by electricity but by her father's genealogy; and the dark hues of her skin put there also by him. But the surprise on her face, the startled, knowing look, was another alchemy altogether her own. Tuyen rightly saw that Carla inhabited a world of fantasy, of distance, of dreams. Her bicycle, like the wheeled apparatuses of Remedios's inventions, extending from her bones as she pedalled her way around the city, her winter sun–yellowed jacket and the courier's knapsack on her back ballooning out like a sail. And the city's smogged air around her seemed painted in decalcomania. All that was why Tuyen was attracted to Carla. The hidden energy, the little shocks secreted in inconspicuous places. The times she came upon Carla in her sparsely appointed apartment next door, standing still as if in the middle of a conversation with unseen people, she fell silent watching. If she were to paint Carla, and she had tried, it would be to copy every painting of Varo's.

In every one of Tuyen's installations—she'd had six now, and had a growing reputation in the avant-garde scene—there was the figure or some aspect of Carla. Sometimes her eyes with their luxuriant lashes, sometimes her mouth in that rich sombre pout. And in each installation her hand on Carla's figure had grown more erotic, painting the escarpment of Carla's cheek or her ankle or her back like a lover.

Tuyen had been drawn to her since the first day of high school. They were both intense, bright girls who kept quiet in class but always had a quirky yet correct answer when asked a question. As when Carla blurted out in class that *To Kill a Mockingbird* was maudlin and embarrassing and why did people need to feel pity in order to act right. Or when Tuyen in a small voice from the back of the history class, during what she thought was a tedious intonement by the teacher about Normandy, said that she was sick of the Second World War and it wasn't the world anyway, it was Europe, and asked what had happened in the rest of the world, did anybody else die? Was anybody else heroic?

Their friendship escalated and expanded to include Oku, a studious guy, when he told the phys. ed. teacher, Mr. Gordon, to eat shit when he invited him to run track. He was suspended for a week because he didn't apologize, and as a matter of principle, Tuyen and Carla, and even Jackie, who was different and odd all on her own, decided to take the week off with him. It was a wonderful week. They played video games at Jackie's house, and Jackie's mother taught them how to play euchre. They ate pizza at Joe's on College, they got high on one tiny toke and giggled at everything and everyone they saw. That was grade eleven. Now that friendship of opposition to the state of things, and their common oddness, held all of them together.

They shared everything: money, clothes, food, ideas. Everything except family details. There was an assumption among them that their families were boring and uninteresting and a general pain, and best kept hidden, and that they couldn't wait for the end of high school to leave home. Only once in a while did they sigh in resignation at some ridiculous request from their families to fit in and stop making trouble.

"Yes, Ma. I'll get a blonde wig and fit in all right!" Tuyen once yelled at her mother. At which her mother looked wounded and told her to stop making jokes and try harder.

They had an unspoken collaboration on distancing themselves as far as possible from the unreasonableness, the ignorance, the secrets, and the madness of their parents. They carried around an air of harassment or impatience about matters at home. "Anyways!" was their signal for dismissing whatever had happened in the hours between going home and coming back to school.

Loners before they met, they were all skimming across high school, all bored with the adolescent prejudices of classrooms. They couldn't wait to get out of school, where they had very early realized, as early as grade three, that nothing there was about them. Their parents didn't understand anything. They abandoned them to the rough public terrain that they themselves couldn't handle but out of which they expected their children to emerge with good grades and well adjusted. So they settled in as mainly spectators to the white kids in the class.

Tuyen noticed the scythe-like, limber, sharp blade of Carla's body, her strange whisper of a voice, and fell in love immediately. Carla would dream off in class—engrossed in a long-ago moment when she had heard a chair falling—Tuyen would nudge her when the teacher spoke to her. Because Tuyen saw a similarity. At home, she herself was caught by a kind of lapping shame. This is what drew them together. They each had the hip quietness of having seen; the feeling of living in two dimensions, the look of being on the brink, at the doorway listening for everything.

They all, Tuyen, Carla, Oku, and Jackie, felt as if they inhabited two countries—their parents' and their own—when they sat dutifully at their kitchen tables being regaled with how life used to be "back home," and when they listened to inspired descriptions of other houses, other landscapes, other skies, other trees, they were bored. They thought that their parents had scales on their eyes. Sometimes they wanted to shout at them, "Well, you're not *there!*" But if any of them had the temerity to say this, they would be met by a slap to the face or a crestfallen look, and an awful, disappointed silence in the kitchen. Each left home in the morning as if making a long journey, untangling themselves from the seaweed of other shores wrapped around their parents. Breaking their doorways, they left the sleepwalk of their mothers and fathers and ran across the unobserved borders of the city, sliding across ice to arrive at their own birthplace—the city. They were born in the city from people born elsewhere.

Only once back then did Tuyen share a family detail with Carla. A letter written by her mother.

Dear My Phuong,

> *You do not know how my heart is open. You have seen my*
> *son, Quy? I am in hopes that he is safe with you. I will give*
> *any things I have to meet him. My days is nothing . . .*

But before Carla could read more Tuyen had grabbed the letter, stuffing it back into her bag, saying, "Anyways . . . my mother's crazy, huh?" Carla had grinned uncomfortably, and they'd said nothing more about it. After that they acted as if the incident had never happened, yet for all its unfinished nature, it brought them protectively closer. When it came to their families they could only draw half conclusions, make half inferences, for fear of the real things that lay there.

Tuyen's father owned a restaurant on Elizabeth Street where most of the help and most of the customers spoke Vietnamese only. When she was little, Tuyen rebelled against the language, refusing to speak it. At five she went through a phase of calling herself Tracey because she didn't like anything Vietnamese. She used to sit at the cash register, her legs hanging from a stool, reprimanding people older than she to speak English. "English, English!" she would yell at them. As a teenager she cut her hair herself in jagged swaths, shaving the left side and having the rest fall to the right over her eyes. Her mother wept, bemoaning the good thick hair she said Tuyen had butchered. Even back then she disobeyed Bo's warnings to stay close to home, scouring the beaches, the railroads, and the construction sites at night for unattended wood. She said she was going to be an architect, and she actually spent two years in college learning draftsmanship. She dropped out before finishing and started doing sculpture at the college of art, but she dropped out of that too, saying that the people there were vulgar, no-talent assholes who only wanted to suck up to teachers and do the conventional.

After she let the others in on her sorties to silent night-time building sites and the railway tracks, she dragged them along with her. They all loved going to the railway tracks with a twelve-pack, some ganja, and a boombox.

She was the most daring of the friends. By eighteen Tuyen had already moved out, living above the store on College Street. She considered herself an avant-garde artist, sometimes doing art installations at the small galleries along Queen Street West. With her bright face, her dark, always-inquisitive eyes, her arms elegant with silver bracelets, she became a ubiquitous figure throughout the alternative art scene, dressed dramatically in her self-designed clothing. She wore embroidered sleeveless vests to show off the muscles in her shoulders, well developed from building her elaborate installations, on which she honed her skills of carpentry, carving, and painting. Tuyen was androgynous, a beautiful, perfect mix of the feminine and the masculine, her face sleek and planed. In the winters she wore the great oilskin coat, which she had found rummaging at the Goodwill store.

There were mice running across the ceiling of the apartments, day and night, but they didn't mind, anything was better than home. The landlord, a Mrs. Chou, didn't take care of the place, didn't sweep the hallway, and didn't paint. Anything that was broken Carla and Tuyen had to fix themselves, like the washers on every tap, the broken bathroom tiles, and the blown fuses. Mrs. Chou called the hovels she rented one-bedrooms, but they were little more than single rooms with a divider, the tiniest of galley kitchens, and a bathroom where you had to leave the door open to sit down on the toilet. Neither Carla nor Tuyen cared. Carla was only too elated when the apartment beside Tuyen became available. The first thing she bought was a stereo so that she could play the Fugees, Missy Elliot, and Lil' Kim and dance. She slept on the bare floor for the first several months, the stereo booming her to sleep, the light brightly lit. Tuyen wondered how Carla could sleep in all that noise, in all that light.

Tuyen's and Carla's apartments became places of refuge, not just for their immediate circle but for all the people they picked up along the way to their twenties. Like the Graffiti Boys across the alleyway, Tuyen's friends from the gay ghetto, a few hip-hop poets, two girls who made jewellery and knit hats, and an assortment of twenty-somethings who did various things like music and waitering. The two rundown apartments were above a cheap clothing store. Mrs. Chou only made appearances to collect the rents and to say, "No parties," and other than those predictable visits Carla and Tuyen had free reign of the place. When they did have parties, both apartments and the hallway were full of smoke and music, beer bottles, and loud talk above even louder music. A cloud of smoke hung at the ceiling and blew its way down the staircase. People didn't go home for days on end until either Tuyen or Carla, mostly Carla, came off the friendly high of Ecstasy to find her face in the toilet or some asshole with his shoes on her bed and turned everybody out. Once, on magic mushrooms, Tuyen saw every detail in the wood on the staircase, she saw that beyond the wood there was a coal-orange glow, and the stairs felt hot and burning for a week after.

Carla had bouts of cleanliness, which could only be called violent, during which she scrubbed and scrubbed her apartment and threw out perfectly good things like plates and knives. Tuyen had no such inclinations. Tuyen's apartment doubled as an art gallery for her installations. Carla's thrown-out objects would find themselves in an artistic creation of some kind.

Tuyen's own possessions, her clothes, her pots and dishes and such, were scattered in small piles around the growing *lubaio* in her apartment. These, her clothing, her dishes, spewed all over the floor, only hid smaller sharp-edged constructions of an earlier idea to build a *hutoung* in miniature, and an idea earlier still for mud terraces and a simultaneous one of ornamental *wenshou*—monsters and lions, horses and fish, phoenixes—all magical animals; some of which she gave to friends when their abundance threatened to clutter even her sense of space. These last she made of wood or soapstone or clay, and they were numerously scattered all around the room. Finally, and not unconnectedly, she had decided on the *lubaio*.

Tuyen had secreted one more letter from her mother's cache like a magical *wenshou*. She had memorized that one and replaced it—the only one in her father's handwriting—addressed to the director of the Chi Ma Wan Camp shortly after the family arrived in Toronto.

Dear Sir,

> *We have lost our child as you know. We were six months in Chi Ma Wan Camp. I am inquiring as to if you have a record of him there. Did he arrive after we left? In case he reaches the camp, here is some money for his passage, and a small amount to get him sweet milk. Also this hat which belongs to his Bo, he will know it. Please take care of him until he can be with us.*

> *Respect to you, Vu Tuan*

She had no idea what she would do with these letters, but she sought them out in her mother's room when she went on visits home and held them like ornate and curious figures of a time past.

She had surreptitiously broken down the wall between her bedroom and the kitchen, making one large room for her installations. One thing with Mrs. Chou's slum apartments— the ceilings were high. Tuyen's dark room was a thick black velvet curtain. The dishes were in the bathtub as the countless paintbrushes were in the sink. Chinese architecture, she said, dating way back, did not use walls for support. Columns were used, she said. She avoided the visits of Mrs. Chou, installed new locks, and made Carla her lookout for Mrs. Chou's possible raids. She had virtually destroyed the apartment. If she ever moved, she would have to do it late at night and very quickly and without a trace.

Still exasperated and a little disturbed by her brother, Tuyen knocked on Carla's door. Why, she wondered, did she find herself still waging that childish war with Binh?

"Look what I have," she said, when Carla opened.

"Oh, sweet!" Carla said, reaching for the two plastic bags of food Tuyen offered.

"Yeah? What do I get?"

"Hugs," Carla said, embracing her gratefully, "but really it's your brother who should get them."

"Don't even mention him. I'm so pissed with him."

"Why? I wish I had a brother like that."

"Oh, you do *not* know him. He is so manipulative . . ."

"Well, I'll exchange him for mine if you want." Carla's tone foreshadowed bad news.

"Sorry, what now?"

"Mimico again. Carjacking."

"Whoa! Christ!"

"Freaking carjacking. How am I going to fix that one?"

"Why do you have to fix it?"

"Because he's mine."

Tuyen had a peculiar feeling of self-betrayal. It was the word "mine." Binh had more or less asked her the same thing—didn't she want to know what had happened to their brother? Didn't she want that anomalous void in her life—in *their* life—charged with some specific substance or body? Did she not feel that sense of casualty, if not fatality, wrapped around their childhood?

Carla had moved to look out the window, and shaking off such thoughts, Tuyen walked across the room to her. She watched the thin muscle of Carla's neck quiver like a tulip's stem. She wanted to caress it, she wanted to put her lips on it. Then the mouth, turned down and sulking, she wanted to kiss it to the upturned suppleness she knew was there. Touching Carla's shoulder gently, as if afraid of breaking it with her desire, she said, "It'll be all right. Don't worry."

THREE

CARLA WOKE UP to the sound of the streetcar along College. The tiny apartment was hot already. She had slept late. She heard Tuyen still chipping away at her wooden *lubaio* next door, and she imagined Tuyen's intense face, the woodchips in her hair, battling her demons, hammering them out on the wooden pole, amidst the ever-present coffee smell enveloping the room.

Carla's eyes took some time to clear before she could see the clock. Ten A.M. Late. Shit. The thought alarmed her for the briefest second. The rest of the room came into its bare view. She heard the man downstairs rolling out the awning on the storefront. Her head felt woolly as if she'd been drinking—she remembered, yeah, but only one beer. Again the brief feeling of alarm. She was halfway off the futon, her head on the floor. This is how she woke up each morning, askew as if some great fight happened during her sleep. The awning downstairs squealed. The light from a clouded sun had already filled the apartment. She struggled to raise herself up, but a lassitude enveloped her. Not the lassitude of sleep but of consciousness. Slumping back onto the futon, she remembered yesterday.

Yesterday she'd come home exhausted, dragging her bike up the filthy stairs. She was streaming with sweat. She had ridden so fast, and she'd ridden, out of her way, all over the city, burning off a white light on her body. First through the downscale suburb of Etobicoke, which looked like the badlands of some alienated city—the low seemingly unfinished buildings, the stretches of uncreative streets, the arid afterwinter look of everything, the down-in-the-heel, stranded feel of the people.

She was riding away from the Mimico Correctional Institute, where she'd gone to visit her brother, Jamal. Her visit with him had only heightened the mixture of anger and fright she'd felt over the last few weeks. She didn't like this part of town, not only because of Jamal but because it seemed downtrodden somehow. A desolate outskirt—railway tracks, wedges of strip malls, and a prison kept like a secret. Gearing up on her bicycle she left the dreariness of it behind, heading downtown. When she made the intersection at Runnymede, the glow was still on her body, searing and damp. The afternoon light was sharp for spring. The sun coming west was dead angled at her head as she rode east, chipping between cars, crazily challenging red lights. The city was vivid. Each billboard screeching happiness and excitement. The cars, the crowds intense in the this-and-that of commerce, of buy this, get that, the minutiae of transient wants and needs. As fast as she was riding, she could still make out the particularity of each object or person she saw, so acute this searing light around her, tingling her skin. Could anyone see her? drenched in lightning?

There had been numbing sluggishness to the prison behind her; a dangerousness, a dangerousness that was both routine and petrifying. That same sluggishness was in Jamal's appearance at the visiting booth. It had been in the waiting room with the reception guard, who seemed chronically skeptical of all who entered; chronically hateful. Why Jamal put her through this, she didn't know. Why, indeed, he put himself through it, let alone her.

She hurtled through the upscale region of High Park, the old British-style houses. The people who must inhabit these with their neat little lives made her sicker to her stomach than usual because she'd just left her brother. The cute expensive stores, the carapace of wealth, seemed unaffected by her lit body. The handlebars of the bike were like her own bones, and like her bones she bent the brace toward the park itself. Perhaps there she might burn off the pace of her legs up the inclines and through the trees. But she was out of the park before she knew it. The trees held nothing. The manicured circle of flowers, the false oasis of the park, only made her sicker. Before long she was out on Bloor Street again, speeding east toward the centre of the city, flinging herself through the lights at Keele and bending southward to the lake; the bellowing horn and pneumatic brake of an eighteen-wheeler flinched her sinuous back, but she didn't stop for the trucker yelling curses at her. She left the drama of the shocked driver and skewered traffic behind. If she could stop, she would have, but she was light and light moves.

Her stomach always made a knot when Jamal was near. He was eighteen, for God's sake. Why couldn't he take care of himself yet? Why did he expect her to come to his rescue always? And why was there this uncontrollable urge in her, this frantic nervousness where he was concerned, as if she had to prevent him from falling, to look out for him as one would a baby with a baby's recklessness?

She was suddenly aware of music. It confused her until she remembered that she had clamped the small earplugs of her CD player in her ears and turned it on as soon as she'd left the building. Oku had lent her Dizzy Gillespie's "Take It as It Comes." The zephyrs of trumpets and saxophones streamed into her at Dundas Street. Out of the horns she sensed the lake and sped down to Roncesvalles. Ordinarily the bike would bump across the streetcar lines, but today she didn't feel them, she was slipping through the city on light. She rode along the shore, feeling translucent. The sun was on the lake, turning its usual muddiness to a pearly blue stretching south and wide. Carla raised her back from its hunch, felt a small hopeful breeze.

"How could you let other people handle you like that and run your life every minute of the day, Jamal?"

They'd been sitting uncomfortably across from each other, a Plexiglas wall separating them.

"Handle me? Nobody's not handling me." He had misunderstood her, thinking she'd meant sexually. "Ghost, them call me in here, you know, Carla! Ghost. You think me a batty man! Batty man in here 'fraid me, you know!"

He pulled the neck of his grey issue aside, showing her a rough, ugly branded G on his breast under his left shoulder blade. Not a tattoo, but a brand rising in an unhealed keloid. It was a furious-looking red, parts of it still oozing. She suppressed a gasp. His face formed the mask of the brother she did not know. The brother trying to be someone she could not recognize. She didn't know why he insisted on speaking in this accent. Something he'd picked up with his friends on the street. He did it to assume badness. She was angry whenever he used it on her, as if she didn't know him, as if she had not practically grown him.

"You don't get it, you don't get it at all, do you? What's the point?"

"Cho to blow!" he said, trying to impress the fellow prisoner in the booth beside him. "Me nah 'fraid nutten, Carla!"

All their conversations in the last few years were conversations of deliberate misunderstanding, it seemed. She couldn't speak to him clearly or reach him in any way, and he seemed to misunderstand her on purpose.

"Do you realize where you are again? And I can't get you out this time. Carjacking, Jamal! What's going to happen now? You tell me." She knew she was pronouncing every word, denying his newfound accent. She wanted to bring him back from the dreamworld he seemed to be in. "They won't let me bail you. And he's not answering his phone. So now what?"

"Him pussy! Me ask *he* for anything?"

"He" was how they both referred to their father outside of his presence, ever since they were small. "She" for Nadine, though Nadine had in effect been Jamal's mother. Carla referred to her as "she," and Jamal, as he grew older, reluctantly went along with it.

"Well, who else can I ask? It's me that's doing the asking. That's the position you leave me in. Who else, huh?"

He'd maintained his sullenness and so she'd said goodbye, promising to leave him some money at the desk outside. She couldn't wait to get to her bicycle and ride away from him. She'd left him standing there, his mouth in a babyish pout as usual. As she rode, she pictured him still standing there, waiting for her to turn around and come back, and all she could do was run, and all she could find was this well of heat and cold depth.

The muscles of highway and streets met down at the lake. All along the underpasses graffiti marred the concrete girders. She recognized the tags. The kids who lived across the alleyway from her apartment were graffiti artists. Kumaran's grinning pig, Abel's "narc" initial, then Keeran's desert and Jericho's lightning bolt. She felt slightly comforted, though she had asked them often enough to paint something else if they were going to paint the whole city over. Something more. They had practically filled all the walls of the city with these four signs, and she would have liked them to paint a flowering jungle or a seaside, the places where her mother, Angie, had always dreamed of going but never went. But she loved the city. She loved riding through the neck of it, the tri-angulating girders now possessed by the graffiti crew. She loved the feeling of weight and balance it gave her.

Jamal didn't see the city as she did. His life was in his skin, in his mouth, in his eyes, in the closest physical encounters. He operated only on his senses as far as Carla was concerned. But she saw the city as a set of obstacles to be crossed and circled, avoided and let pass. He saw it as something to get tangled in. Why couldn't he see just one step ahead of himself, she wondered, one want ahead of itself, as she criss-crossed and floated under the highway bypasses. Everything was immediate for Jamal, everything in the moment. Well, he had to learn, just like she had. Against the flow of the rush-hour traffic making its way to the expressway taking cars out of the city, she pedalled at a demonic pace. Shit, shit, shit, shit. She had to stop thinking, just pedal, just go, go, go.

Her legs were leaden when she'd finally dragged the bicycle up the stairs. Her thighs were boulders. It was as if because she'd stopped she'd become leaden, as if the sluggish prison embraced her again. If she'd continued, she was sure she would fly. But her own weight and the thought of her brother at Mimico Correctional crushed her again. She'd showered in cold water until her fingers were numb, then wrapped herself in a rough towel. Dripping and in between burning and freezing, she'd written something in her head. She thought she'd written it on paper, then searched for it wildly and didn't find it. Her hands were useless, numb and shrivelled from the prolonged shower. She'd tried putting on a shirt but couldn't find the neck. She'd sat naked by the window, freezing and thawing.

For six months she hadn't seen Jamal. She'd convinced herself that if she didn't see him, if she didn't hear from him, if he didn't call her, then things were fine. He was doing well wherever he was. She dreaded his phone calls, especially the phone calls late at night—why he always seemed to be in trouble late at night was beyond her. So six months had passed and she hadn't spoken to him directly. She had heard from him. He'd left two messages on her machine, one sounding sweet: "Carla, just want you to know, see, that I really love you and I appreciate everything you did. I'm fine. Calling because you know how, eh, you say I always call with trouble?" He giggled. "I wanted to tell you that I'm fine and, you know, just checkin' you . . ." The next time he sounded elated: "C, man, I'm really getting it together. Everything is cool, great." She was beginning to get comfortable but should've known, whenever he sounded elated some shit was going to happen.

The next time she heard, it was a legal-aid lawyer who called, asking her whether she could bail him. Then a sheepish collect call from him: "Ah, C, man, ah is like, ah, well, I think I'm in trouble, you know." She was silent, she refused to help him say what he wanted and she refused to play into it with him. Somehow, when he got himself in trouble, she always felt as if she was to blame. She would ask him some incredulous question like, "What the hell were you thinking,

Jamal?" And he would take offence as if he had a right and as if she were asking something unreasonable and as if she should know that it was not his fault, any of it. It just happened to him, he'd say, or it was really the guys he was hanging with. He was a fantasist. She didn't doubt that it *really* happened to him—he was, unlike her, open to things happening to him.

He told her convoluted stories about being in the wrong place at the wrong time, like, he and his friends were just hanging out in the park, chilling, smoking a joint, and some other guys from Flemingdon came along and for no reason started a fight about some girl and he didn't really want to get involved so he stood to the side and somehow the police got there and somehow they picked on him and his friends while the other guys ran off. Another story was that some guy owed him some money and he went to pick it up and just then the guy's girlfriend had called the police on him and they came and started questioning him, not the guy, and said there was a bench warrant out for him because he didn't show up to see his probation officer, "but that was bullshit, Carla," and on top of that the cops charged him with resisting, which everybody could tell was a false charge. "Carla," he'd say, "you know resisting is a false charge, anybody can tell you when you see a black person charged with resisting, it's the motherfucking cops who started it, right, right, Carla?"

It was hopeless trying to sift through to the real story with Jamal. Lurking in everything he said was a glimmer of it, but Carla knew that she never got the whole truth. For one thing, he was never to blame. So while it was true that the police were motherfuckers, Jamal was also troubled and she knew this, he was her brother. He was troubled and black and so the last two facts would outweigh the first when push came to shove. She tried to make him understand this, but he just wouldn't listen. She didn't want him to end up dead or in prison for life, but God, he was wearing her out. How many times had she said to him, "Jamal you realize that you're black, right? You know what that means? You can't be in the wrong place at the wrong time." And he would answer, "C, you think I'm stupid or something? I wasn't doing nothing, C. For real."

This time she had waited for the saga. She had kept quiet on the other end of the phone, and when he'd heard her silence he'd said, "Ah, C, Carla, I was, um, implicated in a crime." He probably thought this sounded official and formal, and he probably thought it said that he was really not involved and that he knew the "runnings," as he called them, he knew the system and the lingo, and he wasn't asking for help just because he was her brother but because he had been falsely accused. *Implicated!* She'd wanted to scream at him. She'd wanted to tear him to pieces, to say to him, You little punk, you idiot. You couldn't stay in school long enough to pass grade twelve, but you can say you were "implicated" in a crime. But before she screamed at him all the rage that the word "implicated" made her feel, she'd put the phone down quietly.

The lawyer had called, asking her about bail and saying it was best if Jamal pled guilty because then he would probably get a judge who would only give him a light sentence or maybe probation, even though that was unlikely since he was on probation when he was implicated in the crime—that's where Jamal must have picked up "implicated." Would she at any rate visit her brother and convince him to plead, since if he asked for a jury trial and pleaded innocent and wasted the court's time, then the judge would definitely be annoyed and give him a longer sentence.

She hated talking to these patronizing lawyers. Their tone suggesting they knew something way beyond what she or Jamal knew, something generic, something unavoidable. So she found herself saying to him archly, "What if he isn't guilty? Should he just plead being black?" There was silence on the other end, to which she said, "I'll get back to you."

Her brother was a piece of work for sure, but she would defend him against that kind of presumption any day. Her father would have to bail him out this time. She didn't have a penny or a pot to piss in. The last time, at least, she had been able to say he could live at her place, but that had brought her only grief—unbearably what she liked about him as a child she couldn't take now. There was never a way to make a bargain with him—you do this and I'll do that. When he was younger she had seen it as cute—breaking stupid convention, being honest—but now she saw it as an inability to show loyalty or to see himself as connected to people. To her, really. She had loved him most, and she thought that he would see that and love her back—enough to . . . to what? Behave? Live quietly? What? She herself had no idea . . . to be safe, at least. But a carjacking, Christ! To get involved in a carjacking, what the hell would be his story this time? She could tell it herself—C, I didn't even know it wasn't the guy's car, he pulled up and said let's go for a ride. That would be the story. He was an innocent again, pulled unwittingly into a plot.

When she'd first got news of his charge, she'd called her father and got Nadine. "Oh my God. He's not here, but I'll tell him. Tell me where Jamal is, Carla, so I can go see him. My God."

"Mimico," Carla answered. "There are certain times you can go." She didn't want to prolong the conversation with Nadine. "You should call them."

"My God, my God, that boy."

She wanted to get off the phone quickly. She couldn't take Nadine's hysterics, nor did she want any assumption of friendship with her. There had always been awkwardness between them, even in her childhood, and Carla preferred that it should stay that way. Loyalty to her dead mother, Angie, dictated that. She never knew what to say to Nadine so she said "goodbye" and "see you" and dropped the phone before Nadine could say more.

Three hours later her father hadn't called back and she'd left another message, this time on the answering machine. When he still didn't answer that, she was so furious her head blazed into an ache. Who the fuck did he think he was? Did she ever call him for anything? Did she ever need him for anything? That was when her body had begun to feel this incandescence. Her face glowed at her in store windows for the next two days, and a nervous kinetic energy kept her awake. Finally she had decided to go and see Jamal and tell him that there was no bail. No bail out of anything any more.

Sitting at the window after the shower last evening, she'd had a smoke to warm her, lighting the cigarette as if all her fingers were thumbs. Ghost, my ass, she'd thought. His ghostliness didn't stop the police from finding him. That's what she had wanted to tell him yesterday. You're such a fucking ghost, every time you do some shit they find you. Or, Ghost, why don't you just disappear from my life. Not that, not that, she felt rotten when she thought that. The smoke hadn't calmed her. Smoking was an affectation she had started early, in high school, in the café across from Harbord Collegiate, in the park on Grace Street, where she and her friends would sit on the embankment, puffing and joking.

When the telephone rang, she hadn't answered. Her father? Not likely. Tuyen from next door or Oku, Jackie? Or was it Jamal calling again, collect? Whoever it was—she hadn't answered all evening. And it couldn't have been Jamal, she'd soon realized, if it was all night. He'd given that privilege up to the suits and the uniforms. Listening calmed her in an icy way. The more the phone had rung, the more distant she became. She looked out the window, blowing smoke into the air.

Tuyen had rapped on her door. Carla had heard her voice calling through the seam, asking her, "How was it, Carla? How is he? Come on, come talk to me." Tuyen's voice soft, then gruff, then giving up. Then she'd heard her go back to chipping away at the wooden *lubaio*. She didn't want to tell Tuyen about it right then. Tuyen was her best friend. They shared everything, but it was long understood that some things, for both of them, were unknowable, unshareable. It was usually Tuyen who pushed and pulled at the borders of these things. Tuyen's artist's curiosity getting the better of their restraint. Carla had ignored her, trying to warm her icy body with her cigarette.

Carla's place was sparse and grew even more sparse after every visit to Tuyen's. She had a futon and three cushions on the floor, a tiny fridge and stove that came with the rent, her stereo and a small television on a few red-and-blue milk crates, and her bicycle hung on the wall. Her clothes, which she kept to a minimum, were neatly, ascetically, hung in two closets. Her shoes she left in a military row outside her door. She didn't want to tread dirt into her rooms, and since she and Tuyen were the only tenants on the second floor, her shoes were safe. She was frightened by clutter.

The street below the window seemed distant, blurred, soft-lit last evening. She'd watched the street people haggling, the store owner trying to move them along, the man who went to the Mars ten times a day for ice cream, the lottery ticket man, the café sitters, the trail of plastic-bag-laden people coming from the market. She watched and watched until the light went and the street lights came on and the crowd changed, with the exception of the regular homeless—the man who always told her, "Have a nice day, have a very nice day"; the chain-smoking woman who, on bad days, declaimed herself ugly to anyone within a few feet; the other woman who waited in the alley each day to tell the unsuspecting passerby that her dog had died; and the short, swollen, barefoot man with black hair. Then she watched the sun set—not the actual setting but the way anyone in a city sees the sun set, taking it for granted that the pinkish orange hues enveloping the buildings reflect the sun's going light. So she had watched from her window, the undivided phalanx of buildings eat away the sun.

Much later, eaten away herself into the gaze of the ebbing street and the perennial clicking of the streetcars, she had fallen asleep below the window. When she woke at the still-open window, the air had gone a little cold, and the jaundiced light of the street lamp had hit her in the face, "blessed" her face, as her mother used to say. "When I blessed my eyes on you." Why had she remembered that? *Blessed, blessé.* When my eyes wounded you, when the sight of you wounded me, which one did it mean? She felt the stroke of light, which is why she must have awakened. The street was now a damp quiet. It must have been three or so, perhaps four, in the morning, the time of the morning when streets seem to be their own selves, reflective, breathing some other breath, going some other way without the complications of people.

She had awakened then with a clarity and thought, *If you expect that I could help you.* She reached for her notebook and wrote it down. She had been dreaming it, over and over again, this line of words said to someone in her dream. "If you expect . . ." echoing under the rest of the line, "that I could know you, that I could see the thing riding you, if you expect that I should . . . if you expect to see God in me . . ." Well, it was a little dramatic but not hard to figure out who her dream was talking to, she thought, throwing the notebook aside. She wished her dreams were more complicated. She always wrote them down thinking they might be, then read them in the mornings knowing they were not parables but just extensions of her day life. She wished they were more cunning, hiding some secret that she might discover there.

One of the arms of Tuyen's *lubaio* was closest to the wall against which Carla's bed lay on the floor. Carla had grown accustomed to Tuyen chiselling all through her sleep. Last night she had dreamed Tuyen asking, "What about that wall?" Meaning the one near Carla's head. Meaning could she take it down too, could she extend her sculpture through to Carla's place? Could she store the railway ties in Carla's apartment? Carla always dreams this when she is nervous.

Last night she'd wanted to lift her head and pound on the wall for Tuyen to stop chiselling. But she only turned, putting her foot to the wall, and dreamed, *If you expect that I should ease some ache in you* . . . She wrote it down in her sleep, as a bit of paper from Tuyen's wrecked room floated toward her. She grabbed at it and, in grabbing, woke up, got up, the feel of paper on her fingertips. She felt thirsty, went to the refrigerator, found a beer, and went back to her bed, closing the window and reaching for her notebook.

The chiselling stopped momentarily. Tuyen was listening to her move around the room now. Carla eased her body down quietly onto the bed—Tuyen had heard her, she was sure, and might come over, and she didn't want that. She sat quietly, her quiet and Tuyen's attention holding up the wall between them. She didn't want to talk. She waited stealthily until she was sure that Tuyen understood. She didn't want to tell her about sitting with Jamal in the Mimico prison. Her brother had sent her speeding through the city with the random logic of an element, and she felt she was unravelling. She wanted that heat in her brain to subside. She heard Tuyen chiselling again, and she put the beer to her lips, drinking it all at once like water, slaking the thirst that light gives you.

Waking up and finding herself halfway on the futon and halfway on the floor, and knowing she was late for work, Carla decided not to go. That decision made her spring to her feet, take a shower, and get dressed. She would call the Asshole—that's what she called him, the dispatcher at Allied Swift Packages. What would be the use of going to work anyway? It was Monday, and sometimes she liked to take Monday off just to go in the opposite direction of the world hustling past her with its Monday morning anxieties. No one wanted to be where they were, which made them all rude and unhappy. Monday was the day of mistakes, which is also why she was glad to be 'off the road, her bicycle weaving in and out of traffic, trying to negotiate opening car doors and being squeezed at right turns. Mondays, she preferred to walk. By Tuesday the city had calmed down in acceptance of the fact that it had to work, that it had no choice.

Today she herself would have been careless.

"I can't come to work today," she said, surprised at the strength of her voice.

"Why?"

"I just can't," not finding a plausible reason she could give him other than she was late and still so fresh from a dream that it was too disturbing to deal with the real world.

He was at the beginning of a new sentence—"Look, Carla, it's Monday, we need"—when she cut him off—"I'll see you if I see you"—and hung up. She didn't care if he didn't give her good calls, she didn't care if tomorrow when she got in he made her wait longer than anyone else or gave her short runs. It was Monday, and she wanted to walk against the current of the city.

She washed her face compulsively again before leaving, trying to remove the phantom blessing of the lamppost from her forehead. She rubbed her face with the towel, still feeling the stroke of light on her, and left the apartment quickly, trying to ignore Tuyen's open door. Lately she'd found Tuyen's attentions too attuned to her, too burning, too difficult. Something was changing ever so slightly between them and she felt uncomfortable, uncertain about what it was.

Waving Tuyen away, she got a coffee at the Mars deli and drifted along College Street in the direction of Yonge.

FOUR

TUYEN'S DOOR HAD BEEN OPEN when Carla left. She was still knocking and chipping at the wood of the sculpture, but she was watching for Carla. The sculpture spread tall like a totem over her belongings. She was working on cutting small stick figures into the body of it. The figures were bending and standing in uneasy positions; some were headless in an extreme agony, or was it elation?

She knew that lately she'd been too intense with Carla. She couldn't help herself. She had done a slow muscular dance around Carla; at first she herself not knowing what it was in all its fullness. But now she'd felt a kind of urgency, a sense that Carla was opening to her. Yet it could all be her vanity, she thought, laughing at herself just as she glanced up, seeing Carla move quickly to the stairs. Tuyen almost said something, then changed her mind, seeing Carla's body flatten against the wall trying to avoid her. Carla passed, waving a defensive hand, declining the unspoken invitation. Despite herself, Tuyen came rushing to the door, calling to the bottom of the stairs.

"C, Jackie and Oku are coming for coffee, don't you want to stay?" Carla waved a hand. "Come on. How's Jamal? Okay?" she asked. "Check you later?" A little hope in her voice. "I have something to ask you. Can I come with you?" She couldn't help saying it. Carla shook her head, no. "Later," she heard Carla barely mumble.

Last night Tuyen had called Jackie and Oku to ask them if they'd talked to Carla. She'd said that she had a bad feeling and that Carla wasn't answering her phone or the door.

"So what's new?" Jackie answered. "You know how she is. Bipolar. But I'll try her, okay?"

Jackie was breezy about everything. It was her way of keeping things together. The breeziness was the surface; underneath Jackie was frantically setting all the disturbances in order. Tuyen knew she would just happen to drop by the next morning.

"Oh, Tuyen, what's the big deal?" Oku asked, when she finally got through his father's annoyance for calling so late.

"Well, I know she went to see Jamal, and you know how depressed she gets with that."

"Yeah, right." Carla had lain paralysed on her futon for a week the last time Jamal was in trouble.

"Give it till tomorrow. I'll come by before class." Oku rang off quickly, his father in the background grumbling about people calling at all hours.

Now they were all three in Tuyen's dilapidated apartment. They forgave the mess because she made great coffee. They had all become used to the mess anyway. It was useful—after visits to Tuyen, they usually went home and launched into vigorous cleaning. Oku and Jackie both headed for the shabby armchair in the corner. Jackie won out with her diva stare at Oku.

Jackie had dyed her hair red and now had a second-hand clothes store, calling herself "Diva," greeting customers effusively, and flattering them into scandalous excess buying. "Girl, you look good!" she would ooze, leading someone to buy the most improbable outfit. She had stayed home alone nights since she was nine years old, refusing to be babysat any more at Liz Dorry's house while Jackie's mother and father went partying. She had watched late-night television, Fashion-Television, MuchMusic, MuchMoreMusic, "Entertainment Tonight," "Lifestyles of the Rich and Famous," "Trading Places," "Martha Stewart," "Emeril Live," and hip-hop videos on Black Entertainment Television. Her argot was one her mother and father could not decipher for all their own hipness. She spoke valley girl, baller, hip-hopper, Brit mod, and French from watching RDI. She had sat there night after night, absorbing the television's language and culture and getting familiar with its speakers and citizens, changing her face into the drawn profile of a supermodel, her smile large and petulant, her ever-present long polished fingernails, her attitude snap, worldly, and dismissive as Naomi Campbell's. She had a German boyfriend, Reiner-Maria, who dyed his hair a dripping black and wore ominous leather and played second guitar in a band. They sounded like Ministry, Throbbing Gristle and Skinny Puppy. Jackie had found Reiner cruising the industrial scene that moved around the city from one ubiquitous dungeon-like club to another when she was in her black dress, black eyeshadow, multiple-pierced earlobe period. None of Jackie's friends ever remembered Reiner's name. They just called him the German boyfriend.

"What's the dillio?"

"Well, Jamal got caught for carjacking. You know that, Oku."

"I don't know anything."

"You hang around with him sometimes, don't you? Up there in the jungle?"

"I see him, but I don't know what he's into."

"Yeah, right." Jackie wasn't impressed.

"Now, you know I'm a grown man, I'm not into that shit. Those are young guys fucking around. I check for him 'cause he's Carla's brother, but you know, them young brothers are hard core, man."

"So you know about it, right?"

"Hell, they see me coming. I'm too cerebral for them. I just get some ganja up there, check some guys I know, older guys, man."

"But couldn't you have talked to him?"

"I did. But it's a man thing, know what I'm saying?"

"*Man thing*? What the fuck!"

"Yes, a man thing, Jackie."

"Well, it's a man thing to be in jail?"

"Rite of passage in this culture, girl. Rite of passage for a young black man."

"Well, your ass is not in jail, Oku."

"No, but you know what I mean, don't you? I can get jacked up any night by the cops just for walking in the wrong place. You know that, Jackie. Don't front like you don't. You talking in another language now? You forgotten how life is?"

Oku needled Jackie, every chance he got, about the German guy. He was jealous. He'd had a crush on Jackie since grade ten, but she paid him no mind except to send him on errands for pop and cigarettes. She was the reason Oku first hung out with Carla and Tuyen, thinking they were Jackie's best friends so they would lead him to Jackie somehow. They'd become close anyway, despite his lack of success so far. Oku was a poet. He lived in his parents' basement, listening for his father to leave so he could raid the refrigerator upstairs. His mother didn't mind, but his father had told him he would never deny him a roof, but he had to work to eat. Bring home good grades from the university—that was his primary job. His father also meant work renovating houses like he did. Summers were hellish for Oku. Fitz, his father, always had a friend who could give Oku a job hauling gyproc or insulation. Oku couldn't bear coming home dusted in plaster and covered in paint and wounded by falling hammers. He listened instead to Miles, he investigated the futurist squeaks and honks of the Chicago Art Ensemble, he travelled the labyrinthine maze of Afro-jazz base and drum, jungle. He worked it all back to Monk's "Epistrophe." He thought his father an unfortunately small man, small in the mind, and one day he would maybe just tell him so. And he loved Jackie, though he knew he hadn't a hope.

None of them took each other home in those teenage years. The only place they went to once or twice was Jackie's because Jackie's mother and father were cool. Or so they all thought, except Jackie. In fact, they took nothing home, no joy and no trouble. Most days they smoked outside school together, planning and dreaming their own dreams of what they would be if only they could get out of school and leave home. No more stories of what might have been, no more diatribes on what would never happen back home, down east, down the islands, over the South China Sea, not another sentence that began in the past that had never been their past.

They'd never been able to join in what their parents called "regular Canadian life." The crucial piece, of course, was that they weren't the required race. Not that that guaranteed safe passage, and not that one couldn't twist oneself up into the requisite shape; act the brown-noser, act the fool; go on as if you didn't feel or sense the rejections, as if you couldn't feel the animus. They simply failed to see this as a possible way of being in the world.

They'd decided instinctively that this idea was scary. "They're freaks," Tuyen would scream, describing her father's outstretched hand telling her, "You get along, yes! Join up and get along!" Tuyen's imitations of Tuan would send them all into fits of laughter, though afterward Tuyen would feel slightly disloyal.

"Anyway"—Tuyen wanted to get back to Carla—"fine, fine, Jamal's in jail. What about Carla? What do we do?"

"What can we do, Tuyen? She's saddled with the little motherfucker."

"He's not a 'motherfucker,' Jackie, he's just a young black man-child who's fucked just like the rest of us. He's trying to find his way. But they won't fucking let him."

"Well, I'm just a young black woman trying to find my way, and I ain't in jail, all right? Who the hell is 'they'? Don't bring me that endangered-species shit 'cause I'm the most endangered species, all right?"

"Black men have no power, Jackie."

"Fuck! And I must be the queen of England. Oku, don't front that lame shit, man."

"Yeah, black women don't have to deal with this crap, you know. You're strong . . ."

"Oh fuck! Oh Christ! Spare my ass that bullshit, please! You mean like your mother? Like mine? You see any strong anything there?"

"Anyways"—Tuyen tried again to keep the morning on track—"guys! Carla, remember?"

"Well, you won't have that problem, will you? With Nazi boy."

"Oh, you did not go there, you did not fucking go there!"

"Fucking heterosexual dystopia."

The snarling stopped abruptly. Tuyen had finally gotten their attention.

"Heterosexual dystopia," she repeated. "God save me from heterosexuality. All that bullshit about men and women, all that raw hatred, all that mayhem, even jail, for what? And you two, why don't you just fuck and get it over with?"

They were both stunned, but as usual Jackie had the comeback.

"Don't get your shorts in a twist, honey, just because the love of your life, who doesn't notice you, by the way, is in shit."

Oku was quiet. Then, "Be serious, Tuyen. I'm talking about serious shit out there."

"So am I, Oku. Why do you guys have such a stake in keeping the bullshit going? Why don't you strike?"

"'Strike?'"

"Yeah, a 'fucking,' like Jackie would say here, a 'fucking' labour action. On . . . on . . . masculinity. If you don't like it, if it's so tortuous, why don't you strike? Like quit."

Jackie couldn't hold it, she sputtered, spraying her coffee, and breaking into her broad, rippling laugh.

"Girl, you're so funny, you're killing me," Oku said dryly. He looked at Jackie with a mix of jealousy, annoyance, and desire. "Funny as hell, you are."

"I'm serious," Tuyen laughed. And when the laughter subsided she asked, "Can you all stay till she comes back?"

"I gotta make money, girl. I'll check you later." Jackie was on her way to her afternoon shift at the store. "Look"—she stopped at the door—"that kid will always be in trouble. He'll never get it straight, and Carla has to figure that out and get on with her own shit. And you, you stop waiting for her to notice you. Talk about dystopia!" She raised an eyebrow at Tuyen, then smiled mischievously and left.

Oku leapt across the room, following Jackie out the door. "Yeah, Tuyen, I gotta go to class." Tuyen heard him plaintively calling after Jackie, "Hey, Jacks, wait up, I didn't mean . . ."

Jackie's last words struck Tuyen uncomfortably. Yes, she had been waiting for Carla to come around. She had humoured Carla's depressions, her faraway attention. All in hopes.

Carla had made it clear to Tuyen that she was straight, but Tuyen could not quite believe her. If she made herself useful enough, if she listened and coaxed enough, maybe Carla would come around. Straight women were never as straight as they put out, Tuyen figured. She had, after all, slept with numerous straight women. They merely had to be convinced. And there had been a few times, after one of their parties, when she had found herself in Carla's bed, cuddling on the pretext that they were both high and drunk. Which was pretext enough for Carla to pretend that nothing had happened and to pull herself away from Tuyen's sleeping body quickly in the morning. Tuyen was cautious with her, knowing that if she pushed too much, Carla would run scared. She was always afraid Carla would move, would cut her out completely. She knew Carla was capable of this. She had cut off her father and stepmother. She had preoccupied herself solely with her brother, leaving no room for other intimate relationships. They'd been friends, but there had always been a space of leave-taking when Carla would abandon their friendship to some region in her brain, which Tuyen found impossible and at the same time alluring.

Carla had abandoned Tuyen to her explorations of sex, telling her, "I'm not interested. I'm just not. It's not my thing, all right," when Tuyen tried to entice her to go to the clubs on Church. Innocently, Tuyen would say to her, "Fine, I'm talking about going dancing. Straight people dance, right? It's just dancing." Tuyen also left books like *Rubyfruit Jungle* carelessly around Carla's apartment, hoping they would spark some latent interest in Carla, but so far her entreaties had been rebuffed and she'd had to settle for near-unconscious probings and feels when Carla could claim drunkenness or drug-induced forgetfulness.

Tuyen would try on these occasions to stay as alert as possible, as unimpaired as possible, so she could make note of and memorize the details of Carla's body, the responses to her touch, the meter of Carla's breathing, and the precise sounds of her murmurs. Carla always said her hands were lovely and begged her to massage away the knots in her back from riding all day long. Tuyen always regretted falling asleep, but couldn't help it, stroking Carla's back, her ears, having Carla respond to her with sleepy moaning. The next morning Carla would wake up earlier than she and wipe out their sexual intimacy with forgetfulness and distance. Tuyen was never sure how to press Carla; she didn't want to spoil the little understanding they had, nor quite frankly did she want to take on alone the obviously troubled terrain of Carla's life. She had her own "shit," as Jackie would have put it.

So yes, Jackie had a point, Tuyen thought. Carla had been more than plain to her after the last drunk. When in the morning Tuyen had playfully kissed her, held her as Carla tried to get up, Carla had pulled herself away abruptly, saying, "Shit, Tuyen, I told you I'm not into that."

And Tuyen, stung, had said to her, "Well, you coulda fooled me." She inferred more than actually had happened. She picked herself up from Carla's futon and left, slamming the door in a tantrum. Then, thinking that she was being childish, she returned to Carla's, finding her in the bathroom. "You think because it's not sex, it isn't desire," Tuyen told her.

Carla paused in brushing her teeth, stared at Tuyen, and then continued vigourously. "It is, you know."

"Look, I have no desire, okay? You have to have desire, don't you?"

"How can you have no desire?"

"I just don't. For anyone."

"Or you're afraid of it."

"Okay, Tuyen, think what you want." Carla rinsed her mouth out.

"I mean, having no desire might mean something deeper, you know. Like, who doesn't have desire? And if you have none, how do you know? How can you be sure? Like everybody has desire . . . so . . . ."

"I know what I like and what I don't like . . ."

"Yeah, but you just said you have no desire, right?"

"Well . . . that's how it is, all right? It's not my thing."

Tuyen sensed that Carla felt trapped, so she let up. Trying to make the moment light, she said, "Okay, you breeder, I'll leave and let you get going to work."

Carla acknowledged that she was being let off the hook and pelted water from the running tap at Tuyen's face. Tuyen grabbed her, kissed her on the ear, letting her tongue linger there softly, and left for her place. That was the week before Jamal's lawyer called. Since then she had not had a chance to broach the conversation again, and now Carla had gone into a depressed cocoon. The doors to their apartments, which were adjacent, were usually left open, but in the last few days Carla had kept hers closed and had talked little to Tuyen about what was happening. Just when she thought she had a slight advantage, a glimmer, Jamal had grabbed all the attention from Tuyen by getting himself arrested.

FIVE

A yellow mote of sand dreams in the polyp's eye;
the coral needs this pain.

The poet Kamau Brathwaite wrote this. It could be this city's mantra. It could escape and mingle with the amplifying city, especially on Mondays.

A yellow mote of sand dreams in the polyp's eye;
the coral needs this pain.

Though it becomes more and more worrisome as it's repeated against the busyness, the sweat and nerves of Monday morning, when rheumy-eyed students blunder up St. George toward the university and workers stand outside the hospitals in cliques of two or three, smoking cigarettes, blowing gusts into the wide air of the avenue, breathing in the exhaust of six lanes of traffic before running back inside to children, cancer patients, and the fickleness of nature and fortune—broken bones, broken teeth, broken muscle, saturated livers, ill-fed brains, fatty hearts, and hungry blood. Meanwhile the crowds of people at the centre of the city itself feel like another kind of storm. There are men eagerly trying to catch the attention of other men. The air now filled with their voices saying "yeah, really" and "right, right" like the chorus of an "excellent, sir" song. The "pick me, sir" lyric, of young execs who'd spent the weekend snorting coke in the bathrooms of Richmond Street generation-next clubs to get ready for the hard week of cutthroat office ahead of them. There are people who don't look at anyone and hurry to deadly lunches or top-priority errands that simply have to be run today or else the world will stop. The world here is full of self-consciousness and seething animosity. Young people come to the downtown to be in the world, or to run away from abusive homes in small towns like Sarnia and Fenelon Falls and Minden, or from suburbs like Vaughan and Malvern. They hang out in doorways, looking dreamy with drugs or alert with wanting. There are old regulars too, who stay here because it is the centre of life and because they cannot find their way back to anywhere.

At Yonge and Bloor, the very heart, the corner is stacked six or seven lemming deep as usual, waiting for the traffic lights. Spike Lee's *25th Hour* is playing at the Uptown. A man wearing a shalwa kamese and a Muslim skullcap is carrying a briefcase in one hand, in the other, he fingers light brown wooden prayer beads in their circle—in his entreaties. To what? His face is beautiful, thoughtful, as if it were the most ordinary thing to do, to pray to Allah in one hand, to attend to the gods of money in the other. He's going west, a sweet peace is on his face. A huge distracting billboard above the southeast corner flickers an ad for a car—a woman smiles from it, and reaches her hands out to her billboard driver.

Tuyen's family is rich, newly rich. They have a giant house in Richmond Hill, where rich immigrants live in giant houses. Richmond Hill is a sprawling suburb outside of the city. It is one of those suburbs where immigrants go to get away from other immigrants, but of course they end up living

with all the other immigrants running away from themselves—or at least running away from the self they think is
helpless, weak, unsuitable, and always in some kind of trouble. They hate that self that keeps drawing attention, the one
that can't fit in because of colour or language, or both, and
they think that moving to a suburb will somehow eradicate
that person once and for all. And after all the humiliations of
being that self—after they've worked hard enough at two or
three jobs and saved enough by overcrowding their families
in small dour rooms and cobbled together enough credit—
immigrants flee to rangy lookalike desolate suburbs like
Richmond Hill where the houses give them a sense of space
and distance from that troubled image of themselves.

When she decided to live on College Street, Tuyen's parents were angry. After all, that was where they had lived
when they first arrived from Vietnam with their two daugh-
ters. In a rooming house on Ulster Street before Tuyen was
born, and before her brother Binh was born, their small terrified family had occupied one room on the top floor, sharing
the kitchen and bathroom with students from the university.
By the time Tuyen came along, the Vus had moved to
Alexandra Park. Then they moved out of the housing development to a damp house near the market. The rooms were
never warm in the winter, and they were sweltering in the
summers. Now they lived beyond all that drama of material
poverty, in Richmond Hill.

Tuyen disliked the house in Richmond Hill. It was artifi-
cial. The whole development seemed highly contrived, as if it
were made all of cardboard and set down quickly and precariously. Someone's idea of luxury, which was really antiseptic,
and for all its cars and spaciousness, it was nevertheless root-
less and desolate.

Each time she came home for a visit, her father would ask, "What you want to go live there for? I'm finished with you this time. Why you want to spend good money on a cesspool like that?" By "this time," he meant unlike the last time, when she dropped out of draftsmanship and started sculpting. He had forgiven her that time because he remained convinced that he could persuade her to go back.

"It's my shit hole, Bo." She knew that he would not abandon her. She was his possession, like his whole family was.

"You bring these children here and this is what happens to them. They disobey."

"You didn't bring me here, Bo, I was born here. Wellesley Hospital. Remember?"

"And on top of everything they talk back to you. They have no respect. Why do I buy this big house for you to go live where we started out?"

"I'm not moving out of the city, Bo. You'll see me."

It had been four years since she'd left, and this was their exchange each time she returned. The same words, the same answers. It had become a kind of play with them. On her visits she raided the refrigerator and borrowed money from her mother and rifled through her sisters' clothing. Tuyen spent nothing on clothes, and even if her sisters' tastes were miserable, she managed to look good in their seconds. She was the youngest, which is why she got away with things her siblings didn't. Her father had been much stricter with them. Ai and Lam and Binh would never have dreamed of breaking the rules as she had. Their father, Tuan, had them on a tight rein. But Tuyen had been able to somehow circumvent or disarm her father. Perhaps he was growing weaker with age, or perhaps he was baffled by her strong resolve in everything. Tuyen never gave in to him when he said that she should do this or that. He found himself having to reason with her, rather than order her. He didn't mind it at all except in important matters.

After she'd spent the morning trying unsuccessfully to convince Jackie and Oku that there was something wrong with Carla, Tuyen shambled her way to Richmond Hill, intending to borrow some money from her mother. The money from her last installation party—money, that is, from the booze and the donations—was just about done. In the daytime she could count on her mother to be home alone. But more importantly she wanted to find out if her mother knew what Binh was up to. She knew that she had to ask this in a delicate way; she didn't want to open up any grief in her mother or cause her any pain. She had hoped to avoid her father and another argument about where she lived.

Her mother was home, still in her room, but so too, uncharacteristically, was her father. She had expected him to be downtown by now, preparing for the lunch crowd. He was in the kitchen, still in his pyjamas. He looked vulnerable, his hair receding and thinning, the skin sagging a bit on his still-fit body. The small scar near his mouth made the lines on his left cheek even deeper. He seemed tired. He smiled faintly at her, a delight passing briefly over his face, and then he launched into his usual.

"Why do I spend money on a big-time education for you to go live without your family? How you think a family works? Same house, same money, same life."

Tuyen knew this was her father's way of welcoming her and saying that he loved her. Love for him meant a kind of gruff duty and care.

"Makes sense for you, Bo, but I didn't leave the family. Am I not here, right here, now? I just have to be on my own."

"That is not sense. On your own for what? What is out there?"

"I don't know, Bo. That's just it, right? I don't know. You don't know."

"Stupid girl. I know. You go. You see."

"Bo, why don't you come visit me, then? But call first," she added too quickly.

"Don't you worry. I won't come there. You stay there with your dirty friends. Let me tell you, friends will take you but they won't bring you back. And don't ask me for any money."

"Oh, for God's sake, Bo! You think because you have a little money, it makes you better? It just means that you sacrifice everyone around you. That's how people make money . . ." It was out before she could stop herself. Then she didn't know what to say. It was not something she was supposed to speak about. About her oldest brother, whom she had never met but who had been lost, literally, years ago. "Bo . . ." Her father gave her a wounded look and left the kitchen.

Lam, one of Tuyen's older sisters, had overheard them. She'd been doing the morning dishes at the sink, her hair open and draped to her waist. Lam had never cut her hair because she thought she was ugly in every other respect. She had a large face with prominent cheekbones. She cultivated the black glistening hair like a treasured crop. She herself had never dared to talk back to her father.

"You think you're so smart, eh?" Her voice slid into Tuyen like a knife in butter. "I know why you live downtown."

"Then why, huh?"

Tuyen was really more concerned with what she'd just said to her father. Lam, she knew, resented the overindulgence Tuyen got from everyone. She would never have had the nerve to answer her father in the way that Tuyen did. She chafed like the rest under his rule but didn't dare disobey him. Tuyen was the baby; Tuyen and, before her, Binh, they were pampered. Lam and Ai were reminders, she suspected, of their parents' past, their other life; the life that was cut in half one night on a boat to Hong Kong. Lam and Ai had become shadows; two little girls forgotten in the wrecked love of their parents. At times Lam had felt wrong for surviving, wrong for existing in the face of her parents' tragedy.

"I know, I know." Lam sounded childish in her own ears.

"I don't care what you know."

Tuyen was dismissive, as she'd always been of Lam. She was still thinking that she'd committed the worst faux pas with her father. Lam looked at her with a mix of sibling hatred and pure envy.

"I will tell them about you."

"Why? Why would you be that evil?"

Lam was taken aback. She felt withered, she felt like the younger sister. She pointed a finger at Tuyen and left the kitchen, stupefied and enraged.

Tuyen hadn't meant to accuse her father of anything. She had meant to humour him, if not get him to understand. She spent a few more minutes in the kitchen thinking about this, convincing herself that her father did not take it as an indictment of what had happened so long ago. Perhaps he understood her remark as criticizing his drive for making money. That would be better. Besides, he had never told her the whole story. And certainly never how he felt. She had merely overheard, here and there, snippets of conversations. She had made sense out of nonsense. She comforted herself that it was just their usual sparring; that her father had not made out any reference to the loss of her brother Quy. She felt no danger from Lam, and anyway, she told herself, she was making a different life. On her own.

The threat from Lam was just childish. Lam would no more hurt her parents than Tuyen would. At least never intentionally. Tuyen knew this. If there were some way she could hurt Tuyen without hurting them, perhaps. So she was in no danger from Lam. Tuyen had known what buttons to push with Lam and Ai since she was small, and growing up hadn't altered her reckless use of them.

She made her way to her mother's room. Her mother and father had stopped sleeping in the same room when they moved to Richmond Hill. What with her mother's insomnia and her father's equal sleeplessness, their schedules of paltry intermittent sleep did not coincide. So as not to disturb each other, or as Tuyen suspected, so as not to have to talk to each other, to go over the worn language of disappointment, they each had a separate room.

Cam was lying in bed, her head propped up on pillows, her mouth slightly open. The room was dimmed to the daylight outside by heavy curtains. Tuyen watched the shallow breathing lift her mother's chest. On the night table was a brass incense burner and the perpetual photograph of the brother she had never met. All the innocence reflected there was doubled in her mother's sleeping face. Tuyen felt a surge of resentment for the boy, a familiar feeling. One that embarrassed her now, but one that had become a reflex to any image of him. Not that she hated him, she didn't know him, he had simply been an impediment to . . . to what? To things she no longer needed, had never needed, but observed as missing. She thought of picking her way through the room looking for more letters—thinking there was some way of using them in her *lubaio* installation—but then, adoring her mother's sleeping face, she changed her mind. Tuyen closed the door quietly, hoping she hadn't awakened Cam, and went back to the kitchen.

Tuyen stayed in the kitchen, waiting for her father to return. Opening the cupboards, she scooped cans into her bag. She was also hoping to find one of her father's stashes of money. He always hid small amounts of money around the house, "just in case," he said.

She always meant to be more sensitive to Lam and Ai, more understanding to her parents. She would arrive at the house with the best of intentions in that regard—to show them all that she had made a different life for herself and was no longer bound by the smallness of family. But on encountering her real family, not the one she had analysed with pity and felt compassion for, her resolve invariably blew up into tantrums. She always fell into the traps of anger and the same pettiness she abhorred in them. She paced the kitchen, counting up the traps she had fallen into in the space of an hour; she had taken offence at a photograph of a poor boy, she had hurt her father, and she had hurt Lam too. Even if Lam had really started it, Tuyen was supposed to be above it.

She had left the embrace of her family—truthfully, not embrace, her family did not embrace. They fed you, they clothed you, they fattened you, but they did not embrace. Yet they held you. With duty, with obligation, with honour, with an unspoken but viselike grip of emotional debt. Tuyen wanted no duty. And perhaps that is what she had arrived at. Yet she wanted an embrace so tight, and with such a gathering of scents and touches. She wanted sensuality, not duty. She wanted to be downtown in the heat of it. Everyone walking in the city was senseless. She loved that. Everyone escaping the un-touch of familiars and the scents of fatalism gathered in close houses. Familiarity was not what she wanted or what would make her feel as if she were in the world. It was the opposite. The alien touch of sidewalks, the hooded looks of crowds. She loved the unfriendliness, the coolness. It was warmer than the warmth of her family in Richmond Hill.

Theirs wasn't warmth, it was readiness, a businesslike readiness to have all the world had to offer by way of things. A voracious getting. They had everything and nothing. They didn't even like or savour having everything, they simply had it as a matter of course. Cars, cellphones, computers, expensive clothes, unused bicycles, unused toys, unused kitchen gadgets, unused birthday gifts, gifts that only had a momentary charge of excitement that was not excitement but agitation. The rooms of their big house in Richmond Hill were stuffed with clumsy furniture. There was a television in each room, turned on endlessly and loudly. Her mother, Cam, didn't throw away anything. So there were generations of furniture and generations of pots and pans and generations of all the things a house can use. Then there were papers of all kinds: pay stubs reaching back to when the family first came to the country from Vietnam, every single receipt for any item they bought over the years above fifty dollars, every bank statement when they finally trusted a bank with their money, and every lease of a room or apartment or house they had rented on their way to Richmond Hill.

Her mother had cried the day she moved out.

"I need to get out," Tuyen told her.

"Why? Why? Why do you want to leave us?"

"I'm not leaving you . . . but look, look around here. It's schizophrenic."

"Don't you use words like that with me. I know what they mean. That's not good of you."

"Okay, I mean there's too much clutter, too many things, I can't think."

"You were always a bad child. You think you know everything."

Her mother's words belied her limp body sitting in a chair, eyes red, tissue paper wet from tears balled up in her hand.

"Ma, Ma, I'll be fine. It's not a sad thing. It's great . . ."

"I am not giving you your birth certificate. You will lose it. You're not good with business. And your health card—give it back to me."

Cam suddenly sprang up, wrestling Tuyen's bag from her.

"Ma, what if I get sick?"

Cam went limp in the chair again. "That is what I'm saying. Why are you leaving? Anything can happen."

"Jeez, Ma, it won't."

Tuyen's mother had a mad fear of being caught without proof, without papers of some kind attesting to identity or place. Cam had laminated everything in sight when she discovered a shop, Vickram's, that did laminating. If she could wrap everything in plastic or laminate it, Tuyen felt, she would. Which is why the carpeting in their spacious house had a path of plastic running over regularly travelled surfaces. And the chairs and couches were not only Scotchgarded but covered in protective plastic that made sitting the most uncomfortable act. Cam's main preoccupation, though, was birth certificates, identity cards, immigration papers, and citizenship papers and cards. She checked incessantly and duplicated them tenfold, keeping them in cookie jars, vanity drawers, and breadboxes. With all that anxiety, Cam was slender in frame and quick in movement.

Her parents' eccentricities by turns amused and frustrated Tuyen. She would regale her friends with stories of her mother's attempt to plastic over every surface, of how Mr. Vickram loved her mother because she was responsible for one-third of his earnings, and that if they ever saw her coming back from one of her visits wrapped in bubble wrap, they should not be surprised. In fact, Tuyen mounted an installation once of herself in bubble wrap, with stickers from various countries pasted on her naked body. Calling the installation *Traveller* she instructed the audience to lift her and pass her around the room in silence for ten minutes. But then there was the other side of the eccentricities: she hated knowing that they came from a real moment of devastation, not personal quirkiness—her mother's insomnia and her frantic retrievals of hidden or lost papers at night, her father hiding money in shoes and books. And the incoherent fights between Cam and Tuan about who was to blame.

"I didn't see . . ."

"What is the point?"

"It was the authorities . . ."

"How long should we have . . ."

"Why didn't I see?"

"It makes no sense to argue. It's done."

"We shouldn't have come."

"Do you remember anything?"

"What life is here, tell me?"

"You write and you write and you write. Do I say no?"

"Why? Why should you? Next time I won't tell you, that's all."

"Quiet."

And about sending money abroad, about who was selfish, who was unwilling. Tuyen had eventually moved out of the uneasy luxury of her parents' house when she couldn't bear overhearing any more.

She not so much overheard as sensed, since her own understanding of Vietnamese was deliberately minimal. She'd only been able to gather in fragments, and in the letters she read surreptitiously and despite herself, the story that haunted them; the one that made her mother insomniac. The story about the beautiful boy Quy, the child they had lost in the South China Sea while fleeing Vietnam. *Quy* meant "precious" and Cam and Tuan tortured themselves in arguments about whether they had made a mistake, whether they had tempted fate by calling him Quy. They argued about who was at fault for leaving him, for taking their eyes off him for a second at the boat site.

Tuyen heard them hissing in whispered shouts, through her own sleep. Cam had been watchful to keep the whole family together. Tuan had paid off anyone they had to pay off for the passage on a boat to Hong Kong. Then Quy had drifted off in the night mist in a boat when one of them thought that he was with the other. Quy, their last child then and their first boy, so he was called *precious*. Their next son, the first born in Toronto, they called Binh, meaning "peace," which was their beseeching for mercy for that terrible loss.

In Toronto, her father had tied them all to a cash register. Tuan used to be a civil engineer in Vietnam, Cam, a doctor. When they arrived in the promised land, the authorities would not ratify their professional documents, and Cam became a manicurist in a beauty salon near Chinatown while Tuan unloaded fruit and other produce from trucks to the backs of stores on Spadina. Cam knew nothing about manicures, of course, except what she had done with her own well-shaped hands weekly. But that was sufficient. The rest she faked. Renting a chair in a corner of the beauty salon on College Street, her quick elegance adding to the pretence, she set up the warm water for the hands, the little white towels, the cuticle remover, the nail buffer, the nail polish, and charged twenty dollars per customer. Pedicure was thirty dollars. On certain days Cam went to English language classes and on others she studied for her medical exams in English. This after being in practice in Saigon for seven years as a family doctor.

Tuan's engineering came in handy at calibrating the weight of crates and boxes on his shoulders and back. His first two years he lifted lichees and jackfruit and sugar apples and star fruit and bean curd and dried mushrooms in all their assortments. Also lettuce and bok choy, Chinese cabbage, and bean sprouts. Fish and ducks, pig halves and the dead weight of frozen chickens. His back was either wet or cold most days. He graduated to selling at the front on the occasional summer day. When they figured out how—Tuan with his contacts in produce and with the money they'd brought with them plus the money they squirrelled away—they opened their own hole-in-the-wall restaurant off Spadina. After that there was no thought of being a civil engineer any more, or a doctor. Tuan knew he would never be allowed to build buildings. Cam was more hopeful, more dogged. She studied and studied, but always, four times, her English proficiency failed her. Never mind that she was probably only going to take care of Vietnamese patients who couldn't understand English-speaking doctors anyway; never mind that she could turn a breach, never mind. She too gave up finally.

The restaurant became their life. They were being defined by the city. They had come thinking that they would be who they were, or at least who they had managed to remain. After the loss of Quy, it made a resigned sense to them that they would lose other parts of themselves. Once they accepted that, it was easy to see themselves the way the city saw them: Vietnamese food. Neither Cam nor Tuan cooked very well, but how would their customers know? Eager Anglos ready to taste the fare of their multicultural city wouldn't know the differences. Luckily, national pride and discerning palates overtook the Vus and they hired a good cook, giving him a one-eighth share of the business, the only way they could keep him. The engineering skills came in handy again. How to fit thirty people into the tiny squarage of Saigon Pearl; the ergonomics necessary to urge them to leave so that another thirty could be seated within forty-five minutes; the right greeting and treatment so that thirty diners felt satisfaction, familiarity, yet not intimacy, which would make them linger. Then the translations that Ai, Lam, and particularly Binh and Tuyen, would have to facilitate.

Binh and Tuyen were born in the city, so they were born under the assumption that simply being born counted for something. They were required to disentangle puzzlement; any idiom or gesture or word, they were counted on to translate. Cam and Tuan expected much from them. As if assuming a new blood had entered their veins; as if their umbilical cords were also attached to this mothering city, and this made Binh and Tuyen not Vietnamese but that desired ineffable nationality: Western. For Tuan and Cam, the children were their interpreters, their annotators and paraphrasts, across the confusion of their new life.

Such power in children. Of course they became oracles of a kind too. Tuyen, perhaps, was the most savvy, and with a combination of her father's affection and indulgence, she used this power to get her way always. Her desires were not as geopolitical as her parents, not as strategic, and because she was a child, they were far more personal. Like wanting a certain pencil or a certain piece of beef or candy or wanting to sit on this chair or that and throwing a tantrum if she was told to behave. Such power in children makes them become smarter than their parents much sooner than expected. And perhaps Binh and especially Tuyen became not only smarter than their biological parents but smarter than the surrogate city— the authorities whose requests and rules they translated for Cam and Tuan. Perhaps they took a liberty here and there, made a deliberate misrepresentation or two along the way. Binh would later finance certain operations in what is called illegal human traffic, but which he saw as the free flow of goods and labour. And Tuyen, a little more esoteric but with the same surrealist bent and without the masculinist charm of her brother, but perhaps with a little more intellectual rigour, would become a Dadaist, making everything useful useless and vice versa in her chaotic apartment.

But back then, right after school, Ai, Lam, Binh, and Tuyen had to report to the restaurant to clean tables or wash dishes or chop vegetables endlessly for the freezer. They served soups with beef and mint and sprouts, and chicken on rice, and Singapore noodles. Ai and Lam and Binh worked dutifully and without chafing, but Tuyen complained constantly. She cut things carelessly, she broke glasses, and she left a mess with the dishes. She bawled the customers out if they didn't use English. Her father put her on the cash register, where at least her passion for numbers and patterns kept her interested. Nevertheless, she was wilful and rude, overcharging and arguing when the restaurant was crowded and everyone feeling rushed. Lunchtime and six to nine-thirty were their busiest times. Then, while they cleaned up late at night, Tuyen did her homework at one of the tables.

She remembered all this in a rush, moving around the

cluttered kitchen, the eternal cooker blinking. No matter the size of their kitchens over the years, they were always cluttered. She felt a sense of comfort and contradiction. What was that unease? she wondered. Why had she wanted as far back as she could remember to "not be them"? Not be Vietnamese. It was nothing that they had taught her. They were so definitely who they were. She felt outside of herself, outside of them. Which is why she'd found Carla. She wanted to be more than them. More what? she asked herself now. Damn. All she'd come here to do was borrow money and get back downtown, and all she had done was dig up uncontrollable feelings.

Her father came back into the kitchen, dressed in street clothes. He grunted at Tuyen, moving toward the fridge.

"You still here? You change your mind?"

"Bo . . ." He raised his hand, stopping her, poured himself a glass of water, added bitters, and drank slowly.

"Your mother's sleeping. Don't wake her, eh?"

"Bo"—Tuyen added pleading to her voice—"are you going downtown? Can I get a ride? I need your help, Bo." She placed her words where she knew he would find them. "Need" and "help" always appealed to him. Her voice was wanting, if not childish.

"Hmmm," he said, giving in.

She would apologize to him on the way into the city. Smarter or not, she loved her father. She had to apologize for touching that vulnerable spot that she had been unable to translate in all her years as her parents' interlocutor. She had not even been able to get the story fully spoken.

SIX

JACKIE WAS SEARCHING for yet another cigarette when Oku caught up with her. Oku wished he had one to give her. He wished that he had anything to give her since he had obviously stepped across a very thin line with her at Tuyen's. He'd teased her before about the German boyfriend, but he hadn't heard himself do it with quite the venom of a while ago. Or quite the childishness. Was it because somehow he felt that he was losing ground, that she seemed more distant? That he hadn't seen her for some time or that they, meaning Carla, Tuyen, and himself, were seeing less and less of her these days? Or was it just his inability to find the words to tell her how he felt? Maybe some fumbling sex between them, once, a long time ago was not enough to be a declaration of love.

It was the women's washroom at the Lula Lounge one night, when Jackie dragged him in, daring him to do it to her right there. The laughing-giggling-blurry high of her pulling him into the stall, opening his shirt, biting his left nipple. Yes, he remembered it was his left nipple. He remembered everything about the sex. Especially the breathless laughing sound she made when he went into her. He remembered everything, but she didn't. At least it seemed to make no difference to her now. They had gone back to the dance floor and danced all night as if they were not in the middle of a packed room but in each other's skin. He had licked the musky sweat off her neck, she'd held him with both arms around his waist, running her hands up his back. When the party was over, they had stood outside on the sidewalk, at first waiting for Tuyen and Carla, whom they'd lost in the crowd, oblivious to them. Not seeing them, they thought of hailing a cab, but Jackie told him to walk her home instead. And they'd walked along Dundas Street hugging and dancing and trying to trip each other.

It was three in the morning and they were both still high and drunk when they got to Ab und Zu, Jackie's store on Queen Street. She let herself in, turning and brushing her hand against his face. Oku hadn't thought of Reiner, but the door closing brought the cold fact of him. He'd quickly hailed a passing cab and gone home. The next time he saw Jackie it was as if, for her, nothing had taken place. She had been so casual with him, he felt upset. He felt like not talking to her, but this tack didn't work either. It wasn't as if nothing had happened, it was as if what had happened was meaningless to her, like hanging out, or laughing, or having something to eat. After that she seemed uninterested in him. So he wrote her poems.

But poems, obviously written for her and declaimed at Tuyen's installations, missed their mark among the people in the room, even though he sent them, as seductively as he could, right at her sharp cheekbones and her full wide lips. Didn't he, in the middle of his most passionate verse, see Jackie lean over, offering her mouth to the German boyfriend? Oku could not bear to think his name or say it. The German boyfriend, or cruelly, "Nazi boy," was how he referred to him. Maybe poetry was too obtuse, too angled for his purposes. Which, if he thought about it, were what? His purposes, that is, he asked himself, fumbling stupidly in his pockets as if he could find a cigarette there for her. He always caught himself doing something that he guessed she would find trifling. But if he was trifling, what did she see in that German idiot with the dyed black hair and the ankh in his ear and the bad imitation of Hendrix guitar playing?

"Fresh out, Jackie."

"You do not smoke cigarettes, Oku."

There it was again—he felt awkward, more so.

"Listen, Jacks . . . ah, sorry about the 'Nazi boy' stuff . . ." He felt insincere. He had meant the "Nazi boy stuff."

"Really! No kidding. 'Sorry about the Nazi boy stuff'?"

He felt her looking right through him, mocking him. They were stopped at the light. She looked at him directly for so long his face tingled. How rich her skin was. Her face evenly beautiful, not a blemish, not an incongruency. And no innocence whatever. A face that knew everything—everything bad—a face that could search out failure and scorn it. Or find it amusing. Amused is what Jackie's face told him now. Oku didn't know which he liked—to be found amusing or to be scorned. To be scorned probably. That at least was charged. To be found amusing made him blush, made him melt.

The traffic light must have changed several times—he had the feeling of other people crossing and traffic moving, then stopping. She held him in a kind of glimmer. He wanted her to look away and he wanted to be held. He didn't want her to hold him like this, when all she had for him was amusement. But to be held at all by her, by her eyes, was thrilling—it was to be held as if by her body. She hadn't laid a finger on him, yet he knew this is what it would be like to touch her again. To be held in some knowledge she had, some substance that was tangy.

"Really," she said again, her voice insinuating yet distant.

He knew that he was losing her attention, even her amused attention.

"Jackie, hook a brother up, huh?" He had intended to say something else, something certainly less inane, something serious, but now he'd said this and it seemed lewd.

"You know, Oku, men are so innocent." She breathed the words rather than said them. "I hear your poems, they all begin as if you're innocent. Like things happen to you that you can't predict. You never know what's going to happen to you. You love innocence, you're fixated on it. I don't trust innocence. I'm not innocent. I know what's going to happen to me." She spoke slowly, singeing him with each breath.

He noticed with a shock that she had not used the word "fuck" once. The College streetcar was at the light. She had always been aware of the traffic, the lights, the streetcar approaching, her particular plans, the everyday world going on around them. He hadn't. Jackie was on it before he could recover.

Oku saw the streetcar moving, the doors closing, and her beautiful back disappearing. He felt like a daydreamer just awakened.

Quy

Other tragedies have overshadowed mine. Look at that Catholic priest in Managua, he got himself shot; a plane will crash in the North Sea; some stupid rage—I know all about that—will hack eight hundred thousand people to death in Rwanda. But nothing will suck all the oxygen out of the air in years to come as what they will call 9/11, then the Americans will rampage the globe like thousands of Vietnams, and I, I will be forgotten. You see what I'm talking about?

In my heart, sometimes, I feel a lightness, a nonexistence. I feel it now riding this train. I have these moments, very dangerous, I feel scattered. But I'm here, and I feel like telling you the rest. Not because you'll get it, but because I feel like telling it.

My life at Pulau Bidong wasn't always unpleasant. I discovered small things about myself, small pleasures. There was a boy I used to play with in the old rotten boat in the bush tangle, near the rock that resembled the Buddha. Along a slimy path to the boat he would push me and I would push him and we would run and swing on the rotting banisters. There was a sapling growing inside the boat and we would swing and bend it and let it go. And it made a loud slapping noise. We tied a rag to it and filled the rag with stones and we would slingshot the stones up in the air and out of the boat. We would balance on the side beams and chase each other. The boat was just like the one that had brought me to Pulau Bidong. One day, the boy fell off the boat screaming. He grabbed the plank as he went crashing down. I ran down and around to see what happened to him. He was crying, his ragged shirt was ripped open, and there was a little cut in his belly. I tried to pull him free, to help him to stand up, but he cried more. I told him to stand up, but he wouldn't listen to me. I told him if he didn't stand up and stop crying, I would go back to the camp by myself. He just kept crying. So I went back to the camp. I knew he would soon come back and tell on me. He would probably say I pushed him, which I didn't do, but I knew he was a wicked boy and would tell a lie on me. So I went to sleep without any food and I hid from him the next day.

I was eight years old. When no one tried to beat me for pushing him, I was sorry I left him and went to look for him by the boat. He was still lying there beside the rotted boat. His hand was over his eyes. I called him, I said, "Hey boy!" but he didn't move his hand from his eyes. He didn't answer me. So I pulled his hands, and his open eyes stared at me. I said, "What you trying to pull, you asshole!" Then a bee flew out of his ear and stung me on the mouth. I saw the merest smile on his face. I screamed and started running. My lips became swollen instantly, and I vowed never to talk to that boy again. He disappeared. No one looked for him. Except me, sometimes. Just to see if he was sorry for playing the horrible trick on me. If he had only once appeared to me, I would have maybe said sorry myself. Anyhow, I did not miss him, and as days went by I did not miss him even more.

A month or two went by, and on a day when I was
tired from the wear and tear of cuffs and scratches from the
other children, I went to the rotting boat to see if my friend
was still there. He wasn't. But he had left his shirt there,
and the zipper from his pants. The place where I last saw
him seemed bleached out, grass ripped up. Of course, it
took me years to figure out that the fall had practically
killed him and that I'd done the rest. A clouded leopard
probably ate him, or perhaps the rats that roamed the camp
like we refugees. Perhaps in all the days that I hadn't
returned for him, they had taken small bites of him and little
by little he was dragged away. But I chose to think of him
then as nothing but a trickster. Perhaps I was afraid someone
would think I had hurt him and they would beat me or
send me away to another camp where my parents could not
find me. After all, they were soon to come for me, so I had
to stay quiet.

Then there were the beatings at the camp. You could
get a beating from anyone. And for someone like me with
no one to retaliate, I was like a bed mat on a line. I can't tell
you how many beatings I got. That boy used to hit me. So,
I played dumb. I was dumb. They let me go finally with a
beating. By now you would understand I was not a lovely
child any more. My legs had sores, places I picked and
picked and ate the skin off. I was unwashed, and lice were
plentiful in my head. I scratched and scratched until my
head was bruised and scabby.

Pulau Bidong was cluttered with ramshackle buildings,
small lean-to shops and houses, barracks really—some stilted,
some open to the weather. Every day more people came,
getting off the boats, walking the wooden pier with whatever
they salvaged, sometimes only their arms swinging, one foot

in front, one behind. There was nothing to do all day but stand around or find things to eat. I would jump off the pier to relieve the itchiness of my head. So I learned to swim, and one day a woman approached me. She used to run the shop where drink was sold. She said I was a good swimmer and she had a job for me. She told me I would have to swim out to a boat and bring back a plastic bag for her. She told me to wait at the pier until the sun went down. And so I began my first career. The woman gave me food in exchange and tar for my head lice. She was not a pretty woman, she had a cleft palate—her mouth was cut in two. She was nothing like my mother that I remember, nor my sisters. Her fingers were dirty, and she tricked me and gave me less than what she said, but that was fair. Who was I?

Who was in charge? I didn't know, how would I? The strong, the cunning, the smart, those who could run fast, those who could hold their breath, those who had money and gold, cigarettes and chocolates, those who could talk; anyone who had a knife or gun or stick. Don't ask me about authorities. They were the authorities. The woman and her gang and the other gangs who fought her. I was glad she took me under her wing because that is how I met the monk and my fate.

The monk told me many stories. When I first met him, he looked me right in the eye and told me this one. There was a boy once who lied a lot, the monk said, he lied until his teeth were green and he stole and he was wicked. One day he went to fetch wood and he met some tiger cubs and he played with them until he was bored, so he decided to break their necks to see how it felt. When he did that, the mother tiger saw him and let out a roar and came racing toward him. He was so scared he flew up into a tree. The mother tiger saw that the cubs were almost dead and she went and got some leaves from a special tree. She chewed them up and spit the mixture on the little tigers and soon they sprang back to life and the mother tiger took them home. So the boy climbed down and dug up the special tree and took it home. Soon he became a doctor, a miracle healer, and he raised the daughter of a rich man from the dead and the rich man took him for his son-in-law. He lived happily ever after with his wife, the rich man's daughter, until one day his wife grew jealous of the tree he had in the backyard, which he paid more attention to than her. She went outside and pissed on the tree, and the tree was vexed because it hated nastiness, so it uprooted itself and started flying to heaven. At that moment, the man came home and saw the tree taking off. He couldn't catch it, so he threw his axe at it, but the tree kept flying, taking the man holding on to the axe along with it. And that is why there is a man in the moon to this day.

When the monk told me this story, I began following him around. That boy's name was Cuoi. There and then I knew the monk could look right into my soul and see who I was.

No one was in charge of Pulau Bidong. The people in charge only wanted us out of Terengganu, out of Malaysia. Don't ask me. I knew nothing about big politics, who ran what wasn't my business. I only knew small things. The way things look to a child. Everything about this island was large, everything was bright, everything was brown or yellow. When you are a child, you concentrate on small pebbles, small looks, you look at the ground, you get shoved and pushed. You get shoved and pushed so much you look for something smaller to push back. You wait, you plot, and you savour it when it comes. That's how that boy fell in the rotten boat. I saw the wood lice; the wood was soft, but he didn't know. He was stupid. I told him to go first. He was stupid, and those who don't hear will feel. That's what the woman with a cleft palate said to me. *Those who don't hear will feel.* And anyway, better to be taken away by a clouded leopard than to live on Pulau Bidong. But I think it's the rats that got him, piece by piece. The rats were vicious and they respected no one. They didn't run when you came near. They would stand up and show their teeth. And me, I was little, so I had to protect myself. I always carried stones. *Troi co mat. Troi phat.* Heaven has eyes. Heaven punishes.

SEVEN

Quadraphonic, Jo Jo Flores, Paul E. Lopez, Boris Kid Conga,
Divine Earth Essence, Live percussion by Tribalismos, Saturday 18.
Oz/Off Centre PJ Patric Forge, Movement, Lond., U.K., Da lata,
computer of rebirth of Cool., Aku John Kong, OJ palma at Roxy
Blu, Konfusion, Design/vice, Soul Power, DJ spinna, with resident
DJs Semois & Kila, Una mas! Ziolay 21st disco, hip-hop house,
soul-funked/Brazilian/OJ John Laumahara, Fiction Design Co.'s
men's and women's summer collection. Exclusive up roc/FDCO
416 Fashion, Juice/solid Garage featuring Jephte Guillarme—New
York—born in Haiti, uprooted to Brooklyn with his family, turning
vodun spirituality into something understood. Hit single "The
Prayer." Voyage Dreams "Mad Behind the Tet Kale Sound"—
Friday 5th—Una mas/Funk d'void—Techno meets funky jazzy
house meets Glasgow Funk d'void/Grand Master Flash "immortalized
by Blondie, feted by the hip-hop cognoscenti, Grand Master Flash
turned the humble record deck into an instrument as potent as the
piano or guitar"/Afrika Bambaata. B. Boy and Dance classics
Saturday 29th (Mancccc Wabanakkk) . . .

Looking for her cigarettes, Jackie had pulled these advertisements out of her bag yesterday morning. She'd handed them
to Oku during her thesis on innocence and hadn't taken them
back. What did she mean, *innocence?* He hadn't done anyone
any harm, ever. He had only noticed that he was still holding

the cards and bits of paper she'd chucked at him as he walked down Augusta Avenue trying to recover from what she'd said.

He'd been looking over them as he sat at the Rose Café. He really should be in a class, but that was over for him. He liked Jo Jo Flores and Paul E. Lopez. He'd danced to them at Tuyen's place. The fashion show trip he just couldn't take, though. Who the hell was Fiction Design? Foolish as he must have sounded earlier, had she seemed the slightest interested? Had she in fact stepped closer to him, deliberately put out that vibe, or was it just he? But he had said the lamest line, the most insipid words in the black vernacular, the most washed out, most overused. Oh shit! Man, he wished he could snatch them back—was he elegant and gorgeous enough to use those words—"Jackie, hook a brother up" and get away with them? Well, they had seemed not to have the right effect, so clearly not. She just took off on him. Would she show up at Tuyen's this evening? Right now he wouldn't know what to say to her if she did. But flimsy as it was, he had something belonging to her and therefore an excuse, if he needed one, to get in touch with her. Not that this junk was important to her, he was sure—just ephemera—but he had looked at them through the day, the cards and posters, hoping that in them was a map to her, to Jackie.

This morning his father's cough had awakened him as usual. He rolled over, feeling the advertisements near his left hand. His father was in the bathroom upstairs now. Oku heard him blowing his nose in that disgusting way he had, and hawking into the sink. Oku got up, put the ads carefully into his knapsack, and prepared himself for the morning ritual with his father and mother. He showered quickly, trying to beat Fitz to the kitchen. His mother was already there. This morning ritual made him feel like a child. For a moment he understood why Jackie would call him innocent. One never feels like an adult with one's parents, and he did experience a slight embarrassment still living with his at twenty-five.

Fitz, his father, never ceased to make him aware of that, either. Oku had tried to move out a few years ago, but Fitz had made him feel both guilty and stupid at the same time.

"Well, if you want to break your mother's heart, I am not the one to stop you. And if you want to go give white people your money while you could give it to your own family, fine. Go follow other stupid black people and treat the white people better than your own flesh and blood."

Nothing about himself, of course. Fitz had put out that it was not on account of any personal regard Oku owed him, but Oku felt ungrateful anyway. There was Fitz saying that Oku was betraying not only his mother but also the race. The combination killed off Oku's idea of a slamming bachelor apartment with a black leather couch, a CD player with multiple loading, a space where he could smoke ganja any time and possibly seduce Jackie without interruption. If he had had that place two months ago, he could have taken Jackie home after the Lula Lounge. He would not have gone cold when Jackie closed the door, disappearing into Ab und Zu, leaving him sick and strangely frightened, picturing her slipping into bed with Reiner. He would have had friends over day and night, he would have spent hours listening to Monk and Miles and Ornette and Dizzy and, best of all, not had to hear Fitz's voice each morning. All that if he had not listened to that same voice confidentially saying, "Now you can stay home and save the little money, which, for me, would be the best thing. Me know say you is a man. Me respect you as a man and as a son, whatever is mine is yours. So you know the right thing to do. You no have to leave. Me as a man would never say you shoulda leave." This was as close as Fitz could come to saying that he was asking Oku to stay; it was as close as he could come to saying he would miss him. And Oku had been seduced by it, thinking his father was finally acknowledging that they were men on equal terms. Fitz was pleasant or at least silent for the better part of six months after Oku's decision to stay. But he gradually reverted to his old self as time went on. By which time Oku had blown the first and last months' rent he had saved and Fitz had the upper hand again.

Oku was waiting for Fitz Barker to speak. Let him talk all he wants, he thought, don't answer, appear interested, even schooled, in all the old-time lessons that are his pleasure. Then leave the room. Every morning Fitz delivered the same history lesson in between chewing his hunk of hard dough bread, thick with butter, and downing his cocoa. Oku's mother, Claire, listened diligently, eyeing Oku as if to say, Please, please don't answer back and please, please take a lesson.

"Boy, when I come to this country, I didn't have nobody, you know!" Fitz paused for accent, searching Oku's eyes to make sure the significance of the point was understood. "You think is one time I wanted to weep here in this place? But I couldn't do that. Who would bother with me? I was a man. Boy, you hear what I'm saying? I was a man."

"Understood, Pops." Oku couldn't help a little sarcasm, a little humour.

"Don't 'Pops' me, boy. You think because you go to school you smarter than me? Is me who send you to school, boy. Don't think you have it on me, you know!"

"No, Pops, I don't have it on you at all."

Fitz fixed him with another searching look, trying to figure out if Oku was joking again, trying to make a fool of him. Oku looked as sincere as he could, sensing his mother.

"You damn right there, boy."

"Damn right, Pops." He was thinking of Jackie.

"Damn right, I tell you." Fitz was lingering over these words with his knife in his hand, making sure that each centimetre of bread was covered with butter.

"You'll get a heart attack doing that, man." Oku tried this as much to halt Fitz as to warn him.

84

"*Heart attack?* I work every day, boy. You ever see a man like me with a heart attack?"

Fitz was on his favourite subject now, the physical and moral benefits of manly work. Let him go on, Oku thought, finding something else to do with his mind as his body absorbed his father's harangue. What an unhappy man. Jesus. He looked out the kitchen window to the garden, where his father grew tomatoes and sweet peppers and mint in the summer. Back of the garden was a garage with at least three broken-down cars, parts, anyway, from three broken-down cars. His father threw nothing away. An old muffler, a leaking carburetor, a rusty fender. Fitz filled every minute and every space with work. Oku had no desire to do any of the things his father did. They shared little beyond genes and the way that DNA makes you walk the same way and lift your head the same way, the way it makes your hands seem as the hands of one person. With one exception—his father's love of music.

Fitz had a trunk of old records, which he opened every Sunday with a bottle of Scotch while Claire cooked their favourite meats. Spinning Miles and Dizzy and Coltrane and Charlie Parker, the Shirelles and the Four Tops right along with Toots and the Maytals, John Holt, and Burning Spear. As with all his things, this trunk was off limits to his wife and Oku. For Oku, it was the only thing fascinating about his father—this trunk. Sundays were the only days that he could say—apart from the times when he was so young as not to remember—Sundays were the only days that he could say he loved his father. "Claire, Claire," his father would call, "you remember this one?"—throwing a forty-five of the Platters on the record player. Fitz still had forty-fives and some seventy-eights. He had the long spinner and the inserts for the holes in the small records. When the music hit him, he'd swoop Oku's mother up in his arms and spin her around, his thick hands becoming elegant and smooth on her back. "This is what you call dancing, boy," he would laugh if Oku ventured into the room. "You could never dance like this!"

On Sundays, if Fitz was in a particularly good mood, he would drive Claire out of the kitchen and start cooking himself. Claire having done all the seasoning the night before, there would be a hyperbole of pots and pans clanging, and oil splattering everywhere, before Fitz emerged with simmering curried goat and aromatic coconut rice, boasting at his prowess and his versatility. All along delving into his trunk and putting the Mighty Diamonds, Beres Hammond, and Gregory Isaacs on the stereo. Of course, when the bottle of Scotch was coming to an end and the music from the records becoming sadder, when he began to play Wilson Pickett and Swamp Dog and realized that he was on the brink of tears, he would have to get angry and turn on Claire and Oku instead. He would tell them they were useless and did nothing but eat him out of house and home. If they were lucky, he would go outside to the garden and slam the back door behind him. And if not, they had to sit very still until his anger subsided or risk having an ornament flung at them if they moved. Not that Claire took it always, but it was better to take it than to object. She didn't want a fight lasting days. And Fitzy was a good man, he only felt that he had been held back, and were he a different man in this country, he would be further ahead.

Sundays were like that—which lately Oku had avoided by staying out all weekend—and weekday mornings were like this: everyone had to wake up at the same time as Fitz, and if Oku made the mistake of sleeping in, Fitz would kick the door in. "I have to put bread on the table for you, the least you could do is be at that table when I'm there."

This used to annoy Oku, but not recently. Recently he would surprise his father by saying to him, "Fair enough, Pops. Level vibes." When he first said it, Fitz was struck quiet. "Hmm." The boy looked like he was pulling a new tack. What did he want now? But Oku would jump up and head to the kitchen close behind him.

"You find a job yet, boy?" That one he knew Oku couldn't answer.

"Soon and very soon," Oku mumbled.

"'Soon and very soon,' eh? All right, boy."

This was Oku's new plan, to humour Fitz. Not to fly off in a rage at him, not to bait him, not to look down on him. But to feel sorry for him and to see him as oppressed, ground down by the system.

"You happy, Pops?" Oku said, looking back from the window and the carcasses of Fitz's plants and cars.

"*Happy!*" Fitz was incredulous. "It don't have happy in that! Happy, boy. You think they put you here to be happy! You damn fool. Claire, this boy need to do a good day's work, then he'll understand. Happy, my ass."

"You don't think that you should be happy by now?"

"This university business making you stupid or what?"

"No, really, Dad, you don't think that you should be happy by now? What's all this for?"

"To put food on the table so that my betters can tell me I'm not happy."

"Why you got to be so sensitive? Why can't you just answer the question I'm asking you? Are you happy? Don't you feel you should be happy?"

Fitz looked as if he was about to burst. "Claire, you hear this nonsense? You hear what this idiot boy, *you make*, asking me?"

"Fitz, mind yourself now."

"You don't see the boy speaking as if he better than me?"

"Ah, forget it, 'old school.' Never mind."

"Why you don't go about your business and make me go 'bout mine?"

"You're right, you're right, Pops."

His father thought he was going to the university, but he wasn't. Oku was doing a master's degree in literature, but he had dropped out in January. He couldn't bear it. And he was weary with the fear of what Fitz would say and do if he knew. They'd already had an argument long ago about why he was doing literature. What good would that do, what the hell kind of job could you get with that, was Oku intending to eat the papers or wipe his ass with them when he got it? Because that is all his "master's" would be useful for. Oku had endured any number of attacks on the efficacy of a master's degree in English literature. He had used aloofness and rudeness. It would be a dreadful comedown to now admit that, though for altogether different reasons, he had arrived at the same conclusion as his father. Every now and then he had an attack of panic so strong that he felt weak, he had pains in his stomach. Each morning he thought he was working up to telling him, but each morning he failed.

When he examined this fear, he realized that it wasn't simply a fear of Fitz. It was he himself who was afraid. He didn't know where to go from here, and he would see that in his father's rage, and the panic in him would threaten to burst out and he did not know where it would go.

This morning he'd started what he now thought was a stupid argument about happiness. His father was intolerable, couldn't hold an adult discussion. He always had to be certain and right about everything. There were no variables in his life, no uncertainties. If there was anything he was uncertain about, he just pretended to know it. So there was no talking to him. He knew everything.

Fitz was a compact man, not a small man by any means, but compact, tight in his big body and tight in his self-assurance. Oku watched him leave the table, his face resolute. He hated him and he envied him. Often Oku, who resembled him, would find himself looking at his own image in a sudden glass window. He would see his father there in himself but with just that iota of doubt that made him himself and not Fitz. The image would catch him by surprise and not a little disappointment that that self-containment, that pig-headedness, could not be his. No doubt he would get along much better in the world if it were. And just now, as his father rose, he remembered only a few years ago, when he was a teenager, looking at his dick in the mirror and wondering if his father's dick was the same length, the same shape. A chuckle escaped him. Fitz spun around and stared at Oku hard, making sure that he held his gaze long enough for dominance. Oku chuckled and gave it to him. "Boy . . ." Fitz finished, leaving the room.

Claire rose immediately after Fitz, following him down the hall and seeing him out. When she returned to the kitchen,

Oku had already retreated to his room in the basement. She had wanted to ask him what was all that about happiness. Fitz might be dense, but she wasn't. She'd been noticing some things, like how Oku hardly picked up a book any more though he left with books each day, like how he crawled into the house sometimes in the small hours of the morning, a wreath of ganja trailing him, after being dropped off by a Jeep full of men, with booming music. Then again for weeks the men would disappear and those girls would call and he would stay out nights, days. She was covering for him. Fitz didn't notice all these things, but she did. What he was up to, she didn't know.

EIGHT

WHAT MADE JACKIE THINK of that train ride to Toronto? She hated complications. The train from Halifax to Toronto. The memory of it came from the time when she had no control of memories—which she would keep and which she would have disappear—when she couldn't shape them into something else. She hated complications. Anyway, she had to compose the letter to *InStyle*. *Dear* InStyle, *what the fuck is up with that Bo Derek piece in October?* Okay they won't print "fuck" in the magazine. *Dear* InStyle, *What is up with saying Bo Derek's corn rows is an example of one of the most imitated hairstyles of all time? Are you for real? Are some of you smoking something? Did you all do some bad coke?* All right, strike the last two questions. *My great-grandmother, not to mention my ancestors, are turning in their graves . . .* Would they get it? Too subtle. *Stop crediting Bo Derek with something that goes back centuries in Africa, America, the Caribbean, and Canada.* Maybe she should start the letter, *Dear* InStyle, *I am a Canadian fan of your magazine. I was shocked . . .* "Hook a brother up"—what made him think that she would be impressed by that line? Not in this lifetime, not in this frigging lifetime. She was not going to get dragged into that tired bullshit.

The streetcar was practically empty. She could have looked around to see if Oku was still standing dumbstruck at the light. Instead she remembered the train, which she tried to put aside for the letter. It had taken the longest time getting here. She could feel her parents' anticipation. She was a little sick from the rocking of the train, or was it from their talk about how different, how exciting life was going to be from then on? She fell asleep so many times, half waking to hear her father's rap on James Brown and Mustangs, his favourite car, or her mother saying, "You sleep, baby," to her, or, "You know it, baby," to her father. What was it that made her remember? It was, yes, it was the same mix of desire and revulsion, the same feeling in that train car of warmth and insecurity, damage and seduction. Standing close to Oku, his limber virility, his lips, his throat growling, "Hook a brother up." It was just a turn in that sentence that lost her to him in that moment. Little did he know that without the accent on "brother," without the hesitation between *u* and *p* in "up," she might have stayed with him at the traffic light. High and having a good time at Lula Lounge was one thing. This was definitely another.

Jackie flipped through the *InStyle* on her lap again ads for Tiffany, Escado, Mercedes, Patek Phillippe, Gucci, Ralph Lauren, Marc Jacobs, Coach. There was Michael Michele in Carolina Herrera, Halle Berry in Valentino, Lucy Liu in Carmen Marc Valvo, and there was where her letter would appear. *Dear* InStyle, *I have been inspired by your feature on Vivica A. Fox. She is such a wonderful actress* . . . No fucking way. He was not what Jackie had in mind. I control my shit, "brother." There was so much more in those four words. As she had told him—she hated innocence. She had detected it as lethal way back on that train ride out of Nova Scotia. She despised people who didn't know what was going to happen to them. Those kinds of people, she thought, lied to themselves and to people around them. She had no pity for that kind of person, and what Oku had been asking for was pity.

Tiring of *InStyle*, she flipped through *Black Beauty* to the horoscopes: "Aries—April is your time of the year romantically but you are in danger of being attracted to those who do little to brighten up your life, so don't give up your heart too quickly . . ." "*Not fucking likely,*" she said loud enough for the few on the streetcar to look at her. ". . . Cash wise, gains come through investments, people, and travel. During May you seem to be saving like crazy because you are quite capable of saving more cash than a demented millionaire on occasions . . ." She laughed, unaware of the attention she attracted around her. She looked up to see her stop about to be passed, and she pulled the cord furiously for the driver to stop. When he didn't, she collected her magazines and walked to the front of the car. The driver slowed to the next stop. Jackie climbed off, saying loudly, "Some people are just assholes."

Alexandra Park is that urban warren of buildings and paths where Jackie and her mother and father lived after taking the train to Toronto. That was 1980. Here they call Nova Scotia "down east" and "down home." In Alexandra Park everyone is hip to the news about who else is making their way across the country, best as they can, hoping to find a job in Toronto or, better still, a way back home with some money.

After Jackie grew up, she didn't want to go back, but her mother and father still always talked about it as if it was a real possibility. Impossible. And they both knew it. They'd sold what little they had in the first place, which was a diamond earring belonging to Jackie's mother from a great-grandmother who went to New York in the thirties and a car with a broken fan belt belonging to Jackie's father. And little by little, in the years following, most of their families, except for some unknown, unfriendly cousins in Truro, most had moved to Toronto too. So there was no one to go back to, but the thought remained a fantasy, and as fantasies do, it pictured Nova Scotia, Halifax, as a paradise on earth and Toronto as a wretched hellhole. Jackie didn't remember Halifax, Nova Scotia, anyhow. Same as any kid, a life is a room, a playground, a mother, a father, not a city by the ocean, small and undulating, not a harbour, not snow cakes out to sea, not a warm Scotch at the Brown Derby on Gottingen Street.

Jackie wouldn't remember Halifax except for the North End Library next to the apartment building where she lived the days of her fifth year. Half a day with her grandmother, half a day at the afternoon daycare. At the library she would linger on pictures in books from the children's section and Miss Towney would get her and other children to sing "Lift Every Voice and Sing" once a year.

Not needing a memory to take with her on a train all the way across the country, all her memorable memories were in the two people she sat between on the train ride—the one who took her to the bathroom and held her up so she didn't touch the seat and the other one who blew on her hot chocolate before she drank it; the one who gave her his change and his rabbit's foot to play with and the one who undid and redid her braids so she'd look nice when the train stopped almost a whole day later at Union Station in Toronto. Jackie was going to be a supermodel ever since her already long five-year-old legs twisted and scrunched themselves trying to sleep on the train coming west. She was decked out in psychedelic pants and a frilly Indian top just like her mother's. They were five years late for that style, but they were still looking good in 1980. The father wore velvet pants and a hat with a feather.

They came to Toronto just when the Paramount—the best dance club in the country—was about to close. They only got the tail end of the dancing and the beautiful aroma of fried smelts. That was after Marvin Gaye came out with "After the Dance," and the Paramount had a huge painting of the jacket cover on the wall. And people were as if they had stepped right out of the painting, the slinky retro-thirties dresses, the men in hats, the saxophone player, the whole smoky intoxicating gyration of the figures in the painting melded with the figures on the dance floor and at the fish-fry tables. The smell of Avon White Linen perfume and the elegance of Chivas and all the crazy moves and all the broken hearts and the girls who were being turned out and the men who tried to look criminal and hard and the drunks who were charming and the drunks who were mean and just the hot, urgent, dangerous feel of the place where scores were made and scores were settled. Jackie's mother and father only tasted it all for a year or so. Maybe two.

Jackie's father found out that there was a crap game downstairs and you could get reefer and blow and whatever, and when the cops entered the Paramount a red light went on and off, the signal from upstairs to ditch everything, the money, the drugs, the works. He thought craps was his game, but every man down there thought that. This is how you could wake up the next day with your furniture going to somebody else's house, all because of a bet past broke. And your engagement ring—somebody could tell you it once belonged to them. And your leather coat with the slit up the back looked just as good if not better when you watched some guy who came to the Paramount in polyester walk away from you with it on his back.

Jackie's mum got in with some girls who had a rivalry with some West Indian girls. Saturday nights they would settle all scores in the women's washroom. The Scotian girls, and she was one, had a reputation for fighting. They would beat you like a man. Because their fathers beat them like men and their brothers beat them like men and their men beat them like men, so they beat each other and those West Indian girls like men. You never just fought one of them, they were all related somehow. If some West Indian girl thought she could bring it on in there and took some Scotian girl on, a crowd of cousins and aunts would be on her. "That's my cousin you messing with, girl." The women's washroom was a place to show off your badness. Your bad threads or your bad fucking skills or your bad fist skills. There were some fights there. Over men, over money, over just looking too good for your own good. Everybody at the Paramount was on edge. You had to mind that you didn't disrespect somebody's woman or somebody's man or just somebody.

They knew about the Paramount from Cape Breton to Vancouver, *they* being a select group. Black people and a few, very few, hip whites—whites who were connected. Just as they knew about Rockheads in Montreal. And every blind pig in Winnipeg, Hamilton, and any city with more than two hundred black people. They were the first places people headed on the nights that the men didn't hit the strip clubs. On the weekends, that is. They were the places people went to feel in their own skin, in their own life. Because when a city gets finished with you in the daytime, you don't know if you're coming or going. After you didn't get the job, or got the job and it was shit, or you were tired of the job, the Paramount was a place of grace—like church. Where else could you enjoy the only thing you were sure God gave you, your body, without getting into any kind of trouble for it? Well, trouble you could handle anyway—trouble you didn't give a shit about, trouble you went looking for. You could dance that thing around the Paramount like there was no tomorrow. You could shake it, shimmy it, let it fall out of your dress, let it step off of your high-heeled shoes, you could dress it up any way you wanted, you could fill it with booze, you could float it on ganja, chill it on coke, you could get it fucked right there on the dance floor, then you could let it fall down near the light post on Spadina or walk it up the street like it was on a loose string. What could be more perfect?

Jackie's mother got caught up in the Paramount on account of Jackie's father and a West Indian girl from Jamaica. West Indian girls loved Scotian men on account of their accents, which were just like American black men's, which meant that Scotian men were close to dream men. So Scotian men got a lot of pussy from West Indian girls on account of that. They got a lot of pussy from everybody. In the pussy line, they were at the front. Jackie's daddy had to come into the ladies' washroom and tear Jackie's mother off the girl from Kingston named Marcia. Well, Marcia wasn't from Kingston, really, but her mother was. Marcia was born in Grace Hospital on Church Street, as Marcia told Jackie's mother when Jackie's mother called her "island bunny" and "Jammie." Kingston Marcia lost some hair and got a cheek almost bit off that night and Jackie's mother found a reputation.

Jackie got parked at Liz Dorry's like all the other children whose mothers and fathers were out partying and hustling and drinking and dancing at the Paramount. These were early days, their first, second year in Toronto. Jackie's mother wanted to take a course in hairdressing, a course in icing wedding cakes, and a course in nursing. She was twenty-two. Fine as refined sugar. Jackie's father had his own set of fights at the Paramount over Jackie's mother. Some dude with a fur coat would start eyeing Jackie's mother or grinding her on the dance floor and Jackie's father would have to break bad.

The fried smelts were delicious at the Paramount, and cheap. There was the obligatory thick greasy guy of a cook with a cigarette hanging from his lips. He would pile those smelts high on the plate, then ring in the money at the cash register with the same oily hands. But man, did they ever taste good. There was the whole incongruity of the elegance on one side of the Paramount and the fish fry on the other and the mishmash of it in the centre. It was a throwback to juke joints and speakeasies, but all legal, well, some legal, right there on Spadina Avenue.

Then there was also the Elephant Walk, where you had to be known to get in, where you had to be certifiably dangerous to get in, or know someone who was. You had to be badass or beautiful. Threateningly beautiful. The kind of beautiful that teetered on the brink of some disaster, like a tooth knocked out or a knife gash that would make the beauty even more beautiful for its gone promise and its evidence of having put itself on the line. Jackie's mother and father were in time to see this at the Elephant Walk. It was up three flights of stairs in a building on Spadina that held a few small sewing factories. It was just south of the Paramount, and the door was barred from the inside. A bouncer would look at you through a peephole and let you in if you hit the standard. Then he would look you up and down if you were a woman as if you could be his or as if you were his when he opened the door. If you were a man, he took your measure, said, "Hey, bro." Or was threateningly silent. Truly only the pimps and whores got into the Elephant Walk with no trouble. If you were like Jackie's mother, fresh out of the Brown Derby on Gottigen Street in Halifax, Nova Scotia, you were out of your depth. Jackie's father only had the look, he didn't have the play of those dudes he imitated in their morning coats and slanted hats. And even they weren't always the real deal. The dudes who didn't front and didn't talk so much about being players, they were the real deal. They looked like death. There was a nothing sound around them, not even a calm sound, just the dead sound of nothing—no compassion, no humour, no feeling.

Jackie's father used to be a barber down home at Al's Barbershop and he went to work at Golden's on Bathurst Street the second week after he arrived in Toronto. He was reckless, though, and recklessness got him into the Elephant Walk, which is where one of those dead men threw him down the three flights of stairs for trying to horn in on the action. His leg was broken, and he'd walked with a limp ever since. He really made a name for himself when he came back on crutches and sliced the man's left quadriceps with an old-fashioned razor.

All this took place at the Elephant Walk without benefit of police or charges. Or, at least, the police questioned but got no answers. That community was so tight that if there was a fight in the Paramount and reinforcements were needed, it would only take thirty seconds before word hit Alexandra Park a block and a half away, and five seconds later they'd be there. It didn't matter the time. It was usually one o'clock in the morning. They had radar—advance-warning radar. And it worked well, especially if cops were in the park. Salt-and-pepper cops was how the police decided to deal with Alexandra Park—one white cop, one black cop. The black cop was supposed to smooth the way. One of "their own" to make them feel comfortable and make them talk. Only problem was that the pepper cop was from the West Indies and the cops had miscalculated racial bonds. Though not even the West Indians would talk to the West Indian cop. To everyone, cops are just another race altogether, and as far as they were all concerned the pepper cop was a race traitor. The time when they were looking for Jackie's father after he worked on that dude's hip abductor, Jackie's father knew before the two salt-and-pepper cops hit 113 ½ Vanauley Way, but he sat waiting for them. He gave them a good view of his broken leg. How could he have? it asked them. What was he—Superman?

Ab und Zu advertised itself as selling post-bourgeois clothing. The store was just on the border where Toronto's trendy met Toronto's seedy. The rent was cheap, and Jackie had had the foresight to think that the trendy section would slowly creep toward Ab und Zu and sweep the store into money. Next door to Ab und Zu was a greasy spoon—Sam's—recently taken over by other hopeful trendies—a couple of women who were anarchists. There, a mix of the old neighbour-hood—the working class, the poor, the desperate—and an increasing number of anarchists—mostly friends of the two women—drank coffee in mutual curiosity. Every morning, the two women and Reiner, because he opened the store, would have to wash the sidewalk of last night's vomit or piss. There was a pimp, Ronnie, who preyed upon the most drugged-out women in the neighbourhood and who used Sam's as his office. When the two women took over, Ronnie menaced them into letting him stay, and in the first weeks he succeeded—until they tried to fix up his workers and get them counselling and rehab. Then Ronnie moved his crew along farther west, but not without a parting touch of vindictiveness.

A broken door that the women suspected was Ronnie's doing. No more trouble though, Ronnie couldn't afford too much heat, just the destitute puking their stomachs out occasionally in front of Sam's and Ab und Zu when they could lay their hands on some alcohol.

Reiner was waiting impatiently for Jackie. He was dressed in his usual gigging black. He was a lean tall man. A tattoo of the planets in their orbits ringed his left forearm. His face, slightly pocked from childhood illnesses, was hard, square-jawed, and roughly handsome. He had his gear near the door. He had a gig in Kitchener tonight. Reiner lived at the back of the store and his band practised in the basement. This all helped with the rent of the storefront, where two women were now browsing through dresses.

"Hey, babe, glad you're here . . ."

Jackie came through the door. "Hey, hon, sorry"—then seeing the two customers—"Lorraine! Lorraine!—Long time no see. I've got just the thing for you, girl."

Reiner tried to get her attention again. "Jacks, baby, Claude's coming with the van . . ."

"I know, I know, sweetie, hang a sec. Lorraine, come on over here." She headed for some racks, dragging the customer called Lorraine behind her. "Missoni, Lorraine, big print, lots of colour, chunky new look, combination bohemian chique—opulent glamour, very northern Italy. You too, honey"—she turned on Lorraine's friend—"very sixties. Try it on."

"Jackie, here's Claude now . . ."

"Yes, sweetie . . ." Her encouraging gaze still on Lorraine and her friend, Jackie walked over to embrace him, kissing him, running her hand over his cheek. "Bye, honey, have a good gig. See you tomorrow, oh no, Sunday, right?"

"Yeah, you gotta open tomorrow, Jackie."

"Of course, sweetie. What did I tell you, Lorraine? Very south Austria, right? Warm, bold, you, honey. Bye, baby."

Reiner loaded the amp into the van at the front door, then came back for his guitar. Jackie felt him lingering and broke off from her sales pitch.

She embraced Reiner again, saying what he wanted to hear, "I'll miss you, babe."

"I'll miss you more." He had been hoping she would have come earlier to spend some time with him. Now he sounded petulant, wounded. She, of course, had forgotten about his gig.

"Don't say that, babe." She touched his roughened face, then took his guitar and walked him to the door. "I'll stay over Sunday, cool?"

Reiner was reassured.

Jackie stood on the sidewalk, watching the van pull away, muttering to herself, "Now that's what I'm talking about." With Reiner, she knew who she was, separate and apart, in command of self. With Oku, she was on that train, liquid and jittery and out of control.

NINE

A MAN ONCE JUMPED in front of a subway train, embracing his three-year-old son. What it must have felt like to be held like that, simultaneously clasped to a bosom and thrown against a devastating object. Why had he taken the boy with him? Why did people kill their children or their girlfriends or their wives or their parents before killing themselves? Why did they not simply take themselves—was it some spite against another, against the world? How does one maintain spite so late, so close to perhaps the one solitary moment one had?

The next week Carla saw the funeral on the television news. What a mess he'd caused—now a lot of people had to put things right, had to mourn him, to bury him, to pick out his funeral clothes, carry his coffin, weep for him. Their lives would be altered forever. His wife had to feel guilt over what she might or might not have done, there would be rumours about how she was to blame. Carla would have gone alone, taken only herself and not in so public a way either; she would have simply disappeared, a well-planned disappearance so that no one would know that she was gone in that way but perhaps only gone on a trip, moved to a new city or country. She would have left letters to be mailed over time, arranged phone calls, she would have left a definite route to another life being lived. She would inconvenience no one. That's how a suicide should be done. It should be a disappearance. A happy disappearance.

What Carla herself remembered from St. James Town was the odd stirring of the air on the balcony. Something bad had happened and no one would be coming back and this was all a spectacle, it was awful and it was also wonderful, an occasion. She remembered smiling as if it was a prize or an enviable event, though all through it she had walked around with the baby in her arms. No one could pry him loose from her. If they tried, her screeching reached the street twenty-one storeys below, even when her father tried. Especially when he tried. She was not supposed to give the baby to him, she said, her child's scream piercing him. Through the dense walls, over the balcony, sirening down the railings, through the discarded summer furniture, the thrown-away carpets, the derelict skates, lamps, beer bottles, the forgotten cardboard boxes, the dried pots of annuals, through all the dreams apartment dwellers store as garbage on their balconies until the next summer. Her screams travelled and fell to the knob of grass at the front of the building, radiating out to wherever Angie might be. She would not stop screaming until she was left alone with her brother in her arms. Then her screaming subsided, and in a minute, the threat forgotten, she was thrilled again at the occasion of having someone die in her own house.

She was five then, twenty-three now. And she could still hear a telephone ringing, which she could not answer because she was holding the baby for Angie; the front door slam, then open—the baby was hers. Her mother had given him to her. Had passed the bundle of him gurgling to her. She had been singing along with the radio, "Trains and boats and planes . . ." She had a pencil in one hand and a last mouthful of doughnut in the other and she was conducting an invisible choir when her mother out on the balcony had said, "Carla, stop that noise, sweetie, and come and hold the baby."

Her mother, Angie, always had her hold the baby when she potted plants on the balcony. She potted impatiens and marigolds and morning glories. She tried a grapevine once and after a few years there were tiny sour green grapes. Carla loved those grapes. She loved to wear the same clothes as her mother. She especially loved a purple velvet skirt. Angie had the skirt. Carla had a dress of the same velvet. Angie sewed a green bear at the front.

"Now put the pencil down, sweetie, don't get it in his eye. Okay, take him inside now. Careful, careful. Hold him carefully."

Carla's stepmother, Nadine, works at Mt. Sinai Hospital, but she wouldn't be in the line of nurses outside grabbing a smoke; she didn't smoke. Carla's mother, Angie, smoked though. She was in Carla's mind yesterday and today, but she wished that she remembered her mother more clearly. Then she might know what to do about Jamal.

Over the years, despite her efforts to hold on to the memory, her mother faded and faded until all Carla had left was the certainty that Angie had existed and the violent loyalty she owed her. There was a small photograph of Angie that she had been allowed to keep as a child. A woman in blue jeans and a checkered shirt with dark shoulder-length hair. The photographer had caught her with her mouth about to say something—a sentence unfinished—her eyes were happy, laughing. She was in a park, a dog and a man and a tree were in the far background. Her skin was pale, and there was a mole on her left cheekbone. Carla had memorized her face.

Jamal, of course, could not remember their mother. Because he was still a baby when she died and it had been Carla's job to tell him about Angie. Her small recollections weren't always enough to support the fierce passion she expected of him in this respect. She had even taken him to where they used to live, showing him the high-rise apartment building on Wellesley, pointing to the twenty-first floor, the railing from which she and Angie had blown bubbles into the air; the balcony where they sunbathed in the summers. Angie had bought her a pair of sunglasses just like her own, and they rubbed suntan lotion on each other, giggling, and lay on towels listening to the radio, to Three Dog Night and John Denver and Credence Clearwater Revival. If she could give Jamal a memory, she thought—something like a lovely secret—he could hold it and it could perhaps make him strong when he needed it. But Carla's own font of memories was fading, and those that she had given to Jamal were only second-hand and worn out, if not fabricated.

Carla loved these Mondays the way she loved snow-storms. The way these two things stopped the world. A city hemmed in by snow was a beautiful thing to her. Cars buried in the streets, people bewildered as they should be, aimless and directionless as they really are. Snowstorms stopped the pretence of order and civilization. The blistering winds whipped words right out of people's mouths, they made all predictions and plans hopeless. She would abandon all warn-ings from Tuyen and the weathermen on twenty radio and television stations and launch out into the city in a blizzard. Identifying the direction of the wind, she would turn and turn in the blizzard and be lost, walk with it, walk against it, driving her feet through the thick gathering wall of it. Nothing like a snowstorm to calm a city and make things safe and quiet.

But there was no snowstorm today, just that same numbness about her brother. Which is why she found herself standing in front of the big apartment building where they used to live when Angie was alive. It had long become a kind of shrine for her.

Carla was thankful that she'd got a job as a courier. It gave her more time to think, and she could ignore the world where you had to fit, where you had to play some game she didn't understand and just wasn't up to. She probably could have if she had wanted to—that's what her friends always said.

She was not phenotypically black either. Only on careful consideration could one tell. She looked more like her mother. She always found it odd and interesting that most black people recognized her anyway. They were more attuned to the gradations of race than whites. Whites generally thought she was Spanish or Middle Eastern. So to disappear into this white world would have been possible. But it would have been a betrayal of her mother's choices as she saw them. Her mother was white, her father was black. Her mother must have made her choice for a good reason: good or bad she had crossed a border. Carla instinctively understood. And it must have meant something profound to her mother. It must have taken some doing and it must have cost something, because when she died no one claimed them, Carla and Jamal, no one except her father. And that reluctantly. Angie had been dead to her family since the day she started up with Carla's father, Derek.

Though Carla had thought many times of running away from living with her father and stepmother, she never did—there was always Jamal to keep her. He had run to Yonge Street when he was fourteen. Their father had eventually found him there, standing in a doorway at the Gerrard Street intersection with two other boys. He was high on glue. That was after Carla and Nadine had pleaded with him to go get Jamal. Well, Carla didn't plead, she hung over the house like an unanswered question. Derek, her father, could feel her brooding and her anger—he was oddly alert to it even when she was a child—so he went to get Jamal. He had been two weeks on the street and was ready to come home. He sullenly followed his father to the car, came home, and slept for a week.

Jamal swore to Carla that he wouldn't do it again. She came to his room and reminded him that it was just the two of them together and alone in the world, and he promised without understanding. She promised him that when the time came, soon, she said, in a year or so, they would move out together. They sat in his room, dreaming of this. About the stereo he'd have and the job she would get after college and how he could finish high school while she worked and how they would be free from their father and this house. He promised the way anyone promises after a rough experience. But it was only the first time he ran away, not the last.

Carla had approached the buildings from the north, from the vista of the viaduct. Angie used to like that spot. Even in the winter and especially that last winter, she would bundle Carla and the baby up and take them to that spot. Walking up past the Castle Frank subway to the bridge looking over the Don Valley. Angie would stand there, staring and telling them how lovely it was and that it reminded her of where she was born, except for the bridge, except for the traffic, and except for the winter. She promised that in the summer she would take them down the trails under the bridge. She hadn't done it that summer after all, Carla thought, though there were summers when she had taken Carla alone. That was before Jamal was born. The two of them, Carla and Angie, would set off on a Sunday morning, finding their way under the bridge, idling along the paths, listening to birds and the snuffed noise of the highway high above them. But that summer, the summer when Jamal was still a baby, was the summer when Carla's job was to hold on to him, tight, while Angie stepped off the balcony. Angie hadn't even waited through the whole spring.

They had argued furiously. Carla had covered her ears to block the noise of the fight between her father and her mother. Her father was screaming, "Don't you ever, ever come to my house and disturb my family again. This is the last time you'll ever see me, you bitch."

"You're not going to get away with this. You liar, you liar, you fucking liar." Angie's voice was thick with disgust and love. Then there was only the sound of bodies against walls and fists against flesh; a dresser tumbling down in their bedroom.

"You're crazy, you're fucking crazy, let me go." Her father dragging Angie toward the door, Angie hanging on to her father as he tried to reach the front door. When he got to the door he succeeded in ripping her fingers from his throat and shoving her hard toward the kitchen.

"Fucking bitch, you want to ruin my life, eh? Leave me the fuck alone."

Angie was whimpering as he slammed the door, then with a kind of roar she grabbed a pot from the sink, flung the door of the apartment open, and sped down the hallway, screaming, "You fucking liar, you shit, I'll hurt you, you see, you see if I don't." The pot ricocheted off the elevator doors, and Angie stood there emptying her lungs with the sound of an enraged wordless scream. Back in the apartment Carla patted a mewling Jamal. He had been awakened by the noise and was fretting. Carla patted him, saying, "Sleep, sleep. Sleep, sleep."

Angie came in from the hallway, went to the bedroom, and collected Derek's clothes. She took them to the balcony and threw them over—his gloves, his pants, and his underwear. Then she cleaned the apartment, turning the stereo up to its loudest, scrubbing her hands under the kitchen tap, her face slack-jawed, streaming with tears.

Carla told Jamal this story once, what she recalled, in an attempt to make him understand why he should love someone he never knew and why she was steadfast in her love for Angie. Jamal only understood it in that it deepened his sense of why his father did not love him. Even as the story came out of her mouth, Carla knew this was how he would take it, not as a sedative against their father but as a confirmation of his fears. More and more she found herself unable to console him or to call on anything she actually knew for certain that would help him.

"Maybe she was a bitch, Carla." He had said the most dreadful thing. She had slapped his already wounded face and strode off. She could not forgive him. Yet she did in the end because he was the best thing that she had of Angie's.

782 Wellesley Street, apartment 2116. Toronto M6H 5E7. Phone number 962–8741 (when the bill was paid). When Carla was four, Angie had taught her the address through nightly repetition. And her last name—Chiarelli. The building looked slightly shabby now. Worn out. So were her feelings, standing in front of it. Carla sat on the small grassy spot out front. She was suddenly exhausted, from the long walk and from the ride yesterday, from the whole thing. Did it happen the way she remembered it, did it happen at all?

All the way here she had felt childish, as if she was going to tell Angie something. But, of course, Angie Chiarelli wasn't here and this place was just a nondescript, shabby apartment building, a new set of people going in and out of it; its occupants must have changed several times in the last eighteen years. Whoever lived in apartment 2116 was oblivious to Angie or to her. This was not a home where memories were cultivated, it was an anonymous stack of concrete and glass. There were no signs of Angie's presence, no old wardrobe, old door buzzer, old dress. The grapevine had been ripped down from the balcony of 2116, the towel and the suntan lotion and the dark glasses Angie bought her were not strewn haphazardly on the floor up there waiting for her. She had overused these memories, wrung everything from them. She could hold them on one page of a notebook. The only way she could make them last was to spool them in a loop running over and over in her brain. The same sentences arranged in different ways. She knew she had probably made up some incidents along the way until they were indistinguishable from the real ones—extensions of them. Had she said, "If Angie were here, this or that could have happened," and then made it so, melting what should have been with what was?

Sometimes she thought that events could not possibly have happened the way she remembered. How could she recall with such clarity things Angie said, things her father said? Wasn't she too young to understand? But she did remember. She would swear by it. Love can make you remember. And what she had left, what she could be sure about, was an utter love. When Angie had said it was time for her to go to school, she had spent hours drawing a picture of herself. She gave it to Angie her first morning of kindergarten, saying, "I drew you a picture so you won't forget my face when I'm gone." What she was sure about was that this love was steady and deep enough to create itself over and over again.

But 782 Wellesley had become less and less cooperative in that love. Today it stood there indifferent and inhabited by other lives, other worries, other dramas. The building would not register these any more than it had Angie's. 782 Wellesley was built especially for disavowal—it was incapable of nuance or change or attitude. It was innocent. Carla felt a stifling lethargy. Wasn't she just thinking about love? "Draw me a picture of you so I won't forget your face, Mom." Angie had laughed, kissing her. That feature of love, the one that recalled something unadulterated, enjoyable, she no longer remembered it. The flush of pleasure never came on its own. Always the invasive clasp of a wilfulness, as if she loved Angie despite things, not for them. She hated her father because she loved Angie, she loved Jamal because she loved Angie, she loved her friends because she loved Angie, she was a bicycle courier because she loved Angie, she hated policemen and ambulances and bank tellers because she loved Angie. Loving Angie was a gate, and at every moment she made decisions based on that love, if the gate swung open or closed. She kept from loving because she loved Angie. She collected nothing like furniture or books because she loved Angie and things would clutter the space between her present self and the self that Angie loved. Carla needed a clear empty path to Angie as a living being. She appeared calm on the outside. She had a cool surface. But the battle to sort out what she could and couldn't love was furious in her. The loop of experiences with Angie needed more and more space in her brain and the invention that maintaining an image of her mother required took all her will and focus. The things that she could touch that reminded her of Angie were few. This building was one. Today it yielded little that could nourish her purpose.

The latest tenants went in and out of the doorway. Carla searched their figures for any familiarity. Doesn't a life leave

111

traces, traces that can attach themselves to others who pass through the aura of that life? Doesn't a place absorb the events it witnesses; shouldn't there be some sign of commemoration, some symbol embedded in this building always for Angie's life here? She guesses perhaps not, though she stands on the lawn as if she should be noticed or acknowledged. What did she actually want here? Acknowledgment or release? She was holding on to a precious bundle; there was a woman's face there and scraps of conversations and what felt like nerves and emotions and sinews—and the bundle was fragile and elliptical and she wished that she were not the only one responsible for it. Angie would disappear if Carla let the bundle fall. And why should Angie disappear, what had she done? She had, yes, crossed a border. But wasn't that daring! Wasn't it hopeful? How come she had to disappear for it? Angie had lived dangerously, as one should. How else could anything be done. That was what Carla was holding for her. If only because Angie had made her and Jamal, if only for that, Carla would hold Angie's bundle of sinews, impressions, and her face.

Jamal was waiting for her to do something to get him out of Mimico. His next bail hearing was in three weeks' time. There was nothing else for it, she had to go see her father before that. She turned away from 782 Wellesley if not energized then purposeful. It was afternoon now, three o'clock or so, and she felt hungry—she would walk across the great arc of the bridge to the Danforth—it wasn't far, but turning to the bridge, her body sank, she couldn't summon up the stomach to go there. Not now.

TEN

TUYEN'S FATHER'S HOBBY was drawing all the buildings in the city as if he had built them. In his spare time, which was brief, after the restaurant was shut for the night, after the produce was put away, and the kitchen cleaned, and the lights dimmed, Tuan would go home and draw. Because after all that work he couldn't sleep. He had gone past tired to that wide-awake state that prevented him from sleeping until three or four in the morning. Tuan would often begin working on his drawings at one of the tables in the restaurant, not bothering to go home when the rest of the family left. He could not always endure his wife's insomnia, which was not a restful one like his, but a continuous pacing, throughout which she went over again and again the scene at the bay when they both lost sight of Quy.

Cam played the vision over in her head, trying to regain the moment when she did not see, trying to alter the sequence of events so that she would arrive at herself in the present with her family and her mind intact. Just a split second would have been all the difference. Why hadn't she noticed that moment as she should have? Why couldn't she reclaim the time? Why had this happened to them? It was she to blame, it was she who could have with one turning of the head caught sight of Quy and pulled him to her. She could taste that moment, she longed to live it, it terrified her. She had such a deep sense of shame she felt inhuman.

Tuan, for his part, worked to stave off his own lessening. No work was back-breaking enough for him. He welcomed the rebuff of Canadian officials and employers to his licensing as a civil engineer as it matched his sense of unworthiness and dishonour. There was nothing they could take away from him, nothing he had that he had not lost already. Though despite both himself and the powers that be he was successful. But he drew buildings as if he was still what he was.

He did not like to think of that moment the way Cam did—if he did, he would have days of paralysis when he could not get out of his pyjamas, his limbs felt weak, and he could not work. He would glimpse himself at the bay, feeling relief that they were finally leaving, ticking off in his mind all the preparations he had made, all the months of secret negotiations on getting his savings out and then the dangers of talking to the wrong people about their departure. Had he hesitated a moment too long or a second too short in all these phases of the planning, and had that hesitation pushed events off-centre? He was only too aware of how important it was to have the right weight of objects, the correct angle of alignment for a stable structure. So too with events. *To be able to stop when seeing danger, is knowledge.* It was all dangerous, but he had not been able somehow to measure the danger, to apprehend the most crucial moment like the weakest point in a structure. *Guard the home you have, and regret vanishes.* This is what in his outward demeanour he strove for. *Keep the order of the household—when people in the home are strict, it is auspicious to be conscientious and diligent.* The household was strictly committed to these mantras. But, still, neither of them, Cam nor Tuan, could find a cure for their alertness.

She paced, he drew.

Tuyen learned to draw from her father. She had imitated his posture and the movement of his drawing hand since she was a child unaware of what he was actually doing. Amused by her mimicry, Tuan gave her pieces of paper and a ruler and they both sat creating drawings of boxes, bridges, pipelines, buildings. Tuyen's drawings quivered on the fantastic, first because she was a child and her lines would become wavy, or as her mind wandered she would include a face here and a kite there, but as she grew older these inclusions became more deliberate. Her father's annoyance only spurred her to perfect the fabulous as a practice. A head growing out of a drainpipe, a river flowing through the roof of a house. Gradually Tuan became used to it, convinced by then that she would not, as he had hoped, become an engineer like himself. Architectural school, perhaps, then. There she could express that creativity. Even with this, though, she had dropped out, and Tuan was at a loss to figure out how to control her. He had in his estimation lost control of his family since the night in the bay. All his efforts were to hold together the constantly slipping limbs.

It was inevitable that Tuyen would apprehend the seepages in her family's life. There was always in the house the double life, the triple images. Not to mention the outside world, which was threatening and which was the engine behind the manufacture of still more fantasies. Tuyen's love of the unexplainable was inevitable. Her parents became for her subjects for observation and intuition. In art school, which she went to next, she discovered Remedios Varo. Remedios Varo's father was a hydraulics engineer. He trained Remedios to draw by having her copy his diagrams and drawings. From imitating him, she learned depth and detail. Added to which, they say, she had a rich dream life that leaked into her own drawings and paintings. Tuyen discovered this coincidence with her own life at art school, and her brief stay there, if it was good for anything, awakened her at least to this.

When Tuyen had found her father at home in the middle of the day in his pyjamas, she knew that meant he had spent the night awake drawing, and that meant a paralysis had overtaken him. Her mother, too, must have been awake pacing, as she had done over the last many years. Pacing or writing an endless stream of letters to authorities in every Southeast Asian country, searching for Quy. Terrified of returning to that part of the world herself, Cam had become involved with a network of officials, charlatans, magicians, crooks, and other distraught parents like herself in her search. Tuyen had once happened on a collection of these letters, whose duplicates her mother kept for easy referral and follow-up, and hope.

> *Dearest Mr. Bowles, UNCHR,*
>
> > *Please excuse my bad English but my state of distress is great. I believe that you can help find my Quy and know where he is. I have no sleep since he disappear from me and my husband. Enclose is a photo of him. If in your list of lost boys, please to find him, and his mother and father is awaiting at Refugee Settlement House, Toronto.*
> >
> > *Please do your best.*
> >
> > > *Sincerely, Vu Duong Cam*

> *Dearest Mr. Chao, Hong Kong,*
>
> > *I am sending the money here which will pay for your investigation. I'm happy that you are close to finding our boy and eager for his return. Whatever is necessary we will do. We left Chi Ma Wan Camp on September 29, 1980, at 1 P.M.*
> >
> > > *Sincerely, Vu Duong Cam*

July 7, 1985

Dearest Mr. Thieu,

> *I was sent your name as a person who could help us find our son Quy. He will be ten years old now. Enclosed is a laminated picture of him. He will not be much changed. Here is a laminated picture of my family so you can know what he would look like. Also money is in close to.*
>
> *Sincerely, Vu Duong Cam*

April 25, 1986

Dearest Sir, Mr. Chao,

> *I'm happy that you think you have found Vu Quy. The money is coming for his passage to us. You brought me so much joy.*
>
> *Sincerely, Vu Duong Cam*

October 19, 1991

Dear Editor, Thai Daily,

> *Please post this ad in your newspaper: Reward of Canadian dollars for information as to the whereabouts of Vu Quy, last seen at bay on March 28, 1980. If you were at that place and have any information about this person, please write to Vu Cam, 5713 Meadow Way, Richmond Hill . . .*

January 15, 1991

Dear Ms. Ebhard, UNCHR,

> *Please also to forgive my English. Your Mr. Bowles has sent me to you. Our boy is lost now few years. We hear of a list of lost people and we ask for it. If in any of your travels you have seen him. Here is a laminated photograph of my family to help you searching.*
>
> *Sincerely, Vu Duong Cam*

Dear Editor, Bernama, Malaysia,

> *I'm looking for a small boy by the name of Vu Quy. He knows his name and his parents' name. If you find this boy, please hold him. There is a reward of money for his return.*
> *Sincerely, Vu Duong Cam*

May 5, 1997
Dear Editor, Lienhe Zaobao, Singapore,

> *Why do you not print my letter any more? Have you no heart? Have you no mother or children? . . .*

June 29, 1999
Dear Mr. Chiu, astrologer,

> *I am sending you $350 today as agreed. The day is indeed auspicious as you promised. I slept somewhat last night for the first time since arriving in this country and I know that must mean that my son is safe.*
> *Respectfully and sincerely, Vu Duong Cam*

Yet Tuyen found her father slightly elated on the drive to the city. He seemed to have forgiven her for her reference to the family secret.

"Where you off to, Tuyen?"

"Home, Bo."

"Oh, home is not where your family is? Home is that nasty place?" She sensed slightly less conviction in him. As if he were joking with her a little.

"Oh, Bo, don't start again."

"Okay, okay. You know, soon maybe we will have some news . . ." He broke off as if he'd said too much. She prompted him.

"What good news, Bo? Did you buy another restaurant?"

"Oh, never mind. New restaurant? No, well. You see."

It was the most confidential the father had ever been with her except when he indulged her in drawing with him. But on serious matters he was a virtual tomb. The rest of the ride to Toronto was mostly silent. Tuyen felt slightly uncomfortable. She wanted to apologize for insulting him, but her usual forthrightness deserted her. She changed the subject to Binh.

"How's Binh? Where was he today?" Did her father know about Binh's plans? she wondered. Was that the news he was referring to?

"Binh? Good boy. You should come home if you want to see him." All conversation led to this point with her father. "And why don't you help him when he asks you? You have a duty . . ."

"Oh, Bo, you know I don't like selling. It would be very bad if I helped him. No one would buy anything."

Her father laughed. "It's true. What? What are you good at?"

"Bo, I'm sorry for hurting your feelings."

"Don't be sorry. You come home and everything will be fine."

He either deliberately misunderstood her or hadn't taken what she'd said in the same way as she thought. She kept quiet for the rest of the ride; he took it as an acknowledgment of his rightness and seemed prepared to leave it at that this time. He did not launch once again into his usual harangue about friends and family, about duty and obligation and honour.

When the car neared the Saigon Pearl, Tuyen asked her father to drop her off. She was always afraid of Tuan dropping by the apartment, even though she often told him to come see for himself that she was fine. He didn't put up the usual fight this time, just said, "Binh is a good boy, you respect him. You call." Tuyen hugged him and hopped out of the car. "You come home," he called after her.

She felt there was something odd about her father's behaviour. Not his behaviour, more like his demeanour. She sensed a lightness about him. Something she'd never sensed before. She wouldn't say that her father was a gloomy man, but he cherished correctness, propriety, and in this he appeared dour. Now she perceived a slight change in him that was startling to her. He was usually so purposefully serious that the hint of any lightness, and it was only the merest hint, seemed extravagant. She would have to call Binh after all. Perhaps agree to help him out at the store again. That twinge of embarrassment she had felt when Carla said the word "mine" about her own brother returned.

Though Tuyen and Binh were not far apart in age—he was eighteen months older—they were in sensibility. They'd never been particularly close. Mostly they had fought each other for their parents' attention. Binh considered Tuyen a usurper in his quest for their affections—he was the only boy and the favourite, it seemed, until Tuyen came along. Then no amount of cherishing was sufficient for him. Tuyen seemed to get attention simply by being the newcomer. It would be easy to say that this sibling animosity followed them to adulthood, but it didn't: their roles were simply different. Binh was the cherished boy, Tuyen the baby.

Yet they could not get along even though they were collaborators of a kind as regards translating the city's culture to their parents and even to their older sisters, they were both responsible for transmitting the essence of life in Toronto to the household. It was a job Binh took tremendously seriously and Tuyen took, as far as he was concerned, with too much whimsy. Binh would translate instructions from teachers or a mailman or the hydro man. He would invariably slant these to his own interests, as when a bill arrived, he added arrears to the amount, pocketing the extra, or when notices from the parent-teacher meetings were sent home, he would suggest that teachers wanted to discuss the fact of his father making him work too much in the restaurant. Tuyen, on the other hand, always threw those notices away, and when the hydro had to be cut off for fixing a main, she would tell the household there was an emergency in the city and that she would not be allowed to go to school for the day. With the exception of when they were quite small, they never fought outright since an all-out war would not be beneficial.

The uneasy collaboration made them wary of each other and therefore mistrustful. So when her father said Binh was a good son with that minutely discernible sense of elation, Tuyen was immediately suspicious—this lightness she ferreted out of her father had something to do with Binh and that dangerous idea he had hinted at a few weeks ago. Her brother was once again trying to focus the drama of the family on himself, and that could not be wholly good. For him perhaps, but not for everyone else.

Binh was a mercenary trained in the trenches of child-hood to get his way. And in the particular war waged in the Vu household, his way was sucking up all the attention. He perceived, like all his siblings, the vacuum left in his parents by that night long ago in the bay on the Vietnamese coast, and in his efforts to fill that unnamed space he went to great lengths. Not knowing precisely what was necessary, he tried every angle. Recently he had assumed more and more of the responsibility for the restaurant. Lately it was packed at night with his friends occupying several of the tables toward the back all evening long. His interest in the restaurant had been spasmodic—usually around some bright idea for a karaoke machine, or small jukebox machines on the tables. Tuan would shoo him away, telling him he had no head for business and asking him how those ideas would make money.

Binh had been sent to the University of Toronto to do business and had left with all the credentials of an M.B.A., namely a distaste for the straightforward and honest, a mistrust of social welfare, and a religious fervour for what was called the bottom line. His education had enhanced his penchant for ungenerousness and solidified his resolve that only he mattered, though he had also been indulged at home beyond the bounds of favourite son. Since he was, in effect, two sons, the one lost and the one found.

But it was a difficult task to stand in for a mythic tragic brother who, not having to do anything, never failed at anything. And who, not having a physical presence, could never be scrutinized for flaws and mistakes. That mythic brother grew in perfection, it seemed, as Binh felt himself struggle for adequacy.

Binh was that strange mix of utter overconfidence and insecurity, utter ruthlessness and squeamishness. So while he invested fifteen thousand dollars in a shipload of migrants from Fushen to British Columbia, he did not want to know the details or, of course, be named if they were discovered. Though if they were not discovered, and even if they were, he stood to make a profit of three or four hundred per cent on his investment. His was not the lion's share in this enterprise. He was a small investor. But he stood to make even more if some of those migrants found their way to Toronto, from which he and several colleagues would arrange their transportation to New York City with proper documents. He also had a small investment in a home-based Ecstasy manufacturing plant, which distributed to high schools and raves. Binh, like all businessmen who run multinational operations, could swiftly pull his money out of one concern or another and invest elsewhere. For safety, and because he did love electronic gadgets if he loved anything, he ran a small electronics store in Korea Town on Bloor Street.

The day Tuyen moved out of the house, Binh stood outside the kitchen door waiting for her. She was heading down to the garage to borrow her mother's car.

"I didn't think you'd make it," he said, grinning at her.

"Well, I did." She was surprised by the almost complimentary sound in his voice.

"Hey, I can drive you if you want."

She felt a softening toward him and a relief. At least he understood her need to live on her own.

"Thanks, I can drive myself."

"Ma said I should drive you, no big deal."

She didn't feel like struggling any more, she'd withstood the crying and the badgering and at least Binh hadn't tried to dissuade her, so she let him take her, and her garbage bags full of clothing, to her new place above the store.

On the drive downtown they said nothing to each other, and Tuyen was grateful for that. It occurred to her that the silence between them was more than silence. It was a leave-taking. It would be solely up to him now to carry out whatever other duties of translation remained.

"This is a dump," he said when they arrived.

"No, it's not. It's great. Look at the ceilings."

"Whatever."

"Don't go saying it's a dump, okay, Binh? I don't want them going more crazy about it."

"You should stay home, save some money, and get a condo. That's what I'd do."

"I'm not you."

"Guess not. So, later. I'll take the car back to Ma."

He handed her the last garbage bag and picked his way down the staircase, squeezing past an old stove on the first landing. Tuyen felt the faintest stirring of fear watching him go. Then she realized with a kind of joy that she was about to be alone, and with unusual friendliness, she called after him, "Bye, Binh!"

Today he still lived at home devotedly. In fact he, unlike Tuyen, had no feelings of restriction at home or urges to find himself. He was himself under the adoring eyes of his father and mother and the watchful knot of his two older sisters. He came and went as he liked, he bought a BMW, and if he had girlfriends, he stayed at their place when he needed privacy. His spiritual motivation, if he was aware of a spiritual side, was to so please his father and mother as to seal that opening in their hearts left by his mythic brother. Yet over the course of his life so far he had not been able to come to that project without a deep-seated resentment. That their love was not given wholly and unadulteratedly, he felt, made him return it in kind. Then too, his lost brother had been a child, and as a man now he felt shame about his resentment for a child. How could he match such perpetual innocence? How could he compete?

Neither he nor Tuyen, nor Ai nor Lam, could say that their parents had ever fully declared them second-rate to their lost child. Cam and Tuan were parents in the way they knew—dutiful, authoritarian, good providers. And certainly Ai and Lam, who were the only other witnesses to that loss, did not think in those terms ever. They were born in the old country and understood their positions before Quy's loss, understood as a matter of culture; and surely if they had har- boured any hopes of changing that, of living out their fan- tasies of the North American teenaged rebellion, with Rolling Stones concerts and independence and free sex, Quy's loss squelched those hopes.

It was Binh and Tuyen who were in a position to feel second-ratedness as a visceral marker. Their culture was North American despite their parents' admittedly ambivalent efforts to enforce Vietnamese rules, and in North American culture they knew it was *de rigueur* to love children equally and for children to claim that kind of love as a right. Binh picked up on that lost right and made all efforts to collect it. Tuyen, on the other hand, was made merely curious by its absence. She preferred to explore other aspects of North American birthright, such as independence, free love, and artistic irrelevance.

Tuyen had never felt the need to keep an eye on Binh's dealings, but as she left her father and walked along College Street toward her apartment, she felt a deeper stirring of uneasy interest. About her family she had taken a superior view. She considered them somewhat childlike since her power over them in the form of language had given her the privilege of viewing them in this way. And her distance from them, as the distance of all translators from their subjects, allowed her to see that so much of the raison d'être of their lives was taken up negotiating their way around the small objects of foreignness placed in their way. Either they could not see the larger space of commonality or it was denied them.

But superiority aside, she was still broke. Watching her mother, she'd had second thoughts about breaking into her sleep to have her mother force money on her. She had become so preoccupied with having hurt her father and wanting to apologize to him, and her sister had put her off with the threat, despite her cool response. She had, as usual, become confused and tangled up in their presences. Some day she wants to mount an installation of the characteristics of her family, if only she could imagine the science with which to do it. It would be a hundred boxes of varying sizes made of a transparent translucent material floating in a room, suspended by no known element. The floor of the room would be water, and she would walk through the room bumping into the boxes, which would not be discernible to the naked eye. As she collided with the boxes, things would fall out, spikes and keys and mouths and voices.

She would have to go to the restaurant later and borrow some money from her father; though she hated giving him another opportunity to scold her and lecture her about dropping out of school, about living downtown, she was desperate and would have to endure it. Or she might take Binh up on the offer of money for keeping the store, which would also give her a chance to scope him out; to see what he was up to. She had told him she wanted nothing to do with his idea of digging things up, but she had no illusions that that would stop him. Admittedly, she had abdicated to him her role as arbiter between the outside world and the family, but she might have to intervene if his scheme—she was sure there was a larger scheme behind it all—placed them in jeopardy.

But her father was shrewd, she assured herself as she neared the apartment. She and Binh might have been the translators, but her father ran things. He determined from which version to abstract the family's course. Still, her parents had a vulnerability that she had known for as long as she could remember, and it made her feel protective of them; it had sometimes motivated her interpretations of the exchanges between officialdom and her family more than self interest.

Stopped at the light, she laughed at this partially disingenuous assessment of herself. She remembered her child self, her teenaged self, impatient with her mother's repeated attempts to get accreditation, tired of making phone calls for her, writing letters of explanation and not mailing them as she was instructed, knowing that her mother's letters were so convoluted that they likely would only prove her unqualified for consideration. Bureaucrats, Tuyen knew, were not impressed by long letters containing life stories. There were forms that had to be filled out with no addendums, no laminations. Anyway, she had been a petulant child, thinking her parents incompetent and wishing they were different, similar to some perfect parent she had in mind who was not Vietnamese and for whom she did not have to translate the world.

"Hey, what're you laughing at?" Carla had come up to her on the street, caught her laughing to herself.

"Oh, Carla!" Tuyen snapped around. "I was so worried about you last night—and this morning. Where'd you go?"

"Walking. What's funny? People will think you're mad or something."

"You didn't talk to me this morning, what do you care?"

"I'm sorry . . ." was all Carla offered.

Seeing her about to dive back into the morning's mood, Tuyen said, "I forgive you. See how easy I am?" She brushed a hand over Carla's left cheek. "Jackie was over this morning and Oku. They came for coffee. They might check by later."

Tuyen chatted the rest of the way to the apartment, trying to keep the mood light. She was happy simply to be in

Carla's company again. She didn't mind caring for people who were not her family—it was so much easier; they actually did not expect it and were more than grateful for it. With other people you could begin from the beginning, together you could create your own forces, your own stories. Love was easier, it was unexpected, pure. Because it was unasked for, unsolicited, yes, unexpected. Like Carla. She loved Carla.

With her friends, Tuyen could be lavish. They took it as a gift. They took each other as gifts. They were marvellous each time they met, bringing each other messages from the realms of their families and poring over these messages like found jewels, turning them over in the hand and listening to the sounds of them as they clinked on each other. Now that they were older, the details of their families lives loosened on their tongues, becoming fantastic when they lay together on the ratty couch at Tuyen's, examining them. This was Tuyen's interpretation, at any rate.

Now, walking toward home with Carla, the uncomfortable feeling she'd had observing her father seemed already to belong to another world. The fear she felt—no, she would not call it fear—the presentiment she had now appeared as just another secret box for examination.

ELEVEN

THEY WERE ON THE STAIRCASE up to the apartments when they smelled the cooking coming from Carla's place. "Oku!" they both said together. Oku was a great cook and he would often come to their place and cook elaborate meals from their scanty cupboards. They loved those visits, when he would throw together what to them were impossible ingredients and come up with sumptuous meals. They each had an aversion to cooking. Tuyen's was easy enough to understand. Throughout her childhood she'd spent from four o'clock in the afternoon to midnight in a restaurant, falling asleep on the table to be awakened and taken home half walking, half dragged. She could count the days since her father acquired the restaurant that there had been a meal cooked at home. If they didn't eat at the Saigon Pearl itself, they ate leftovers from the Saigon Pearl. Tuyen made every effort not to learn cooking and developed a dislike for what was called Vietnamese food.

"Why can't we eat like normal people?" she used to ask when she was little; when she was sent to school with minty soups and bean curd.

"Don't you see normal people coming here to eat, Tuyen? They like our food," her father would point out, but Tuyen was never persuaded. She only felt exposed in the restaurant when European clientele were present, and when the customers were Vietnamese or Korean or African or South

Asian, she hated, then, the sense of sameness or ease she was supposed to feel with them.

It took her years to admit to friends that her family owned a restaurant, and she was still not comfortable taking them there. Tuyen's favourite food was potatoes, cooked any style, but mostly just plain boiled potatoes with butter. They were easy to cook, took no attention whatever, and to her taste they were the most delicious things. She could eat potatoes any time of day or night, huge bowlfuls. Potatoes were perfect, neutral, and glamorous. Meaning not at all like her family. And milk. She loved milk. Despite the fact that her stomach reacted violently to it. But she insisted on drinking it. Or now buying it at least. She thought of this violent response as something to be conquered, like learning a new and necessary language. If nothing else, her tiny fridge could be counted on for storing putrefied sour milk that she had not had the courage to consume.

Both their childhoods, Tuyen's and Carla's, had been of navigating different and sometimes opposed worlds. At every turn it had been treacherous. And food was the dead giveaway. On Saturdays Nadine, Carla's stepmother, would take her to Kensington Market, where laden with bags Carla would wait and wait, her body in an impatient and resigned burning, as Nadine talked to the storekeepers, haggling an extra piece of fish, an extra lime, an extra pepper, mistrustful of the weighing of every item. Her stepmother's happiness in contrast to her unhappiness and discomfort was most evident at the Saturday market. Carla stood waiting, her nose rejecting the smells, her throat gagging on rotten fish and rotten vegetables, her face turning away from the appalling blood stains on butchers' aprons at European Meats, her whole being wishing to be elsewhere. Carla hated Nadine's exotica.

She was uneasy among the pawpaws, soursops, plantains, goat, fish, gizadas, and cans of ackees. "Your father likes this," Nadine would croon. She'd taught herself how to cook Jamaican just for Derek. Carla despised the smell of the stores that carried dried cod and fresh thyme and mangoes. Her ears registered discomfort at the sound of accented voices pausing in self-derision, in boastfulness, or in religious certainty. She hated this language that she made herself unhear, unthink, and undream. She never actually learned it except to understand her father, Nadine, and their friends, and to translate it to her teachers and anyone official. She had been a translator herself, knowing a language the way a translator whose first tongue is another language knows. She did not live in it. She considered her father's customs foreign, embarrassing oddities that she would try to distance herself from in public. Nadine would take her to the patty store, bestowing on her a patty in cocoa bread and a cola champagne as a treat. Carla stood uneasily eating while Nadine insisted that it tasted good. She found the floury depth of the two breads distasteful. The centre of meat and spices burned her and set her tongue on fire. The cola champagne added heat where she wanted coldness, water. So overwhelming was the whole market that the taste in her mouth was sweet and sickly at the same time. She vowed never to come here when she grew up.

So food was not their specialty, nor cooking. If not for the potatoes, which Tuyen shared freely with Carla and had in abundance, Carla would be bone thin. And so they both fell on Oku, hugging him, when they got to the top of the stairs.

"If I was straight, I would marry you," Tuyen said.

"You're a dream, Oku." Carla hadn't eaten since the day before. The smell from his cooking made her notice how desperately hungry she was.

"Oh, you don't want to marry me too? Still noncommittal?" Oku teased her.

"Closest you've come." She moved to the sink compulsively. "You're a great cook, but you use every pot, pan, dish, and spoon in sight. Everything's dirty."

"Oh, Carla, leave that. Let's eat first."

"We need dishes to eat on, Tuyen. Girl!"

They were sitting now on the floor in Carla's apartment, savouring the meal Oku had cooked. He had no culinary antipathy registered in childhood discomfort. He loved his mother's cooking, he loved his father's cooking. He learned to cook lovingly what Carla had rejected from her stepmother. The graffiti crew from across the alley was there too, scattered around the floor: Kumaran, Keeran, Abel, and Jericho. They had smelled the cooking across the way and asked Oku if they could come over. He bargained with them for rice and cardamom and cloves and chilies, and now there was a curried chicken dish with the odour of cardamom, cilantro, and burnt cumin. Then there was rice, saffron-coloured, with peas and raisins. Oku hadn't learned to cook rice this way from his mother but from the graffiti crew—well, not the whole crew, but Kumaran, whose parents were from Tamil Nadu. He had also crushed a papaya and tossed it into a vanilla ice cream for dessert, and he had brought from home one of his father's precious eighty-eight-proof bottles of Wray and Nephew rum. He had taken his mother's training and augmented it along the way with all the training of all the mothers of the friends he had. His father would probably not approve, preferring the monoculture of Jamaican food, but Oku's tastes had expanded from this base to a repertoire that was vast and cosmopolitan. On their lucky days Tuyen and Carla would come home to fried snapper in a mole sauce or cassava frittes with burgers, or chicken's feet soup. Odd that the same foods they were averse to in their childhoods they now revered in Oku's hands.

Today he was really hoping that Jackie would return as they had loosely agreed, for Carla's sake. But so far she hadn't shown up. He wanted to make some type of amends for that ineffectual, rude remark he had made to her on the corner. He wasn't sure really what her response had been, but he'd taken it as dismissal; in his long unrequited approach to Jackie he had always been able to balance himself between meaning and not meaning. He was waiting for her to take him seriously, but when she didn't he prided himself on being able to laugh it off as she seemed to do also. He had watched carefully over her different relationships with men, knowing that if he was snide enough about them, they would disappear. He thought that it was his doing—their disappearances. The German boyfriend, however, was proving difficult, and he was getting slightly panicked.

"Jackie said she was coming, right?"

"Oh, and here we were thinking this was all for us, Carla."

"Oh, come on, of course it was. I'm just asking. So she should be coming, right?"

"She'll show up, I guess. You know she's got the store now."

"Ab und Zu! What the fuck is that anyway?"

"Here and now, honey. Or is it now and then, Tuyen?"

"Now and then, I think. They're doing well, Jackie says. Reiner's living at the back of the store to save money. And the band is practising in the basement."

"*Practising*? Bunch of fucking Nazis imitating that Guns N' Roses shit!" Oku was beside himself. "Can't she see?"

"Chill out, man." Kumaran laughed, trying to laugh Oku out of it.

Oku turned to him, slightly embarrassed. He'd forgotten the graffiti crew in the room. "Yeah, what you guys do lately?"

"The subway, end of the line at Sheppard. You can see the pig there when the train slows." Kumaran licked his fingers. "And see that bank at the corner of Dundas and Spadina? Right at the top? We did that."

"You guys are nuts, man. How'd you get up there?"

"We hold each other by the legs."

"Out of your mind, man, y'all are out, frigging crazy!"

"It's art, man. You should come with us one night. Tuyen does."

"Now you got to be out of your mind. I'm staying on the ground. On the ground, man. None of that high-wire shit for me."

The crew laughed, getting up as if by signal. Kumaran's graffiti crew prided itself on fluency, stealth, and agility. They had made themselves shadowy and present in the city, as in the room. If anyone had looked into the apartment, they would have seen Tuyen, Oku, and Carla right away, and only after searching for something sensed but not seen would they have grasped the leaning, slouching, posed outlines of Kumaran, Keeran, Abel, and Jericho. They were critical presences, unnoticed until they felt like being noticed. They saw their work—writing tags and signatures—as painting radical images against the dying poetics of the anglicized city. The graffiti crew had filled in the details of the city's outlines. You could see them at night, very late, when the streets seemed wet with darkness, agile and elegant in their movements. The spiritual presences of Tuyen, Oku, and Carla's generation. Their legs straddling walls and bridge girders and subway caverns, spray-painting their emblems of duality, their dangerous dreams.

"Check you guys later," one of them said.

Tuyen jumped up, following them to the door, promising to go out with them again soon.

Oku turned to Carla, "So, Yardie, what's the dillio on Jamal?"

"You got ten thousand dollars or a house I can borrow?" She heard a betraying resentment in her voice. "No, I'm serious—that's what I need to get him out."

"Why do you have to do it? Why can't your father?"

"Pleeease. He washed his hands a long time ago."

"Isn't Jamal still a juvenile, Carla? Isn't your father obliged?"

"*Obliged?*" She laughed this time. "He's not obliged to do shit. Jamal is eighteen. He's not a juvie any more."

"That's some dope shit." It was inconceivable to Oku. His own father would never let him out of his sight. He thought of this with fear and relief.

"You know, Carla, maybe this time he's just got to figure it out himself."

"You don't understand. You have people, Tuyen, right? You, both of you, always had people."

"He had people too, Carla."

"Not like you. Anyway, he's my brother. I'll deal with it."

"Carla"—Tuyen's voice was soft—"we're not saying . . . you know, like, abandon him, but he always does this and then you're the one who has to . . . you know, clean it up, fix it."

"Yes, the point is, you always rescue him, see. He expects it. So we're saying you can't keep up. He never takes care of you! He's not a baby! So maybe just let him handle this for himself, like a man, this time."

"Would you want that for your brother, Tuyen? You don't have anybody, Oku, so you don't know. If you did, you think you'd just let them stay in jail?"

"I don't know. You're right, okay, but what I'm saying is why doesn't he ever think of you? Where you going to find ten thousand dollars? That's just whack!" Oku was incredulous.

"Well, I'm probably back to where I don't want to be, I guess. Gotta go see Derek. I was on my way there this morning, but . . ."

"Your father?"

"Yes, the fucking asshole."

"Well, he should take it on, Carla. Why should you have to alone?"

"Okay, okay, done already. I don't want to talk about it any more."

Carla started briskly packing up dishes again. Tuyen made no move to help. She poured another rum from Oku's stolen bottle.

"What the hell is this made of, Oku?"

"Good stuff." Oku smiled at her, wandering over to the stereo.

"Hey, Carla, take one, let's just chill out. Kick back." Tuyen rose. Going toward Carla at the sink and holding Carla's head back, she poured a shot into Carla's mouth. Carla gasped from the bracing fumes, bent over. Laughing now.

"Hey, Carla, where's my Dizzy?"

"Doesn't look like she's coming, Oku." And they laughed together drunkenly.

Quy

Time. All of them have time. I had waiting. They have their
friends and this city. I had shit. I guess you'd say I should
have made better of myself. I didn't have anybody sacrifice
a whole life for me. Every one of them had that. A city like
this is built on that. I can feel it all around.

After a year and a half at Pulau Bidong I learned a little
English. My first step to humanity. My father had hung
around the assholes of enough Americans to know the
value of English. He came home with words like "cool"
and "Charlie." At Bidong I buzzed around the UNCHR
people, hoping one of them would find me interesting or
cute and take me with them. I almost did it. There was
one lady who looked at me fondly, and whenever she
came, I made it my business to be less hungry-looking and
more charming. It's hard to look cute after a year and a
half of loneliness. I offered her little objects I made with
twine and sticks and bottle caps. I collected plastic debris
and gave it to her. And after all that, the bitch didn't take
me. She was French. My father spoke French. The
UNCHR people kept looking at us and asking us how we
were treated. Us, the children parents had abandoned or
lost. We punched each other out for their attention. All
they did was count us and write reports.

When I first saw Pulau Bidong, I've got to say it was

beautiful. The boat I was in was called the *Dong Khoi*. We had drifted for the last ninety-six hours without water or food. Mercifully, although I don't believe in mercy, we looked up one dawn to see Bidong. The water between the *Dong Khoi* and the island was blue-black. The air was cold, even though it was hot. The water—did I say?—was a wonderful misty blue-black, and there out of the mist rose Pulau Bidong. Green and greener where the sun hadn't touched it yet. If I got to that island, I thought, I would stomp all over it. But this is the future and I'm recasting. I didn't feel that. I thought instead that my mother and father, my sisters, would be there waiting for me. I thought all boats went to Bidong. The sight of the island lifted my hopes. I've never been able to get rid of the feeling I had at the sight of Bidong in the dawn. The sky was a blue-grey mist too, yet all three hues of sea and sky and land, I could see clearly through to the waking sun. It may have been about four or five in the morning. There was a silence. Sometimes I wish that I had stayed right there in that picture in that dawn. I see me leaning off the *Dong Khoi* with the beautiful island in front of me and that feeling of expectation. Right then, nothing is wrong. Nothing.

I could've had a different life if that moment—ah, sure. My father and mother had already dragged me from a certain trajectory. Truly, the war had already dragged us up and ripped up our planned course. People like me don't have control of life. Anonymity is a useful thing. In some places they think people like me are preparing to bomb buildings and murder children. My mother and father and my sisters went off to join them, and I suppose I would've gone right along with them and never had these thoughts if I hadn't followed those legs onto the *Dong Khoi*. Perhaps I would've had these thoughts anyway. Perhaps they're having these thoughts but have stuffed them so far down their own gullets they're inexpressible.

I'm grateful in the end for the *Dong Khoi* and Pulau Bidong if I'm grateful for anything. But gratitude is not one of the outcomes of this story or my life. My brother got my father and mother at the thick point of their guilt. They don't see him, they see me. They imagine me in the dense mist in the South China Sea, me on Bidong. They pour all their senses into him, paying and paying out till he's sick with indulgence. I've got no pity. You think I would look at his face and not see the years he's been fattened instead of me? Brotherliness is another feeling I can't come up with. Self-interest is what moves the world. People bunch together because they're scared. I'm a loner. Don't expect me to tell you about the innocence of youth, that would be another story, not mine.

What happened to the master who made the servant swear never to tell his stories to anyone else? Did I tell you that story? The monk who came to Pulau Bidong once told it to me. I'll tell it to you in case you think I don't have a sense of humour.

Once there was a servant who had a young boy for a master. Every night the servant would tell this boy fantastic stories, and the stories were so good the boy didn't want anyone else to have them, so, the son of a bitch that he was already, he told the servant never to tell anyone else these stories just so he could have them to himself. He made the servant swear never to tell the stories outside his room, and the servant, ass-licking servant that he was, vowed never to do so. The boy grew up and was to be married. He dressed up in his finest clothes and went out of the house to his carriage to leave for his wedding. The servant happened to be passing by the boy's room when he heard voices from inside. Who could be in his master's room? he thought, and he leaned his head against the door to listen.

One voice said, "We have to do something about this damned boy today!"

Another voice said, "Yeah, that *cac* is going off to get married and we'll be locked up in this room forever."

"Okay," said a third voice, "here's the plan. I'm a story about a poisoned well. When he gets into his carriage and they're halfway to the wedding, he'll get thirsty and I'll appear and he'll drink from the well and that'll be the end of the selfish *lo dit*."

"Great idea," said the first voice. "But just in case he doesn't drink from the well, I'm a story about flaming hot coals. When he reaches his bride's house, they'll run out with a footstool. I'll lay under the cushion and burn him to death."

"Yeah," said another voice. "Fantastic. I'm a story about a deadly venomous snake. Let's say he doesn't drink from the well, let's say he doesn't put his foot on the stool. I'll lay in his honeymoon bed next to his sweetheart's face like a beautiful embroidery. When he lays down, I'll kill the *du-ma-may!* And we'll all be free from this room."

"Yeah," they all agreed.

Just then the frightened servant, who didn't know a good thing when he heard it, burst into the room, but there was no one there.

When the master went out in his carriage to his wedding, the servant begged to go with him. On the way the young master said, "Oh, I'm so thirsty, servant, get me some water from that well."

The servant, risking a blow to the head, said, "Oh no,

master, you'll be late for the bride. They've prepared better than water there for you."

The master said, "Okay, you're right."

When they got to the bride's house, the footmen brought out the footstool for the young master's feet. The old servant grabbed it quickly, burning his own hands, saying, "Oh, master, the coals are too hot, these idiot footmen. Climb on my back and I'll take you inside." The master was astonished but went on his back.

After the wedding, when the bride and groom had retired to the bedroom and the bride was all naked in the matrimonial bed, the servant snuck in and stood behind the curtain. Next to the bride's lovely face was the most exquisite embroidery of a languorous snake. And as the bridegroom was about to lay his head on it, the servant jumped out and grabbed the deadly venomous snake and smashed it to death, apologizing and explaining the conspiracy of the stories he had overheard in the master's bedroom.

What makes a guy so slavish? This is a fairy tale, the kind you know. Now who would make up a story like that?

TWELVE

AT THE ATM MACHINE in the bank, Tuyen found a photograph. It was lying there as if waiting for her. This always happened to her. She would turn around and find frames filled in with the life of the city. She would find discarded looks, which she tried to trace to their origins, or alternately their flights. On any given day, on any particular corner, on any crossroads, you can find the city's heterogeneity, like some physical light. And Tuyen found herself always in the middle of observing it.

She's taking her last twenty dollars out of the ATM machine, and when she looks down, there's the photograph lying on the floor. There are two people in the small photograph, a man and woman, against a tropical tree, with a church steeple in the background. The man is wearing light pants, a suit, single-buttoned, with a tie; the woman is wearing a white boat-necked dress. Tuyen turns the photograph over and reads: "*Recuerdo de nuestra noche*, 1968." She was torn between taking the picture, that was her first instinct, and leaving it for its owner's return. Such a photograph, someone would return for. The idea of using it in her installation came to her immediately. A token, *a memory of our night, 1968*. Whoever they were, they would be in their fifties now, they were in the heat of a love affair then, and they were in love with themselves; they were stylish, young. She wondered what they were like now and which one of them had lost the photograph thirty-four years later. That's what made Tuyen decide to leave it where she'd found it. In case that woman, or that man, came back in a terrible panic at having lost a moment in 1968. She put the photograph down gently, feeling it's afterimage in her hand.

Reluctantly she appeared at Binh's store. He looked up as she entered. There was an unusually grateful smile on his face.

"Don't be too happy yet . . ." She stopped, noticing that there were other people in the store. Someone small and cute who must be Binh's current girlfriend, and two of Binh's friends—Elliott, who Tuyen had never liked and who had been Binh's friend since grade nine, and another guy Tuyen didn't know but didn't like immediately. She was predisposed not to like anyone around Binh. And they all looked at her warily.

"Everybody, this is my sister Tuyen," Binh said, his voice proprietary.

The two guys got up to leave, the girlfriend stayed seated, trying to make even less of herself. Elliott threw Tuyen an appraising look before going out the door behind the other man. Tuyen noticed the other man bite his fingernails and spit them on the sidewalk, then examine his hand and put it in his pocket. Elliott said something to him, and they parted. The girl made a movement, and Binh introduced her.

"This is Ashley."

"Ashley?" Tuyen asked with an impolite curiosity. "Where'd you get a name like that? What's your real name?"

"Hue," the girl said defensively.

"Well, nice to meet you, Hue." She looked at her brother, rolling her eyes.

He said, "I see you changed your mind about helping me? Or you just snooping?"

"I figure, how hard could it be?"

"Yeah, right."

"And I could use the money."

"Ah," Binh said, a small triumphant look on his face. "I only need you to help Ashley out."

"Ashley? You mean Hue."

"Yes, Hue. For Christ's sake, since when are you so politically correct. She wants to be called Ashley, all right?" He sounded peevish.

"She does?" Tuyen asked looking over at the girl, who made no comment. "Well, whatever. So Hue's gonna be here. Fine. So what do you want me to do, then?"

"Ashley," he said firmly, "will open up in the mornings. I know you don't like to get up early. And do you have to wear that tatty old coat?"

"What are you? Donatella?"

"Fine, so you can close the store at nights?"

"Why? Trying to hide me from the customers?"

"Can you do mornings?" Tuyen looked disgusted. "No, I didn't think so."

"Okay, okay. Hue can do mornings, I'll close up. Every day?"

Binh was getting frustrated, and Tuyen sensed it. She wanted to be different with him. That was why she had come. That sound of the word "mine" from Carla had kept tugging at her. After all, he was making an attempt to find their brother, or so he said. And though she was suspicious of his motives, it wasn't a bad thing that he was trying to do. So why couldn't she summon up a warmth about him? Perhaps they had spent too much of their lives, all of it, sparring with each other. Perhaps Binh wasn't likable. Perhaps she was unlikable.

"Look," he said, pulling her aside, his arm around her

shoulders, "I just need you to keep it together here for me while I go. Just check on Ashley . . . Hue," he conceded. "She'll do all the work."

Tuyen felt his arm around her shoulder more than she heard what he said. How come he held her with so much familiarity?

"Fine, fine," she said, drawing away from Binh. "I'll help Hue." She directed a deep smile at the girl, who responded tentatively. "And what about Elliott and that guy?"

"They got other things to do."

"Oh!" She had a fair idea of what "other things" meant. The guy spitting his fingernails into the street looked like a piece of work to her, and Elliott, she'd never liked, not the least because he had tried to show her his penis once when he was sixteen and had sworn her to secrecy, begged her not to tell Binh. Which she hadn't up to this day. "They're not gonna do them here, are they?"

"Jeez, Tuyen, Jesus. Are you here to help or not? No, all right, no."

"Don't get so upset. I'm just asking. Just want to know, that's all."

A silence ensued. She felt petty. She had brought all the hostility into the conversation when, in fact, she had intended to be nice, or at least vaguely agreeable. Instead she had found herself instinctively nasty.

"So, Hue, we'll work it out, right?" she said apologetically.

"Sure. I do this all the time. No problem."

Of course, Tuyen thought, realizing that apart from their floating animosity she really did not know her brother well. She had created an archetype of him, and there it stood.

"Great. So, my brother treats you okay, does he?" Tuyen

tried joking, but it sounded lame even to herself.

"Yes." Hue giggled.

"Hue, can I talk to Binh in private for a second?"

"Sure." The girl took her purse and went outside. Tuyen watched her rummage for a cigarette, light it, and lean on the window, smoking.

"She seems nice."

Binh didn't answer. He arranged the receipts in the cash drawer, then said, "You know how to work this, right?"

They both knew how to work a cash register. For a moment they were back in the restaurant as children, self-important and studious. For a moment she felt a comfort with him, accompanied.

"Yeah, I know. But listen, what are you going to do exactly?"

"Well, Ma's been ripped off for years. Both of them. So I'm going to track him down one way the other."

"But why? He's probably dead and probably died a long time ago. He was so small and . . ."

"So they need to know."

"And if he's not dead, then he has a life."

"So they need to know. You don't see them."

Compassion wasn't a feeling she thought her brother experienced.

"But suppose it only brings them trouble."

"How?"

She couldn't answer well. "I don't know. Maybe if he's alive, he's a shit, you know."

"You were never afraid of anything. How come you're afraid of this?"

Her brother's assessment took her aback, both in terms of how he saw her and how he appraised her feelings now.

"I'm not afraid for me," she said, feeling dishonest.

The truth was, she didn't want to be drawn into a family drama. Binh, she thought, always wanted some kind of touching, even if it was painful. He always sought out the rawness of human contact, the veins exposed. She wanted to leave well enough alone. She was content to witness at a distance, to go over the bones dispassionately. She looked at Binh now, thinking that in some ways her brother was more sensitive and she more ready, more needy, and all the calculation that she had ascribed to him was probably not so hard core after all.

He was saying, "I'm not going to let them get fucked over, you know. First of all, I'm not telling them about it, in case it doesn't work out."

Selflessness was another attribute she knew her brother definitely didn't have. He must have told Bo already, otherwise why had Bo hinted something of it to her? She decided not to reveal this to Binh, let him think she didn't know.

"Well, you gonna do it anyway, so . . ."

"Yes."

"Do not bring trouble, Binh. The danger of the sky is that we cannot climb up into it."

Tuyen heard herself saying what her father said to them when they were growing up. Binh laughed at her.

"I didn't know you were so old-fashioned. Speaking of which, you can take a coat off the rack in the back if you want."

"I like my coat fine. Your girlfriend looks like she's freezing. Too small for me, if you ask."

"I didn't ask, and don't try to fuck around with her."

"Scared?"

"Anyways!"

Hue had finished her cigarette and was looking at them

through the window.

"Not my type," Tuyen joked. Binh beckoned to Hue to come in.

"So, Hue, see you next week, will I? Here's my number. How long is this for anyway, Binh?"

"Ten days, maybe."

"Okay, we'll hold it down, right, Hue? So, later."

She left, feeling a mix of pleasure and discomfort. She had at least paid a debt, owned her brother as "mine" to a greater extent than she thought she could. She had at least left without biting at him. But she was apprehensive about what this journey to find their brother would open up in their lives, her life.

She wrapped her too-big coat around her, walking slowly in the damp late-spring wind. The sun had been in and out all day. She could use a cigarette, quite frankly, she thought. Pleased as she was with herself, it had been a stretch of good behaviour. It was just like Binh to get everything in knots once she thought she was well away from her family. She passed two black men near a parking meter, one of them gesturing to the other.

"*A janela já foi consertada, ele só queria dinheiro. Eu não vou . . .*"

"*Bom, ele nâo me disse isso. Eu tenho os canos de metal prontos . . .*"

Their voices spoke in another language—Spanish, she thought, no, it was Portuguese. An older woman, white, went by, looking at the men. Tuyen caught her dismay at their language. She said, "Spanish or Portuguese?" to the woman, catching her off guard again.

"Portuguese!" the woman replied, the thickness of that

accent underlying her own English. "You never know when you're talking, other people could be listening." The woman put her fingers to her lips, and Tuyen grinned.

Yes, that was the beauty of this city, it's polyphonic, murmuring. This is what always filled Tuyen with hope, this is what she thought her art was about—the representation of that gathering of voices and longings that summed themselves up into a kind of language, yet indescribable. Her art— she had pursued it to stave off her family—to turn what was misfortune into something else. She had devoted all the time to it, and here they were—her family—returning again and again.

"Africa, I suppose?" The woman still engaged her.

"Or Brazil."

"You never know, you have to be careful when you speak."

"'Careful'? About what?" Tuyen asked, but the woman had already gone into a fruit store. "Hmm," Tuyen sniffed. So much for unities.

In the closing door of the fruit store she saw her own image. "I like this coat," she said to herself. Her face was as unfamiliar as it always was to her when she caught herself in a mirror. Yet all her installations were filled with self-portraits, like Varo's. Curious faces staring, in her case openly, even rudely. Varo's face was mysterious, hers was inquisitive, candid. She would go along with Binh's little project. She had no choice. "It is not in your hands," she told her image in the glass door.

That was mid-May, and Tuyen had every intention of following through with her promise to Binh. She went to the store to relieve Hue by 2 P.M. for the first few days. Hue was perfectly capable and more knowledgeable than she about Binh's affairs. Tuyen realized that when Binh wasn't there Hue's voice was efficient and even bossy. She corrected Tuyen when Tuyen did something wrong, like pile gadgets on the counter, and she ran to serve customers before Tuyen discouraged them with her intrusive stares or probing questions. Left to Tuyen, the store would have made few sales.

Her *lubiao* project was foremost in her mind, and she asked each customer, "What do you long for?" as they came into the store. The idea was to write these longings down and post them on the *lubiao*. Hue interrupted her each time, pushing the person toward the expensive electronics that Binh sold. Some customers were actually struck by the question. "Reading, a whole year to read," one said. "To feel safer," another said, "safe, like when I was a child." A Somali man, who was a taxi driver, and who came in for a new radio, told Tuyen, "Enough money to go home and marry four wives." Tuyen broke into laughter and so did the man.

"You're kidding me."

"No, no, my uncle has five. He has a schedule. One night with one, the other night with another, and so on. He has a paper with all of it written down."

"And that's what you long for?"

"Yes, I would be very happy."

"And tired!"

"No, no," the man laughed, "never tired."

After the Somali taxi driver left, Hue scolded her.

"You can't carry on conversations like that. Then people don't buy anything. You're chatting too much about irrelevant things."

"Oh, chill out, Hue. What do you long for?"

"Not me. I don't long for anything."

"Oh, come on!"

"I have work to do. I can't. That's foolishness."

"You long for my brother."

"I'm not answering. You—you're too chatty!"

"All right, sell, sell, sell." But she didn't, she scribbled the taxi driver's story in her notebook, sketching an image of him beside it, giggling to herself.

This book she called her book of longings. She had happened on the idea of collecting these stories when she found the signed photograph, "*Recuerdo de nuestra noche, 1968*" at the ATM machine. The city was full of longings and she wanted to make them public.

A Bengali woman had asked her, "Why long for anything? Longing is suffering. We have to stop desire. Desire nothing." Tuyen accosted people on the street as well as in the store, and the Bengali woman was waiting for her daughter outside an ice cream parlour. They watched the Bengali woman's daughter buy an ice cream and lick it deliciously.

"Now she'll be sick with that. Lactose intolerant. See what desire is?" the woman said. "I would like better knees," she confided, pointing to her heavily wrapped knees under her sari. "But what to do, eh? To desire is to suffer."

What did she herself desire? What did she long for? A bigger studio, Carla, another family: yes, all along she had wished that her family was different.

Tuyen came to the store on the third or fourth day to find Elliott and the other man talking with Hue. Conversation stopped when she entered.

"Well, don't mind me," she said.

"They were going."

"Elliott, what're you up to?"

"Oh, nothing much. Some stock for Binh, in the back."

The other guy looked impatient and said something to Hue in Vietnamese to which Hue agreed. He ignored Tuyen and spoke to Elliott—"Let's go, I'm busy." Elliott seemed no longer interested in Tuyen, and they both left.

"What was that about?"

"Just business."

"Business? Shouldn't I know what the business is?"

Hue looked bored and headed into an explanation of how many electronic cards of RAM memory were ordered and how many computer cables, an explanation so deliberately tedious that Tuyen raised her hand, begging off. Let them have their complications, she thought, what do I care? She got her book of longings out and waited for the next customer to come in. Opening the book while Hue hovered busily, she saw Carla's longing. "Sleep. A deep, dreamless sleep. Totally knocked out. The kind of sleep that feels like food and when you get up you feel new." Tuyen had written below, "Mine: to be seduced, utterly seduced. By you." It was so strange, she thought, how people see qualities in other people—things that probably aren't there at all. She, for example, saw something deeply seductive in Carla, something Carla didn't see—it always baffled Tuyen. Jackie would tease her, "The girl is not home, honey."

Lost in her book of longings, Tuyen only looked up when Hue said loudly, "I'm leaving now."

Tuyen took her head out of the book to see Hue pacing indecisively.

"Okay, see you tomorrow."

"I don't like that one," Hue blurted out.

"Who—Elliott? He's harmless."

"No, the other guy. If he comes back, don't talk to him."

"Why would he come back? For what?"

"Whatever, don't talk to him."

"Well, I've nothing to say to him anyway."

Hue still seemed reluctant to leave. "He runs girls. He calls it a spa."

This was more than Tuyen had got out of Hue on any subject, and she hadn't even asked.

"Really?" The curiosity in her voice seemed to propel Hue to the door. As if she had said too much.

"See you tomorrow, then."

Tuyen followed her to the door. "Is Binh in on that too?"

"Of course not! I just don't like that guy, that's all." And she escaped out the door.

Okay, Tuyen thought, something else I don't want to know about. Binh probably had his finger in it somewhere, but thank heavens her brother had a very healthy sense of self-preservation. At the back of the store was evidence of that. While XS sold mainly computer parts and other electronics, there were boxes of men's clothing, office supplies, shoes, lamps, clocks, and anything Binh could get cheaply just to diversify his investment in the store. Oddly, Tuyen had thought that once she was alone in the store she would have rifled through Binh's affairs to see what he was up to generally—but she hadn't felt the urge to do it. And even now, with Hue's unsolicited declaration about Binh's shady friend, she was still completely uninterested. Besides, she thought, Binh was not stupid, he wouldn't leave any damaging evidence around.

Her intrigues with her brother were lodged in their childhood and so too her suspicions. They were both grown up and probably quite different people, just people unable to let go of a childhood game. What did Binh long for? That was obvious. To be the only boy. No, again that was the only trajectory of thought that their relationship led her to. He probably longed for something quite different. She promised herself to ask him. Maybe it was she who longed to be the only daughter.

Enough psychoanalysis, she told herself, and enough of this scene. She suddenly decided to close the store early and go to the studio. She pushed the book of longings into her bag, made a mental note that Hue had already emptied the cash, and locked the door behind her. She breathed in relief. She didn't know how people held on to that kind of work, rather, she told herself, she knew how but not why. Why wake up every day to slug it out at some mundane, numbing, repetitive small act? Why be satisfied with that alone, and happy— some people were happy with it.

Heading home, she looked at the city around her. Now, in fact, she noticed lots of people like her staring idly into store windows, sitting in doughnut shops, touching fruit in outside fruit stands, washing clothes in the laundromats, reading newspapers. Tuyen stopped into the Bubble Tea Café and ordered a coffee, took out her book, and waited for someone to sit near her to ask them what they longed for.

It's like this with this city—you can stand on a simple corner and get taken away in all directions. Depending on the weather, it can be easy or hard. If it's pleasant, and pleasant is so relative, then the other languages making their way to your ears, plus the language of the air itself, which can be cold and humid or wet and hot, this all sums up into a kind of new vocabulary. No matter who you are, no matter how certain you are of it, you can't help but feel the thrill of being someone else.

She called Hue the next afternoon at the store to ask if Hue really did need her to come and if everything was all right. She had become caught up in how she was going to execute the collection of longings. She thought of glass, small glass pieces on which the longings could be written and which she would then embed in the *lubiao*; or should she use paper, perhaps in newsprint, or if only she had the technology, tiny video enactments, or . . . At any rate, Hue said that she did not mind at all, and one day led to the other and Tuyen promised that for the rest of the time she would call in until Binh returned, but if Hue really needed her, she should call her. It wasn't that she had lost interest in Binh's project of finding their brother, it was just she pushed her initial anxiety about it away, thinking that (a) it was highly improbable that Binh would find him; (b) if he did, she would deal with that when it happened; but (c) the chances were so remote; and (d) what was she getting so freaked out about? Binh was off doing the nasty in Thailand. He would return, tell their parents he went looking, get credit for being a good son, and put their minds at rest that everything possible had finally been done, but it was all their fate . . .

So perhaps cloth; she had decided on cloth. She had strung a huge diaphanous grey-white piece against a wall and was using a calligraphic pen to transfer in her fine handwriting the entries from her book. After several hours of work, she happened on the idea to insert her mother's letter into the cloth. Of course! She felt a surge of creative recognition that the idea had begun somehow from there. Pen poised, she taxed her memory for the first one she'd read when she heard from the open doorway, "No luck, after all." She was startled to see Binh in her studio.

He never came up here. He looked dejected. She was uncomfortable. There was a kind of intimacy in his coming to her place that she found alarming. And an intimacy in his look of disappointment.

"You mean, you didn't find him? Well, what did you expect?"

"He exists, he can be found."

"But I keep asking you, why? Why do you have to find him? Who cares?"

"They do."

"Why didn't they go looking themselves? Long ago then?"

"How can you ask that? They couldn't leave here . . . they were scared . . . they were refugees. . . . You have no pity."

"Look, I think they need to forget it. Not forget, but make peace with it. Why do you want to start it up again?"

Binh stared a while at the grey-white hanging cloth on Tuyen's wall. He read the longings she'd written there.

"So you—you only care about other people. Look at that crap! And look at all this shit on your floor. We're not Chinese, eh! You're always pretending. People are real, eh? They're not just something in your head. You always play around as if everything is a joke. You don't care about nobody, just yourself."

"You care about the wrong things. You always did. I know people are real, but everything isn't fate. They taught us that, but it isn't true." She heard herself having the first conversation she could remember with Binh where there wasn't raw animosity. "I still don't get what you're doing."

"You weren't the boy. You didn't get the shit. I want to find him. Let them see who he is, then maybe they'll get off of my back."

There was a violent petulance in his voice.

"What shit did you get?" Tuyen rose to challenge him. "Please tell me. It looked pretty good to me. And who cares? You're grown up. If they're on your case, why do you live there?"

"Forget it." He stuffed his hand into his pocket and pulled out a wad of money. "Here, for taking care of the shop. Hue said you really helped her."

"That's too much." Tuyen wondered why Hue had exaggerated.

"No. Take it—I know you don't have money."

She didn't refuse, and an awkward moment followed. They had nothing more to say to each other, but she sensed some hesitation in Binh. He must be a lonely person, she thought. Perhaps in their family it was he and she who were the closest, if not in affections then in all other ways; in the geography of their experiences.

She watched Binh go down to the alleyway, get into his silver Beamer, and drive away. She should have given him something, she knew, some show of recognition, if not affection or support. She'd done what she could.

Poised in this reflection, her inky hands pulling the hair at her left temple, Tuyen didn't hear Carla come in.

"Hey, I just saw your brother. God, he's gorgeous." Carla was standing at the door, and Tuyen felt a minute pang of childish jealousy.

"You just don't know how to say that I'm gorgeous."

"Probably, you're so alike."

"We are? How do you know?" She said this, half questioningly, half certain. "Alike"—the word revolted her; it gave her some other unwanted feeling of possession. To be possessed, she thought, not by Binh only but by family, Bo and Mama, Ai and Lam, yes them, and time, the acts that passed in it, the bow, the course of events.

"Did you say you probably think I'm gorgeous?"

"Wow, *that's* gorgeous!" Carla was looking in awe at the

large hanging Tuyen had been working on. "That's beautiful."

"Not yet"—Tuyen came to stand beside her—"it's not finished."

The longings seemed to race down the drape of cloth on the wall.

"I have to make some translations too, I want to put different languages. I'm going to fill it with every longing in the city."

"The hideous ones too?" Carla's voice sounded shivery.

"I'll have to, won't I? Otherwise it would be a fake."

"Ah." Carla made to leave.

"Hey, where you going?" She touched Carla's face.

"Nowhere."

"Then stay with me." Her fingers stroking Carla's cheek. She always felt like covering Carla's mouth with her own. Especially now. "Help me write them? Anywhere you like."

"Okay, but not the perverse ones." She took her face away from Tuyen's fingers. "What about the *lubiao*? What're you doing with that?"

"I haven't decided. This new idea came to me and I'm trying to make it fit but. . . . Maybe the *lubiao* is a relic, maybe I'll use it as a contrast. We'll see. Here's the book—choose the ones you like and tick them off when you're done."

The hideous ones. Those were the longings about bodies hurt or torn apart or bludgeoned. No one had actually confided details to Tuyen. She had intuited these, perceived them from a stride, a dangling broken bracelet—a rapist's treasure, each time he rubbed the jagged piece he remembered his ferocity— a muttering, a woman off her head sitting on a sidewalk—her longing for that particular summer in Beausejour when she was between leaving that life and coming to this sidewalk.

Some Tuyen had got from newspaper articles—one

about twin brothers dying at a karaoke bar: Phu Hoa Le and Lo Dai Le. The four men in bandannas came into the bar and started shooting. What were their longings—the ones dying and the ones shooting? Or, on the same page, the owners of a puppy farm with a hundred puppies mistreated in a filthy barn. Their longings would certainly surprise—she knew how people lived two lives, one most times the antithesis of the other. And the previous week she'd scoured the newspapers to find that Janakan Sivalingam was dead too; he was slashed in his belly with a machete in front of a school. She'd written down his longing for almonds and his attackers', which were for the sight of Julie Andrews in *The Sound of Music.* And looking at the whole page of the daily newspaper—several deaths, a kidnapping, a pathologist's report, a man charged with having an "up skirt" video—all surrounding a photograph of the Stanley Cup with adoring boys decked out in hockey gear. The longings of the page designer, the editor, what were those? For relief? From killings, from misery? Or was it from multiplicity? Vass, Kwan, Hyunh, Sivalingam, Shevchenko—those were the names on the page of the dead or the vicious—the editor's relief from the cumbersome, the unknown, the encroaching. They might all be encroaching on the city, encroaching in the editor's mind, on the pure innocent ideal, violating the heroic Stanley Cup, the cherubic faces around it, pushed to the borders tenuously. Perhaps she could put that page itself there, somewhere, among the longings.

They worked in silence for an hour.

"Tuyen . . . Tuyen . . ." Carla had been repeating her name for several seconds.

"Yeah!"

"You can really disappear, can't you?"

Tuyen grinned. "I guess. Break?"

"I'm gonna leave you."

"No, stay. Want to go for dinner? My treat."

She wanted to be in Carla's company; she always felt a deep pleasure in her presence even though she knew Carla's quiet was not quiet at all. But it would be good to drink some wine and maybe find herself later in Carla's bed, her arm around her middle, her lips on her neck.

"Since that's a rare thing, I'll take it."

Did Carla feel as attracted to her? Sometimes, like now, she sensed that was true.

"It's gonna be good, huh?" Carla was looking at the wall of cloth they'd been working on.

"Yes, I think it's gonna be."

She was looking at Carla, not at the wall. It was going to be good, she thought. She wrapped herself in her oilskin and followed Carla down the stairs. It was balmy outside. She really didn't need a coat; she let it fall open. Binh had been mollified by his trip in search of nothing, Carla was yielding in some way, the installation was coming together fabulously since she'd set on the idea of the longings of the city. She felt a bliss.

THIRTEEN

IT SEEMED AS IF JACKIE had avoided him deliberately. He'd gone to Tuyen's and Carla's frequently over the last two weeks. He even spent a few nights, but she hadn't appeared, and when he asked Carla or Tuyen, they said she hadn't called. Why didn't he simply call her, they asked, or go by the store on Queen Street?

He should be able to do those things, after all, what about the Lula Lounge? Why couldn't he simply leave it at that, though? One night—a shared high. And fucking. People did that every day, casually. Jackie felt nothing for him. Nothing or simply amusement. Coming on to her two weeks ago had apparently annoyed her to the point that she didn't want to see him, even as a friend. But maybe all of it was only in his mind and Jackie was going about her business being Jackie, who appeared and disappeared as she liked, and could have sex with him at the Lula with three hundred people dancing two feet away and forget it the next day. So he would make an ass of himself calling her. He felt like a child with her, not the man he wanted to show her; the man who would be devoted to her, who would love her. Christ, just thinking this made him cringe at her response. Jackie could be so cool, so off-centring, so distant.

The phone rang early. He grabbed it before his father could reach it upstairs. It was one of his "boys" from Eglinton. Kwesi.

"Hey, what's up, man? You awake?"

"Yeah. Yeah, I'm cool."

"So we're down for next Wednesday. You know, like, at Syreta's."

"Yeah, man, I know. I'll be there. Why you calling me so early?"

"Just checking, man. You know. What you up to later?"

Kwesi was the guy with the black Navigator. Oku hung out with him now and then when he needed "smoke" and a few dollars. Kwesi had taken a particular liking to him even though Oku didn't seem to be interested in his schemes to get rich. "You're a smart brother," he told Oku. "We could do some great shit together."

Oku usually laughed at this flattery, saying, "Yeah, man, but I'm not into that shit. It's too time-consuming."

But Kwesi persisted nevertheless, as if he thought that one day he would wear Oku down or one day Oku would face the inevitable. Kwesi and most men he knew lived by their wits.

Kwesi's business was a mobile store held at his girlfriend, Syreta's, or at her friends. The latest Nike, Reebok, leather coats, bags, designer dresses, anything you wanted, could be had. Racks of dresses, blouses, stands of shoes would be moved in just like at a department store and discreet invitations would be put out, though invariably too many people would be lined up outside a house or apartment on the appointed day. Oku helped with the traffic. Everything was marked down to thirty per cent of the original price. There was a slight sense of danger for Oku, but it was understood that he'd go no further—despite Kwesi hassling him about how he didn't need a university degree to make money. Oku called it capitalist bullshit and Babylon, and they both laughed, but Kwesi's logic sat uneasily with him. Kwesi was driving around in a Lincoln Navigator, had a leather coat for every season, a nice apartment. Oku couldn't help but be envious sometimes. Envious not only of the money but of the balls, the certainty. He had a dilettante's curiosity about Kwesi's life, though he was much more tempted lately and found his objections wearing thin. If he continued his friendship with Kwesi, he would have to commit to going the whole way.

"Listen, you wanna help me pick up the stuff today?" There was the usual hesitation from Oku's side. "You know, I'll give you—what?—three per cent?" Kwesi was talking about pick-ups. He had other guys who helped him do this, but Oku knew that he wanted to draw him in deeper. "No sweat. No hassle. It's inside stuff." Three per cent would certainly get rid of his anxiety about his dwindling student loan. "Come on. You down with this or not?"

"Got things to do today, man." Oku wimped out, and he felt like it. There was a disturbing feeling in his stomach. His voice couldn't take on the aloof quality it usually did with Kwesi. "I'll check you at Syreta's Wednesday, all right?"

"Cool, bro. But you know what I'm saying, right?"

"Yeah, yeah. Peace, man." Oku rang off.

His own logic was falling apart. He could get busted at one of the sales just as much as on the other side of the deal Kwesi was offering him. He had convinced himself that being caught actually and undeniably stealing stuff was worse than being caught selling it. He knew he was splitting hairs and Kwesi was testing him and would punk him out soon.

Oku had stayed good friends with Carla and Tuyen because he'd found hanging with the guys exhausting. Yes, he could become the bad public hard-ass kind of black man everyone appreciated. Everybody knew it was bullshit. The leather coats, the dark glasses, the don't-give-a-shit attitude. Life was all about getting the car, the bling-bling, the honey. All that television talk had made it to the street, or was it the other way around? You slapped a few bitches in the mall and faced down a few dickheads in the alleyways. Underneath it all you loved babies, played video games, and loved your mother's cooking and loved nobody like your mother. So much energy put out just fronting. And you sometimes forgot you were only fronting. You were dangerous. There was a kind of romance about that dangerousness, and Oku teetered at times in that alluring space. Which man wouldn't want to be thought of as dangerous? Yet who wanted to have that mantle drawn around his shoulders all the time? Some, but you couldn't crack into the full register of yourself.

One night when Oku was eighteen, he was walking up Beverley Street. It was about 2 A.M. and he'd just left a blind pig on Baldwin, and he was thinking how quiet it was and how he loved the city. He was thinking that he was all out of money and had to walk home, and he was thinking that it wouldn't be so bad because it was balmy, and anyway, the quietness of the city would help him write a poem as he walked. He was high. He'd had two beers, but mostly he'd smoked ganja and danced by himself. He was at Baldwin and Beverley. A car sped south, leaving a silence behind it, then another car came north behind him. This one slowed; he saw the flashing turning light as it swerved into him. He stopped. Two cops came out of the car. He can't remember if they called him, if they told him to stop. His arms rose easily as if reaching for an embrace. One cop reached for him. He can't remember what they said or what they wanted. He only remembered that it was like an accustomed embrace. He yielded his body as if to a lover, and the cop slid into his arms. That was the fucked-up thing about being dangerous. It was a surrender to violence, to some bruising, brutal lover. He remembered how instinctively his arms opened, how gently, as gently as they would have opened to embrace Jackie. But this was another kind of impeachment. A perverse fondling. Another car sped by, slowed to look and then sped on again. The cops didn't find anything on him, and he said nothing to them, just smiled and shook his head. They asked him his name, he smiled again. Their fondling became rougher. Oku let his body go limp. The cops folded him into their car with a few more shoves. He laughed. He was still high. They took him to fifty-two Division. They couldn't find anything to charge him with and let him go around 6 A.M.

He had come to expect this passion play acted out on his body any time he encountered authority, and it was played out at its most ecstatic with the cops. Whenever he encountered them, he simply lifted his arms in a crucifix, gave up his will and surrendered to the stigmata. Some of his friends didn't. They resisted, they talked, they asserted their rights. That only caused more trouble. They ended up in the system fighting to get out. They ended up hating everyone around them. Homicidal.

Perhaps it was his father's tenacity that took him the other way. His father was so voracious, yet so bitter—and that was the part that Oku hated—that in the middle of loving, or eating, everything seemed bitter.

Jackie, he thought, Jackie was somehow the solution to it. If he could one day find the precise words, she would come around. There was some specific thing he had to say, and then the two of them would fall into place. It was like a series of locks: when particular words were said, each lock fell open.

Which is why he'd been silent with the cops. There were no words for the doorway they emerged from, no word that would send them back or pacify them. The words to Jackie, on the other hand, were only hidden. He knew, too, that Jackie was only half of it.

Twenty-five years old, living with his mother and father, and heading nowhere. The university was such a straitjacket, it all made him hunger for another world. Maybe he was fooling himself that he could think his way out of this box. Did Jackie want a man like that? A man who was stable? And what did the Nazi boyfriend have that he didn't? His white skin, for one. Oku laughed at himself. Not fair. Okay, a mother with a lot of rundown properties across the city. Okay both, white skin and a mother who was a slum landlord. This cynicism aside, wasn't he, Oku, depending on the dark tenor of his own skin to woo Jackie? So why couldn't the Nazi boy use what he had?

Oku would spend hours going over the arguments he would put to Jackie. When he did see her, it came out in intolerant bursts, like the last time he'd seen her at Tuyen's. He didn't yet have the words to make that lock fall open.

And what about the lock for himself? His father said he lived too much in his head. The truth was living in his head was what kept him safe. Living in his head meant he didn't react reflexively to the stimuli of the city heading toward him with all the velocity of a split atom. That's why he kept pretty much to himself. That's why he risked being called a "flake" and a "faggot" by the guys in the jungle. That's why he cultivated the persona of the cool poet—so that he wouldn't have to get involved in the ordinary and brutal shit waiting for men like him in the city. They were in prison, although the bars were invisible.

"Don't be a faggot, man. You never, never let people fuck with you," Kwesi had lectured him.

"You bide your time and you take your opportunity," his father had lectured him.

Christ, he was scared sometimes, scared of something lurking in himself, in his body—some idea threatening to overpower him. It took all his power to shut down the crazy person inside of him who wanted to tear things up. He avoided the guys from the jungle more and more. And soon he would have to move out because his father's alchemy was just as potent.

He had nightmares of putting his fist through his father's face; of lifting the breakfast table and smothering him with it. He was afraid that one morning he would wake up and do those things. He would actually wake at times in fear out of a dream thinking he had done just that. He would lock his bedroom door to prevent himself from sleepwalking into these acts.

Oku stayed in his room in the basement until his father left. He didn't want to talk to his mother. His mother could get things out of him. She probably already knew that he had dropped out. He heard her come back to the kitchen. He let himself out the basement door, yelling to her, "Bye, Ma!" He heard her faint calling but pretended he didn't.

Exams were supposed to be happening now. It was the end of May. His father, making him feel like a child, insisted on seeing grades. "Let me see what I'm paying for, boy." He would have to move out.

Instead of the university, he would go to Kensington Market. It was his every day except Wednesdays, when his mother went there. He'd always checked with her each week in case she varied her movements—he'd make a pretence of asking her to get something for him, like guineppes or gizadas. There he would sit at a coffee shop, watching people go by and reading Amiri Baraka or Jayne Cortez. He'd found them while trying to put some life into a class in American poetry at the university, though he hadn't been able to last out the class even with Baraka and Cortez. So what if he knew the classics, if he understood figures of thought? He himself was a figure of thought in those classrooms—an image and not a being, not a solid presence. So what the fuck, he thought, what the fuck was he doing there? Better to read Baraka and Cortez and Neruda and Lorca and Yevtushenko and Brecht on his own. The classes were a waste of time—holding him back as a poet. So fuck that.

He read and watched the street, and depending on his mood that day he might spend the afternoons with Tuyen and Carla, then in the evenings he would sometimes go up to see his boys in the jungle, though less and less these days—get a smoke, tool around, and then go home when the lights were off and his mother and father sleeping.

It was in the market that he'd met the old Rasta and the musician. Not together, but he'd come to think of them as together. As parts of the same person or the same state.

The Rasta was in his sixties. He worked the blocks of the city, panhandling. Some days he was at the corner of Bathurst and Bloor, some days he was at Spadina and Queen, and some days in the market. On the days that he disappeared, Oku learned later, he was playing the horses at Woodbine. His hair was roughly dreaded. He had a hoary beard, which he tied with green and red rubber bands, his pants were sometimes held up with a piece of twine, and he wore boots, winter or summer. He knew the Scriptures by heart. Oku had met him outside the parking lot, close to the Caribbean food store.

"Beg you a money, dread," he said to Oku, surprising him. His face close, the smell of outdoor life reeking on him. Oku stepped back, his senses shocked.

"Hey, college bwoy, dread, beg you a money. The street them hard, you know, dread. The air is abstraction me tell you. Give a likkle something for the I and I." He was aggressive and biblical. "Beg you a likkle something to hold I soul together, man. The spirit massive but the body weak." He followed Oku down the street.

The poetry of holding the soul together stopped Oku. He turned, fished in his pockets, held out a dollar, waiting for the Rasta to open his hand. He didn't want to touch him, still scornful of the man's appearance, but the Rasta grabbed his hand warmly and roughly.

"Blessings on you, brethren. Is the fate of the world you one decide right there so now. Seen? Jah guide, dread. Is I heartbeat unno save. Selassie I."

Oku escaped across the street to the coffee shop, the Rasta continuing to call after him, "Walk good, dready." He sat at the coffee shop, a little undone. His hands quivered from a mixture of scorn, fear, and elation. He had sensed what he felt was all of the man in that grasp. The man's scent repulsed him, but the man had drawn him into a kind of embrace. There was something genuine and plain about it, something vigorous. The man had definition. He was living on the street, but he had definition.

"True brethren, what a merciful morning!"

The next time the Rasta came up on him as he was daydreaming his way past.

"How the I and I today, Rasta? His anger endureth only a minute, for his favour is life, dread. Anything today, Rasta? It rough out here, you nuh know?"

Oku fished in his pocket but could only come up with fifty cents. He gave it apologetically to the Rasta.

"Ah know, nothing, Rasta. Weeping may endure for a night but joy cometh in the morning. You nuh see it?"

The Rasta grabbed hold of him as if to hug him, and Oku shrank with the same feeling of revulsion and allure.

"Is nothing, man. Is only fifty cents," he said, brushing aside and trying to recover himself. The Rasta had rejected something, some way of living, some propriety, and with all his derelictness, Oku envied him.

"Me ah learn, Rasta, me ah grow and me ah learn." Often the Rasta stood at his post in the market, his arms over his head in a gesture requesting mercy.

One day he said to Oku, "Me ah give up the business, Rasta. Me ah give it up. What you think? It too rough, the begging." Oku couldn't help but burst out laughing. "Me nuh joke, Rasta, it rough. You nuh understand?" he said, as if he and Oku had become such familiars that he expected Oku to dissuade him from leaving the begging business.

He was a gambler too.

"Bwoy, the pony business steep! Jah Rastafari. Schoolbwoy, me was one length from millionaire. But Jah know what is not for you, is not for you. Seen! So me ah struggle. Is what you ah read, read so, Rasta? Is only the one book, dread, only one book."

Oku wished he could be so single-minded.

And then there was the musician. Some afternoons the musician sat in the coffee shop muttering, a short pencil in hand, scribbling musical notes onto a tattered fragment of a brown paper bag. He kept a worn leather folder of music under one arm, sometimes shifting it to the inside of his grungy coat, sometimes to the table, then back to his armpit. He was a tall, lean man, his deep dark skin setting contrast to his pink palms. You noticed his palms because his hands were so large, his fingers long and slender.

On their first meeting Oku made the mistake of looking at him too long and nodding to him in greeting. Thinking the musician was an ordinary black guy, he said to him, "Hey, bro, what's happening?"

"I'm not your brother." The musician jumped up, spilling a small table over. He flew at Oku, his face livid.

Oku reached out his hand in front of him, "No problem, bro, no problem."

"I am not your brother, I say."

The musician's sudden looming scared Oku. His outstretched hand touched the musician's coat, offending him even more. He grabbed hold of Oku, spinning him around. Luckily for Oku, the leather folder fell to the floor and the musician dropped him and scrambled for his music. The small clasp on the folder was broken, and the music sheets slipped onto the floor. The musician became frantic, whimpering as he collected the sheets. Oku moved away from him, disappearing out the door. But he appeared to have forgotten Oku, and tears of relief filled the musician's eyes when he had put his folder back together. And he appeared to have forgotten the whole incident the next time Oku saw him.

He was a pianist, classically trained. He held the folder as if it were his life; the leather was blackened and dog-eared. All the sanity he ever had, had been poured into a symphony, *Sepia Ceremony*, which he had created as homage to Shostakovich's Symphony no. 11 and Duke Ellington's sacred music.

He would walk up to perfect strangers in the street and show them his reams of notations for his symphony. He would launch into explanations about this or that movement to surprised passersby.

They wanted him back home in London, he said, they wanted him to go to Munich, but he had come to Toronto on the promise that his composition would be played by the Toronto Symphony. But when they realized he was a black man, their promises had dried up, he said. Bewildered people skirted him, thinking he was a panhandler. He rushed out to them to reassure them. They fled or threatened to call police.

He inundated the Human Rights Commission with complaints against the Toronto Symphony Orchestra and Roy Thomson Hall. Leaders of the black community had taken him seriously at first, but his deteriorating mental state would make him launch into outbursts that made his claims confused, if not dubious. He was an artist, a great genius, and they were all fools—his supporters as well as the commission and his persecutors.

Oku came out of the St. George subway one day, and as he walked toward the university, he saw the musician sitting on a concrete embankment, his leather folder in his lap, his large hands making a gesture of piano playing. Oku slowed his pace, trying to decide whether to take another route and avoid another unpleasant encounter. But he saw that the musician was heedlessly playing his symphony. His face was a beautiful mask of pleasure, his long fingers lustful on some arpeggio.

Oku walked by close enough to observe these things

and far enough away to run if the musician recognized him. The musician looked up and met his eyes, but there was no recognition there except as an artist to his audience, a great pianist to his adoring fan. Oku paid the musician the compliment of listening, then after some minutes, when the musician seemed to have come to the close of his solo, Oku applauded. The musician bowed his head to receive the accolade. From then on when they met at the Market Café there was no trouble. Oku never made the mistake of calling him "brother," and the musician went about his business, composing his music on brown paper bags and securing his leather satchel full of the contents of his sanity.

The musician was never as lucid or as friendly as the Rasta, so Oku came by his name through the Rasta, whose own name Oku never found out.

"See him there?" The Rasta pointed to the musician. "Him a mad, you see! Is talent what have him so. Talent and Babylon take him. Not like the I and I. Babylon don't down cry me yet."

He was patting himself warm in the cold spring day, standing near the parking lot in the market. He waited there often to arrest shoppers as they exited the lot. Oku was on his way to the café.

"See him? See what me tell you?" The musician was playing his phantom piano outside the café. "Him mad!"

Oku felt like laughing. Between the Rasta and the musician, who was more mad?

"Nuh take things to make jokes, dready. Him is a genius. Him name Clifford Hall. Him get scholarship from yard to go a London when me was a big man. Look pon him now! You nuh see it? Follow the white man ways and you doomed. See, them make him mad."

Clifford took money out of his mouth, and the Rasta said, "Is how me supposed to compete with a madman? You nuh see me trial! Cha, man. Anyway, ah nah nutten. Make him live. Jah will take care of the I and I. Seen."

The Rasta and the musician had become a strange source of friendship for Oku. Though, of course, he had a home, albeit increasingly uncomfortable. A mother, a father. A roof over his head. And the anxieties of a failed career were still in the future for him, if at all. And the elixir of faith, which held the Rasta, was not anything that Oku could say firmly he desired. His was for a sense of sovereignty. How had they started out? he wondered. Like him? He knew he hadn't experienced the moments, he hadn't visited the scenes that would lead him where the Rasta and the musician had gone, but he had a presentiment, a moment when he glimpsed all directions of this possible life.

The Rasta and the musician would be an embarrassment to men like Oku's father. They had gone mad, the worst kind of giving into the system that could be imagined among black people in the city. Violence could be understood, but not madness. Violence at least had a traceable etymology—it protected your life, your remaining will, and all your sense of beauty. But madness, madness was weak. Oku's boys in the jungle felt the same: "You see that crazy motherfucker playing air piano? What the fuck is wrong with him? Shame." The Rasta got a little more respect, even though they still thought him mad. At least he answered to higher powers, they said. That a steady stream of them lay open-chested on sidewalks and in the parking lots of after-hours clubs was just how the world was.

Did he want to end up bled out in a parking lot outside a club? Did he want to float out of his body like the Rasta and the musician? Or did he want the hard-headed bitterness of his father, living in the fantasies of *if only*?

"If only what?"

He was sitting at the café, his thumbs on a page of Baraka's *Blues People*. A hand was on his shoulder. It was Jackie's. He hadn't seen her come in.

"If only what?" she repeated.

For a moment it seemed right. He felt as if he was in a room, an accustomed room, alone with her, and had merely drifted off. Her hand was utterly familiar, as if they, the two of them, existed in a particular universe, their particular universe. But, of course, it was the Market Café and they weren't alone. He smiled at her, shaking himself awake.

"Nothing, nothing. Hey, what are you doing here?" He didn't hear her reply. He was suddenly aware that Reiner had also come into the café.

"Hey, man," Reiner greeted. "What's happening?"

His happiness at seeing Jackie became all awkward. "Yeah, cool, man, cool," he answered Reiner.

"Get me a cappuccino, Reiner," Jackie said, sitting across from Oku.

"What do you want on it, hon? Cinnamon?"

Oku flinched at the intimacy between them. He felt like making an excuse to leave. Jackie reached over for his book. "So this is where you are these days."

What did she mean "these days"? "You're the one who disappeared."

"I haven't disappeared. I'm at the store. You know where to find me."

Was she saying something to him? He could never quite figure her out. A simple conversation was soaked in double entendre. And if he made the mistake of acknowledging the double meanings, she withdrew.

"Do I? Do I know where to find you?" He leaned over the table to take his book back.

"Yeah, you do." She thumbed the pages, looking at Oku with an appraising sensuousness. Just then Reiner came back with cappuccinos. "Check you later," Jackie said, rising.

"Yeah, man, see ya." Reiner followed Jackie to the door.

Well, that was confusing, he thought. He watched them cross to the other side of the street. He hated the easy way Reiner put his right hand in the small of Jackie's back. He hated him seeming to guide Jackie with this very hand across the street. He took comfort in a fantasy—Jackie had seen him in the café and had come in to tell him that she missed him. That was what the conversation meant. She could have passed by, he thought, trying to dismiss the other interpretation, namely that Jackie's mother and father lived not too far away, a block, really; in fact, Jackie still lived there sometimes, so it had been sheer coincidence and her words meant just what they said, no more.

But what the fuck did she see in Reiner? That's what he wanted to know. Well, given the things he'd been thinking about before Jackie came into the café, perhaps it was obvious what she saw in Reiner. Reiner was safe. Reiner was white. Musician, bullshitter, and Reiner did not, could not possibly see the city as a prison. More, Reiner must see it as his place—look at how he took possession of it, took possession of Jackie's back, guiding her across the street with one hand, warding off traffic with the other, in which he balanced his coffee. Look at his face, it spoke of someone in control and certainly not threatened. Someone comfortable, easy. Oku hated the familiarity with which Reiner spoke to him too, as if they shared something, a language. He had the sense that for Reiner it was a second language, the "Hey, man, what's happening?" As if Reiner had switched into the second language to arrive at Oku's level, so to speak—to talk to him in his own tongue. Those few words were so charged. In any other situation the meanings would be simple. Here, they were the difference between being white and being black, in control or out of control.

FOURTEEN

WHEN THE PARAMOUNT CLOSED, Jackie's mother and father were lost. Everyone in Alexandra Park was lost. Even some up on Bathurst Street and Vaughan Road and Eglinton Avenue. As far out as Dawes Road and Pape Avenue. All the glamour left their lives.

Le Coq d'Or—the nightclub on Yonge Street where American acts used to play and where Jackie's mother and father saw Parliament-Funkadelic and the Ojays, the Barkays, and Rick James, who was put in jail after some freaky behaviour—that had closed down a few years before too. And then the Piccadilly Tube, where they danced till three in the morning, went under. And then Mrs. Knights, where they danced too and sat in the raised section and a man from Ghana had tried to pick Jackie's mother up right in front of Jackie's father, and he did it so directly and as if it was such a bargain that even Jackie's father would have gone off with him to Accra. The guy took Jackie's mother on the dance floor to "Me and Mrs. Jones," and Jackie's mother almost didn't come back.

"Come and go with me back to my country," he said. "You will be loved by my whole family, you will have my children. It is not like it is here. You are lost here. No one loves you here. In my country you will be a queen, life will be your plaything, the sky will always be blue when you are there, the rains will only come when you remember a sadness."

Mrs. Knights closed. And These Eyes, where the marquee was a purple-rimmed eye, that was gone too. Jackie's father loved the deejay there. His name was Maceo, and he could spin some rhythm and blues like nobody's business. The Web was gone too—DJ Ghetto Soul used to play there and Grand Master—and the Upstairs Side Door closed last, and anyway it wasn't such a funky place. All the glamour left, in other words, the chance to show a bit of style and flash. All the people who looked like they were famous, like the pimps and whores, all the athletes and the intellectuals, the jazz aficionados, the new-comers from down home, the just-comes from the Caribbean, all of them had to fly solo, go places where nobody knew them.

Jackie's mother and father could take hard time, anyone in the Park could. But the thought of hard time without even the relief of the Paramount was unbearable. What's life with-out a little fantasy, a little Diana Ross, a little Chilites, some Bobby Womack, some Billy Paul, Harold Melvin and the Blue Notes? Well enough if your fridge didn't work, if your sofa was on credit, had a spring busted, if, Jesus, you were one dime short of a dollar, but what was life if your imagination didn't work? If you couldn't see yourself strutting into the Paramount to the appreciation, the love of other dreamers like yourself? If no one else could verify your state of cool existence? Not a single soul who could say that last Saturday you were the fly-est, the baddest, the most solid dancer/lover/dresser; the one with the edge like a razor, the slickest, funkiest, the most crisp, the sleekest, the foxiest, the most outta sight, the wickedest in the whole damn place. Well, that's the end, isn't it? That's the bottom, that's the final. And Jackie's mother and father weren't thirty yet when the Paramount closed.

But Jackie couldn't wait for them to find bottom, she had to save them from the downstroke. The bottom was the Duke of Connaught, and she had no intentions of going in there to find them. The Duke wasn't dangerous, it was just sad. Full of might-have-beens and should-haves. It was a dive on Queen Street across from the Kentucky Fried Chicken long before that side of Queen Street became trendy. And even now the Duke still maintains that down-and-out feel, as if its ugliness were so congenital that not even the trendy makeovers all around it could change it. All the glamour and daring of the Paramount had come to a colourless rest at the Duke. Some didn't have the heart for it, so they stayed home. The Duke just wasn't made up to be glamorous. It smelled of wet carpet and beer spills, the walls were a dishevelled cousin of moss green, the lighting was sickly. No, the Duke depended on lost hopes, it depended on crushed spirits, it was not there to cheer you up, it was there to trawl in all the phlegm of your life; the I-never-got-to-do-this-and-that, the wrong-headed mistakes, the unavoidable ones, the inevitability of ending up at the Duke, which you had always seen in your face when you woke up in the morning but disregarded in your enthusiasm for life, your love for someone, and your lust for fun. The Duke was always lurking in the mirror—the bald-faced bad luck of it, the straight-up knowing of it. There was the Duke, waiting to swallow you. There was the Duke, ready to swaddle you in its seedy arms; there was the worn-out shuffleboard table, the deep bar chairs, the smell of spunky beer on tap. Didn't make sense putting a good dress on to come here, didn't make sense trying to hold up any attitude. If you came here, dressed in your fly threads, the Duke showed up that they were really cheap, that they were bought down on Spadina off the back of a truck. Didn't make sense going to Gabriel Kay's apartment to see what he had heisted from Holt Renfrew; it would be wasted at the Duke. The Duke stripped you naked in an ugly kind of way. Every person in there looked like they were ashamed to be there, like they had lost respect for themselves and therefore each other. If you strutted into the Paramount, you slid into the Duke.

So when Jackie heard her mother and father talking about going to the Duke—"Well, maybe I'll just step down to the Duke tonight," her father said. "Yeah, think anything's shakin' there?" Her mother. "Gotta hook up with Gabriel, said he had some business thing." Her father. "Well, maybe I'll tag along. Leave Jackie with Liz," her mother said—she knew it was the end. She had felt their restlessness for weeks, ever since the Paramount closed down. First they had been mournful. "Sheeeet, why'd they have to go and do that, man? For all the money I spent up in there, just that shoulda been enough to keep that place open." Her father. They'd even sworn they would never go to the Duke. "Never find me in that place. Ain't got enough room to swing a cat and they play some country shit in there." Her mother. They held out a good few weeks, Jackie's father stroking that particular spot in his beard, switching from the television to the stereo. He loved Wilson Pickett. He played "When a Man Loves a Woman" over and over again, saying to Jackie's mother, "Hear that, girl! Hear that? That's what it takes, that's what it takes."

He took Jackie up in her lessons. "You gonna have a high school diploma, Jackie baby. Do better than me. Do better than your mother."

"Yeah, Daddy."

"'Yeah, Daddy'? You say 'Yes, Daddy.' No yeah this and yeah that."

"Yes, Daddy."

Jackie's father didn't get a high school diploma, not because he couldn't but because there wasn't time. There wasn't time for that among the six brothers and one sister that he had.

They had to work, and besides, when the older ones were ready, Nova Scotia wasn't ready, what with de facto segregation and what with Jackie's grandmother and grandfather needing the help. And when Jackie's father was ready, it still wasn't worth it for a black person to have an education. Where would you put it? What would you do with it, what good was it? What kind of job would you get with it? Jackie's father had the kind of sense that mattered—street sense. That's the kind of intelligence that was worth something. Here in Toronto he'd come to a feeling that it wasn't worth passing on. It was good enough for him and Jackie's mother. He figured they were country, they were from down home, but Jackie was going to be from *here*.

Jackie liked the attention. She loved the few weeks when there was no Paramount and nothing up to standard for her mother and father to go to. It was like being on holiday. She already had a picture-postcard idea of how her family should be, and it was coming true.

"Jackie, go over to Liz and see if she'll take you tonight." Her mother, testing the waters.

"I ain't going."

"'Ain't'?" Jackie's father.

"I am not going."

"That's right now, but you going."

"No."

"Do like your mother says, girl."

"Can't. Won't. Cannot, will not. Stay with Aunt Liz."

"You cut a switch to beat yourself there, my man." Jackie's mother to Jackie's father. "She's telling you now. But, girl, don't let me have to get up."

Much as she tried, though, Jackie couldn't keep her mother and father away from the Duke.

———

They had turned the Paramount into a liquor store by the time Jackie grew up. There's no sign of the life it once had. When Jackie's mother and father pass by these days, it's all a different place. All their good times, dancing and fighting and styling, gone. All their nights with Marvin Gaye's "Here, My Dear" and Stevie Wonder's "In the City," all their youth has been jackhammered open, dug up, and cemented over in a concrete-and-glass brand new liquor store with small red-and-green tiles on the front. There's no sign of their sweet life, the dancing—that's what they mostly miss—the high-platformed shoes, the thrill of meeting the R & B bands after hours, the particular night when Jackie's mother almost ran off with the bass player from Parliament Funkadelic and Jackie's father had to stage the drama of his life—walking out the door as if he didn't care, so she would know that if she was gone, she was gone—to get her back.

How does life disappear like that? It does it all the time in a city. One moment a corner is a certain corner, gorgeous with your desires, then it disappears under the constant construction of this and that. A bank flounders into a pizza shop, then into an abandoned building with boarding and graffiti, then after weeks of you passing it by, not noticing the infinitesimal changes, it springs to life as an exclusive condo. This liquor store that was the Paramount will probably, unnoticed, do the same thing in three or four years, and the good times Jackie's mother and father had here—the nights when nights weren't long enough, when they all ended up at a blind pig on St. Clair Avenue because they couldn't go to sleep with so much life lighting up their beautiful bodies, or at Fran's on College, eating greasy eggs at three or four in the morning—all this, their lovely life, they would not be able to convince anyone it had existed.

FIFTEEN

HE WANTED TO PLAY her Ornette Coleman's "Embraceable You." He wanted to play her Coltrane's "Venus," Monk's "I Surrender, Dear" and "Don't Blame Me." So he did. He called her and left them all on her answering machine. One every other day. He said nothing in case he put his foot in his mouth again. She would know, he told himself. She would know if he played Dexter Gordon blowing "Laura," Charles Mingus's "Better Get It in Your Soul," and Charlie Rouse's "When Sunny Gets Blue." And he would've played her Billie Holiday singing "You've Changed," except that he couldn't play Billie Holiday without bawling his eyes out, and he wanted to be limber strong so that he could seduce her. So he sent her Charlie Rouse playing "When Sunny Gets Blue" twice. He thought that Rouse's hoarse velvet horn best described all the levels of his love for her, the slow and quiet way he wanted to talk to her, the intimacy he wanted to evoke. And he played her "Venus" more times than he could recall because he felt that tender, that undone with her, that out in space, that uncertain of boundaries, and that much in peril if she didn't love him back.

After Oku did all this he felt shy, stupid. He never thought of himself as stupid, only with Jackie. It occurred to him that she must be annoyed coming home to crazy music on her answering machine. She could mistake him for some kind of freak stalking her, and he didn't want her to think that, but he couldn't stop. He became so engaged in this seduction, he hardly worried about his father any more. Fuck it, he thought, it all had to come to a head soon anyway, and he had to move out of the house. If he loved Jackie, he was beyond Fitz; if he loved Jackie, he could do anything. This mission to send Jackie all that he felt about her kept him up late and woke him early. When he felt desperate, he sent her Sun Ra and the Chicago Art Ensemble. When he felt certain, he sent her Cecil Taylor and Miles Davis. He wished he could play some instrument himself. Then he would go to her door and blow, like Anthony Braxton, all of the mathematical calculations of his love. More often he felt the sense of failed genius or felt simply failed, like his musician friend from the market. But even failure drove him on, as it had Clifford. So perhaps, he thought, if it really came to that, he would go to her door and play the air between them on an imaginary instrument, play the rays of the sun through the smog or the cold air, just like that Varo painting Tuyen had shown them, and then Jackie would recognize his love.

At home the sparring between him and Fitz subsided into a seething quiet in the mornings. Fitz wasn't the type to remain quiet long, but Fitz's voice, querulous and grumbling, receded against Oku's preoccupation with Jackie. When his parents talked to him at breakfast, they seemed far away. He heard them, but didn't hear them. He dropped his usual "Yeah, Pop" into the conversations, and they both noticed that he did it at inappropriate intervals. It irritated Fitz, who became more incensed at Oku after several mornings of inattention to his dominance at the breakfast table.

One morning in June, through the webbing of his daydreams of Jackie, Oku heard Fitz.

"Me no know, Claire, but me never see no report card come here. Me pay my money. Me put nuff energy in this here boy. Is a man he is, Claire. Me don't like minding big man and no return 'pan it."

Oku was about to interject with "Yeah, Pop" when the meaning reached him. A fury crept up his neck.

"Report card? Who're you talking about?"

"You! Who else there 'bout?"

"Man, chill. You're tripping. You must be out of your mind. I'm a grown man. Report card! I don't have to answer to you!"

His mother felt the temperature of the room rise. She said nothing.

"Who you have to answer to then? Who put food on this table? Claire, you hearing this?" Fitz appealed to Claire as if he felt slightly off balance. She didn't respond.

"Your bullshit is tired, man. You should pay us for listening to you crap all over the world every morning. Jesus Christ! Listen, I don't owe you shit, all right?"

"Watch your language in front of your mother, boy."

Oku burst out laughing at this, so sweet a laugh that his mother couldn't help the muscles of her face jerking into a smile, her shoulders perilously close to collapsing in mirth. Fitz was the last one to talk about foul language. He looked at them both in shock. He rose with a wounded look and left the house, brushing Claire away as she followed him to the door.

"Mom, don't worry," Oku said when she returned. "I'll move out. I have to anyway."

"What about the university, then?"

"I'll go back next year," he said, acknowledging that he had not fooled her. "Promise. Just have to get my head together this summer. I'll get a job and figure stuff out . . ."

"Don't leave until you're ready. You know Fitzy doesn't mean anything by it."

"He does, Mom. He's so bitter, man. Jeez, he's toxic. He's always like pissed, you know. He should want better for me. But he just wants to drown me in that. I don't want to live like that."

"Well, I can't tell you different. Only he didn't start out like that."

"You always forgive him."

"He's not a bad man. He doesn't mean half of what he says. He's not the only one like that. Striving makes you bitter." She was thinking of all their friends. People just like them. Perfectionists, really. People who could not look at something beautiful without finding fault. There had to be something not so good lurking behind every smooth surface. If they worked hard for something and got it, it was not good enough. People who took nothing for granted. "I'm not saying you shouldn't strive, mind you. I'm not saying you shouldn't look for better. But understand, your father was only trying to do good for us."

"No, he wasn't. You worked too. You made this too, but he acts like a tyrant because . . . because he can. Jeez, I'm fed up. I'm not taking no stuff from him no more."

"Well, as you say, it's not him you have to please. It's yourself. We can't want things for you. You have to want them. So . . ."

"I'll figure something out. Don't worry, it'll be fine." He reassured her as much as himself. He didn't know where this feeling of evenness had come from. There had been a shift in his anxieties. He examined the new feeling now, turning it over, hoping it was going to last.

———

Around lunch he left the house, going . . . going where? he asked himself. Filling his day was suddenly no longer secretive. He'd sweated all winter over a confrontation with his father about the university and there it was. Simple. He felt relieved. He felt oddly self-conscious now that he wasn't hiding from Fitz. He didn't check to see if his mother was going out to the market today. He had nothing to do and he was embarrassed. All his actions so far had been against Fitz, against what Fitz represented, and now he was free and it felt strange. At least free of the pressure from Fitz. Free enough to take Fitz's Buick sitting in the garage and drive up to Eglinton. He parked outside the barbershop and got out.

A couple of men had been in an intense conversation on the sidewalk. One of them addressed Oku.

"Hey, poet, what you saying, star?"

"Chilling, you know, man. What's up with you?"

"Poet, brethren, tell me this. I'm trying to tell this man that communism could never work on this earth."

"Why?"

"Because man is too greedy, right? You don't see it?" He was a regular on the sidewalk outside the barbershops. Each day he had a new topic, but this was one of his staples.

"Well, I don't know . . ."

"Look, let me give you an example. Let's say there's four of us, right? And we decide to . . . make some dumplings, okay? And we only have enough flour to make twelve dumplings, so we boil the dumplings and we leave them in the pot for everybody to share. Let's say it's four of us. Three apiece, right? Believe me, some man knowing all we go through for the twelve dumplings will go in the kitchen and take four dumplings. Don't laugh. Man is greedy, that's why communism can't work."

"Righteous truths, man," Oku humoured him, going into the barbershop.

The barbershops on Eglinton were sites of great philosophical rumination on the world. Here everything from the war in the Middle East and genocide in Rwanda to the cost of toilet paper and the existence of God were rigorously gone over—examined from every possible angle. Oku came to the barbershops sometimes less for a haircut than for the conversations.

"You hear that? 'Righteous truths'!"

He got a haircut from Paul at Castries Barber Salon after an hour's wait and strong debate on the state of the world. The barbers were in-house philosophers. They commanded a chair and an audience—people waiting for their hair to be cut. They rivalled each other for the fineness of argument and their depth of knowledge. The barbershops were universities of a kind and repositories for all the stifled ambition of men who were sidelined by prejudices of one sort or another. And also a lock-box of the vanities of men so hamstrung. These men became pig-headed about how they thought a life like this should be handled, about the order of the sexes, the order of children, the order of everything. One moment they were radicals preaching communism, the next they were putting women in purdah, the next decrying the pope, the next rooting out the devil from homosexuals.

Paul dusted Oku's neck and face with a brush of baby powder. Oku slipped him a couple bucks extra with the embarrassing thought that his student loan was practically gone and he'd better find a job. He might have to haul gyproc and wood this summer after all. Fine, he would have to bite his tongue and get Fitz to hook him up to the job, but it would be on different terms. He didn't want Fitz hassling him and berating him. That fight at the breakfast table would give him some leverage. He got the sense in that small moment that he had put Fitz in his place once and for all.

He shook himself out of Paul's chair and left the barbershop, walking through a gauntlet of arguers on different subjects on the sidewalk. The whole strip of Eglinton between Marlee and Dufferin was full of West Indian stores selling hot food, haircuts, wigs, cosmetics, and clothes. There were stores selling barrels for stuffing goods to send to families in the Caribbean and there were stores selling green bananas, yams, pepper sauce, mangos, and salt cod, all tastes from the Caribbean carried across the Atlantic to this strip of the city. Wrapped in oil and sugar and pepper, waxed in onions and thyme; modified, hardened, and made acrid and stale by distance; hardly recognizable if any here were to really take a trip to where they once called home.

This was how Oku experienced his mother and father each day. As people who somehow lived in the near past and were unable or unwilling to step into the present. But then in some ways they were ahead of him, he thought. Hadn't he been dogging behind Jackie since high school? Hadn't she moved on? Had herself a German boyfriend, a second-hand clothes store, a life he could not enter? And he had hung on anyway to the idea that one day she would notice him and bring him into the present. And he had been passive in this, seeming to do nothing to actually get there with Jackie; afraid that if he pushed it she would definitely say no. He had thought that if he left it like a possibility, it could still happen.

Oku pointed the Buick south on Oakwood, leaving the Eglinton strip behind. He headed to Queen Street, where Jackie's store was. He hadn't heard anything from her. He had to know if she'd heard his music. Maybe it was the way the morning had begun that made him bolder. When he first took the car he had no idea he was heading for Jackie. Nor when he got the haircut, a small vanity that said the idea was lurking in him. But now he was there and certain.

He parked, and walked a block looking for the store. He saw the sign from across the street, Ab und Zu, and it hit him that Reiner might be there. Just as he thought it, Reiner walked out the door, his black guitar bag on his shoulder. Jackie held the door open for him, then waved as he walked down the street. Oku stood poised, not wanting to be witness to this domestic scene, let alone be caught doing so.

Jackie retreated inside the doorway, but then she stopped, catching sight of him across the street. She raised her hand in greeting, or was it beckoning him to come? He couldn't make out the expression on her face. It wasn't happiness, which he wanted. It wasn't distaste either, which he dreaded. It was that closed, smoky look she always gave him—half derisive, half curious, as if there was something she was waiting for him to do. Now he followed the invisible string in her hand, crossing the street in the middle of moving traffic. He felt as if he was colliding with something as he entered the doorway.

"So, hey," Jackie said, standing close to him.

"Hey," he managed to get out of his throat.

They stood this way for what seemed a long time. Then Jackie moved, going to the back of the store, and then he heard Charlie Rouse playing "When Sunny Gets Blue." He stood listening, his eyes felt swollen from desire, from recognition, and from a joy. That hoarse muted horn held her as he wanted to hold her. And she stood still, watching him in that smoky, curious way. He wanted to reach out and kiss her throat. He wanted to drop to his knees and kiss her thighs, but he didn't want to move. He wanted to stay right there in "When Sunny Gets Blue" with her. He wanted all five minutes and forty-eight seconds of it, like this, with both of them in the full and absolute meaning of things between them.

In the silence after, Jackie slowly brushed a hair from his neck, looked into his eyes as if still trying to find something conclusive there, and said languidly into his ear, "Fuck me, then."

He inhaled her skin, held her in all the shocked passion collected in him. He laughed, chuckled in the well of her throat, kissed the smooth cool surface of her neck.

They were in Reiner's bed, but he didn't think of it as Reiner's bed until after. He only thought of how they were one muscle made out of the same material, how he wanted to be inside her, how he was finally seeing her naked body, its dark brownness, its pitched sinews, its toned angles, how he felt weak and limber at the same time. He thought only of how he pushed and pushed and held her, how her legs framed him, how she bit him on his breast and his shoulder, how her arms were liquid, how she stroked his ass, how she smelled, and how she mounted him, that same cool look behind her half-closed lids; how they turned and turned, never exhausting that rhythm, the wetness between them. How she told him, "Give me your sweet cock. Fuck me." How he said to her, "Here it is, here it is, take it, fuck me, fuck me." How slippery he felt and close to crying when she said, "Don't cry now, eat me, come on, eat me." How he put his mouth on her, how she held his head, kneaded his shoulders to make his tongue obey her rhythm, and then pulled him up again, guiding his cock into her. How he wanted to come, but he wanted her to come. "I want you to come, I want you to come, I want you . . ." pressing her, balancing his cock in her, waiting for her. How he felt her muscles contract, her thighs shiver, a long breath in her cresting, how he wanted to scream for the thickness in his cock, how it burst when she put her hands on his ass and pulled him even closer. Then he wept, feeling so come apart. Then he kissed every part of her glistening body. She, still heaving for breath, grabbed him tightly.

He heard her breathing become steady, felt her arms loosen. He kissed the path between her breasts. She held his head, then let him go, rolling out of the bed and finding her clothing. "Come back," Oku said softly. Jackie shook herself into her dress, then stooped beside him to run her hand along his back. "We can always fuck, Oku. Fucking's easy." He grabbed her, rolling her onto the bed again, lifting her dress. He put his cock inside her again. She was impassive. "Not with me," he said, and held her face, kissing her lips. Jackie climbed off of him. He let her go. That's when he became aware that he was in Reiner's bed. He didn't care; he would do anything for her. Even lie in Reiner's spunk. Now Reiner would have to lie in his. He dressed, went to the front to meet a coolly restored Jackie smoking a cigarette.

"So what does it mean?" he asked.

"That we fucked."

"Okay. If that's . . ."

"And it was good."

"Yeah." He tasted her in his mouth, he smelled her on his face and hands. He reached for her, taking the cigarette away and burying his mouth in hers.

"It is what it is," she said, pulling her mouth away, putting her lips in the cavity of his neck near his ear.

Oku felt charged and useless at the same time. Sure, he wanted Jackie this way. What he had dreamed of since Harbord Collegiate had happened. He was so high, so electric, his legs were trembling. But what was she saying?

"So that's all you want from me?" He sounded threatening, as if he had found some leverage with her for the first time. As if he had become irresistible. But beneath that feeling he knew lay all his uncertainty. She was like a thing he did not want to drop and break.

"No, it's what I want . . . all I have to give."

That hesitation between "want" and "have" crippled him and gave him hope. He read ambiguity in it a hundred ways, but qualified by "all," he realized, that hesitation meant nothing. She was just finding a softer way of letting him know where he stood. All these calculations flew through his head. He looked for any weakness in what she said or in her tone and decided that if he hadn't found it, he would pursue it anyway until he did. He'd followed Jackie a long time, and he'd never been this far. So he would take whatever she gave him, whatever she had, and he would find the rest after.

He put his hand in his pocket, found the car keys, realized that he was still holding her burning cigarette with the other, and put it out in the ashtray. "And what . . . what will make you give me more?"

"*More?*" The sexual innuendo thick on her tongue at first, then becoming serious, she said, "Hmm, I don't know."

"Okay," he said and headed for the door.

Jackie moved ahead of him to unlock the door. So, he thought, she knew this would happen. He hadn't been aware of Jackie locking the door in the first place. She must have decided when she saw him across the street, she must have decided in that moment she would fuck him. They both smiled cunningly at the door, coming to the same fact together. Oku cupped her breast, pulled her to him, and made a deliberate bite on her shoulder. Jackie laughed, "Be that way, then," she said, opening the door for him.

"See you soon, maybe," he said, lingering on the "maybe."

He walked to where he had parked the car. All he could feel was her body, her legs all over him. Her scent was in his nostrils, in his hair, on his face, on his clothing. He pictured himself over and over back there in the bed with her.

Quy

I was twelve years old when the monk took me from Pulau
Bidong. He was a Hoa Hao monk. He followed the prophet
Huynh Phu So. The prophet believed in hard work, and for
sure the monk's hands were rough from something. He
was from Saigon, he said. The war churned up everyone.
He ended up in Laos and in Kuala Lumpur, and when I met
him he'd come to Pulau Bidong to bring the teachings of
the prophet to the refugees, not to mention the trade in
Thai sticks. He had a scraggly bunch behind him. Two guys
and a woman you could only mistake for devotees if you
were as desperate as all of us on Pulau Bidong.

Pulau Bidong was a thriving place. There were little
businesses everywhere. Under the hopeless look of things
there was a lot of life going on. I was very enterprising,
myself. I washed clothes and dishes for a living, and I did
errands. I owned two rafts, and I ferried to the middle of the
ocean to get things for the cleft palate Ba Chang. At first
I slept outside her place, then I made a lean-to. I must say I
was good at making things from nothing. The monk was
supposed to teach us how farming the land was practising
the way of the prophet. I never saw him farm anything
except people's stupidity. I admit that if by then I could say
I loved anything, I guess it would have been him, but look,
how was I supposed to understand the Four Debts of

Gratitude? Gratitude to your ancestors, your country, the treasures, and mankind. But I played along.

He was a city monk, but he said his father had studied with the prophet. I don't believe a word he said now. But he taught me to read. He told me I was good talker. What you need to know is what's on paper. Talking only gets you so far, it's on paper you get cheated. He used to be a politician too, he said. He won a seat once in the Constitutional Assembly back in Vietnam. If life were so good with him, I wondered why he was here. Anyway, I took to the reading. Didn't hurt. A fast learner. On Pulau Bidong you had to learn fast, change quick, or you're the bottom shit. I broke my head on his letters, then I learned to read the papers and his books and soon any print that came my way. The things that get hidden in paper! The lies! No wonder I never got off that island till the monk. A paper for this and a paper for that, and when I got there I didn't even know my good name well enough. And papers, of course I didn't have any. They were all gone with my mother and father.

Well, after the monk taught me about paper there was no looking back. I read everything I get my hands on up to this day, from the labels on cans to the scratches of birds and monkeys. Don't you worry, they've got their plans too. I read and reread the newspapers that made their way to Pulau Bidong. I chewed up the monk's book with the verses of the Buddha. My palms sweated the ink off the prophet's teachings.

By now you have to realize that the monk was doing more than helping people to free themselves from the cycle of reincarnation. All who ended up on Pulau Bidong knew their past life must have been shit. We must have fucked up in our earlier lives. But a clear mind was one of the gifts of

Pulau Bidong. The one goal was to get off of that island.
And in the meantime grab all that you could. The monk
helped with this. You want anything, you ask the
monk. He corkscrewed in on the Ba Chang's business in
cigarettes and condoms and matches and ginger and radios.
And moneylending. But the cleft palate Ba Chang didn't
believe in the third debt of gratitude—gratitude to the
monks. So a low-level war broke out. I was caught in the
middle. One day I said to myself, One day I will own myself
and not get caught in other people's mess. Anyway, I chose
the monk's side because he was a man. Everybody knows
women don't win.

It started with the fire at the prayer pagoda. That
could've been anybody—the Christians who wanted to
civilize us or the Muslims who wanted to do the same. But
then the Ba Chang sent her attackers to say that the monk
had better get off of Bidong and go back to where he came
from. The monk decided to fight and sent his pack to burn
the Ba Chang's place down, but she caught one of the men
and gave him a public beating. Then, of course, the monk
was in trouble with the authorities, who told him to fix his
business and move on. He protested, but no one believed
him. He had to sell all his stock and quit Bidong, complaining
that the Ba Chang was a sorceress and that she had bribed the
authorities to harass him.

I went with Loc Tuc—that was the monk's name—to
the mainland as his convert to Hoa Hao. He might have lost
everything, but he did not lose his gift with papers. So I was
born again as Loc Cuoi. We ended up in Singapore, where
Loc Tuc had contacts and where I myself became a monk.

Singapore is the best city in the world. That is where I
discovered Loc Tuc's real book. Sun Tzu. Though you would

think with such a treasure he would have defeated the Ba
Chang on Bidong. This book he hid from me. Loc Tuc was a
cosmopolitan man. He made me wade through the *Tao Te
Ching* of Lao Tzu, though I admit I like poets; the Analects
of Kung Fu Tzu, though I am a practical man myself. Not to
mention the verses of the poet emperor Ts'ao Ts'ao. As a
matter of fact, Loc Tuc traded in stolen bamboo slips from
raided archaeological sites, the graves of the ancient Chinese
noblemen, and these were a particular pleasure to me. Of
course, what he coveted were the actual words of the
Buddha, and he conspired at length trying to acquire the
Kangyur in its earliest known form, even though that was
not his kind of Buddhism. He said that there was a version
written in the hand of the Buddha himself and that he
hoped to have it before he died. The tortures he put me
through memorizing and memorizing. I ask myself today,
Why? What did he see in me? Because he was not a man to
do anything for nothing. Of course, I was his lackey, his dog.
He was teaching me to bite anyone he didn't like. But what
else? Because you don't need to teach a dog good manners.
But maybe I was his insurance. A dog will bite you too, and
if you let go the chain, he will ravage you. So Loc Tuc
chained me up with his books and paper. But I was still a
dog. He knew. I knew.

You would say, then, that I was lucky to be taken in by
this monk, Loc Tuc. You would say that he saved me from
worse things that could have happened to me; that he
calmed my life, took my tears away. So why complain about
the way the darkness made us all hallucinate, made us all
see the water ripple in a certain direction, made my sisters'
hearts quiver, my mother and father think they were each
holding my hand? Why quibble about what made the boat

lift and pull southeast or southwest, what made me fall asleep thinking of my father's hand in his pocket or his hat waiting to be touched the next day? Who knows why we left on that particular evening? Perhaps this was my fate. Perhaps you're right. I didn't have a hard life. It was simply a life. A life like millions of lives.

We may pretend to have control of things, but we don't. It's up to the heavens, as laid out for us by destiny. Why question the stars? Wars are inevitable and we have to pay the price, human nature can't be changed, the laws of nature prevail no matter how we fight against them, the strong survive, the weak perish. Blah blah blah blah! Crap, *lo dit!* Yes, I learned the strong survive, all right, the weak perish. But take it from me, the strong are just strong, not best. The most ruthless, the greediest, but not the best. I know what got killed in me. I know where he is, the weak little shit who kept waiting for goodness, the *geum*, who wanted to jump up and trust anybody; who was ready any time to forgive.

So luck had nothing to do with it. I chose the monk. He didn't choose me. I saw him in his brown hassock with his frigging bells. I knew he wasn't a good man. Who is? I knew all I had to do was flatter him. Not too big because he would see through that, but small, you know, a look of admiration here, a favour there, get him a little lump of opium. You know, quiet, quiet. He would scold me and tell me it was wrong, but he'd take it, and then I'd find him listless, his body slow as oil, in the prayer pagoda, his eyes filmed over and his fingers burned. I don't believe in destiny. If you follow the Buddha, you know you have to make your own path. So I made my path by choosing the monk.

I remembered nothing of Saigon. The shanties of Pulau Bidong had been my city for seven years. By now I had almost forgotten my father and mother. My mother in her red dress, my father in his hat with his hand in his pocket. In the years that passed this is all that remained memorable— the red dress over a fading figure and the hat and the hand in a pocket. When I close my eyes at night, I see the glow of the red dress and this hand reaching into its pocket. And when I open my eyes in the morning at the end of my last dreams, there again is the afterimage of a red dress, a hat, a hand. No matter my dreams, that would be the beginning and end of them. Long after it matters I still see that image like the skin under my eyelids.

Singapore—when we came to Singapore I knew I would live there for the rest of my life. It was clean like a good glass of water. I had never seen anything like it before—the glass towers, the swept streets, the orderly manner of everything, the birds—I felt like a rough and dirty stone put down in the middle of it all. We left seven months later. Loc Tuc couldn't get a good foothold there. He said he needed some place more fluid. We backtracked up the testicle of Malaysia to Thailand. It was a raggedy retreat. It took us a year and a half, maybe two, maybe three—I don't know how many times we were beaten up or jailed. But Loc Tuc would squirm us out of it with the teachings of the prophet, and his pretence of being a devout man and an important man who had suffered under the communists in Vietnam.

He was from Loc Ninh, so he said, but he had spent the war in Saigon, and when the country boys from the north walked into Saigon his teachings about hard work got a going over. He claimed he was connected by family to a general in the southern army, and though he was questioned

and questioned and sent to a camp for re-education, he
finally bought his way out with money from the family.
One minute he was from Loc Ninh, one minute he was from
Khe San, the next time he was from Ha Tien, then from Nha
Trang. Sometimes he was a friend of Thieu, the next his
cousin's sister-in-law was General Diem's mistress. He even
claimed to have made a daring escape from Chi Hoa Prison.
He even claimed to be a friend of Thich Quang Duc, the
monk who had doused himself in gasoline and set himself on
fire in Saigon. That is when Loc Tuc wanted to seem elegant.
That monk, he told me, was protesting the persecution of
Buddhists. I don't know why he told me these stories, they
didn't matter to me. But I suppose I was his only audience,
and as meagre as that was, a storyteller always tries to
impress. I didn't have any stories, so what the hell, I listened.
I was the wrong person to impress.

SIXTEEN

EVERY FOUR YEARS, June in the city is crazy. Cars speed about flying emblems of various nationalities. Resurgent identities are lifted and dashed. Small neighbourhoods that seemed at least slightly reconciled break into sovereign bodies. It's all because of soccer.

The World Cup is this year, and today it is raining. Korea is playing Italy in Japan. Up on St. Clair Avenue, in the Italian neighbourhood, they're biting their nails over espressos and San Romano beer. Any minute now they hope to launch out into the street waving the tricolour and screaming Francesco Totti's name. They're prepared to wear black and go so far as to cut their wrists if the blues don't win. In Korea Town on Bloor Street, the same, except their hopes are more modest, given that Korea's team has gone farther than any in history and the Italians are formidable. When Ahn Jung-Hwan scored the golden goal, from St. Clair to the old Little Italy on College Street the Italians declared days of mourning. In Korea Town, where Binh has his store uncomfortably wedged between a grocery store and restaurant, red flags, red T-shirts, red headbands, "*red devils*" screams, have burst out of the bars and restaurants, honking cars full of people have suddenly jammed streets. Exquisite screams of exaltation can be heard. The Koreans have erupted in a street party too sweet to mean anything less than world domination. The rain is incessant, yet it doesn't stop some; the sidewalks are crammed and tears are flowing so much it's impossible to make out what's falling from the skies and what's falling from faces.

Tuyen loved World Cup. She loved being in the middle of whirling people, people spinning on emotion. She'd been with her camera to every street party this June. To Little Italy, to the English pub, where the reactions are exuberant as a soccer riot in Manchester but contained within four walls; she stood outside of the German pub and was shy to take pictures; at the Brazilian *cevejaria* on College Street she danced the samba in between shots. Today she heard the honking horns heading up to Bloor Street, and she collected her gear and raced up Bathurst to Korea Town. As she left the apartment, she heard a television announcer say, "I didn't know we had a Korea Town in the city." Asshole, she thought, you wouldn't. You fuckers live as if we don't live here. She wasn't Korean, of course, but World Cup made her feel that way. No Vietnamese team had made it, so today she was Korean.

The fool on the television made her fly all the faster up the street. Tuyen began snapping photographs as soon as she hit the intersection. There was one of six or seven teenaged boys streaming a twenty-foot red flag; there was the rain beating down on a girl, her body outstretched through a car window. Tuyen found a vantage point on top of a parked car. The owners were so happy themselves, they didn't mind. The traffic was backed up for blocks. Korean flags drenched with rain slapped about. Car horns made a rhythm, and the whole of Korea Town was lit up despite the downpour.

Tuyen felt elated, infected by the mood on the street. It reminded her of a year ago, when she and Oku went to Quebec to demonstrate against globalization. Oku had joined the black anarchists. They were both always trying to find something tingling on the skin, something where their blood rushed to their heads and they felt alive. She had taken her camera and Oku his balaclava and thick gloves for throwing back tear-gas canisters. The night before, they had watched videos of Japanese demonstrators, impressed by the riot gear protesters in Tokyo had. "There," Oku said, "they didn't have this bullshit talk about peaceful demonstrations, they came out knowing there would be trouble." Carla was nowhere around for this. She watched the protest on TV, disconnected and passionless. Tuyen had tried to persuade her to go with them, wanting to get her out of that stark apartment—a futon, a crate for a table, two stools, some bricks and board for her few books, her stereo, four plates, four cups, four spoons, four forks, four knives, a skillet and a pot, her clothes, a clock that ticked loudly, an old black-and-white television. She was going through an extra-antiseptic phase at the time. "Bullshit," she said, when Tuyen asked her. But Oku got his foot sprained when an undercover dragged him into a van. He was one of the first ones to climb the fence. He made up the opening lines of poems, calling them out to the group he was with. He was enjoying himself, screaming poetry about the downfall of everything. He even enjoyed the arrest. Until his father almost blew an artery when he came home.

He had borrowed his father's broken-down car again. This time without telling him how long he would be or how far he was going. "He's just going to have to understand that it's service to the people, man, service to the people." Tuyen was clicking away with her camera throughout the whole thing. She was going to use the photographs for an installation called *Riot*. She photographed the legs of the policemen on horseback as the horses skittered toward the crowd, planning to title it "Dance." She may have lost Oku when she stopped to photograph the arc of a tear-gas canister, broken glass, and police shoes—she would call this photograph "Overkill." Oku yelled to her for help, but she didn't hear him; she saw him as she saw everything, as she imagined.

Her eyes took in every human experience as an installation, her lids affecting the shuttering mechanism of a camera. It must have been a milky evening: the water was grey milk, the sky was stone grey, the boat was disappearing in a noisy rush, and Tuyen's mother and father must have seen Quy like this—slowly, slowly moving away. Floating, floated away, in the China Sea without a trace. Her mother's insomnia was caused by this sight. When she closed her eyes at night, she herself saw Quy floating away. So Tuyen kept clicking. She kept looking at what wasn't being seen, as her brother must have been unseen, and her mother noticing too late, harried with irrational fear. Tuyen saw, heard first Oku's voice unlike his voice, then saw, turning with her camera to click and click the declensions of Oku's body being dragged to the van. The arm of the cop entwined with Oku's flailing arms. She photographed this aggressive embrace, Oku falling to his knees, then pushed, pulled away by two friends, then the cops beating the friends back and shoving Oku into a white cube van with lines down the side. She called this "Tree Falling Against Van."

Months later, announcing *Riot*, an installation in her apartment, Tuyen mounted these photographs on the staircase coming up. Oku was very proud of them and brought people he'd met at the riot to see them. The photographs made Carla queasy. She told Tuyen and Oku that they were sick. She rushed up the staircase and into her apartment quickly each time she came in. The photographs, something about the motion in them, their sequence, reminded her faintly of the dream of her mother climbing onto a chair. As a concession Tuyen removed the photographs from the stair-well and hung them inside her apartment. She saw Carla's flinching ascent on the flight of stairs, her left ear bent to her shoulder as if against the sound of the pictures, as she would have as a child. It was all Tuyen could do to restrain herself from taking a photograph—a way of caressing Carla.

She loved June anyway. The fresh womanly sound of the word, and the way the month never disappointed in any year. The opening of summer. Today, music blared from cars and from the open doorways of dress shops, restaurants, cyber-cafés, and tea places. Tuyen was ecstatic. She spun around, her camera clicking off shots. She didn't yet know how she would use them. Through the lens she saw a familiar face and stroked the button to open the aperture; she clicked twice, trying to remember who it was. Binh! She hadn't expected to see him here, so the face of her own brother was familiar and unfamiliar to her. She was shocked and ashamed at the same time at not recognizing the sibling with whom she had so many recorded and unrecorded fights. Perhaps there was something in her misrecognition that told of those battles, how a brother was both a stranger and a loved one, more than a loved one, the same as you; and seeing his face outside of yourself, of the family, was to see him anew.

Binh was grim-faced, talking to another man whose back was to Tuyen. It dawned on Tuyen that she was standing diago-nally opposite Binh's store, XS. He was using his hands to talk, pointing at the man as if telling him what to do. The man was tall and slight, his head angled as a boy being berated, dangling on the slim stem of his neck. Oddly, the man's body itself was rigid, a hand reaching out to touch Binh, to hold his pointing finger. Tuyen's lens caught this hand and the other reaching onto Binh's right shoulder. The embrace was both sinister and affectionate. Binh broke into a smile, then spun the man around, his left arm taking the man's right shoulder. Tuyen snapped this series of shots, her own shock translated into mechanical clicking of the shutter. Her camera almost slipped from her hand when she saw the man's face.

It was the face of a boy, a baby, innocent and expectant. There was something wrong about it. It didn't go with the rest of his body—something she'd suspected when photographing his back. Binh clapped. Then they turned to watch the celebration in the street and Tuyen kept clicking her camera at them until the roll ended.

Something stopped her from raising her hand to signal Binh—it was the ridiculous face of the man beside him, the feeling that she had just spied something intimate or secret. The revellers in the street kept moving along in throngs—she had almost forgotten them. A pool of light set itself on that little familiar-unfamiliar knot of her brother and a stranger, a friend, an associate, a partner. The rain continued falling; all of Korea Town was awash in joy.

Tuyen climbed off the car and struggled along the sidewalk, heading home. She wanted to go home quickly to develop the photographs. She wanted to look again at her brother and the man. There was something there that she had to suss out, some intimate fact that she seemed to know but could not put her finger on. She cradled the camera from the rain.

She gradually became aware of someone calling her.

"Tuyen!"

She heard her name above the traffic and car horns. An electric current ran down her neck. God, no, not her brother. She was so sure he hadn't seen her. "Tuyen, hold up!" The voice was loud and excited. She walked faster, trying to think of where to hide the camera.

"Tuyen!" The voice was closer and breathless. She swung around defensively.

"Tuyen, isn't this great? Shit, I've never seen anything like it. It's fantastic." It was Oku, his face streaming wet.

Tuyen was so relieved she grabbed him hard, hugging him. Why, a minute ago she'd been so frightened. And frightened of what? Her brother? That was nonsense, she told herself now, but she looked furtively over Oku's shoulder to the intersection.

"Where the hell are you going?" She tried sounding nonchalant but heard her voice choked on the rain.

"I'm meeting Carla for coffee. Come with me. We were gonna watch the party and then go to the bar—she's on the corner. Come on. This is so fucking beautiful out here!"

Tuyen was caught up again in the enthusiasm of the day. She hadn't thought to check for Carla when she rushed out of her apartment—she'd assumed Carla was at work. She suddenly realized that she had been holding on so tightly to the camera that her fingers hurt. What had she been afraid of? She slipped the camera into the bag on her shoulder. Why hadn't she done that before? Instead, she had carried it like some, some . . . yes, it came to her—Remedios Varo's painting *Solar Music*, in which a figure is pulling a bow across rays of light; in the air small glass prisms break open, revealing scarlet birds. She had been carrying the camera like a delicate glass prism in which she had captured a stunning red bird.

"Come on, come on, come on. Let's go."

"All right, I'm coming, I'm coming." She plunged after Oku back into the throng at Bathurst and Bloor. They found the usually subdued Carla waving a Korean flag and singing, "*Oh, Pil-seung Korea.*"

———

When they made their way to Cyber's, a bar on Bloor Street, a half an hour later, Tuyen had put the disturbing thoughts of her brother aside.

"God, I love this place. The joint is fucked up today."

"Yes, and I'm wet like a mother."

"Here, use my scarf." Tuyen pulled a bandanna from her bag and wrapped it around Carla. The camera tumbled around inside. They ordered a jug of draft, three shots of tequila, and French fries, each hopeful that one of them had money to pay. Carla usually paid. She was the one with the steadiest job.

"Word," Oku started. It was a game they played whenever they went to a bar. Someone would say "word," and each of them would have to riff on some subject.

"Let me get my drink down first." Carla threw back the shot and chased it with the draft.

"Stall. You go, Tuyen."

"No, you go, I'm cold still."

"Lame. I'll start." They both did this to Oku each time. He loved this. He was bursting with it today. "Okay, this city better be ready, this shit is coming down, check it. Days like this are a warning. A promise. I heard one Korean guy say just now this was the happiest day he'd ever had in this city. Now why is that? See this place, some world shit is coming down and some of us are ready and some not. Now why would he say that today? See, some might see that as pitiful. And it is. But, man, I think it's visionary. That guy just saw possibility. This shit is going to get more fucked up after this June. I like it when shit is all messed up like this. So here it is—millennium, man, the millennium is come and gone. And if not, if not for this sweet gasoline of time and our great beauty, they'd be drowning in this quick rain; if not. If not for my hand in

Jackie's, my throat singing this hymn to the boy visionary in the street in the red rain, this city would burn us all."

"Word! Word!" Tuyen and Carla acknowledged him, laughing.

"Your turn," Carla said pointing at Tuyen.

"Okay, okay. I'm not good as him, but here goes. Madonna, Madonna, repeating, repeating that brutalized beaten-up Marilyn Monroe. White folks' culture is just repetition of some old hackneyed images. Jesus, I'm sick of Madonna. I can't understand how she can stand walking around in that body. It's the dried-out pupa sack of Marilyn Monroe. Every generation of Americans gets to fuck over Marilyn Monroe all over again. They get to batter her, jerk off over her, and kill her. The main scary thing about that image is it all depends on bleach, the hair is bleached, the skin is bleached, the body is bleached. They get to corrode her in public. The eyes do damage to her body. I'm tired of them killing Marilyn Monroe over and over again and saying it's sexy."

"Word! Word!" Carla and Oku said together.

"And Eminem is only Elvis Presley, another repetition. Like I have to say more?" Tuyen warmed.

"Hey, no, Tuyen, Eminem's my boy, he's for real."

"Sure, kill women, kill the homos. That's for real. What's that make him? A homeboy?"

"Word!" Carla chimed.

"See, Elvis was for real once too," Oku explained "Poor boy, like Eminem, but the system only knows how to co-opt so they even co-opted his poor ass in the white suprema- cist shit."

"Well, what do you think's happened to Eminem? And don't think for a minute that you're trumping me with that. It's still kill women, kill the homos, whatever. I'm dead either way."

"She got you there," Carla threw back another shot of tequila.

"Word. Hey, your turn," Oku conceded, reluctantly turning to Carla.

"Okay, Angie was a border crosser, a wetback, a worker in the immigrant sweatshop they call this city. On days like this I understand her like a woman instead of a child. Everybody thought she was a whore. She wasn't. She tried to step across the border of who she was and who she might be. They wouldn't let her. She didn't believe it herself so she stepped across into a whole other country."

The table fell silent.

"Word," Tuyen said finally, softly grabbing Carla's hand around her beer bottle. "Hey, Carla . . ."

"I'm good, I'm good. It's just I get it, you know."

The game was over. They sat drinking and feeling, looking at the rain still falling outside and listening to the blare of horns and the clatter of forks and dishes around them. As disturbing as all they were living was, they felt alive. More alive, they thought, than most people around them. They believed in it, this living. Its raw openness. They saw the street outside, its chaos, as their only hope. They felt the city's violence and its ardour in one emotion. It was dark now; the rainy summer light had descended. The water glistened on everything—cars, neon signs, newspaper boxes, people. The blind singer across the street in front of the movie theatre packed up his tuneless voice, going home; teenaged boys hobbled along in too-big jeans; girls holding cigarettes between French-tipped nails walked briskly by. Next door the Lebanese shawarma place, which had been a doughnut shop, and had once been an ice cream store, and would in another incarnation be a sushi bar, now exhaled odours of roasted lamb. A stream of identities flowed past the bar's window: Sikhs in FUBU, Portuguese girls in DKNY, veiled Somali girls in Puma sneakers, Colombian teenagers in tattoos. Carla had said it all, not just about her mother but about all of them. Trying to step across the borders of who they were. But they were not merely trying. They were, in fact, borderless.

"Anyways . . ." They all started laughing at the same time as Tuyen broke the moment. "Let's stop this cerebral shit."

"Where's Jackie today?"

"At the store!" Carla and Tuyen said together. "Where else, Oku?"

"Look, man, get over yourself, okay?"

"I know. I'm just asking."

"Christ. You're gonna lose out, man."

"You better think of something, Mr. Poet."

"Have you done anything? Have you called her, talked to her? What is the big deal?" Tuyen was always impatient with Oku in regards to Jackie.

"She's got a white boy, man. I saw them in the market the other day. It looked really intense."

"*Intense?* Jackie intense? Which girl are you talking about?"

"Yeah, Jackie holding hands and shit. The shit looked critical."

"So, you got nothing to lose, right? Man, you are so slow."

"I've got to do some research, all right?"

"You're just scared." Carla said quietly.

"Nah, I've got to figure out this white-boy thing. I'm not going out like that . . ." He hadn't told them about sex with Jackie. He wanted to keep it to himself.

"What's to figure out, Oku? Jackie's really wise," Tuyen said. "She doesn't want any hassle, no trouble, and Reiner's like that."

"Well, if she don't want it hard, it's not me, right?"

"*Hard!* Listen to you! You give it hard, do you?"

"I don't mean that, okay, time out." They were laughing at him. "That's not what I mean. You all are dirty, man. Hey, let's burn."

"No, I have to develop some film tonight." Tuyen felt for the camera.

"You do that high all the time."

"Yeah, that's when I want it to come out fucked up."

"You and me then, Carla?" He needed a place to crash. He hadn't shown up to Kwesi's, and he didn't want to explain. He couldn't explain.

"Okay, for a bit, then I need sleep. I'm gonna get fired because of World Cup."

"There's hundreds of courier services. You're like Miguel Indurain on the bike. You can always get a job."

"Yeah, right, Poet. Let's get the bill."

"Word. What's Canadian in 9.79 seconds and Jamaican in twenty-four hours? Ben Johnson," Oku joked as they were leaving the bar.

"Oh, that's lame, that's so tired."

The rain hadn't let up, nor had the party in Korea Town. The police had moved the crowd on farther along to Christie, clearing the intersection of Bathurst and Bloor of the pile-up. The car horns still blared. Korean flags flying intercut occasionally with Brazilian and Japanese ones. Tuyen, Carla, and Oku stood watching and waving and singing, "*Oh, Pil-seung Korea! Oh, Pil-seung Korea!*"

Quy

Of the eighty-one poems of the sage Lao Tzu, Loc Tuc liked number forty. "The motion of nature is cyclic and returning. Its way is to yield, for to yield is to become. All things are born of being, being is born of non-being." But me, I liked number twenty. "The sage may seem to be perplexed, being neither bright nor clear, and to himself, sometimes he seems both dull and weak, confused and shy. Like the ocean at night, he is serene and quiet, but as penetrating as the winter wind." See, that's me. I look stupid, I play dumb, but I'm working. *Penetrating as the winter wind*—that's me.

Some ask if there were times that I enjoyed my life. To know this is to know the way. And why, others may ask, did the monk latch on to me? I would catch him off guard, staring at me when he thought I was not looking. I could feel his gaze burn my face from time to time. I spoke less and less as time went on. What is the use? I thought. And so when I uttered any sound he would perk up with curiosity. If I fell asleep, I would wake to find him watching me. When we arrived in Bangkok, I began to feel uneasy about his attention. You have to know that I wouldn't recognize love if I saw it. So I thought he meant to do me harm. How would I know that he saw in me one hundred years of meditation, that I had lived several other lives before my present reincarnation. Garbage, I said when I found out, and anyway it was too late by then.

We settled in Bangkok in the Klong Tocy district. Settled is not the word. We had a room in the back of a store that sold nails and tin and wire and keys. Bangkok was a city in constant dust and smog, the movement of it was turbulent. Bees, I heard the city as if a hundred thousand bees were buzzing in my ear. The bridge over the river had a constant hum of traffic resounding over the tin roofs of the hovels below, which was Klong Toey. There we made a prayer place. The three of us, his followers, were emaciated like reeds. It was strange how Loc Tuc seemed to stay healthy, looking through all of our hard travels. He wanted to be like some monks who had patrons, but he wasn't as charming as he thought, and in Bangkok there were many monks ahead of him. The three of us, his followers, had more of a chance to end the cycle of reincarnation than Loc Tuc. We broke the rules of devotion, of course, smoking and drinking and such, but Loc Tuc was insatiable. More insatiable than all of us. We were his shadows, we performed all the tasks of meeting Loc Tuc's desires. The female he fucked, the male cleaned and fed him, and I got his opium and submitted to his teaching, and we all three did his bidding when it came to delivering messages and bringing them, beating up on someone defenceless, stealing and doing the same duties for Loc Tuc's associates in the dirty places of Bangkok.

Once I beat a man up, a man who owed us money. He ended up in the hospital, and I followed him there and beat him some more. I broke his wife's jaw when she came at me. I don't like people taking things from me. It was in the news-paper how daring I was and how I was low-life from Malaysia.

This is all hindsight. I sound bitter. I'm not. I didn't hate Loc Tuc. After all, he took me from Pulau Bidong. He gave me a direction. He taught me who I was.

As I said, we lived off a tiny alleyway in the back of a store that sold nails and spanners and nuts and pails. Nobody came to buy any of this that I ever saw. A card game kept things going. Here you could bet on anything— where the rain would fall, whether two ants would go in a certain direction, anything. Sometimes there were dog fights and rooster fights and fights between men. Our room was small, and the four of us stuck close to it for the first few months while Loc Tuc put out his feelers for clients of one kind or another. Women wanting their fortunes told or men wanting a job done, like unloading a truck of TV sets or computers or American sneakers or cellphones. This was the beginning of the economic boom, the Asian tigers, Japan, Malaysia, Indonesia, and Hong Kong. Tigers. You could get a job in an American factory, a German factory, an Italian factory—all right here in Thailand. Those stupids tied to those machines would stumble back home with less than what they went to work with, if they were lucky. Not we. We lived on the fat. We weren't big. Not as big as Loc Tuc would have liked. Again it wasn't his country; we couldn't be too conspicuous. We ran into a lot of competition too, a lot of knives, a lot of treachery. Treachery. We ran into people like us. People wanting to get by. To live.

I'm not a liar. Every time Loc Tuc sent me to do something, I put a little aside for myself. If we stole television sets, I skimmed two per cent off the profits, same with dresses or video recorders or watches. Loc Tuc knew. Why would you trust me if I didn't steal a bit too? Just like he did. What was I supposed to be? A sage? I made my own contacts, I cut my own deals. Stole vegetables, sold them to food vendors, stole cigarettes, sold to tourists and children. I was swift. I am swift. I learn fast. Anything. I pick up anything. I watch everything. I had a black bag full of cigarettes, watches, cellphones, pens, tapes, computer disks. I'd peddle them in the tourist district and all along Silom Road. From the old market, around the White Orchid, all over.

I often ask myself why I wore this disguise as a monk like Loc Tuc. No answer. I was a monk. I renounced the world. I didn't know the world. It's all self-deception, anyway. I'm not about to apologize for what I did.

Most days, when things were busy, we worked until one or two in the morning. When things were slow, we walked about all day, begging alms or sitting near the filthy river Chao Phyara. Our room was hot and dusty and suffocating in the daytime. At night the other guy and I listened to Loc Tuc do nasty grunting things with the woman. It got to be like music we fell asleep to. The other guy, Kien, jerked himself off to this tune every night. He wanted the woman, but he was such an ugly man she wouldn't have him. At night I listened to the three of them, and it just turned me right off. You would think that I'd be spanking it myself, but the sound of them made me shrivel up. I would clamp one of the stolen Walkmans on my ears and go to sleep to Mallaria or the Stone Crows.

One day Loc Tuc took me into his confidence. I don't know why. I'm not a person to be trusted. People always trust me, though. I'm the kind of person you think you're having a conversation with, but I'm not there. If you look, my eyes are flying all over. Maybe Loc Tuc thought that loyalty was the least he could expect from me because he had rescued me. If you are ignorant both of your enemy and

of yourself, you are certain to be in peril in every battle.
Why did I think of myself as Loc Tuc's enemy? Perhaps it was
boyishness on my part. Loc Tuc said he was going to return
to Ho Chi Minh City because he was tired and old and
there was one last score of computer chips and cellphone
batteries he would make and then he was leaving. He told
me this when I was tying his arm off for his daily dose, and I
asked him when we were leaving, and he said I was free.
And in a fit of jealousy I told him that the ugly man, Kien,
was fucking his woman. Then he fell asleep and I left to go
to the market with my bag.

When I came back, the monk was lying on the floor
with his right arm in blood. Kien was sleeping and the woman was not around. I had waited for Kien at the railway
station for our usual sweet tea, but he had not appeared.
It was there that he used to show me the panties of the woman,
which he had stolen. He would grin and place them to his
nose. Loc Tuc, I suspected, had tried to tie himself off again
and the butchered veins in his arm had bled. But as I went
closer to him, I saw that he had a bicycle spoke in his hand.
There was blood on it. Then I noticed that the room was
more wrecked than usual. The goods, which were usually
the only orderly things, were in a mess, and Kien did not
answer when I asked him why he had he kept me waiting at
the station. I kicked his foot and he didn't move. Then I saw
his face, which was a mask of black blood. I tried to shake
Loc Tuc awake, but he was gone into his dreams, so I waited
and waited until he woke up.

Kien was still dead when Loc Tuc woke up weeping. We
doubled Kien into a mat. We threw him into the murky face
of the Chao Phyara River. Loc Tuc could not control himself.
He was weeping so much, thinking of the reincarnations he

would have to make. I told him, "Shut up! People disappear all the time." He was like a child. "Nobody comes back," I said, "and nothing happens." He looked at me strangely, and calmness fell over him.

You would think he would be more anxious to leave Bangkok after this. I expected him to take off right away, but he didn't. We went back to the routine in our room behind the store, except that Kien was in the river and the woman was never seen again. "Loc Tuc," I said to him one evening, "when will you leave for Saigon?" He lay listless on his mat, his veins a twist of broken strings, his arm like a discarded guitar. He had done something, it would seem, beyond shame, beyond life. He would stare at me as if he didn't know me, only lifting himself, slowly reaching a bedraggled hand out for the dirty heroin I brought him. Other times he would pace and flutter about jerkily, making another plan to leave for Saigon, only to fall into weeping again.

But sometimes I caught him staring at me as if I were an evil man. I would ask him then, "Loc Tuc, what did Kien say to you? He was a liar, you know. He was planning against you. Did he tell you something?" Loc Tuc would pretend he didn't hear me. But my questions would quiet his accusations, which he never voiced but which I understood. So in war, the way is to avoid what is strong and to strike at what is weak. I determined that as soon as I found out what I wanted from Loc Tuc, I would let him go.

SEVENTEEN

TUYEN WAS WET from the rain. She mounted the stairs ahead of Carla and Oku and felt around in her bag for her keys.

"Sure you won't have a smoke?" Carla coaxed.

"Nah, next time. Tomorrow, save me some." Her fingers touched the camera. She felt nervous. "See you guys."

"Are you gonna be pounding on my head again tonight?"

"No. I'm kinda stalled on that one."

"Thank God!"

"You're kidding! After you made us haul that fucking thing up, nearly killing ourselves!"

"Anyways! Later." Tuyen opened her door and entered her studio, leaving them in mock shock on the threshold.

Her small darkroom used to be part of the kitchen. She drew the camera from her bag, looked at it, and seeing that she had two more frames in the roll, at a whim shot them off at her own face. Then she rewound the film and removed the cylinder from the camera. In the darkroom, the only neat space in the apartment, she approached the three trays and scissors that lay on the counter. The lights off, she pulled the film out, cutting it smoothly from the spool, then with a dexterous motion she pulled it onto the reel in the light-tight tank. She poured the developer into the tank, tapped it to dislodge any air, covered it, and breathed. Exhaled, as if for the first time since entering the room. Her mind ran to her mother in another photograph. A picture of Cam, whose name meant "orange fruit, sweet mountain sunset," and Tuyen's two older sisters. Her mother luminous, the two girls laughing. That was long before they left Vietnam, long before Tuyen was born. The picture was on the mantel at the house in Richmond Hill—Tuyen had asked her mother for it, but her mother refused. Then she'd tried to persuade her mother to let her borrow it to make a copy, but her mother still said no, she could not part with it even for a moment. Her father had taken the picture, and whoever developed and printed it wasn't very good. But her mother's face and the girls laughing was illumination itself.

Tuyen poured the developer out and poured in the stop bath. This is where that other photographer may have faltered. She, or most probably he, may have done this too quickly, leaving some of the silver on the film or perhaps it was at the next stage. Tuyen emptied the stop and poured in the fixer to clear the negative of all the silver, and then hung the negative to dry on the line strung across the small room. She ducked out of the room, shaking her hands dry. The picture had been taken before Quy was born too. He was the small rise under her mother's red dress. Red? Why had she assumed red? The photograph was black and white. She had not asked her mother the colour. She must have assumed, she thought now, from the darkish hue and the luminous face. It could just as well have been blue, but Tuyen liked to think of it as red, bursting with life.

Wiping her hands on her skirt, Tuyen realized that she hadn't changed, she was damp from the rainy walk down Bathurst. She hadn't put the lights on either, and it was completely dark. "Why is this place so messy?" she heard herself say aloud, then laughed at herself. Carla must be invading her head, she thought. The white drape of the city's longings seemed illuminated. The *lubaio* stood erect in the middle of the floor of the main room. She had cut arms into it and had every intention of carving symbols into the whole structure, but for the moment her clothing hung from the arms, along with a bag of onions and another of her beloved potatoes. This to keep them away from the mice. Her futon lay like a messy nest under the window. Her windows faced only the alley, unlike Carla's windows, which faced both the alley and the street. She changed, gathering desperate pieces of clothing from the floor and the signpost. She felt cold even though it was June and warm. The rain was still falling mistily outside. She wished she had a fire.

There had been another photograph on the mantel in Richmond Hill. Identical except for her father's presence. And identical except that their features were now tense, the two girls grim. The rise in her mother's dress was no longer there, and the boy whom it represented was also missing. Someone had taken the photograph of them as they were leaving Chi Ma Wan Camp in Hong Kong. They were among the fortunate. After six months Tuan's grease-handing had finally paid off and they had left. As awful as the place was, Cam was reluctant to go. She kept expecting the disappeared boy to miraculously disembark from another boat. Tuyen's mother removed and replaced this picture every so often from the mantel. As if she could not decide whether she admitted or could bear the reality it suggested but that she occasionally had to face.

Tuyen turned the stove on under a pot of water. She poked into the bag of potatoes and gathered three in her hand, peeled and cut them in halves, and put them into the boiling water. For all her apprehension earlier in the day, she felt safe now, the negative of her brother drying in the darkroom, the potatoes boiling on the stove. Uncharacteristically, she hadn't looked at the strips. She felt safe in that too. She had captured something, she was sure, and she had brought it to her cave. The thought of this studio being her cave amused her. Jackie called it that, and that is what it felt like now. Some early place where the inhabitants had no signs for decorum, no standards for neatness; where they observed an order that was purely utilitarian. The *lubaio*, the bits of wood, the photographs, the longings were what she brought to the cave to be handled, and thought about, and made into something she could use to create alternate, unexpected realities, exquisite corpses. That's what Tuan and Cam were, exquisite corpses. Or were they her surrealists and she their composition? Their exquisite corpse? Not she, Binh.

Seeing him across the street in the rain, his arm around the man whose face was like an angel or a ghost or a child, she had made some discovery that she was yet to understand. The two seemed both real and metaphoric. She guessed that's why she hadn't looked at the negatives yet. She was still absorbing the images, freshly. She knew that by the time she looked at the images on the negative they would acquire other significances, and by the time she printed them they would be art, open to a thousand interpretations. There was one interpretation that she needed to catch. The one that had led her memory to her mother's photographs disappearing and reappearing.

How many times had she rummaged through her mother's possessions, going over the signs of their former life? There was only so much they could bring with them, of course, but her mother's sentimentality could not have allowed her to come away with nothing. Perhaps their opposition to the new Vietnam had been so strong that they abandoned even memory. Yet from their talk she could not sense any strong political opposition, just a fear that had taken hold of them over the course of several months and propelled them to a bay one night. Her father had not been involved politically; he had, in fact, avoided the army. Her mother was the only doctor in a small clinic. They were part, to be sure, of the striving middle class who felt themselves vulnerable under the communist government—Tuan had had hopes of being on the ground floor of real-estate development in Da Nang after the American victory. But in all this they were ordinary people living an ordinary life who were suddenly caught, the way war catches anyone, without bearings; the way war dismantles all sensibility except fear. Only when they arrived in Toronto would they fully construct their departure as resistance to communism. That is the story the authorities needed in order to fill out the appropriate forms. They needed terror, and indeed Tuan and Cam had had that; they needed loss, and Tuan and Cam had had that too. And perhaps with this encouragement, this coaxing of their story into a coherent wholeness, they were at least officially comforted that the true horror was not losing their boy but the forces of communism, Vietnam itself, which they were battling. Whatever the official story, her mother's cache of photographs told another, a parallel story, a set of possible stories, an exquisite corpse.

There were two photographs of Quy. One as a tiny baby on his back, surprised by the flash of the camera. Then another, the one that her mother sent around the world in her quest to find him. A small, intelligent-looking boy, curious. Cam had made many copies, which she sent out with her letters. When Tuyen was little, these photographs littered the house.

Their subject was the source of strange outbursts and crying. Over the years the photograph was less and less in evidence until it had virtually disappeared. It was not on the mantel of the house in Richmond Hill. It lay in the recesses of her mother's room now with the baby picture. Well beyond the time that he could possibly still look like the curious little boy in the photograph, Cam had sent it along with her letters nevertheless. Tuyen hadn't seen the picture in years.

Tuyen was sitting in the dark; she still hadn't turned on any light. Only the glow of the one good burner of the stove could be seen. The pot of potatoes was crackling as if the water had all evaporated. A faint tinge of burning starch could be discerned. Tuyen ran to the stove, rescuing the potatoes from parching. The handle of the pot was hot, and she let out a sound of pain but didn't let go until she'd put the pot in the sink. She scraped the potatoes out, putting them into a bowl, poured salt and butter over them, and mashed them by the light of the refrigerator. She closed the fridge and walked to the *lubaio*, and leaning against it she slowly ate the potatoes. Then she turned the lights on and went to the darkroom.

Tuyen slid the negative into the enlarger, suddenly in a hurry to see what she had captured with her camera—what secret of her brother's. Perhaps she was too suspicious; perhaps she had simply seen her brother in his life, and this was the texture of a moment that she had apprehended and shot. She worked quickly, eyeballing the paper, figuring out the range of light, then deftly, one after the other, she printed the photographs in sixteen-by-twenty. When she was done, it was way past three in the morning. She wished she had had that smoke from Oku and Carla. They were across the hall, playing music. She could hear them giggling now and then. She hoped Oku wasn't trying to move in on Carla, given that his hopes for Jackie were fading. A momentary panic struck her, then her vanity kicked in. No—Oku did not stand a chance, she thought. He could not begin to unravel those microwaves of kinetic energy that were Carla's.

She strung a line across from the *lubaio* to the window and pinned the pictures to it. It had been dawning on her ever since she had taken the first shot, the one with Binh's face and the stranger's back, and now it was apparent.

"Shit, shit," she heard herself say, looking at the pictures in sequence. The figure raising its hand, then turning, something like anger on Binh's face, then a smile. She was convinced she saw a rough wiriness there in the body. Then the face, innocent, as a ghost's. But unmistakably the face of an intelligent-looking boy. The face her mother, Cam, had coveted and sent all over Southeast Asia and Europe. Quy. Why did that face resemble this one? And why did Binh and the man appear to be in a quarrel? She felt disoriented, drawn to the babyness of the face against the body springy as violence. All the structures and translations of her childhood swept her, all the uncomfortable moments of explaining her parents to the world; all the insomnia endured, the regret her parents had translated into efficiency, all dwelled in the face of the man so much like the boy. Quy.

EIGHTEEN

"LOOK, ORNETTE PLAYS all this dissonance, right, and he plays it so long you're out of breath and you think that you can't stand it any longer and then . . . listen now, listen now, right . . ."

Ornette Coleman was playing "The Jungle Is a Skyscraper" on the CD player. Oku's face was glowing. "Then when you can't take it any more, right, when you have had so much confusion, but it's not confusion at all, you see . . . but anyway, then he gives you the melody, see, and guess what, guess what? Then in the middle of the melody, which you wanted, right, you find yourself longing for the dissonance."

"Yeah." Tuyen was in the hallway looking in. Carla was looking out the window. Oku was always talking. That's why Tuyen liked him. He could fill any space with talk. Sometimes she barely listened to the details. She loved his voice and his continuous enthusiasm. Even now he was dancing about the room, talking wildly about Ornette Coleman.

"Check it out!"—as Coleman's horn chattered desperately—"Hear that thick mass of horns? They do this harmolodic modulation, different instruments playing in different keys but in another communion, right, and all that rushing energy, dozens of themes just rushing together. See, everything makes sense when you listen to this, right?"

"Yeah, that's cool. Every horn is alone, but they're

together, crashing," Tuyen said moving into the room. She and Oku were both on the same thought.

Carla hadn't turned from the window. Down on the sidewalk the man who sold lottery tickets was passing by. Oku turned up the music; it seemed to move the glass window pane in front of Carla. He grabbed Carla and began dancing her around the room against her will. Finally she started to laugh and dance around the room with him.

Oku had slept over. Where? Tuyen wondered, her misgivings surfacing again about Oku and Carla. "You two must be still high from last night." She thought of running to her place across the hall to get her camera but didn't.

Oku scatted along with the music. They danced and danced, then they whirled around Tuyen, swinging her back and forth, whirling her around the small room. Ornette Coleman punched notes from his horn like a fighter, jabbing and uppercutting; Charlie Hayden thrummed and pulled on the base; the drummer went mad; and it was as if the musicians were there in the room with them. From across the alley, Kumaran put his head out his window and shouted, "Hey, what's that?" "Ornette Coleman!" Oku shouted back. Even when the music went into its short melody, their bodies stayed in confusion, waiting for Ornette to take them back. Carla lost herself in the dance, she wanted to be lost, her scythe-like body leaned on Oku's, it hung on Tuyen's like a leaf on a stem. Tuyen's misgivings vanished again. No way they had slept together. She began laughing hysterically. It was a hysteria that was infectious. They fell on the floor when the music stopped.

"See what I'm saying?" Oku laughed.

Tuyen wanted the music to last longer. She tried to untangle herself from the two to go play it again, but she felt comfortable with Carla lying on her shoulder. She didn't want to move.

"My father would never understand that," Tuyen said. "Order and practicality is all he sees. It's like anything that's complicated they see as waste."

"Not mine. Mine would see it, right, but he'd ignore it. He'd say, 'Boy, that can't feed you.' And he's the one who turned me on to Ornette Coleman."

They waited for Carla to say something. She sensed their waiting. This time she would say something, but she stayed quiet until it seemed that they had accepted, acknowledged, her accustomed silence. She was fighting herself, fighting her whisper. "There was never any sound in my house. There was never any music after my mother." She'd heard, of course, the coarse songs of terror each time she remembered the day her mother died.

Oku felt like telling her about hymns, how wonderful they could be, but she had offered a lot again in that whispery speech and he didn't want to spoil it.

"Let's eat," he said. "I feel like I haven't eaten in a month."

"Well, don't look at me, bro. There isn't a thing at my place. I almost burnt the last of my potatoes last night." Tuyen rolled over.

"We could smell it. How could you burn potatoes? That's like burning water. Who would think you grew up in a restaurant?"

"Anyways . . ."

"You know what? I gotta go see my father." They fell silent. "The thing is," Carla picked up, "while I'm listening to the music, I can hear it. It's like a puzzle. It makes us seem understandable. Like why Jamal is in jail and everything."

"Whaddya mean?"

"I mean, why he would be in jail, you know, like why not? What made me think that he wouldn't be . . . that he could be free or something . . . but what makes him not scared of that?"

"Babylon, star. You can't let them frighten you." Oku was scared of jail himself, of course. All the time. For no immediate reason. He felt the hair at the back of his neck rising at the mention of the word.

"I wonder if he'll let me do a body cast of him when he comes out? For my installation? I think the body must record something. An imprint . . ."

"You're a freak, Tuyen. Shit, you're a freak."

"Carla doesn't like my installations. She feels her way up the stairs with her eyes closed."

Carla didn't think that Tuyen had seen her, closing her eyes on her way up the stairs. But it would be like Tuyen to be watching. She kept still. The truth was that Tuyen's photographs stirred some response in her that she wasn't quite sure of. Just disturbing, that's all. And how Tuyen could keep taking pictures that time while Oku was being roughed up or some horrible thing happened, she couldn't understand. But Oku didn't seem to mind. He'd never said anything about it. He acted as if he was a movie star, acting a part for Tuyen's pictures.

"Gotta go." Carla jumping up from the floor.

"Whoa, listen, can I stay here for a few days?" Oku asked.

"Are you hiding out from somebody?" Tuyen probed.

"Hey, lend me some money, Carla, and how about it, a few days?" He didn't answer directly.

"I notice you're not asking me."

"Tuyen, where can anybody stay in your place?"

Oku was really hiding out from Kwesi. He was used to hiding out at Carla's when his father was on the warpath.

He would spend days there, then finally go home because his mother wanted him to come home to help shoulder his father's boorishness. This time it was Kwesi he was avoiding. He knew that Kwesi would be looking to tell him that he had punked out. Fine, he would cope with that later. God, he thought to himself, he was tired of people wanting things from him. He was tired of hiding out against it all.

"Cool, cool," Carla said, throwing him twenty dollars, "but don't make a mess, eh, please, please." She and Tuyen had to take their chances when he got too creative.

"I know you people don't eat unless I'm here, you know! You two are just lazy, man. Look at this," he said, holding up a loaf of stale bread from Carla's kitchen. "How old is that?"

"Tuyen will help." Carla laughed.

"Hell, no, I won't. I have work to do."

Carla took the wheels of her bicycle down from the wall. "Figure it out." She hooked them onto the frame in the hallway, gathered her knapsack, and clanked down the stairs. "Later, people."

Upstairs Oku looked out the window to watch her go before asking Tuyen.

"Why you figure she doesn't like your pictures?"

"Issues, man, issues. I don't think it's personal. I don't take it personal or anything."

"Yeah, but why do you think?"

"I don't know." Tuyen didn't want to venture. She didn't talk about her own things, and she didn't want this intimacy with Oku.

"Secret, eh?" He wanted to know what Tuyen knew, but he didn't want to appear overly curious. He looked at her over his slightly raised arm, but she was noncommittal.

"Come go to Kensington with me then." When she hesitated, not wanting to keep on with the same conversation, he gave her a look of truce and became his joking self again. "Hey, you wanna eat? I can't carry all the bags, can I?"

"Not to mention you don't want to meet Jackie and Reiner."

It almost slipped out of him, but he kept his silence. He didn't want to tell Tuyen about making love to Jackie. He wanted to hold all they'd done in the time it happened. The minute he said anything about it, he knew it would disappear. So he allowed himself a joking boast.

"Girl, I've got that under control. I'm scoping it out. Don't you worry. When I come on that it will be like a motherfucker." Even this felt ugly to him, like an intrusion or a betrayal, so he said no more.

"All right, big Daddy Mac. Hang on a sec, wait here, I'll get my stuff."

"Sure, sure, I'm right behind you."

"No, no, wait, I'll . . ."

"Whoa! What the fuck is that?"

Tuyen's door had been closed, and as she opened it, Oku had a glimpse of a line of photographs of the same face strung across the room.

"Don't look! It's not ready yet." Tuyen's voice was slightly panicked. "Hang on, I'll get my bag, okay?" She closed the door behind her. After a few moments of rummaging around inside, she came out again.

"Hey, no sweat," Oku said. "I know the creative thing, you know."

"Yeah," Tuyen offered, and nothing else.

As they opened the door to the alley, they saw Kumaran waiting for them.

"Hey, man, lend me that music you were playing. What was it again?"

"Ornette Coleman, 'The Jungle Is a Skyscraper,' man."

"Fantastic. Sweet."

"Give it to you when I get back. I want it back though, okay?"

"No doubt, man, but come on, man, just get it for me, huh?"

"Okay. All right." Oku ran up the stairs and was back in the alley in a minute.

"Don't forget, man, I need it back, like today."

"Yeah, thanks." Kumaran's happiness followed them down the alley.

The streetcar was squealing by. The profiles of its passengers struck Tuyen as another idea for her installation. Then she remembered the face in her studio and quickly shoved those thoughts aside.

NINETEEN

JAMAL WAS ON THE PHONE. He'd been languishing now for two months at Mimico. There were cracks in his voice where his bravado was leaking out. Carla had gone to his hearing in the courthouse on Jarvis Street. He sat with an uninterested slouch in the Plexiglas prisoner's box. The hearing was routine—a postponement until his lawyer could appear, then another postponement until the police discovery. The Crown imposed bail conditions Carla couldn't possibly meet on her own.

"When you coming to see me?" he said over the phone.

"I can come on Saturday. I got to pull some long shifts."

"Oh . . ."

"What's up, Jamal? You okay?"

"Nothin.' Nothin,' same old, same old." He giggled a bit.

"Did Nadine come to see you yet?" She had expected Nadine to pick up a bit of the slack.

"Yeah, she came, but she didn't have no ID so they didn't let her in."

"Oh, shame."

"It's nothing. She left me some money. Didn't want to see her anyway."

"Oh, don't say that . . ." Carla stopped herself. She was not going to fall into that trap with Jamal any more. "You holding it together, right?"

"Yeah, yeah. Look, Carla, ah, anyway, you know, you could get me out?"

"Jamal, I don't have the money, you know that, right?"

"Yeah, yeah . . ."

"This time it's big. They want big money and . . ."

"Okay, okay, no biggy, eh? Just come and see me, okay?" He sounded plaintive. Carla felt an opening in her chest.

"You know I will. You know I will. No doubt. Right?"

"Okay. See ya." He hung up, trying to sound light.

Carla had been trying to come up with the stomach to go talk to her father. Nadine had been unable to get him to bail Jamal out of Mimico—there was clearly no respect left there, no leverage. Apart from that, the month had passed with a kind of calm. Ironically, she didn't have to worry about Jamal. When he was out on the street, she lived with constant anxiety about the next phone call, the next trouble. Now she at least knew where he was.

But on the phone he had sounded jittery and lonely. He had taken himself so far away from her, she could not even be sure of her readings of him. Was it nostalgia on her part to read his call as loneliness? Was it rather she who was lonely? Her affection for him had never kept him safe or close. She knew that she loved him with a possessive passion, but she had never felt that love returned. He had always felt himself disconnected. She sensed this. As a child he seldom listened to what he was told. He barrelled ahead despite warnings, through the living room, breaking Nadine's miniatures; down tobogganing hills, breaking his leg; against traffic, causing horns to honk. He never took advice, he never ever seemed to be in the same conversations as you. His eyes always flitted to something ahead and beyond you. His body had a wiry alertness, his face a vulnerable tenderness that could be seen now only sometimes below the blank pose he had gradually assumed over the years. Carla imagined this face now, the tender one, leaning into the public phone at the jail, hiding itself from the other inmates and guards.

She had resolved to go see her father and tell him to bail Jamal out. Make him bail out Jamal. Now that resolve was strengthened by what she sensed in Jamal. And in herself. Perhaps he was in danger. More danger anyway, a different kind of danger, because danger was what Jamal was in at birth and what he had always gravitated toward. But she felt a different danger in his life now, the danger of his losing, yes, her.

Carla felt weaker than she'd ever felt. As if she could not hold him up any longer. Whatever Jamal thought, however he located her exhortations to get it together, however he dismissed these and went his perilous way, he depended on her to be there. And Carla was losing faith in her ability to support him. She'd helped him find a room, staked him for two months' rent. He'd been thrown out, of course. The nice Portuguese family, as Carla called them, did not abide the ganja smoking and the friends and the music in their rooming house. She thought afterward that she must have been crazy to imagine that Jamal would be cool and get along in that house. But they had seemed nice people who would look out for him. She was, she understood deep down, under the ridiculous fantasy that Jamal wasn't too far gone yet, too savvy. Or that all he wanted was independence, as she did, and he would take hold of his opportunities, becoming the reliable, loving brother she needed. But that, she knew, was fantasy, though she tried often enough to impose it. Truthfully, he had only been for a short time the cuddly baby brother. At any rate it was a fiasco, and she had to forfeit the two hundred and fifty dollars surety she had left with the Medeiroses before the damage Jamal and his friends left in the room. She'd even gotten him a job with Binh, but that too had been brief when he showed up late every single day and finally not at all.

It wasn't merely these kinds of things that she could no longer support him with, it was the faith that he needed from her that was waning. Between holding him up and mining the short memory of her mother she was exhausted—so exhausted she didn't feel exhaustion, just an empty dryness. A distraction that made her leave packages undelivered till the next day. It made her want to wake up each morning and simply wander about; it made her want to sit at the window all day watching the street below or watching the changing light of the spring unravelling. The only one she could think of handing Jamal over to was her father. Not because he had any interest but because she could think of no one else. No one else was implicated except herself, and her dead mother, who had handed Jamal to her because her father wasn't there. Okay, she decided, time for the bastard to take over. The venom of that last thought was half-hearted. She didn't even have that left, though no doubt when she came face to face with her father, it was certain to renew itself.

She used to be curious about her father's vanity. Vanity was all it could be called. How could he have survived her mother's death and a life after of denial if not for some deep, thick artery of vanity in him. A vanity that he could not suppress even for the well-being of a baby. He had acted as if Jamal were his rival and not his child. His rival for Angie and then for Nadine and then for life. As if Jamal had replaced him. At first she had loved her father as her mother had, as a child would, in the exhilarating domestic space of her mother's apartment—their home—where he would visit with gifts, but where she would be banished to the living room while he made love to her mother. When her mother died, her feelings turned to ambivalence. She felt the same excited joy to be in his presence, but something momentous had disrupted the bonds between them, and so she shrank from him out of uncertainty and then out of loyalty to her mother. At twenty-three, there was no longer any doubt or ambivalence in her about him. There was downright hatred. She detested him.

Going to the blue house all those years ago with Angie was a vivid memory. Even after Carla herself had come to live in the house, the memory of it, in the way she had experienced it with Angie, remained. As if it was a different place altogether. Carla's hand was sweaty in Angie's palm. They were walking toward the house. They stood across from the house. A blue house with rose bushes in front. It was across the bridge, toward the east of the city. They would leave their apartment on a Saturday afternoon, take the subway to Chester station, and walking through the Greek section of town, turn down a small street off the Danforth and another twisting street and then another and come to the house. A family lived there. A man, a woman, a teenager as tall as her father. Angie came here to watch them. They were not anyone Carla knew. Except the man, her father. She saw him kiss the woman once on leaving the house; they said goodbye to each other and waved. He got into his car and drove off. The woman stood at the screen door until he drove off. Carla and her mother simply watched. Angie tried to remain invisible at first, but sometimes she didn't care and stood on the opposite sidewalk, watching. Sometimes she muttered to herself. Sometimes the man looked across the street to where they were. He seemed not to see them. Carla thought he would come over, but he didn't; he went to his car and started the engine.

In the summer or in the winter, whatever season, her palms sweated in Angie's. She didn't mind going in the summer, but she did not like the winter, standing there, watching with Angie. Standing in the falling snow, arrested like trees unable to move, they neither of them brushed the snow away. Her balaclava damp and warm, her breathing visible, she waited for Angie to turn and leave as usual. They must have seemed like statues humped against the weather. There was some timing to it. They would be there for what seemed like hours or what seemed like minutes depending on the season. Then Angie would squeeze her hand slightly, not a squeeze but a pressure, and they would turn and leave.

Some days the blue house across the street seemed empty. No one came out or went in. Those days Angie was restless, unhappy. Carla could sense the fine difference in Angie's unhappiness, the fluctuations in intensity, that the dead look of the house produced. This she was learning even before her mother's death. The calibration of happiness and unhappiness. Somehow she understood as one understands air the changes in the people she lived with, her mother, her sometimes father.

They were already a family of quietness. She was a watchful child, not a child of too much exuberance. She would come into a room and know to be quiet just by the look from her mother or her sometimes father, just by the location of their bodies around the room. Even when they were in pleasant conversation, the tenor of a word or a pause would alert her as to someone about to misunderstand someone else. For that reason she was a slender child, a child who made room with her own body so that she would not occupy so much space that she would be unduly noticed. Or call too much attention to herself. She cultivated a reediness to intercept their tones, their changes in chord. The efforts to hone this faculty became physical in her. There appeared no room for her despite the fact they all seemed sometimes to be fighting over her.

When Jamal was born, she felt a small relief in his wailing cries, his sudden tantrums that would throw the apartment into a panic. That is when she had fallen in love with him. He screamed and kicked and would not be shushed. He woke up at odd hours and woke everyone else up. He misbehaved, if a baby could misbehave.

The man crossed the road once, walking slowly toward them. Carla could not make out the emotion of the man's body, if it was threatening or not. He seemed to be looking at them. Her hand slipped in Angie's. Angie held it tighter. Her sometimes father came, stood inches from them. No one said anything. She felt rather than saw Angie's body grow erect. Carla's own head seemed to receive a blow, though she had not been hit; she felt weighted down. Her slippery hand was held in a stronger and stronger vice. Then her sometimes father turned and crossed the street again toward his car. She heard Angie gather phlegm from her throat, she heard it land softly in the snow.

From then on when they came, the man ignored them, and Carla thought she had probably made up the confrontation because life went on, sometimes there was even a festive feeling about their journey. Angie would pack a ham sandwich for Carla, she would stop on the Danforth and buy her an orange pop. Only the woman at the screen door seemed irritated. Though she never approached Carla and Angie, she stood at the door for a moment longer after the man's car took off.

Carla heard the wheezing and gargle in Angie's throat when the man appeared. The sounds boiled and gathered but then subsided when the car left. At times she suspected some strength in her mother, some purpose that if unleashed would devastate the man. Carla always anticipated Angie, suddenly agile, leaping at the man who was both not her father and her father. And then at other times there was a weakness: just after he left, for a moment Angie seemed on the verge of tears or falling.

Even when the house seemed empty, Angie still went. Carla felt an anxiety in her. In fact, Angie went more frequently then. More than once a week. She seemed agitated, hurrying, not stopping to buy Carla an orange pop or an apple, muttering to herself about hiding. He had ruined her, she said, lied to her, hurt her. When the family stayed away from the house, Angie seemed to burn. She became more and more voluble. She hurled sentences at the house. He took her for a fool, he was a liar, he promised her; her mouth thin, exhausting on her words until her lips were ash white. Then Carla felt a sweat around her neck and covered her eyes so that people passing would not see her.

When they returned on their next visit, Angie rushed toward him with all her intention, leaving Carla on the other side of the street. The sometimes father turned from locking his car door; he seemed not the man Angie needed to berate. He was sighing, taking a deep breath as people do arriving home, happy to have left work. His face was relaxing, his hand was reaching for his pocket to find a cigarette. Angie was disarmed for a fleeting second by his casualness. She was expecting something to be burning in him too. She was expecting a face creased in worry or sin. Surely deeds leave a mark, she thought, but no, his face was settling into placidity, into coming home like any ordinary person. She would have to figure this one out, but she rekindled what was left of herself and flew at him, saying, "How could you? You promised, you promised."

The man raised his arms as if to ward off a blow. He felt numb from another day wondering what the hell he had got himself mixed up in. She was crazy. Angie surprised him and frightened him. His instinct was to run or fall to the ground. He did both, running toward his door, fumbling his key in the lock, putting the screen door between them, and falling into his hallway. Why he hadn't hit her he could not make out. His instinct should have made him do so. But he had felt flushed and heartsick for a moment, a sudden dejection had washed over him. Behind the door he felt ashamed for running and thought of going back outside to assert himself, but he simply locked the door when he heard the balmy sounds of his home and family, the smells that filled the house—the roast and fried potatoes from the kitchen. Finally, he opened the door, but Angie and the child were gone. He came out farther, looking down and up the street. There was no one there, the street was as usual: his street, his car sitting outside, the darkness of early evening had greyed everything. Perhaps it hadn't happened.

The street was quiet, a neighbour putting out garbage. He had to do something about her soon. She couldn't come to his house like that with the child. It had been a mistake on his part. She was such a small woman, he hadn't thought she would run him down like this. He'd promised her, no doubt, and at the time he had intended to fulfil that promise. Such a pretty woman, and she had seemed to need him and she had made him feel powerful and important. He had not looked at her clearly beyond those things and beyond the fact that a little something on the side was not unheard of with him.

When Angie first became pregnant, he did not discourage it entirely, but he told her that she would be on her own; he would support the baby, but he couldn't be there the whole time. When she had Carla, he had second thoughts. Perhaps this was the family he was supposed to be with, perhaps he had made a mistake initially with Nadine. He moved in with Angie for six months, but then something pulled him home again. Indecision plagued him, even as facts multiplied. The fact of Nadine, the fact of Angie and the baby, the fact of a family he had already, the fact of a second family, the fact, the fact . . . He felt fear and self-scorn and rage and self-doubt. But he also felt excitement, passion. Another kind of rage. He was in the middle of a crisis. He was in the middle of love. Ownership. A contest for himself. It seemed as if he was always awake, always startled. He noticed everything with a brightness. There was the other side of that too. If there was a smudge on his black shoes, it made him panic, any dust and disarray annoyed and frightened him, the faint mould on the bathroom walls disturbed him.

When he saw her a week later, after he had run away from her, it settled him. He went to the apartment. He fucked her hard. He told her not to come back to his house. He told her he was going to leave Nadine. He needed time. If she didn't leave him alone, he was going to leave and never come back, never fuck her again. He told her everything, many things, all contradictory and all true. He said he loved her; he said he couldn't live without her, Angie; he said he couldn't leave Nadine at this moment. He said he was staying for his boy. He said never, never come to his house. She was standing across the street the next day. It should have disturbed him, but he was relieved. He didn't want the feeling of crisis to end.

She held the threat over him that at any moment she would kill him, betray him—she had already done that by coming to his house. They both understood. They were beyond betrayal. Otherwise he would have done something. He could easily have charged her with stalking him, with threatening him. She had established with him that he would never rest, and she thought he had accepted it. What else was this choreography between them? What else was it but his acceptance of a thing he owed.

Early one morning when Carla was still a child and Jamal was just a baby, Angie had taken them with her to the bank. On the way Angie played a game. A game where the rules shifted at every turn. After all, it was her game and a game she was making up as she went along. A superstitious game. Here's how it would go, she told herself, if someone said hello to her on the way, she wouldn't do it. No one said hello. If the bus came before she arrived at the corner of Church and Wellesley. The bus was already gone. If she saw a man in a yellow shirt, she wouldn't do it. She saw no man in a yellow shirt. If, at the bank, someone seeing her with children made her go ahead. At the bank no one gave her leeway. Angie was waiting for a look that said that she existed, that her life was understandable. That was what the game meant. She tried to suggest it with her own eyes, to say, Hey, how's it going today? I'm tired, what about you? But cold stares came back at her. Or what she thought was coldness.

She turned and walked out of the bank after taking out twenty of the fifty dollars in her account. But Angie knew that she had come for more. She had come to feel as if she were here and alive. Well, no reason to think that the teller in her own life, with a boss over her and her hopes in lottery tickets, could possibly know that she needed this, no reason at all. But she was depending on the teller anyway—as a compass. She hoped. But didn't see the woman who sold her tomatoes and flowers at the corner store, from whom sometimes she could see a glimmer of familiarity. With what? With life, with the fact that Derek was off, perhaps, with a woman; this wasn't the real thing, but it had caused her to look at the real thing, which was that she was of no interest to anyone. Except the children, and that was instinctive, just as Derek's need for her was instinctive. Or perhaps his was vanity. Someone to bed, to feed him, and someone to mistreat, which she gathered was instinctive too. But all this hadn't to do with Derek. She realized that if she was to do it, she had to be clear, and this game was cheating because she had already decided. Except today she needed a sign. A simple sign would have done it. Maybe going to the bank was the mistake. Who could expect a sign from that? But perhaps she was going at cross purposes all the time, knowing that nothing could deter her from the decision she had made. On her way back to the apartment, she still played the game. If the baby didn't cry, she wouldn't, if the next person she saw carried a green bag, if, if, if . . . When she arrived at the apartment building, all of her ifs had run out.

Angie remembered a headline in the *Globe and Mail* newspaper box on the corner of Parliament and Wellesley, "Breastfeeding prevents cancer in women." She burst into a laugh. Well, fine, let the whole city get on her tits then. She had ended up being the same milk cow as her mother and sister-in-law. Soon she'd be wearing black too, in living mourning of the sin of being a woman. What, after all, had she wanted? Passion. Not secret passion but public passion. Public red-glowing passion. And that had led her here anyway. Well, she sure wouldn't die of cancer. The thought put her in a silly mood.

She got to the twenty-first-floor apartment, took the children's light coats off, straightened the living room, put the baby down, gave Carla a pencil to draw with, hauled a chair to the balcony, picked the baby up again, chuckling to herself over the headline. She smoothed the baby's cheeks, and he chuckled too. Then Angie went back onto the balcony and stood on the chair, and as if suddenly remembering herself, the baby in her hand, she called to Carla, who was singing that song she'd taught her and which Carla had sung all the way back from the bank. "Carla, stop that noise now. Come here, luvvy, and take the baby." Carla came and held Jamal. "Put the pencil down now. Hold tight, dear, and go inside and put him down on the sofa. Stay there till Mummy comes, Mummy has to do something. There's Mummy's girl. There's my baby." Angie waited until Carla had gone into the apartment, then she stepped off the balcony.

Carla stayed singing to the baby until she was tired. The baby was screaming. She left him on the sofa and went back to the balcony to tell her mother, but Angie had disappeared. Perhaps she was in the bedroom, Carla thought. Then she noticed the chair was tipped over. She forgot about the baby. She'd always wanted to see over the balcony, but Angie wouldn't let her. She straightened the chair, climbed up, knelt on the seat, and peered over the balcony.

A woman was lying on the knob of grass at the front of the building way down below. She would tell Angie. No, she wouldn't tell Angie because then Angie would know that she had climbed on the chair. A skinny brown-haired girl and a man naked to the waist on a balcony below looked up at her, screaming, "Get down from there." Carla jumped off the chair and ran to the sofa to hush Jamal. Angie didn't come back. She heard sirens and more yelling, but she was afraid to go to the balcony again. Angie was a long time. The baby blubbered and sniffed himself to sleep. She remembered to put his comforter in his mouth. His eyes were wet, his mouth turned down in a sob. Carla sat on the sofa with him in case he woke up. Angie was taking so long. She got her pencil and sat writing squiggles to herself. A big *A* meant *Angie*, a wormy line meant *said*, a dash meant *to*, another wormy line, this time to the length of the page, meant *hold the baby*.

Carla approached the blue house now with some apprehension. This is how Angie must have approached the house. With a desire that was primal yet a certainty about how dangerous it was and how improbable. The house was not actually blue any more. Hard winters and neglect had scraped the blue paint off the front porch and the window flashing. The porch sagged forward into the patch of forsythia in the yard. Lavender sprang in the rest of the yard, and rose bushes that Nadine had nurtured for years were still stunted against a small trellis near the roadside where Nadine had tried to make them into a front hedge but the snow salt had defeated her efforts. Carla remembered Nadine year after year optimistically pouring dirt and manure around the bushes, clipping and watering, encouraging reluctant branches to grow.

A surge of memory about her days in this house came over her. In her last years here Carla had hung about like a question mark. Her father told her that she had grown tall and angular, though none of his people were tall, none of Angie's, either, that he knew of, so why was she so tall, so bony? He also noticed a hitherto allusive danger in her. Just like her mother. Carla was then eighteen, and Nadine no longer asked her to go to the market or to clean up. She did not want to be met with a recumbent defiance. To be truthful, Carla no longer needed to be asked to clean up. She did it swiftly, unasked. She did it, it seemed, as a way of avoiding trouble, avoiding contact. She took care of herself, always had, perhaps to the point of asceticism. She cleared away domestic chores with a briskness. But she took no pleasure in them as she had surely been taught.

Nadine had shown her how to cook lovingly, how to polish tables and floors as if the people you were doing it for, your family, would enjoy it and therefore that would be your joy too. She had shown her how to shop for the best fruit, the best food. Her stepmother had smoothed her soft hands over a seam, showing her how her appearance must be lovingly put together. Carla had taken all this and turned it into competence. She glided through these lessons like an impatient note taker. She completed what they both asked of her not like a daughter but like a clerk, marking off their needs, completing their emotional desires like an office manager.

All her efficiency was to make the time she had with them shorter and shorter; to reduce conversations to a minimum, to limit anything they might want from her. The only time they got an emotion out of her was when she would jump to Jamal's defence. Though on that score she was mostly watchful, a kind of seething watchfulness that even Derek was slightly afraid of. Otherwise she had sculpted her face to passivity; cheerfulness or anger were imperceptible. She had thought that was what was needed in this house. She had learned not to call attention to herself. Outside or inside. She had stopped bringing any worry home to them. This house was full of enough hurt. Nothing could compare with what was already there. So any small trouble she took care of herself by giving it to the linden trees and the maple trees and the forsythia bushes on her way home. Lingering in the playground and park, she would stand under the bare limbs, watching the snow skiff against the bark, and recite her fear. Anyone walking by would see a girl thin and sickled against a maple, resounding its stillness and winter quiescence. From the brittle forsythia she would break off sticks to beat the pavement or run along fences, scolding like a teacher whoever had bothered her that day. By the time she arrived home her face was placid and even.

She could not bear being in the same room with her father. She noticed this strangely one day when she had turned fifteen. She walked into the living room at four-thirty and rain was falling. It was not a rainstorm, just a steady rain. The couch was wet, and the chair was wet, and rain dripped with a tinny sound into the light fixture. The ceiling was that dreary watery grey that the sky gets. Through the window she could see that it was still the sunny crisp autumn day she had left outside. But in the room rain was falling. Her father was making a list of some kind, his lips moving as if counting, his head bent over the table, and his face drenched. His shirt stuck to his skin. There were puddles of water around his feet and the chair he sat in. Water dripping from his arms. Her father looked up from his pen like a struggling swimmer and stared at her as if to say, What is it you want now? then bent his head again to the table. Carla backed out of the rain-drenched room. Water seeped to her feet at the doorway. From this moment she started calling her father Derek. He did not stop her.

After that each room in the house felt foreign, if it had ever felt like a home. She touched the furniture, looking for raindrop stains or softening of the wood. She examined the corners, looking for dampness. Though the room seemed dry when she was there alone, she couldn't help feeling a strangeness, a peculiar chill or breeze on her skin. Carla began walking in socks on the dank floors.

She saw that her father was home—his latest car was parked in his usual spot. She knew it was his car because of its shine and because of where it was parked. The house had no garage in the back, so he commandeered a precise spot in front of the house. Derek changed cars every four years. He knew nothing about cars, but he knew about fashion. He spent hours cleaning and buffing his car on the weekends. The car sitting outside the house today was a black Audi. He had a black car, sometimes green, but mostly black. Selling that could bail Jamal out of jail. Carla tried to suppress a surge of anger. It wouldn't do to begin this way. Her father was vain; she had resolved to appeal to his vanity first. Anger was a last resort, and it would probably be useless anyway. And she wanted him to do more than simply bail Jamal out. She wanted him to be present. Take over the responsibility for Jamal. She didn't know how she was going to put it. Derek would surely say he had been a father to Jamal; he would say he had rescued the boy enough. Enough for him meant only what didn't put him out, she knew.

Carla waited in the living room. Nadine had let her in and gone upstairs to get Derek. He came into the room, an expectant look on his face. Nadine hovered behind him, then decided to go to the kitchen.

"I'll get you both some lunch. Then we'll have a nice visit." She trailed off to the kitchen.

Derek walked over to Carla and hugged her. As usual, she was sticklike in his arms.

"How you doing, eh, how you doing?" He had clearly decided to meet her with bravado. "You don't call me, you don't come around. Don't you wonder what's become of your father?" He let her go, sensing her reserve. "Well, sit down, sit down, and tell me what you're doing."

Which world exactly was he living in? she wondered. She sat quickly in the single chair in case he wanted to steer her to the couch with him. The living room had been done up in a springy pattern. There was an odd gayness to it. Derek dropped into the couch, reaching in his pocket for cigarettes. Nadine returned with a tray, a beer for Derek and a glass of juice for Carla. Carla watched as she served Derek. She was happy that Carla had come, she chatted in a manic tone.

"Oh, Carla, it's so good to see you. We don't see any of you children any more. Your big brother is still in Montreal. Doesn't look as if he's coming back to Toronto. He's got a great job there."

Carla bristled at the "big brother" reference. She hardly knew Anton. He had left home when Carla and Jamal arrived. There'd been a row with his father and he'd taken off. He was nineteen at the time. She only remembered scornfulness from him on his rare visits. And rudeness to Nadine about how she could stand taking care of that white bitch's children. Nadine would say something about innocence and tell him to keep his voice down.

Nadine gave her the glass of orange juice, her hand trembling. "Carla, darling, it's so good to see you. Anyway, let me stop, stop fussing. I'll get us something to eat. You used to like my chicken. I have some ready to go."

"No, Nadine, don't bother."

"*Bother!* No bother. No bother at all. I don't get to do this often."

She faded into the hallway. Carla took a sip of her drink. It was tepid.

"So tell me how things are with you," Derek said, dragging on his cigarette. "I know that boy Jamal is in jail again. Nadine said she went to see him."

"That's what I came to talk to you about."

"Carla, I've done my best for that boy. I have sacrificed— I can't have him jeopardizing my home."

The glass flew out of Carla's hand uncontrollably, it hit the wall on the left side of her father's head. He was stunned, dropping his lit cigarette to the couch and ducking.

"You've done your best!" She was enraged; she felt as if she had completely lost control of her body. Or rather, she thought later, gained control of her body. "*Sacrificed!* Sacrificed what? You vain, awful, disgusting man! You sacrificed my mother!" Carla was screaming, words tumbling out of her mouth. The same words she had told herself to hold back on. Nadine flew into the room.

"Now, Carla, Carla, Derek, Derek, what's the matter in here?"

Carla was standing at her end of the room, ready, it seemed, to advance on Derek. Derek crouched, momentarily touching his face and searching for the lit cigarette in the folds of the couch. A piece of the glass had made a small cut on his cheek, another piece had landed in his collar. He gingerly removed it, at the same time trying to get to his feet. Nadine stood between them.

"You never did nothing for Jamal. You just thought that he—me and him—messed up your fucking life. What did you do, huh? What? You're such a fucking asshole. Let me get out of here."

She had to get past Nadine and Derek to leave the room;

they both stood transfixed. "*Move!*" she screamed. She saw in her father a mix of terror and aggression. He couldn't decide which one to act on, and she realized that she'd always found him weak at the core, there was always a cowardice there, a shrinking, under expensive shoes, expensive cars, his face shaved so precisely around his moustache and his smell of rich colognes. Today she'd noticed a small protruding gut and an old conceit that in his younger face must have seemed like daring but now was a calcified lechery. "*Move!*" she screamed again.

"Please, Carla, wait a minute." Nadine reached out to her pleadingly. "Just a minute, we're a family. We can't be like that."

This had always been Nadine's foolish, thankless, and unrewarding project. She alone had had the right to say no, and yet she had taken it on. Carla felt a small pity for her. What torture it must have been to spend all those years raising another woman's children and understanding her husband's deep betrayal.

"Look, Nadine, it's not you, okay? I just can't breathe the same fucking air as Derek." Derek—she called him by his first name as if he were a sibling.

"So why'd you come here, then?" Derek found his voice.

"Because I was hoping I was wrong about you. I was hoping that you were human, you fucking jerk."

"Don't talk to me like that. I'm your father."

"What the fuck does that mean, Derek? What the fuck does that mean? It means nothing to me, it means nothing to my brother, and it meant nothing to my mother. You made her walk off the edge of a building, it so didn't mean anything."

"She was a crazy—"

"No, Derek!" Nadine was appalled.

"Say it, say it, 'bitch,' right?"

Carla flew at him, slapping his face and kicking him. He fell over onto the couch again, his raised arms warding off her blows. He'd completely lost the composure he'd tried to affect. He'd known all along that beneath Carla's calm lay a rage, rage that she could not express as a child but that would break out somehow. He was not a man who was afraid of women. He handled them emotionally, and if not emotionally, physically, without compunction. But this was not a woman, it was his daughter, and her rage was so primal it seemed to drain his own pretensions at violence. He lay on the couch, letting her hit him; he tried to fight her off, but she seemed stronger. Then he heard himself say, "Sorry." It was the smallest sound, and he didn't mean it so much as it escaped him. Carla didn't seem to hear it. She just kept hitting him until Nadine, recovering, held her. She wrenched herself away from Nadine and without another word left the house, slamming the door.

Outside on the sidewalk she searched in her jeans for her keys. The shiny black Audi sat at the curb. Beginning at the closest tail light she scored the skin of the car all the way square to the far tail light. "Fucking prick!" she yelled at the house. An old neighbour out digging up his spring garden looked at her, surprised. He and her father used to come outside on Saturdays in the summer and polish their cars together. "What are you looking at, asshole?" she screamed at him. She unlocked her bike and rode down the street and across the Danforth. She felt exhilarated. She didn't feel worried or troubled, she felt refreshed. She had turned something on her father. What it was wasn't clear. The ride across the city would tell her. She sped along beside the traffic over the Bloor Viaduct.

TWENTY

THE RESEARCH HE'D BEEN DOING was walking through the park. If he got to know Alexandra Park, he figured he'd know something about Jackie. So he would take the walk through the park not to run into her by chance, well, not wholly, but to gain something of her that he might have, like everything else perhaps, taken for granted. The one time that Jackie had allowed them to come to her house was when they were all suspended from high school. He only remembered vaguely. Her mother teaching them to play euchre, a glass of Southern Comfort at hand and a cigarette to her lips. Jackie was uncomfortable, he remembered. She kept emptying her mother's ashtray and wiping the table. That was years ago, but now that he revisited the occasion in his mind, that is what he recalled. Jackie's discomfort. None of them had thought anything of the surroundings. They all lived in houses with their parents, but Jackie's parents' tiny apartment did not strike them at the time as so different. His walk now told him something else. His parents weren't rich or even well off by any means, but they obviously lived better than people in Vanauley Way. And this is where Jackie had always lived.

He knew, as a black man his age knows, that the park had a reputation. It was turf in the low-level war for such places waged by poor people. If there was history being made in the city, if history was the high-level war rich people waged for their own turf in the city—those wars about waterfront developments and opera houses and real-estate deals and privatization contracts—then the poor waged wars for control of their small alleyways and walkways, their streets and the trade in unofficial goods. Their currency was not stocks, wealth and influence peddling, but tough reputations and threats of physical damage; their gains weren't stock options and expensive homes but momentary physical control and perennially contested fearsomeness. This war was a more volatile war, perhaps. There was no cushion of security to land on if you lost a skirmish.

Come to think of it, now that he recalled, that experience hadn't brought them closer to Jackie, hadn't brought him, to be exact; she had become more aloof with him. Her mother had taken a liking to him and had said to him jokingly, "You sweet on my Jackie, eh, boy? You'd make a fine man, you will," and Jackie had frozen him out after that. Though he was so stupid, he thought now, that he'd kept asking Jackie how her mother was. He had liked her. There was a sweet drunken look in her eyes and a faded beauty to her face—something lurking that had come alive when she said, "You sweet on my Jackie, eh, boy?" A glint in her language, something smoky and seductive. Jackie had given her a hateful look and said, "Mom, puh-lease!" And the disdain gathered in that "puh-lease!" had fallen on him in some ways ever since.

Fair enough, he thought, nobody wanted to have the approval of their parents for their love life—after all, look what a mess they'd made of their own, for God's sake. His own parents' marriage went through seasons of emotional drought bordering on hatred, then periods of what only seemed to be nostalgia for their younger, more exciting selves. He certainly wouldn't take a drop of advice from them about love. And he would suspect anyone they thought would suit him as a lover. But that was then and this was now. Come to think of it, he had been faithful to that moment of Jackie's mother's seduction. She had added her own allure to what he felt for Jackie.

What he felt now was no teenaged crush but a big man's love and lust, a powerful pull that told him he would not enjoy his life fully if she were not close to him, if he could not talk to her, if he could not always be in the orbit of her face. So he had resolved that if he wanted her, he would have to know what she knew, walk where she had walked, and figure out the things that had given shape to her. Alexandra Park was one of those things.

He'd never met Jackie's father, but there was a tall man, just as tall as he, coming toward him who was unmistakably him. Oku felt nervous but realized that Jackie's father didn't know him, so he could easily pass him by. The man had a limp to his walk, probably not a limp from any injury but from some sense of style. His head leaned to one side the way black men in sixties movies leaned their heads. A comfortable thought passed through Oku. The brother was old school. It was that lean of the head that told him this was Jackie's father. Jackie had the same slant, the same way of sizing you up at the same time as making you know that she was dangerous. Jackie resembled her mother more than her father, but his height and that threatening lean of his head Jackie had taken from him. He limped toward Oku, and assessing him as no threat, he walked by. Oku called to him: "Mr. Bernard."

Jackie's father stopped. "I know you, man?" he asked. Oku felt as if his answer had better be correct. In that "I know you, man?" was a challenge for respect. Oku recognized it. It was couched in another generation, but the machismo was recognizable. It was a question about dominance, and territory, it said, Don't be trifling, and what the fuck do you want?

"No, sir," Oku said with the required deference. "I'm a friend of Jackie's, and I saw you and I just knew you had to be her father."

"Oh yeah, that's my girl, how you know her?"

He hadn't said the right thing. The interrogation would get deeper now, the stakes were higher. "We went to high school together, sir." He dropped the second "sir" in to reassure Jackie's father of his total respect.

"She ain't around today. Haven't seen her in a week or so, you know. She down at that store . . ." Jackie's father trailed off as if he'd found something disturbing in what he'd said.

"Oh, I was just passing by. You tell her I said hi, eh?" Jackie's father looked at him quizzically. "Oku's my name, sir." Oku reached his hand out, and Jackie's father took it.

"All right, young brother, all right. See you on the tip." He limped on, going toward Queen Street.

Oku watched him go, then regretted not asking him to go for a beer or something. Maybe he'd lost an opportunity, but he didn't want Jackie feeling he was prying, he didn't want to repeat that incident years ago when her mother's attention got him the cold shoulder. So he watched Jackie's father go. There was the old player in her father; the hand clasping his had been cool yet brotherly. The face was slightly twisted in the way that older black men's faces invariably were. Something wry seemed to be constantly slipping across their lips; some knowing tale, as if to say, "Yes, I know that bullshit. Took me a life to figure it out and I still ain't got it. Beat that." One day his own face would register that truth, but he hoped not.

As Jackie's father disappeared west along Queen, Oku felt wistful for him. He felt the concentration of the man, the insecurities that had to be gathered up, the opportunities that were imagined but never came, the vanity that his body allowed him, all gathered in that limp like some bird feigning weakness to protect what was valuable. He looked around at the perilous stuff of Alexandra Park.

What must have scared Jackie was Vanauley Way. The scarred brown buildings. The dry hot walkway in the summer, the dry cold walkway in the winter. Her coats with the polyester stuffing coming out, the nylon tearing so easily. Why couldn't they have planted a good tree anywhere here, why couldn't they have laid out beds of plants and flowers, a forsythia bush or two, a grove of hostas, some forget-me-nots, some phlox, smoke trees now and then, mint bushes and rosemary, why had it been so hard for the city to come up with a bit of beauty?

The narrow winding walkway, virtually empty in the daytime, scarred-looking, teemed with a ghostly, sometimes scary life at night. With one thought they could have made it beautiful, but perhaps they didn't think that poor people deserved beauty. Lavender, for instance, could grow anywhere. No reason at all that the walkways, which were not built for cars, could not have been made into an oasis of flowers, grasses, bushes, with perhaps a cobbled walk. But at least lavender. Then at night it wouldn't be that shadowy, that dim. And in the daytime people would have come out to front yards and puttered around, had a coffee, said "hello" and "how you doing?" to children, and "careful there, careful now." In the nighttime the gloom would have been lit by people sitting in their gardens with lanterns, a little laughter would have passed in the air—not the kind of laughter that was derision and self-mockery or smirking at someone else's folly or misfortune but real laughter from the small joy of life. There would have been wine and music, and not the kind of wine that you drank eventually to numb the inconsequential-to-anyone-else disaster of your life, and not the music that makes you remember a perfectly lovely time at the Paramount bitterly, but the music that makes you remember that time self-indulgently.

A rose bush in the front of 113 ½ Vanauley Way would have tasted the rains of fifteen, twenty years in Toronto and thickened and twisted its wood over that doorway like loveliness. Yes, why not a plantation of rose bushes all along Vanauley Way, millions of petals growing and falling, giving off a little velvet. It's amazing what a garden can do. And Jackie could have sure done with a place like that. They themselves tried a few perennials in window boxes; they tried to make the best, but then had it been a garden instead of that dry narrow roadway, Jackie's childhood might have been less hazardous.

People defended that park, saying to the city, in so many words, Don't drop all your negative vibes on us, we're trying to live the same as everybody, but if you couldn't see it in your heart to put a garden in here, if you tarred over every piece of earth, then don't blame us. Would it have killed them to splash a little colour on the buildings? Yes, it may have cost a little more in the first place to make the ceilings a little higher, the hallways a little less narrow, but in the last place think of the perspective: the general outlook might have been worth it. The sense of space might have triggered lighter emotions, less depressing thoughts, a sense of well-being. God, hope! The park wouldn't have driven Jackie's father and mother to drink like it had. And the dream of going back down east for good wouldn't have faded and died right there on the narrow asphalt paths of Vanauley Way.

Even the dream of staying in this city would have survived. A barbershop of his own, maybe, for Jackie's father instead of the penitentiary in Guelph for two years less a day—which turned out to be eight months that time—for receiving stolen goods. Another stint for B and E at a computer factory when he sold IBMs for ten points on the street. And why did he have to come back to Jackie's mother hanging out at Wilson's on Bloor, some asshole following her around and calling her up and hanging up in his ear? So she said to him that she couldn't be waiting around for him forever, and he said, "fair enough," but she knew that he was doing time for them, doing time wasn't recreational, what did she think, he was up in jail partying? And why'd she have to rub it in his face, bring it in his house, and what about Jackie, did Jackie have to see all this shit going on, what kind of woman was she going to turn out to be if her mother was a whore?

"Whore, whore," she said. Now he'd gone too far, now he'd gone just too far; did he want her to leave his ass this minute, this very minute, 'cause if she was a whore, she wouldn't be with him, he should be glad she wasn't no whore, a whore wouldn't have time with his sorry ass, and look, look here, he had promised her a good life down here, and there it was, he was in jail half the time and they were starving or ducking the police half the time, and the nasty words he saved for her, and where was the sweet life when he could not even hold down a chair at Golden's Barbershop for one half second and he was running the streets and had her tailing behind him and they had a mouth to feed, and where did he think she got the money to feed herself and Jackie while he was gone? Think some government cheque was enough to cover their ass, and time, doing time for them, yeah, all right, true enough, but do some time outside, do some time here with her and Jackie. Had she, she, not stayed as long as she could in that godawful job in the comb factory? Packing one green comb, one yellow comb, one pink comb, and one red comb in a box all day long for four dollars and twenty-five cents an hour. She'd packed combs until she was dizzy; she'd given combs to friends, sold extra combs at the hair-dresser's, until the novelty of working in a comb factory had worn off and she was sick of packing one green, one yellow, one pink, and one red comb into a box the whole livelong day. And love, love was about finished, where was her joystick, where was her man, she was a young woman still, where was her loving?

Jackie's father said that he could feel his "boy," meaning his dick, growing deader year after year. He could feel it beginning with the tip. Each year another centimetre would go. Which is why Jackie's mother began to get terrible bruises on her face and arms, raccoon eyes, and just a low-down feeling in her gut the whole time.

They weren't the same people who had taken that train to Toronto fifteen years ago. Well, no one ever is, but they weren't those two people much more so than they'd imagined. They weren't the people they were going to be or had set out to be, the people they had envisioned. Look, okay, they hadn't *envisioned*. Who does, except rich people? You simply throw yourself at life, and the narcissism of being young and beautiful and handsome and strong and eager and ready is supposed to see you through. So when Jackie's father asked Jackie's mother to marry him and they had a big wedding at the Cornwallis Baptist Church in Halifax and everybody turned out and Jackie's mother got pregnant that very night when they rolled around on satin sheets at the Four Seasons Hotel for that one night for which Jackie's father had cut hair and shaved chins like a demon, they were young and in love with each other and themselves and the world. And when Jackie's father's uncle phoned up and said, "Come on out here, boy. It's a happening town," they got on the train in their psychedelic pants and cocked hat and Indian blouses and came just like that because they were still young and still in love with each other and themselves and the world. What's wrong with that kind of narcissism? So they didn't *envision*, no, they thought that they were young and beautiful, and it wasn't a lie, and it ought to have been enough. It's enough for a lot of people, why not them?

Jackie heard all this when her mother and father were trying to keep their arguing low and when they were so mad they didn't care to spare her. Between her parents and Vanauley Way, she wondered what she was going to do. She did them all a favour by making a plan. If the city didn't have the good grace to plant a shrub or two, she would cultivate it with her own trees and flowers. And so she did. In her mind.

Every day she walked down paths of magnolia trees and lilac bushes; wisteria hung over the arbour and doorway of 113 1/2. In the spring she walked around complimenting the tulips: the parrots, the Rembrandts, the triumphs, the double early, the viridiflora, the double late, the hummingbird, the clusiana. She loved lobelia at her feet and just the names helianthemum and habranthus. All these and more she found in a book called *The Expert's Flowers* by Dr. N. T. Humphreys. She walked from Vanualey Way to Harbord Collegiate in tumbling, arching cream shrub roses. And if her mother and father couldn't love one another or could only love one another in this reckless, undefined, unreliable way, she would love them with a passion but with a discipline.

It was riding the tip of his tongue; it was hovering in his brain. He knew it wasn't simple. Jackie hadn't left Alexandra Park. She owed a loyalty to her mother and father. That faithfulness didn't mean that she wanted to have it burn her as it had them. Hence, the white boy. Oku knew this logic. He knew that to Jackie he probably looked like so many burned-out guys in Vanauley Way. Young, but burned out, so much wreckage. How could he tell her that he wasn't wreckage? How could he, when he was depending on her to tell him that? What could he tell her then? Number one, that he wasn't a player. He would have to shed any ambivalence about that. Number two, he wasn't her father. He would never allow that look to come into his eyes, the wry look, the defeated look, the bitter look. He was going to work the rest of the summer, the rest of the year, then go back and finish the master's. Why? Because he loved that, and what he loved he wasn't going to have taken from him or give up. Next, he had held her, he had felt her, he was certain, he simply had to be there. Jesus, who was he promising all this to? All right then, himself. He was promising this to himself.

TWENTY-ONE

TUYEN HAD GONE to the market with Oku, and she had joked around with him in their way, teasing him about Jackie, discussing John Coltrane's "Venus," but her brain felt lit. She was frightened of the face in the photograph she had taken. Could it be him? After all, the only photographs of Quy she'd seen were of him as a baby. His face would have changed. And she had never ever seen his real face. Perhaps she was hallucinating. He was a ghost in her childhood, the unseen, the un-understood, yet here he was, insinuating himself in a simple meeting with her brother that she had foolishly photographed like a spy. Throughout her childhood Quy had looked at her from every mantel, every surface, and now she thought she had looked at him. And there at the end of the roll of film was her own face too, wet, her hair clinging to her cheek, the flash of the camera making her seem startled. She was so frightened she'd ended up in the doorway of Pope Joan, longing to be seduced.

She'd thought briefly of talking to her sisters, but that idea came and went quickly with the memory of her last encounter with Lam when she was home. She had little contact with either of them, and besides she didn't care what they thought. They were older, it seemed, by millennia and simply didn't see the world the same way as she did. Yet she was always surprised by the venomous passion that jumped out at her from her sisters each time she was in some kind of trouble with her mother and father. When she was little, they always suggested to her parents some much harsher punishment than her parents had settled on. Far from enhancing their power over her, it diminished them, but the intensity of their hatred always surprised her. Even when she tried to be helpful to one of them, whoever it was would spin around and attack her.

Like a year ago, when Ai wanted to go to Montreal to live and their parents objected, swearing to cut her off, screaming that she was breaking up the family. Ai seemed determined to go despite this, she seemed to blossom in the drama all around her. Until, in a moment of sisterly conspiracy, Tuyen had said to her, "Ai, it's gonna be great for you."

"You little whore!" Ai had spat at her. "Who asked you? You would like me to go, wouldn't you? Then Binh would have no one to support him."

Tuyen was stupefied. What intrigues had she missed, and how did her family really see her? That last, she thought, she didn't care about, but obviously she was not immune to their opinions. Recovering herself, she had said to Ai, "Oh, do whatever the fuck you like, then, I was just trying to help you."

Ai ended up staying in Toronto, and Tuyen suspected that it was all an attempt to be the centre of things, and if she really thought about it, Ai didn't have the backbone to go off on her own. She had been tied to Tuan and Cam ever since that night in the bay.

None of them could see themselves without the others set in that particular tableau. There was an invisible string between them beyond the pull of family as Tuyen knew it. Something had slipped out of their hands; they would always feel absence. It was this overwhelming sense of regret that

Tuyen had fled. It would descend on her if she spent any length of time at the house in Richmond Hill or in the too-long presence of any of the family, even Binh.

There were moments, then, when Tuyen had to go somewhere to be seduced. Openly seduced. And seduced in no way imaginable within the confines of that family story.

Pope Joan was a bar on Parliament Street. A bar that stood as the last eastern outpost of gay life in downtown Toronto. It had had several reincarnations, the previous one being the Rose, where they played Patsy Cline singing "Crazy" at the end of each night. It was primarily a lesbian bar, though a few gay men and a few voyeuristic straight couples could be picked out on any given night. There were several pool tables on the lower floor where butches expressed their angular prowess and their sartorial charm. They drank strictly, and voluminously, beer. And they hogged the pool tables, treating any women who didn't measure up with cold dismissal. Their dates were usually upstairs dancing or slumping on the leather sofas, smoking and eyeing each other pointedly bored.

Generations and variations of butches had occupied the lower floor and the pool tables in the relatively short life of the club on Parliament Street. So quick, so incandescent was the life of the women who came to the club, it could only be measured in months. There was an urgency to the place and a packed force. All that couldn't be lived outside was lived in here, in the six or seven hours between when the doors opened and when they closed. The meetings, the courtships, the marriages, the break-ups could be done in the small public space of the Rose, or Pope Joan as Tuyen knew it. The butterfly lives lived here, the sweet-winged existences—the telephone operator, a real-estate broker, a welfare mother, a girl from North Bay, or the woman from Timmins who knew the place as the Rose, a woman from Regent Park, any woman—anyone could become invisible, whole and erotic, on this dance floor. Any woman could drop her necessary defences to the city, put her legs up on a stool, and drift.

It was from Pope Joan's that Tuyen brought women home. Women who smoked too much, drank too much, did too much dope. Women, therefore, whom she didn't have to keep. Or women who were professionals at something— lawyers or real-estate brokers who were fascinated that Tuyen was an artist until they saw that she really was an artist when they woke up in the mornings in Tuyen's dishevelled bed. Or women who thought of Tuyen as the Asian girl who could share certain bizarre erotic secrets with them. Once she laughingly told Carla that those women didn't know that she was so much not what they imagined.

"Why would you sleep with them?" Carla asked.

"We're not sleeping, all right? We're fucking. Jealous?"

"No, but why?"

"Because they're interesting."

"How?"

"They're just people, Carla. It's fantasy. You learn things about yourself."

"Like?"

"Like . . . like, Carla . . . like having sex is just human, you know, experiencing your physical self, your flesh, like I feel like I'm in life. My skin is alive, all my senses are open. You feel it right here," she said, tracing her hand up Carla's abdomen to between her small breasts.

"Well, whatever."

"Sure you're not jealous?"

She used to ask Carla to come with her to Pope Joan, to cover for her in case there was someone she couldn't shake. But she'd stopped doing that. Oku wouldn't come with her because despite their friendship he would not go that far, and Jackie vainly told Tuyen that Tuyen wouldn't get any action if she came along. Tuyen actually invited Carla in the hopes that some lever in Carla's mind would switch on, some desire discovered. That Carla might recognize herself in the lean girls against the bar, the girls in slender-cut suits with silver rings on each finger and thumb who looked so compact and secretive, so much as if all their essences were perfectly locked and kept, and only if you managed to please them could you unlock their fingers and pry them out. They smelled of a different perfume, they never quite met your eyes except in a swift and thorough appraisal whose conclusion you became aware of immediately when their eyes averted without the longed-for approving smile. You longed to go with them to secret apartments in the suburbs or condos on the lakeshore and there have their fingers brush down your back and have their maroon mouths kiss your thighs.

Tuyen entered Pope Joan's looking for a woman like that. She didn't want to go home tonight, back to the image of Quy's face. The Quy she had imagined. The music was techno, the deejay was the regular Thursday night deejay, Angela. She played house and techno music. She stood on the raised dais, earphones to her left ear, held there by her shoulder, her hand moving from one album to another. Tuyen felt relief at the pounding, fast, whirling music and thanked the song for replacing the frenetic buzz that had taken over her head for the last two days. She moved to the bar and ordered a beer above the music, sizing up the women at the rail, looking for that one with the coolest, most-remote look. She saw a woman with a dark, angular face sizing her up. She returned the glacial look, and the woman smiled a half smile both challenging and easy. Tuyen smiled back, and they headed for the deliri-ous dance floor.

Two hours of mindless dancing later, she had gathered that the woman's name was Iman, that she worked for an insurance broker, doing accident claims, that her family was from Eritrea, that she had fled their happy life in the suburb of Brampton. And that Iman had a small condo on King Street that she rented with a friend.

"What kind of friend?" Tuyen asked above the music.

"Not that kind of friend. Someone I used to be involved with, but it's nothing now."

"Ah."

"No hassle," the woman assured her, sensing Tuyen's dejection at possibly having to deal with a jealous ex. "Or we could go to your place?"

That prospect didn't appeal to Tuyen. "No, if you say it's all right."

The music had simmered to R & B ballads, and they danced closely in the steam of each other, the woman putting her lips in the cup of Tuyen's shoulder. Tuyen bought her another tequila, and she laughed, downing it and biting into a quarter moon of lemon, saying, "I don't drink, you know. I'm a good Muslim girl." When the set was over and the music picked up pace again, the woman led Tuyen off the dance floor toward the door. They left the cocoon of Pope Joan, hailed a cab, and went to Iman's place.

The sex was casual, performative and muscular, rather than passionate; the kind of sex two strangers have, physical and unartistic except for the natural artistry of bodies. They would meet again and glide by each other at Pope Joan, per-haps nodding as if what had happened between them was the simplest of exchanges. But the sex they had needed no promises, except the work of thighs and hips and tongues and hands. They didn't talk, they only held and squeezed, and wet and exhausted and too drunk to do more, they fell asleep. The next morning they parted as casually—Iman going to her job at the insurance broker and Tuyen making her way to her place on College Street above the store, across from Carla.

It was eight in the morning, and though it was unusual for her to be awake at that time, she had wanted to leave when Iman left.

As she walked the distance home, she felt as if she were still drunk—she hadn't been able to sleep off the tequilas. But something had resolved itself in her mind. She simply had to confront Binh. She would do that and then she would go to Richmond Hill to size things up herself. After all, maybe she was imagining things. She had warned Binh not to make trouble, and he hadn't called her with any news. After their last encounter she thought they had developed a kind of understanding, so she must be wrong about the photograph.

TWENTY-TWO

WHEN CARLA LEFT THE HOUSE after throwing the glass at Derek, Nadine turned on him. "You have a lot to pay for, Derek. She's right. Why did I spend my life with you? How . . . how could you be so selfish?"

"I don't want to hear about it, Nadine. Ever since the day those children came here, you turned on me."

"Turned on you? They were children, for God's sake! You're a grown man. Take some responsibility."

"*Responsibility!* Didn't I take them in? Didn't I?"

"You were duty bound. You were supposed to love them too."

"You sided with that bitch against me. You and your family took her side. How the hell you could take her side after she ruined my life."

"My God, Derek. She killed herself! You made her kill herself."

"I didn't make her kill herself. Don't blame me for that."

"Who else?"

"Just like I said. You take her side and turn against me. She was crazy. Shit, she had a mental condition!"

"Well, she wasn't crazy enough to stop you from putting your dick where it didn't belong."

Derek wheeled on Nadine, raising his hand to hit her.

"Go on, hit me, Derek. It will be the last thing you do. Go on."

"Fuck you, woman," he said, pushing her aside to leave the room. "I don't have time for this! You can go to hell."

"You're the one going to hell!" she yelled after his back going up the staircase. From the kitchen, a few minutes later, she heard him slam out the front door.

274   Derek hadn't pushed Angie over the balcony, but he might as well have.

His friends, his family, had formed a protective circle around him after the inquest. Nadine felt like a bystander. Derek's arms had gripped her shoulders in a nervous vice. She was his prop, his evidence that Angie was just a crazy bitch trying to come between him and his family. His grasp of her shoulder confirmed for Nadine that Derek was to blame. Angie's mother had spat at him in the courtroom, shouted at him, "*Figlio di puttana!*" Outside, after the inquest, she walked over to him, reaching for him in what seemed at first a gesture of forgiveness. Nadine knew it wasn't peace, it wasn't forgiveness, it was vengeance. Derek saw Angie's mother and made a strangling sound before she grasped his neck. "Fucking get her off me!" he screamed. He closed his eyes, she had something in her hand that was cutting into the right side of his neck. "*Bastardo! Figlio di puttana!*" Nadine watched in sweet horror, wishing the worst. It was a St. Christopher medallion. Derek thought it was a knife and tried to wrench himself away, yelling, "She's got a knife!"

After the suicide they had taken in his children by Angie. Angie's sister had dropped them at his door, the little girl, Nadine knew about her, and a squalling baby she didn't quite know about. Derek had denied it, his face in that soft way, as if he had been wounded. He had promised her that it was over, that the woman, Angie, was a madwoman. That yes, the first child was his. It had happened at the time that he and Nadine weren't doing well. But the baby, he swore, was not his, not at all. He had had nothing to do with that woman again. She was crazy, following him, coming to his home. He was paying her child support and that was all.

Nadine wanted to refuse, she would not raise another woman's children, she wanted to leave him but she hadn't. He had chosen her, hadn't he? He could just as easily have taken off with the white girl, but he had chosen her, chosen to stay with her, and so some vanity in her, a vanity, of course, tinged with racial vindictiveness, made her take his choice as an honour.

The truth, she knew, was that Derek was a vain man, not a forward-thinking man. He could not start over again with another woman. He had been quite comfortable living in that way with Angie on the side. Nadine calculated, counted on that streak of conservativism in Derek. When she finally agreed to take his children in, it was with another calculation. That he would never be able to thank her. That would be their pact. Something else involuntarily crept into the bargain. Nadine gradually and sometimes violently ceased to love Derek. What she felt for him was certainly strong but it was not love. Another fascination took hold of her—why Angie? What did Derek see in Angie? Nadine was tortured by this. The thought also occurred to her that taking the children would reveal this. That Derek could betray her for someone less worthy was to her impossible. So how was Angie more worthy?

She searched the children's faces for what element there might reveal Angie's attraction. But what it took for her to take care of another woman's children without cruelty was every ounce of her sense of herself as a good human being. It wasn't hard with the baby. He was like an unformed bit of matter, he knew nothing. But Carla was a brooding, watchful little girl who was grieving for her mother. She would sometimes ask Derek when Angie was coming for her and the baby. Derek would bark at her eventually, saying that Angie wasn't coming back and that she should be quiet. The child was unhappy, and in those early days Nadine could not bring herself to comfort her. Carla would sink into quietness and strangeness. All Nadine could summon up was a prissy reprimand of Derek: "The little girl has lost her mother, you're her father. You should explain it to her." Nadine really meant "You'll spend a lifetime explaining it to me."

You can't resent children for long. Or at least Nadine couldn't. She didn't have it in her. Some did—there were stories of child abuse in the papers every day. One poor boy beaten to death by his stepmother and father after he'd come to the city from Jamaica. Nadine knew where her anger was. Derek was the one who should suffer. She ignored her sisters hissing at her on the telephone about why she should not be taking care of Derek's bastards. She made Derek blunder through the first month of feeding and dressing and taking care; begging his mother to help out. She wanted him to know just what he would owe if she took on the task of caring for Carla and Jamal. And despite herself she came to give them a kind of love, especially the baby, who didn't have the reserve of the little girl.

The sisters found her behaviour unusual. In the years that passed they shook their heads at her, saying she was either stupid or a saint for taking on the burden of Derek's children. And they did not know and Nadine did not confide in them what a struggle she had in damping down her hurt and resentment, her feelings of utter betrayal. She had turned a corner morally in being able to bring anything like love to her relationship with these children. She took it as a triumph over Derek, over herself, over conventional wisdom, to come to the point of considering Angie's children her own. The complexities of this triumph—some distorted, some like an epiphany—she never revealed or for that matter understood herself. She felt guilty about Angie. Why? Because Angie had killed herself in some respects because of her, Nadine. Her existence, which stood in the way. Was that vanity too? she wondered. Angie had killed herself because of Derek's callousness. Or perhaps Angie was mad, as Derek said, and had killed herself because of that. Whatever it was, Nadine felt guilty. She should have put a clean stop to it long ago.

There was a terrible flattery also in Angie's death. For Derek. Nadine had overheard a man at a social function pointing to Derek as they passed by and saying in an appreciative tone, "Woman kill herself for him, you know?" She shared in this flattery, as women in her social circle told her better Angie than she, and complimented her on sticking it out or encouraged her to leave his ass now. So for all this terrible praise she took extra care of Angie's poor children. It was the sign that she had no malice toward Angie, no malice for a dead woman; that she was better than Angie. And anyway, why should these children suffer because Derek couldn't keep his fly zipped? And she was not about to let them suffer so that people would say that her jealousy made her mistreat them. She would take instead the beatific garment offered to her, taking Carla and Jamal in and loving them.

And she had. She had loved them. Beyond what she had thought possible. That's the thing with children. They opened a person up. They came with their own presences and opened you up. Now Nadine could not recall with the same intensity ever not loving Carla and Jamal. Perhaps there had been in her a small resentment toward Carla. She bore a resemblance; unlike Jamal, Angie was there in her. Perhaps she had been unable to completely love her for this. Perhaps it was why she had been unable to form the words to tell Carla that it had not been her fault. She had not meant to leave her without an answer. She recognized a whinging smallness in her hesitation. She told herself that she did not say anything because Carla was too young, not because of these resentments. She told herself no, she would never transfer these to her. And she didn't, at least she thought so. Self-doubt made her think everything twice, made her mistrust her best feelings. She loved Carla. As much as she could.

Nadine's love for Jamal, however, was unreserved, so uncontrollable at times that she never made the right decisions about him. He got whatever he wanted from her. Whatever whim of his needed satisfying she gave in to. With Nadine, Jamal had no compass for right and wrong, and when Derek stepped in, he bludgeoned his way in, his meter of hatred for Angie as clearly present as his wounded passion. Between them Jamal was a temperamental bundle seeking continuous attention yet blowing up because of it. Sometimes Nadine was speechless with this love, confused at the depth of it, as deep as if Jamal were her son in flesh. In fact, this love had alienated her from her son by blood. He found her weak because of it. But she would do anything for Jamal. There had been many confrontations with Derek, some coming close to violence in defence of Jamal. She'd stolen money from Derek for Jamal, she'd hidden the fact that he had dropped out of school, she'd covered up his lying, and on the numerous occasions that Derek had put him out of the house, she had gone looking for him with Carla and brought him home.

———

Carla had left home at nineteen, by which time she had grown lank and long as if from too much rain and small portions of strong sunlight. When she first told Nadine and Derek her plans, they both involuntarily screamed "no" at the same time. What about college, university, how was she going to make a living? Nadine took it back, quickly saying, "If you really think so, Carla. If you're ready." Yes, go, Nadine thought. She had lived with this brooding, watching child for eleven years. Relief is what she felt. She would not have to answer any questions. If Carla stayed at home, she would be a child who had to be answered, but if she left home, then she was an adult with a separate life and Nadine wouldn't have to feel any more guilt for Derek, or for the death of Angie.

So as quickly as she had said no to Carla moving out, Nadine took it back. "Yes, yes, darling. You're big enough now. As long as you think you could manage." She would do her best to help Carla, help her fix the place up. She would visit her. They would be different. They would be adults together, they would go to the movies together, meet on their lunch hours and have a laugh. She wouldn't have to love her any more. Carla would find people that she could love. She had not exercised this muscle at all with them.

"I can manage. I have a job. I found a place already." And that was that. Carla wasn't asking them, she was saying that she was going. She was saying, if they heard her right, I'm leaving you both. Don't need what I never got.

Nadine searched herself for some word that would ease them over into friendship. She wanted Carla to know that she was happy for her, but Carla was gone, retreating, or rather advancing into her life. Who were her friends, and how did she know the city enough to have found a place, to be ready to live on her own? What Nadine had not said had cut her off too. She would have to wait for Carla to come to her. One day she was sure it would happen. Carla would see how she had protected her and shielded her from the bad things in life. But Carla circumvented every effort she made to come by and visit her. When she baked something and said she'd come and bring it, Carla said no, not to bother, she'd pick it up from her at work, or she'd merely say, "Don't cook me anything," in her exasperating whisper. Nadine wasn't the kind of demanding mother that others were. She knew where to stop and she knew why. She didn't want anything boiling over. She didn't want that whisper to turn into a growl.

Today Nadine dressed for work feeling an unusual absence. She would tell her that she, Carla, was not to blame for anything. She would tell her that she was too small to understand at the time, too small to be burdened. It was too late, but she wanted to tell her, she wanted it to make a difference. An urgency moved her. She would tell her the whole story. But she was going to find Derek first.

She left the house and could hear far off a train lumbering and squeaking along the tracks at Cherry Street. She looked at her watch, she should get to work. A sweet smell of fresh bread was coming from the bakery, a recorder was playing music at the school next door. She walked toward the Chester subway, feeling a sharp light on her, her head tingling as if she had inhaled water. The city around her seemed new, soft-skinned and tender.

She handled the facts of the day briskly—the white counters, the green screen of the computers, the ruby coagulates, the sharp needles, the shiny sinks. By lunchtime she had decided to skip the rest of the day and go talk to Derek. She'd been to Derek's workplace infrequently. She was going to leave him, now finally, if he didn't do what he had to do.

Derek managed a car wash in the west end of the city. Good weather or bad, six or seven men would by turns be shivering from the cold or wet, rubbing cars down with wet rags, lit cigarettes in their hands to keep them warm. Over the years Derek hired an assortment of the city's down and out, men who had the good fortune of being the latest wave of immigrants: Sikhs, Caribbeans, Vietnamese, Sri Lankans, Russians, and Somalis. Somalis and Ethiopians now made up the majority of the crew. Two old Caribbean men and one Ukrainian had been with the shop even before Derek. Most days Derek sat in the small warm kiosk taking money from the customers while the crew ran the cars through the wash and then wiped them to a shine. That is, unless a pretty woman came to get her car done. Then Derek would come out, ordering the crew to make sure that her car was waxed well and all the running boards wiped. He would turn on the charm, holding her by the shoulder and giving her a free coupon and his assurances that she could call him any time, come by any time; managing to get her phone number and, if she was married, implying all the while that she may not be happy and that he was available to talk or have a coffee. Derek's game was a quick and slippery charm. In the middle of the oil-stained, deluged, smelly car wash, among the ruggedly dressed, rough-handed, broken-faced men, Derek was immaculate, well dressed, and sweet smelling. He always exuded the lover, the charmer.

Walking toward the car wash and seeing him standing with the men, pointing to the hood of a car, Nadine felt a wave of both desire and revulsion pass through her. Yes, she had loved Derek for this very thing, his virility, his easy lust.

And here it was, more than twenty years later, still intact despite everything that had happened.

Derek was startled when he turned to go back to the kiosk and saw her. He hurried toward her, assuming she had come to make a scene and to squelch it before she did so in front of the men. He turned a smile on her as he would a customer and made a grand embrace as the crew would expect him to behave toward his wife. The crew, today a Sri Lankan, the two old Caribbean men, and the two young Somalis, looked on appreciatively. Derek called, to one of the older man, "Roger, take over the kiosk for me. I'm going to take my wife to lunch." Then he checked his pockets for his keys and guided Nadine to his car.

"I want you to go get your son out of jail, Derek."

"Get in the car, Nadine."

"I mean it, Derek. I'm tired of this . . . tired with you now." She sounded exhausted.

"You see what that girl did to my car, Nadine?" He showed her the scoring around the body. She looked at him pitifully.

"It's nowhere near what you did." Something in her tone told him this would not be their usual bickering.

"Do what you have to do. I'm done," she said before he turned the key in the ignition.

Quy

It's late spring in this city. Seasons mean nothing to me. Money is my season. Korea beat Italy. You never know, they could beat Germany next. But I doubt it. That Teutonic bunch have no creativity, but they have order. I'm the opposite. Sometimes I think I haven't the heart for another city. It's just that I haven't the bones to reach my hand into another set of lives, feel the sweat of stupid dreams.

What am I doing here, anyway? Well, I lost the compass for knowing where I was long ago, I suppose. So it's useless asking who I am. You're more interested in how I got off of Pulau Bidong. How I got here and how grateful I am. How I know the alleyways that lead to the back doors of Chinatown in this city. What if I told you that there's a web of people like me laying sticky strings all over the city?

You want to know how a person like me could get into such esoteric matters. After all, what pause would I have between scuffling off a boat in the South China Sea, the eternal boat to Pulau Bidong. Get this, a person like me gets to know things. And if you were a boy like me, you'd wise up soon enough to the way things get told and what the weight of telling is.

Well, I was rescued by monks from Pulau Bidong, and they had a good thing—begging. I shaved my head and put on a brown robe and learned to solicit alms on the mainland.

We were like a gang, like any conglomerate of businessmen. We had territory, we had monopolies, we had wars, we had alliances, until a schism broke out between the monk who was my father, an ascetic with an opium habit, and a high-tech monk with a laptop computer, a Web site, and a dream of expansion into America.

I was fed up with Loc Tuc. The other side was more promising than that black hole of an opium high. The *Dong Khoi* had freed me of allegiances. By this time I was a bone of a man, my body looked older than my face. My face always saves me; I'm told it has the innocence of a child's. That face remained with me. I myself don't recognize it when I look at it in the mirror. Who is that? I ask. That clear-eyed weepy boy, the waiting look, innocent, innocent like a banded kingfisher. I've managed to change everything except that face. It's waiting for its mother and father to come back. You would fall in love with it. My body has done everything hurtful, but that face keeps hanging on.

The new boss with the laptop had his hands on everything. I used to call him *"du-ma-nhieu"* behind his back. He had a mobile cellphone and partners on every continent. He would find somebody for you as far away as Alaska. But I didn't want to find my mother and father any more. I told him that. I was finished with that long ago. You should see our crew of monks, orange-gowned and macerated, we moved like a dust cloud. But we had uzis and palm pilots. We controlled the unofficial refugee trade from Malaysia and Thailand to China and out; we hacked into offshore bank accounts. Of course, other residuals and commodities came our way. Use your imagination. We exported the *I Ching* for idiots and took a shared interest in pirated *Thoughts of Mao Tse-tung* and replicas of Michael

Jackson's *Thriller* album. In our dim corner of the world we unravelled languages while we traded in everything from plastic hair combs to liberated Ford Broncos from New York. You may not understand this, but the world came to us and we ate.

The monk with the laptop was a dangerous man until he fell in love with the girl sewing tongues into Brooks high tops. When he looked at her ravaged fingers, it became personal. We blew up a factory, and the girl dropped him for ruining her life. She had the police hunting us down because we made it political. It's all right when the economic wheels are turning—theft is nothing—but turning principled is another matter. You have to know how to run your life, you have to take the highs with the lows. Never get used to an easy life—it'll slip out from under you any time. Years, years we spent living well, under the radar, then he goes and does this thing. So I had to find another way; it was getting ideological. I didn't want to make it into the newspapers any more. I stole the laptop and the cellular and cut out on a boat to Fushen. Hopped a freighter and ended up on the Pacific coast of Canada with some teenaged girls heading for the tenderloin district of San Fransisco. I'm doomed to boats.

You want to know how I felt? Did I grow, did I believe, was I hopeful, was this a journey to start a new life? How could I have betrayed the new boss, how could I steal from him, am I redeemable? Did I have a moment of revelation? Can I turn my life around? You're better at that.

For some of us, the world is never forgiving. And anyway, we don't believe in such things, these ideas of forgiveness, redemption—it's useless. That high-tech monk is probably dead by now and has figured out another incarnation.

The ship ran aground in the Juan de Fuca Strait. I bailed out. Me and some others hit land before the Coast Guard came. The laptop and the cellular were wrapped in oilskin. I knew they would be my collateral. "The danger of the sky is that we cannot climb up into it; the danger of the earth is the mountains, rivers, and hills—constant pitfalls— seek and you gain a little."

By now the monk was a blade of grass, but he had kept files. There were correspondences on the laptop, letters from and letters to. Some woman had been sending letters to the new boss for years, searching for a boy. There was a network of middlemen and pharmacists, payoffs and bribes that the monk had a hand in. Someone was searching for their sister, someone else for a grandfather. "For the weak at the outset, good luck is a matter of following along." How was the monk supposed to find them? Boys would not be boys any more, this sister not a sister, this grandfather is a pile of dust. But they kept writing, and the monk kept taking, and sending hope from Klong Toey. Sometimes he may have found someone, but they had to pay too. Hitchhiking the Trans-Canada Highway, I knew the laptop was my capital.

My body keeps moving out of wilfulness. What is physical is uncontrollable. If I didn't have to take a piss, the Mounties would never have caught me. There's my face again in the cameras of the world. This time I'm ducking, shielding it with my handcuffed wrists. Looking better, looking better, though. Only biding time. They gave us orange overalls. The men and the girls. I suppose it's a blankness of another kind. I suppose it's the same picture as at Pulau Bidong those many years ago. But I can't complain. There's something to anonymity, stereotype, being part of the hordes. It can be a camouflage. Let others try to escape it.

Let them complain. I'll slip into it and disappear. Did I tell
the Amnesty people who I was? Who I'd been? No. What
for? To complicate things? Let them have their picture,
I say. Yes, I'm innocent of all things. Yes, I'm guilty of
all things.

When they relaxed the detention rules, I took off with
two girls worth eighteen thousand dollars apiece. Thirty-six
thousand on delivery to Margaret Yao in Toronto. I searched
quickly for the laptop, which had been confiscated. One of
the girls found it, while the other one chatted up a guard.
Then, waiting for early-morning changeover, we ran off.

There were fears and figures and dates in that computer
and then there were those stories which I must confess I
found seductive. The transactions that the monk made in
identity. Everything is mystery. As cold as those dealings
were, the way he wrote those stories was poetry. I suspect
he and I were brothers beyond what we told each other. But
perhaps not. He was sentimental, after all. Look how he got
caught up in that factory girl's life. When I read the monk's
poetic meanderings, the laptop went soft like blood.

He'd been taking money from that one woman for
more than ten years to find a boy named Quy. He inherited
this mark from the monk he deposed and destroyed with
the best dose of opium since the Buddha made heaven.
Every four or five letters he would give her hope and relate
how he had seen her boy and the boy was now a holy man,
and then he would plunge her into despair, saying no, it
might not be him after all. Then he would ask her to send
as much money as she had so he could go to the sacred
temple in the interior, where he was convinced the holy boy
had gone. Then he would berate her about how little she
loved her son that she would send such a pittance. This was

the monk's most intense relationship, I could tell, until the factory girl came along. I came to believe that he was Quy himself; otherwise, why would he keep up so many letters with this one mother when with all the rest he robbed them and moved on? But then again the subject of all this could just as well have been me, for one of the names I go by is Quy and I was lost one night in a bay, or so I've told myself.

The new boss never showed any particular interest in me. How would I know that he saw in me one hundred years of meditation, that I had lived several other lives?

Innocence is important for a hero. I'm not innocent; neither was the monk. Innocence makes a story more appealing to some. It's dangerous where I'm concerned. How many times did I have to repeat my own story to some stupid new humanitarian. My words passing like through a sieve. No amount of relating would help. It was always new to them. It got so that to amuse myself, since I was so bored with it, I made minor changes to the tale, or in the end I fantasized wildly. Either way, I was a liar or I was mad. Either way, my listeners went away as if they'd heard nothing. So much for innocence as arbiter of any situation. I never tried to find myself or who I belonged to. The thought made me weak. It paralysed me. Whenever my mind wandered there, I became a child. This *Lon* inside me would whimper, "Why don't they come for me?"

When the monk fell in love, he called this danger on himself. Maybe he was weak. I warned him. He had moments, reclusive, when we would not see him for days. Away on business or just lying on his mat. Perhaps then he longed for the woman in the letters, perhaps then he dreamed of going to her and forgiving her. He stole more from me than I care to say. I don't blame him; I would have done the same. And I warned him.

As I said, spring. Me and the girls sat on a train to the city for three days, and then we arrived. It wasn't hard to convince them that I was one of the bosses, that I knew people and they owed me. I fucked them both. I missed my tape of Mallaria and the Stone Crows. Ku Yie playing guitar with Carburetor Dung would have been nice. Well, what can you do on a train for three days? I had to ditch them. They were planning to do the same to me. But they weren't my only ticket. The laptop was a gold mine.

TWENTY-THREE

BINH WOULD BE just opening his store on Bloor Street. Monday. It was 10 A.M., and that was the time he generally got there.

Tuyen tried working but could not concentrate on the signpost or the little carvings. Then she tried transposing the longings in her book to the wall but was too distracted. She still felt drunk from the weekend. She was not a good drinker. Drinking actually made her face red and swollen. So she'd spent Friday lying on the floor with cold towels on her face. She had pulled down the dried photographs as soon as she came home and put them in a pile on the table. Lying with a cold towel on her face, the photograph of the man burned her retina. Between the ache in her head from the alcohol and this image of Binh's companion, she fell into something that wasn't really sleep. She woke up around 1 P.M. and looked at the photos again. The red light on her answering machine blinked. Binh, she'd thought fearfully. She pressed the button, heard his voice begin a word and snapped the button off. Uncharacteristically, she washed the dishes in the sink. Called Carla across the hallway, knowing that she wasn't there, then went to Carla's to see if there was anything to eat. The bareness of Carla's apartment stunned her. She looked around and had the sense of something missing. No photographs. No family. Lucky, she thought, then took it back.

Carla had her own shit. Tuyen, at least, didn't have a brother in jail. She phoned Jackie.

"What's happening?"

"Nothing. What's happening with you?"

"Nothing."

"Okay." Jackie was curious.

"Okay, then." Tuyen rang off. The phone rang, she hesitated, thinking it might be Binh, then grabbed it, but it was Jackie.

"Hey, what's going on?"

"Nothing. Same old."

"You don't sound 'same old.'"

"No, I'm cool. Hey, Jacks, what if we did the installation at your store?"

"Oh, sure"—Jackie was hesitant—"but how're you going to get that thing down the stairs?"

"It's changed, it's changed, Jacks. Anyway, Oku will help. I'll do it in pieces."

Jackie hesitated again. "Oku . . . Oh, well, fine. Fuck, come to think of it, that would be great. More people will come to the store and shit. Yeah, all right."

"Okay, then, check you, right?"

"Yes, later. Hey, when—"

Tuyen hung up before Jackie finished. She thought she might have said something to Jackie about the pictures, but she couldn't. Jackie would have put it in perspective. Carla was too brooding. Jackie had the ability to cut things off, to truly live her life despite everything, and to dismiss what she couldn't control. But it was still too intimate. She couldn't get the words out of her mouth.

Tuyen burst into the store as Binh was bringing a box from the back to the front. All her remonstrations to herself walking up

Bathurst Street, to be calm, observe his moves, don't jump to conclusions, left her. "What're you up to, Binh?" She heard her voice sounding threatening and childish, something of their old rivalry cutting through.

"Well, hello, and what's up your ass?" He put the box down and started opening it.

He looked contented, she thought. She didn't want to say, I saw you, you're scheming about something. Everything that came to her head sounded petulant. His look of contentment made her even more suspicious.

"No, what're you up to? What's happening? Bo said the other day that you were doing something?"

"What are you doing here, anyway? You never come to see me. I asked you to take care of the store and you fucked off on me. How come you're here now? What? Need money?" As if she would ever come to him for money. As if. He reached into his pocket in exaggerated magnanimity.

"I don't want money from you. I want to know what's going on." Tuyen threw the pictures on the counter.

"What are these? What the fuck?" He caught sight of himself in the photographs. "What the fuck you doing? Why you spying on me? What the fuck!"

"Who is that?" Tuyen asked.

"Who's that? What the fuck you doing spying on me? When did you take these?" He saw the World Cup crowd in the background. He knew when she had taken them, and he used the word "spying" twice.

"So, there's something to spy on?"

"Look, you come here, show me pictures of myself that I don't know you've taken, and then accuse me of something? I don't know what—"

"Okay, I'm leaving, but don't think—"

"Wait, are you nuts or something? What are you taking pictures of me for? And I don't even know? Are you crazy?"

She saw her opening. "Well, who's the guy?" Tuyen danced with him the way she used to as a child, neither of them considering what the other said. And so she stepped aside the accusation that she had done anything wrong.

"Well, if you honoured your family and if you listened to me, you would know that I've been helping Mom and Dad. I always take care of them, you know. You never do. You're off living your artist life. Don't think I don't know about it. I have my eyes open, you know. But I haven't said nothing to them about you."

"My life is none of your business."

"You think you're so different with your shitty paintings and crazy nonsense."

"Yeah, and what're you doing? Saving the whales? Making money, right? And Bo has to always bail you out of some stupid idea."

"Stupid idea? I'm not the one running home broke all the time!"

They came to a small impasse. Each forgetting the new start they had been on the border of only a month ago. Instead, each contemplating the devious machinations of their childhood, the strokes and plays they had performed to hoodwink, outwit, and misrepresent their parents until, bored and frustrated with translation, they had set off to live another life outside the knowledge or apprehension of Tuan and Cam.

"Well, I did a good thing. I finally found him like I told you I would!" Binh exulted, stabbing at the photograph.

"Who is he?" Tuyen's voice was small. She hadn't wanted confirmation of her guesses, but she wanted Binh to say the word all the same. The word hanging over them all, the word like a jewel of air that would break open their existences to the dreadful. The word that had caused their parents such pain and that had to be said sacredly or not at all.

"Quy."

"How do you know it's him? How did you find him? Mom's been looking for years and never found him. How could you have done it? You don't know that for sure." Jealousy, resentment, suspicion erupted in Tuyen.

"It is him, and I found him."

"You don't know that for sure. Tell me, tell me how you know it's him. It could be anybody. You never saw him. You never knew him."

"So what? Of course it's him. What do you think I would do? Mum's not good with English, you know that. That's why the whole thing was fucked up and she got taken so many times. There are records, like I told you. People don't just disappear. Hello, it's 2002. If you had any love for them, you would've tried to find him too."

"Oh, please! He was a boy, for Christ's sake—a baby almost."

"See—you don't have faith."

"Well, how come . . . ?" How come what? Tuyen couldn't finish the question. Her suspicions of Binh were stronger—he never explained anything, and here he was trying so hard to do that.

"I asked you, didn't I? You fucked off. You think I wouldn't find out? Anyway, I haven't told Ma and Bo yet, not really. I hinted to Bo months ago, I said I was looking. I didn't want to get their hopes up and then it wasn't him. I wanted to make sure. Listen, I did my homework, okay? I checked him out good first."

"I don't believe you." She was petulant.

"Believe what you like. Anyway, why were you sneaking around taking pictures and now coming to bully me, huh? You must have seen it too. The resemblance. You did, didn't you? So what's the problem? It's gonna make them happy."

"But how?"

"Look, I tracked him down. I checked all the possible places he could've gone. He was old enough to remember his name. A common name, all right, but I tracked him down. It's taken me a year. You probably figured I was going for drugs or porno or something. You always think the worst of me. So, anyways, I found him and I checked him out."

"And now he's here?"

"He's here."

"And you haven't taken him home yet? Why?"

"Now, wouldn't you know if I did? I'm preparing them."

"So where is he, then?"

"In back. Helping me unload stuff."

"*Stuff*? Where?"

"Jeez! Yes, stuff—drives, belts, shoes. He's going to come into business with me. He'll do that end. You'll see. And they'll be happy."

"I don't know, I don't know, I don't trust this."

She should be feeling elated, happy for her parents, happy for their life, she thought. She should be hugging Binh. She should at least be shocked and pleased that Binh had found Quy, but all she felt was a tingling of things coming apart.

Her mother would be vindicated. She cannot imagine the look of utter pleasure that would spread over her mother's face—the nights of sleep Cam would finally get, the change that would come over their lives, how her sisters would be released from their shame of not watching, of not witnessing, of surviving. How her father would stop the intense self-punishment he had undertaken ever since Quy's loss. And how, finally, a brother who was lost would find his people, his home, would hear all of the sorrow that loss had given, would be told of the frantic searches for him, of how not a piece of bread was eaten without the taste of his absence, how life had been limped through since his departure.

All this Tuyen knew she should have felt—instead, there was a sense of foreboding rather than relief. Was she afraid that she would no longer be the centre of attention; that she would be replaced? Binh obviously didn't feel that, so in the end was he a better person than she? These thoughts tumbled through her mind—she felt slightly ashamed and now expectant. Quy was fifty feet away, and she wanted to flee. She should be bursting out the back door, welcoming her brother; instead, she felt like bolting. She suddenly realized what she had heard.

"He's out back?"

"I'm here," someone said behind her.

She turned to see the boyish face of the photograph. The man smiled through it, giving the face a ferocious look. Tuyen was frozen. Her fingers twitched to her mouth. He had been standing in the recess of the blinds near the dressing rooms. For how long?

"Sister?" he asked.

Binh was beside Tuyen, pushing her toward the man. "Yes, big brother, this is our little sister."

She felt small and speechless.

"Good, good," the man said in a thick accent. He bowed to her. Binh pushed her closer.

"She's shocked," he said to the man. Then to Tuyen, "Is that how you greet your brother? Go."

Tuyen was propelled by Binh's hand and an ineffable dread toward the man. She reached involuntarily for his shoulders. He felt like nothing, a ghost. She sensed something malevolent and withdrew her arms.

"She's in shock," Binh said again. The pressure of his hand increased on her back, urging her forward, willing her to be nice.

"Much time to know my little sister," the man said haltingly, the words sounding like new stones on his tongue.

"When . . . when did you arrive?" Tuyen managed.

"Not long. Not long. Brother Binh is caring for me gratefully."

"When . . ." She began another question, but Binh jumped in.

"Well, we'll go later today. I've told them that I have good news for us. They have no idea that he's here. I only told Bo that I may have found our brother. I didn't want to tell Ma in case. But now, now everything is fine."

"Today?" She seemed only able to deliver one or two words, like a child. No coherent thoughts came to her except that something was wrong. Her brother couldn't be this man. This man had a contained tightness, a light presence; this man she was sure could harm you coolly, arbitrarily. But what had she expected? Why shouldn't he be such a man? After all he had been through? Why shouldn't he be ferine and cold? He was entitled. He could not simply live in their imagination perpetually innocent, perpetually pure. Things had happened to him. Probably bad things. She—they were all transfixed in the past, but he had been living. Living out their distress as well as his own. What leads people into certain lives; what molecules of air and senses and events make them veer this way or that? Of course it was her brother Quy. Of course it wasn't. What difference would it make? This man had arrived in their orbit, and he was therefore theirs. What had she expected? A boy poised on a boat, waiting to be picked up and led back to his real life? She wanted to ask him, Where have you been? She wanted to ask him, Who are you? She was tongue-tied.

"Today?" She turned to Binh, aware of the man as one is aware of a gecko, a spider, a shadow.

"Yes, today. I'm going to find him a suit."

"A suit? What for?"

"To wear." Does a shadow wear a suit? How could Binh think of these things now? *A suit.* "You can come up with us. That'll make things nice for them."

"When?" She was hating this inability to compose a sentence with a verb in front of this man, Quy. And had he overheard their whole conversation? She had the feeling that he had, and she knew she didn't like the idea of that.

"This evening. I'm looking forward most sweetly to meeting my mother and father." His voice only gave Tuyen more to worry about. There, there in that sentence it was over-something. Overweaning, overconfident, overly formal. Then the quality of it—like someone trying to hide a self, a more ravenous side.

"Binh, it's going to be such a shock. Did you talk to Bo about it, at least?" She turned to Binh, suddenly wanting what they had never had—cooperation.

"Yes, yes—no, look, I wanted it to be a great surprise for everyone." He was opening another box, pulling out shirts and measuring them against Quy's body. "I left you a message. Bo called you too. He said he told you to call me."

Yes, she had avoided the messages. Now she was sorry. But really, she thought, what could she have done? Binh was in charge.

"What do you think, Tuyen? This one right?"

He was acting too strangely, she thought. How did it matter what the man wore? Maybe it was as it seemed and her imagination had run away with her, her mistrust for Binh. Maybe she'd had too much to drink over the course of the last three days and she was the one acting strangely.

"I apologize," she said, abruptly facing Quy. "Welcome. My mother and father have never recovered from losing you."

"No I," Quy replied.

Again she heard that formal tone faintly secreting a crudity. She felt embarrassed at thinking this.

"Can I go up with you both, Binh?" And now her brother had the upper hand—having to ask Binh was hard, but no way she was leaving him unobserved.

"Of course. I'm taking him for dinner. It's Monday, remember?"

The restaurant was usually closed on a Monday, and the family usually had dinner together at Richmond Hill, with the exception of Tuyen, who wounded them all by missing this time frequently. It was a ritual she had found as tedious as the restaurant itself ever since she was a teenager. Now she felt justly reprimanded.

"Football again!" Quy rushed to the store window. There had been a gathering crescendo of car horns outside. Tuyen became fully aware of the brewing traffic jam outside on the street. Red flags washed past the window. "Korea! *Du-ma-may!*"

The coarse expletive jarred Tuyen. Binh laughed, waving at the passersby, giving the victory sign.

"Our big brother, Tuyen! He's home!" he said, grabbing her shoulder. She squirmed at this show of affection from him.

"Yes. Well, I'll come back," she said. "What time?"

"How about five, five-thirty? It'll be hell getting out of here."

She remembered to grab the photographs, shoving them into the bag sheepishly. "Okay." She made a small shy gesture of goodbye to Quy as she opened the door and plunged into the growing red crowd outside. The noises rose. Korea had almost scored a goal against Germany.

Tuyen made her way through the crowd grimly. Christ! Was she so hateful as to prefer that Quy had not been found? She turned right and headed south to her apartment. One thing, she decided, her mother and father could not be hurt. She'd see to that. She would do her part, even if this Quy gave her the creeps. That was unfair, she thought. She didn't even know him. At any rate, whatever, she would stick by her mother and father. It was all well and good to have a tragic story in the past, but what if it returns? What if it comes back with all it has stored up, to be resolved and decided, to be answered. She couldn't foresee an easy time, as Binh must have envisaged. The lost boy would have to have been sad, lonely, angry, hurt, angry. Was that the scraping sound she had heard in his voice? Would he have had a life with love? A girlfriend, a wife, children, perhaps? She had been rude, and not very clever—she hadn't asked him any of this. Would he have let the past go as chance—unfair, but chance—and made the best of what he got? Yes, of course there were stories of refugees made good no matter the circumstances. God. What did she mean, *made good*? That was so weak, that was so lame. She couldn't believe she was thinking it. Would he be kind to her mother and father?

In the end that is what she meant, she realized, that is what she wanted. They deserved kindness, and Tuyen doubted whether this ghost could deliver it.

When Tuyen arrived at the alleyway leading to her apartment, a black Audi was practically blocking the doorway to the stairs. Music was booming from speakers at Kumaran's window. It was Oku's "The Jungle Is a Skyscraper." And the walls of the two buildings caverning the alley were now covered in paintings. On one side there was a flowering jungle, lianas wrapped around the CN Tower, elephants drinking by the lake, pelicans perched on the fire escapes. On the other side there was a seaside, a woman in a bathing suit and hat shading her eyes, looking out to sea. The black Audi was parked outside a cabana, a boat rocked against the radio antenna of the car. Tuyen recognized the scenes. The places Carla had talked about, the places where Angela Chiarelli dreamed of going. Tuyen hadn't noticed the paintings earlier. Kumaran must have done them during the weekend, which had been a boozy blur for her. The one time she'd come home she hadn't seen anyone. The Audi parked outside now was real. She didn't recognize it. No one in this alleyway could afford an Audi. She called to Kumaran over Ornette Coleman's shrieking in loops, but Kumaran probably could not hear her. She edged her way around the car and opened the door to the staircase. She heard laughter upstairs from Carla's side. "Carla!" she called, climbing the stairs. Maybe Carla could help her think this out, stop her from being paranoid, offer her a way of seeing the new apparition of her brother Quy as a blessing. *Precious.*

"Tuyen, Jamal! Jamal got out!" Carla stood at the top of the stairs, beaming.

"Great! Hey, Jamal!" Tuyen replied, as he appeared behind Carla. "What's happening, how are you?"

"I'm chilling . . . you know." His eyes looked red. They'd been doing a joint.

"Come on in, we're having a celebration. I was looking for you all weekend to tell you. He's been out since Friday. Where you been?"

"Oh, you know . . ." Carla seemed unusually manic to Tuyen. She was disappointed that she would not be able to talk to Carla about Quy, and she didn't have time for a party. "Listen, I'm just here to change to go to Richmond Hill. Home for dinner."

"Oh, come on. Come in for a minute." She pulled Tuyen into the room. Tuyen reached to hug Jamal.

"Okay, but just for a minute. Jamal, how are you? How're you doing?"

"You know, no problem, no problem. Just getting my head together."

"Great, great." Tuyen had no idea what to say that hadn't been said. No one could be expected to be optimistic about Jamal, except Carla, of course. And right now she had her own trouble to deal with, so the words on her lips sounded distant and insincere.

"Tuyen, here, have a beer with us."

"No, I really do have to go, love. You know. Hey, whose car is that blocking the door?"

"Oh, it's Derek's. He lent it to me to go find a job. You know, new life and all that shit, right?" Jamal said the last sentence slowly and with sarcasm.

"Great, so you all are fine now?"

"Well, fine as it gets, I guess." There was something odd going on, but Tuyen didn't have the time. Carla's eyes were glassy, as if she wanted to wring some genuine happiness out of the occasion.

"Hey, your brother still got that sweet Beamer X5?"

"I guess. Is that what it is? I don't know cars."

"Cars! That's not a car, Tuyen, that's like phat, man, that's the bomb." His eyes were animated, and his fingers snapped on the end of his arms.

Tuyen caught a glimpse of the brand on his chest. "Why'd you do that?" she asked, pointing.

"Ah, that's nothing," he said, his hand coming to pull his shirt tight. Then, "So, like, what'd he pay for that?"

"No idea. Jeez, I gotta go, I gotta go. Glad you're all right, Jamal." Tuyen got up.

"Don't go yet." Carla sounded pleading, following Tuyen to the door.

"No, really, I got to." She felt Carla grasp her hand, interlacing her fingers with an intimacy that at any other time she would have loved. "Check you later." Even now she wanted to hold her and kiss her.

Tuyen hurried over to her place, dropped her bag, and sat on the floor, holding her temples. She closed her eyes and exhaled a gush of a breath. She was trying to sort herself out. She had to be calm, she told herself. That way she could observe the way things were going. She felt dazed too. What would all of it mean for her? She saw it only as binding her closer. Not that she hated her family. She just didn't want to be in their everyday life. But now she had been drawn back into it. Look, she told herself, on the other hand it could be good. No skeletons, no ghost. The universe restored. She knew that Tuan and Cam would've given up anything they had for this moment. Though deep in her heart she blamed them for not doing just that, and for surviving and dragging her into their survival. But now it was going to be fine. She could unblame them. Binh had redeemed them.

She breathed deeply, got up, and walked to her window, which faced the alley. An iguana was climbing through the opposite window, a parrot soared to the chimney, a peacock leapt off a tree near the garbage cans. The Audi was gone, and Carla was getting on her bike near the Amazon, her face an electric radiance. Tuyen smiled. Everything would be fine. She remembered Varo's *Exploration of the Sources of the Orinoco*. She had her art, she had her life. Whatever. Anyways.

TWENTY-FOUR

THE RIDE TO RICHMOND HILL was suddenly too short. Tuyen sat in the back seat of the Beamer. They seemed to be moving so quickly. When they were on the highway, she said, "How are we going to do this, Binh?" She spoke to him, but the back of Quy's head concentrated her.

"Well, how do you want to do it?" He tried to keep his exasperation out of his voice, but she could hear it.

"I think that we should go in first. Tell them. You know . . ."

"Okay, fine."

"So it's not a shock . . . totally . . . or . . ."

"Fine," he said again.

He was humouring her, she felt it. He'd made the big catch, and she could play with the small details if she wanted. Silence fell again. She could hear Quy's breathing. Why couldn't she ask, So what was your life like? So where were you? So anything?

"This is the highway," Binh said, as if he was a tour guide and as if Quy had never seen a highway before. Quiet again.

"I mean, I think that's best," Tuyen started up.

"I said okay!" he warned.

"Okay." Her body was tense and prickly. The man looked straight ahead. Maybe he was tense too, she thought. What would she say to Bo and Ma? Binh was in control, but his control always felt chaotic to her. She would have to make up for him, to anchor them for disappointment. This man was disappointing, she knew.

There was a sunny haze on the buildings seen from the highway. The traffic felt slippery. As if they were gliding unencumbered through a slick, silvery air.

When the Beamer pulled into Ridgeway Heights Crescent, Tuyen noticed irritatingly the incongruity of its name. There was no ridge, there was no hill; these had existed only in the imagination of the developer. Yes, they had driven the scythed asphalt of the street, but that was all that was true about the words on the street sign.

She had not spoken to Quy the whole way. Repentant now, or perhaps only to keep down her rising anxiety, she heard her voice bellow in his ear, "Won't be long now. That's where we're going." She pointed over his shoulder to the rounding white porch of her parents' house. "Stop, stop here, Binh." Her voice was so high pitched that Binh stepped heavily on the brake.

"What is your problem?" he asked, putting the Beamer in park.

"I—we should park here. Don't go into the garage yet."

"Stop telling me what to do." They were five hundred metres from the house.

"No fighting," Quy suddenly spoke, silencing them both. "It's fine. Everything. I stay here. You go first. Everything is fine now."

"Okay, big brother." Binh smiled. "Everything is fine."

Tuyen grunted assent and opened the door, climbing out of the Beamer. Binh followed. They walked in silence for a few steps. Tuyen began to say something, but Binh's resolute face dissuaded her. It reminded her of when they were children. At night in the restaurant, after all the customers had left, he would sit on a table playing his Pacman, which she was not allowed to touch, his brow furrowed, his mouth pursed; she would sit on the cash register stool, both of them waiting while their sisters and Bo and Ma cleaned the restaurant around them. Then, much to his annoyance, she would burst into loud renditions of "Itsy Bitsy Spider," her arms waving like a choir master, building the song with more and more gusto until he screamed for her to shut up. Either Ai or Lam would slap them both to quieten them down. But it didn't, it only made them wail louder to bring Ma or Bo to their rescue.

Rescue. Were they now on some mission of rescue? Who was being rescued? she thought. Ma, Bo, her sisters, her brother, this one, or the man they'd left in the car? Quy, the eldest? She must stop annoying Binh; she must help him rescue Ma and Bo. They must, she and he, translate now the years between that man and their parents. They must stand between them to decode the secret writing of loss and hurt.

She put her arm on Binh's to slow him. He turned to her at first brusquely, then, seeing the understanding of their mission in her face, slowed himself, as if to savour their mutual intuition. This is what they'd done all their lives, she thought. She felt comforted by their commonality, the same commonality that had made her so uneasy most of her life; it had made her long to be unexceptional. Yet, here was their specialness now carried between them to the door of the house, the recognitive gaze of an exception cherished through all this time. Wasn't that what her art was all about in the end? She had a vision of the cloth on the wall in her apartment, the scores of scribbled longings, then she felt for the photographs of Quy still stuffed in her bag. She would make tiny copies of the image, yes, and insert them among the records of longing in her installation. She would take photographs of the people of the city too, and sprinkle them throughout. She would need a larger space for the installation, three rooms really, very high ceilings. In the middle of each room a diaphanous cylindrical curtain, hung from the ceiling, that the audience could enter. At the centre of one cylinder would be the *lubaio* with all the old longings of another generation. She would do something with the floor here too, perhaps rubble, perhaps sand, water. In another cylinder there would be twelve video projections, constantly changing, of images and texts of contemporary longing. This one would be celebratory, even with the horrible. Again here the floor, the path, what material? The last cylinder would be empty, the room silent. What for? She still wasn't quite certain what she was making; she knew she would find out only once the installation was done. Then, some grain, some element she had been circling, but had been unable to pin down, would emerge.

Quy

There are times when I've said to myself, Who the hell are
you? That's a dangerous question. And this is a dangerous
city. You could be anybody here. That is what first took me
when I walked among people on the streets. Then one
morning I sat on the subway train and I heard a laughter
and it reminded me of when I was little, and right away
I knew it would be easy to disappear here. Who would
know? The man living across the street from you could
have fought in the Angolan war, he could've killed many
people, and there he is sitting in a deck chair with his wife
as if nothing happened, and one day he will mention the
simple fact to you with a look of triumph as he remembers
it only as a youthful adventure. That woman whose ass you
love when she walks down the street, she could've been
tortured in Argentina and the last thing she wants anyone
to love is her ass, her genitals were wired with electrodes,
once. And the taxi driver you strike up a pleasant
conversation with could've been her torturer or a torturer
of a similar woman in Burma with similar equipment. So if
this guy from Angola can sit there in his shorts and tan
himself and remember killing people like a youthful prank,
like a necessary job, and if the taxi driver can devote
himself to sharing pleasantries and directions, thinking of
the electrodes he put in a woman's cunt as routine, just

trying to get the job done, like driving a cab, well, who am I really? Who the hell am I?

So I'm sitting here thinking, Margaret Yao turns out to be the girlfriend of one Alex Turgenov, who happens to have been a sports doctor from the old Soviet Union and who is now a mechanic but more importantly runs a whorehouse; the girls turn out to be only three thousand dollars apiece. Alex is going to store them in a whorehouse called a spa, above a retail shoe place that used to be called the Elephant. One day the cops will find them and they'll be on TV and Alex will disappear and Margaret will walk across the screen looking sour, but that's another story. By some coincidence, if you believe that kind of thing, I come to the name of a guy, Vu Binh, in the monk's e-mails. Young guy, M.B.A., all the money he wants, all the pussy he needs. And by some stranger coincidence, this one perhaps love, he's looking for a man who was a boy named Quy. Well, see for yourself. I already put two and two together. I appear. The guy is either very cunning or a *lo dit*. I arrive; he's convinced. I'm convinced. He turns out to be my brother. Isn't my name Quy? Wasn't I lost so he could come to me in his expensive shoes, in his silk shirt, his mouth slow and vulgar on his mother tongue, with his silver Beamer? He knows everything, he's a swift man, he looks at me like Picasso devouring an African mask—how can he use it, how can he change it, which part of his belly can he put it in? So I say to myself, Fine, let it play.

But I'm so full of rage, a kind I've never felt before, and I want to take a swing at him and I want to hug him as my brother. But I know that I'm going to take him for everything he's got. It's the things that were mine, and he got them double. He's got my mother and my father and my two sisters. He's got the world in front of him. He's got the store, and we're in the store when the World Cup match between Korea and Italy is playing. And he's got happiness like the people outside in the street when the Korean redhead scores the goal that beats Italy. He's got everything.

I look at the crowd outside and I say to myself, How come, how come this can't be me? And I say to myself, Quy, it is you.

We have another sister, and she's harder to convince. The minute I hear her voice, I know she's no pussy. So I listen close to what she says, and I decide there's no need to play her, the rest of them will work it out fine. She wants them to be happy, she wants me to be happy. So I make her know I'm standing in the room, watching her, waiting for her to decide whether to kill everything again. And it is as if I'm standing in the bay, about to follow someone onto the *Dong Khoi*. And suddenly she turns around, recognizes me, and says she's sorry, and I feel lifted up by my father or my mother. The crowd is outside the store window again. This time the Koreans are playing the machine, Germany. They won't win, but they're there. They're on the pitch in the semi-final. Everything comes together. "*Du-ma-may!*" I scream, "*Du-ma-may!*"

So now I'm here in the car, waiting to go meet them. Little brother will come to get me. He and my little sister are preparing them for the shock, and I'm sitting here in the Beamer, and I'm thinking, People disappear all the time into cities. Why not me, eh? Why not me? I could run a store like Binh. What do people need? Movies, video games, yes, I could do that, sell videos, I could become close with my little sister, me and my older sisters will remember games we played. My brother and I will go to the strip clubs together. My mother will cry and my father too. They'll forgive themselves now. I'll marry someone, I'll have a kid or two, and just like that man I'll sit outside, I'll find someone to tell this story to, and I'll laugh because all my predictions and interpretations were wrong. So I'm waiting, I'm going to rest my head here and wait.

TWENTY-FIVE

CARLA DIDN'T RIDE into the Amazon. She rode through the city, now feeling free. Free of Jamal, free of Derek and Nadine. She would never be free of Angie. She didn't want to be free of her. She only wanted the memory to lose its pain, not its intensity. Derek had bailed Jamal out. Jamal was going to live with him. Whether that lasted or not now was up to them. She wasn't free of Jamal, really, and she didn't want to be—she only wanted to be free of his pain. And of her protectiveness toward him. This was a step then, that it wasn't she who had bailed him out, that Derek had taken the responsibility, and however that had come about she didn't need to know, nor did she care.

She rode up the Bathurst Street hill just for the taste of lactic acid in her thighs, then down under the bridge and back, then along St. Clair Avenue. She stopped in Little Italy, secured her bike, and sat down at the Eden Trattoria and ordered an espresso. Carla imagined Angie growing up just off this avenue when times were different and when Angie was a rebel.

There used to be a black club above Chiarelli's Espresso Bar on this street. Angie used to work downstairs nights serving espresso to old men from Calabria playing cards and talking, while people dressed to the nines went upstairs on the weekends to dance. It was on the sidewalk outside the espresso bar that she'd met Derek. After weeks of listening to the pumping disco music upstairs and feeling a deep thrill from the cool hip bodies laughing and wheeling by the window, Angie had volunteered to close up that night. She wanted to go upstairs, to be enveloped in the smell of perfume and the taste of Southern Comfort, the heat and dark of the dance floor, and that laughing that seemed somehow to her not light at all but knowledgeable and dangerous. She didn't listen to the gnarled old men talk, over their cigarettes and espressos, about the "monkeys" upstairs. She didn't hear the absolute proscription laid down there in those curses plain and ugly as anything. She only saw the easy way Derek smiled and the way that smile said she was gorgeous and young and sexy and that they both of them together would be incendiary. She didn't hear Derek joke with his friends that she was fresh meat, or if she heard it, she'd already decided that she could take that lascivious name tinged with something racial and envious, something special. Angie didn't want to be anyone ordinary in Little Italy. She was scared of the Saturday shopping and the Sunday churching and the Sunday dinners where her brothers' wives and her mother and she would busy themselves with cooking while her brothers and her father drank wine and scowled at the television or insulted each other about not knowing what real work was. She was scared of the screaming nieces and nephews and the inane talk about babies and wedding showers and houses in the new suburbs of Toronto. So Angie cut all that off with one flight into the most forbidden place on her family's earth.

I'll never know quite what that was like, Carla thought. She heard around her the language of her own childhood, a language she didn't speak or understand now, but whose tones she felt comforted by. "To Angela Chiarelli," she said aloud, raising her coffee. She made a new vow to remember Angie, not with the same frantic effort at preservation, at loyalty. She had held on as if she could lose loyalty. Now she knew she couldn't. And she couldn't hold the baby any more either. She knew all this when Jamal came by in the black Audi. She knew Derek hadn't lent it to him. Derek would never lend anyone his car.

She'll go back to her apartment and live her life. She'll have parties with Tuyen, she'll go to the Roxy Blu, she'll go to jazz concerts, she'll wait in line to hear U2, she'll go with Tuyen to Pope Joan, to Afrodeasia. They'll dance together. She'll check out the open-mike spoken word at Caliban with Oku. She'll cut her hair, she'll go to Jackie's Ab und Zu and get a new wardrobe. She'll be seduced by someone. She can't hold the baby any longer.

It won't matter that Jamal left Carla's place, cruised up Weston Road, turned into a small street with an apartment building, waited outside until a friend came down, who then sat in the passenger seat; a friend who greeted Jamal with, "Hey, J-man. Shit, it's great to see you," clasped his hand, and hugged him. Jamal put the car in gear with a flourish and first drove through the growing neighbourhood of ex–West Indians, ex-Eritreans, ex-Somalis, ex-Vietnamese, and ex–South Asians. His friend Bashir, the son of an ex-Somali, was born right here when you could still smell the beef terminal from the Junction; when they hadn't yet turned the abattoir south of here into town houses.

"Fuck, this is a sweet ride," Bashir said. "You're living very large, J-man."

Jamal grinned at the compliment and turned left onto the main drag, with its brief mix of used-car dealerships, dollar stores, cheap, ugly furniture stores, food stores, banks, and panicky "stop and cash" booths. He nosed the Audi through the sluggish traffic up toward the highway.

If it means anything, the conversation they had was about how smooth the ride was, how sleek this Audi looked, how it was his father's, the fucker— "the vain old fuck-head," Jamal said. "But I wouldn't buy no Audi like him. I know this guy with this X5, sweet, man."

"Beamer X5? Whoa! Put some Pioneer speakers in there . . ."

"Pioneer! Are you crazy, man! No way. Some Anaconda with subwoofers, like twelves, right . . . real bass, built-in equalizer . . ."

That conversation was punctuated by drags on a spliff and chuckling. And then his friend Bashir said, "Let's roll, man." And then Jamal said, "No doubt, man, I'm ready."

Carla has already decided on the new course of her life when Jamal drives the Audi to Richmond Hill because there are rich motherfuckers there and they got great cars to boost, in garages off roadways called crescents and drives. They got monster houses and monster rides and his friend is the garage-door specialist and a strong man and he's the driver. And really it should be three of them, but they are two. They spot the silver Beamer X5 outside near a stop sign, and there's an Asian guy in the passenger seat. The guy looks middle-aged to them. His head is laid back on the headrest, and his eyes are closed; the windows are open because it's a nice evening, not so hot as earlier in the day. And maybe the middle-aged Asian guy is waiting to meet someone; maybe he's resting for the first time in a long time, and is waiting until someone comes out of the house not far away to get him. The Beamer's silver skin burns like a fish in the dark pond of the evening.

They circle him once, twice. And Jamal wants to take this one, so he gets out and gives his friend the wheel of the Audi. He has a small black object in his waist, and he slides up stealthily on the resting man. He practised two or three times in his head, *Get out, motherfucker*, as he's heard in the movies. So when he gets to the car, he says these words and presses the gun to the man's face. And the man seems insulted and stunned—how could he have been caught in this way?

Adrenaline makes Jamal wrench the door of the Beamer open violently, grabbing the man and dragging him out of the car, flinging him to the pavement and kicking him in the ribs. But the man, surprised and suddenly charged himself, hangs on to Jamal's left leg.

The gun falls, clatters against the pavement, and slips under the car. Then the friend in the Audi jumps out and comes running, kicking the man loose of Jamal. The man is stupidly fighting as if he has a life that's precious. He realizes that they want the car, and he says, "Take the fucking car" in Vietnamese, but no one understands him. So they beat him and kick him beyond recognition and Jamal jumps in the silver Beamer X5 and his friend takes the Audi and they drive away, leaving the man half-dead by the road.

And the man lies there thinking, Not Bidong, not Klong Toey, not in any of those places had he let himself down like this. His mouth is full of the brittle, rusty taste of blood, and the sky looks like the sea that first morning on the *Dong Khoi*. And he leans his head as he had over the side of the boat, longingly, and Bo and Ma are finally running out of a doorway, running toward him, and the road between them is like water, and they both grab him as they should have and his mouth splits open and all the water spills out.

This is long after Carla drank that espresso and rode home. She put on some music when she got there, and she sat by the window, looking out on the street and the coming evening, at the young man who sold houses, the woman who worked in the abortion clinic, the girl who talked to her dogs as if they were human. The lottery man was heading from the

Mars. Downstairs the storekeeper had drawn the awning in. She would wait up until Tuyen came home. Listen to music, drink some wine. Tomorrow she would miss work and have everybody over. She longed to hear Tuyen chipping and chiselling away next door.

ACKNOWLEDGMENTS

ALONG THE LENGTH OF TIME I spent writing this book, I was accompanied by five most searing critics, Louise Dennys, Leleti Tamu, Leslie Sanders, Claire Harris, and Constance Rooke. When I came to the end of the writing, I found myself rereading Pablo Neruda's "The Book of Questions" and discovered the question I had asked each of them—*"Tell me, is the rose naked / or is that her only dress?"* To which they all replied patiently and repeatedly, as I've now realised in Neruda, *"From what does the hummingbird hang / its dazzling symmetry?"* I humbly thank them for their generous collaboration. Many thanks to Bernice Eisenstein, Angelika Glover, Deirdre Molina and Sue Sumeraj.

DIONNE BRAND won the Governor General's Award for Poetry and the Trillium Award in 1997 for *Land to Light On*. In 2003 she won the Pat Lowther Award for Poetry for her book *thirsty*. Her novels *In Another Place, Not Here* and *At the Full and Change of the Moon* have been published in the US and the UK to great acclaim. Dionne Brand lives in Toronto.

A NOTE ON THE TYPE

The typeface Berling was designed by Karl-Erik Forsberg for the Berlingska Stilgjuteriet in Lund, Sweden in 1951. It belongs to the modern text typefaces and like most of these markedly shows the influence of the Neorenaissance.